Masterpieces

OF

Mystery

Masterpieces

OF

Mystery

The Grand Masters

Selected by ELLERY QUEEN

C O N T E N T S

INTRODUCTION

Some of the details are now lost in the mists of memory. The survivors of that bold group agree that it all started one day in March 1945 when a baffle of detective-story writers met in an apartment in New York City. I recall that it was the apartment of Marie Rodell, although at least one of us later insisted it was a duplex borrowed for the momentous occasion from Fannie Hurst.

The consensus is that eight of us gathered on that auspicious day—Marie Rodell, Baynard Kendrick, Ken Crossen, Anthony Boucher, Mignon G. Eberhart, Mabel Seeley, Clayton Rawson, and Ellery Queen (the last named represented by Frederic Dannay); and before the historic day ended, that small band of merry men and women had founded Mystery Writers of America, an organization dedicated to making the lot of the mystery writer a happy one.

MWA (as the organization came to be known in the fashion of these acronymic times) was not intended to be a social club, although it has often been that; or even primarily a guild in the craft sense, although it has always been that. Our chief function was to build a non-secret society and operate as a union, although MWA has never called itself that, and in earlier years the mere mention of the word "union" horrified some members and even caused others to stalk out of meetings. Our main goal, on that frabjous day, was (and still is and always will be) to improve the basic contract between publisher and author, and I recollect that it was the late Clayton Rawson, creator of magician-detective The Great Merlini, who, in a flash of inspiration, gave us our imperishable motto: Crime Does Not Pay—Enough. I also recollect that it was Baynard Kendrick, creator of blind detective Duncan Maclain, who was the proximate cause, the prime mover, the true Founding Father of MWA, and public acknowledgment of his indispensable role is long overdue.

Well, in the course of time MWA achieved miracles (although more miracles cry out to be performed). In the course of time MWA grew and branched out with new chapters—in northern California (San Francisco), in southern California (Los Angeles), in the midwest (Chicago), in New England (Boston), with "At Large"

7

members throughout the United States and "Corresponding" members overseas. In the course of time MWA chapters socialized, conducted craft sessions, produced anthologies and textbooks, and most important to the Founding Fathers' and Mothers' original purpose, made happier the mystery writer's lot. And in the course of time MWA began to take pride in its accomplishments and signalized its pride by bestowing awards on deserving colleagues, usually at its gala annual dinner in New York City—awards for excellence in the fields, among others, of novel, first novel, short story, motion picture, radio, television, and fact crime, including awards of merit for individual tours de force, special anniversaries, and lifelong contributions to the genre.

The awards take the form of scrolls and ravens, and of busts of Edgar Allan Poe, creator of C. Auguste Dupin, inventor of the detective story as we know it today, and the Patron Saint who has made us all his epigones (and note that the word contains his name). The modest ceramic bust of Poe, designed by Peter Williams and executed by Louise Larabee, is called an Edgar and is comparable as a reward for achievement to the solid-gold Oscar of Hollywood.

Every MWA award is a high honor, but unquestionably the most prestigious is that of the Grand Master of the mystery story. As of this writing, 15 Grandmasterships have been awarded—to Vincent Starrett in 1957, Rex Stout in 1958, Ellery Queen in 1960, Erle Stanley Gardner in 1961, John Dickson Carr in 1962, George Harmon Coxe in 1963, Georges Simenon in 1965, Baynard Kendrick in 1966, John Creasey in 1968, James M. Cain in 1969, Mignon G. Eberhart in 1970, John D. MacDonald in 1971, Judson Philips (Hugh Pentecost) in 1972, Ross Macdonald in 1973, and Eric Ambler in 1974.

This anthology, Volume Three of MASTERPIECES OF MYSTERY, is a tribute to the 15 Grand Masters. In this book you will find examples of the work of all the Grand Masters—a treasure-house of 'tecs— and we are deeply privileged to bring these distinguished authors to you.

Happy reading!

ELLERY QUEEN

THE TRAGEDY
OF PAPA PONSARD

BY VINCENT STARRETT

Vincent Starrett, newspaperman, critic, editor, teacher and writer, was born in Toronto, Canada, on October 26, 1886. He worked as a reporter on the Chicago *Inter-Ocean* and the Chicago *Daily News* and for a time he taught short-story writing at Northwestern University. He lived in New York, London, Paris, Rome, Reno, St. Louis and Peking. His more than 100 books include verse, essays, biographies and mystery fiction. His *The Private Life of Sherlock Holmes* (1933) is considered by most critics the best book ever written about the Master Detective. He died on January 5, 1974.

WITHOUT HIS BOOKS PAPA PONSARD would have been lost indeed. But he no longer read them. Instead he catalogued them, every day, in his little shop in the Rue St. Jacques, behind the Pantheon and not too far from Notre Dame. It was a sorrowful and delightful task. For what is more delightful than cataloguing one's beloved books, and what is more sorrowful than writing after them a price? However, when one is a bookseller these things must be.

Three steps led downward to the bookshop of Papa Ponsard. Then a door opened with a tinkle of bells, and beyond the door was the shop, a bit dim and dusty even at the hour of noon. For rooms, like brains, are dusty things when one is old and eyes are dim with years, and there is perhaps a contagion about it all that even the doctors do not understand. Across the shop three steps led upward to the darker mysteries of chambers beyond.

Papa Ponsard, seated on a high stool behind his high old-fashioned desk, where the light was best, could look through his window and watch the feet of those who passed along the sidewalk. This also he did daily, often for a long time, his quill pen poised above a page in the old ledger in which the cataloguing was going forward. At such times his mild blue eyes were anxious behind their little panes of glass. There was a pair of feet he knew and feared to see. At such times, too, his granddaughter, standing on the highest of the three steps at the rear of the shop, would chide him for his negligence, her own eyes anxious.

"How comes the catalogue along, Grandfather?" she would ask. And then as like as not she would add, *"Fie!* You are looking again for Monsieur Gebhart. He will not come today. Depend upon it, his threat was all the merest stuff and nonsense. He would not dare."

When she had said this, or something very like it, Papa Ponsard would take his eyes away from the feet that passed along the sidewalk and bend his head again above the ledger. He would dip his quill into his inkhorn and write:

> *Gaboriau (E.). Le Petit Vieux des Batignolles.*
> *Paris: E. Dentu, 1876. Somewhat worn and shabby, but a sound*
>   *copy of this scarce little book by our first great master of the*
>   *detective story. Rebound. 3000 fr.*

Or perhaps he would write this:

> Leblanc (M.). *Arsène Lupin, Gentleman-Cambrioleur.*
> *Paris: P. Lafitte, 1907. Vaguely soiled, but in the original*
> *wrappers so often missing. The earliest book about this Prince*
> *of Thieves, now becoming quite rare. 6000 fr.*

And sometimes he would add a little star and an additional line: *"A genuine bargain."* But indeed they were all bargains, and francs had fallen sadly, in those unhappy days after the second World War.

Yes, without his granddaughter Papa Ponsard would have been lost indeed. It was she who, in the darker chambers behind the shop, prepared his cheese soup and called him to it when the clocks of the city were striking the hour for that delicious repast. It was she who kept his mind away from the feet of Monsieur Gebhart. A pretty girl, and sweet as a princess in a fairy tale.

It had been a number of years since Papa Ponsard had issued a catalogue of his books. The difficulty was the printer: he insisted upon being paid. And of the many feet that passed along the sidewalk before the door of Papa Ponsard's shop, there were so few that turned down the little flight of steps and heard (if a pair of feet may be said to hear) the tinkle of the bells above the door, that printers' bills had come to be a memory of the past. Almost a happy memory, if bills *can* be a happy memory. It was a situation not without its discouragement, as Papa Ponsard was obliged to admit; yet one that might after all be corrigible. If, for instance, there were no Monsieur Gebharts to harass and annoy one.

Meanwhile, the cataloguing must go forward. Who could say at what moment an American, loitering in the neighborhood, might drop in and purchase for 30,000 francs his wonderful copy of Voltaire's *Zadig*, so long the pride of Papa Ponsard's heart.

Thirty thousand francs! Curiously, it was the very sum he owed Monsieur Gebhart. A remarkable coincidence, as often he had mentioned to his granddaughter. Yet when the day came, would not his heart fail him? To see his superb *Zadig* leave the window in which for so long it had reposed! To be bereft of *Zadig*! One of only forty copies on gray paper, and bound for a king's mistress! Already his heart had failed him many times at the mere thought of it. Without his *Zadig*, Papa Ponsard would have been lost indeed.

To be sure, there were other old companions in that wonderful window. Passers-by, if they had been interested, might have read some interesting titles. For Papa Ponsard loved not only his Voltaire and his Gaboriau and his Leblanc, but the whole realm of what is lightly called detective literature. He was in his way a scholar; but better still he had been for most of his long life a reader. Now his eyes were tired, but the clandestine celebrity of Monsieur Lecoq and Joseph Rouletabille and more recently, of Inspector Maigret, were part of his tapestry of memory, and the fame of London's Monsieur Sherlock 'Olmes was not unknown to him. With only a little stretch of his neck he could see the titles of some of the books in his window display.

They were a miscellaneous lot designed to catch the popular fancy; but a few "high spots" were there also, for the specialists: an indubitable English first edition of *The Hound of the Baskervilles* (London, 1902); an indubitable French first of *Les 13 Coupables* (Fayard, 1932); an indubitable first in translation of *M. Ashenden, Agent Secret* (1930), in the pleasing format of the Editions de France; and that admirable rarity, the *Histoires Extraordinaires* of the admirable Edgar Poe in the translation of Baudelaire. Could he orally bring himself to sell them if opportunity offered?

Sometimes Young Valentin Nadaud ran in from next door and added his encouragement to the situation; but he looked oftener at Papa Ponsard's granddaughter than at the fabulous *Zadig*. This was not surprising, however, for she was very pleasant to look at; and books, after all, are only books when one is a Valentin Nadaud—even such a treasure as *Zadig*. There were but forty copies of Papa Ponsard's *Zadig* in all the world, as Valentin had often heard; but there was only one of Josephine Joly. She was unique.

Papa Ponsard took his eyes away from the hurrying feet in the Rue St. Jacques and observed that his granddaughter was watching him. She stood as usual on the uppermost of the three steps that led into the chambers beyond. As always he felt abashed. He spoke quickly.

"My darling, I was about to catalogue the glorious *Zadig*. I was upon the very point of taking it from the window."

"That is excellent," she smiled, "and you will just have time, for the cheese soup is almost ready. I was about to warn you."

"It is a magnificent volume," said Papa Ponsard, "and it would grace the catalogue of any bookseller in the city. The price, of course, is ridiculous. It is worth forty thousand francs, if it is worth a sou."

"Then why not ask that for it? You who love your books so much must not be too modest when you come to sell. It is no compliment surely to the books."

"Ah, if I might keep it for myself! How happy I should be! I know I shall miss it when it is gone, as I should miss you, Josephine, if you were gone."

"Well, well," she laughed, "we are neither of us gone yet, Grandfather. I, at least, shall not leave you for forty thousand francs or for one hundred thousand."

"You will leave me whenever the young rogue of a Valentin says the word," said Papa Ponsard sadly. "You will leave me for ten francs, or for none."

"I shall never leave you while you need me," said Josephine, "whatever Valentin may say, or anyone else."

"That is my good girl," said Papa Ponsard, "but I should feel easier, my dear, if Monsieur Gebhart had already come and gone and we were safe."

"Safe!" cried his granddaughter. "Safe for another month, Grandfather? That is not safety. But he will not come today. And if he does, what matter? He will go away again, as he has done before. One cannot give what one does not have. His threats are the merest *pouf!* It is only in books that poor people are thrust into the street because they cannot pay their rent. Come now, in a few moments I shall call you to come in and enjoy your soup."

"In the newspapers too," said Papa Ponsard. "Every day I read about them. It is a dreadful thing. And all my books! My *Zadig* . . ."

"It is worth forty thousand francs," said his granddaughter, "and you must not catalogue it for a single franc less. The idea! That glorious book! Remember, then, in a few moments I shall call you."

This conversation, also, had been repeated many times. In all its lines both were letter perfect.

But on this day Papa Ponsard did indeed reach into his window and remove the glorious *Zadig*. He laid it gently before him on his high desk and turned its leaves with loving fingers. He knew it almost by heart—from its title page to its colophon he could have recited its enchanting pages. Not its contents perhaps, but its pages. Upon page 7, for instance, there was the broken letter that occurred only in copies of the right edition. It had been corrected in the later smaller copies for the trade. And at page 40 there was the errata slip so often missing in otherwise perfect copies of the original issue. Oh, it was a superb book!

Papa Ponsard dipped his pen into his inkhorn and wrote:

> *Voltaire. Zadig, ou, La Destinée. Histoire Orientale.*
> *Nancy: Leseure, 1748. Red morocco, with the original wrappers bound in.*
> *The rare first edition of this charming little introuvable in a binding especially designed by Padeloup for Madame de Pompadour and incorporating her arms. One of forty copies on gray paper with the errata slip so often missing and the broken type face on page 7. A magnificent copy of this rare and desirable volume.*

His quill hovered for a moment over the page, and then he wrote courageously: "*40000* fr." In another little note he added almost confidentially: "*I have seen only one other copy of this book in fourteen years.*"

For an instant his heart almost failed him. He had done it at last and his immediate impulse was to strike out all he had written. Could he really see it through? For some minutes he was immovable on his stool. Then his hand stole to the drawer of his desk. He opened the drawer a little way and peered in. Yes, *it* was still there. Not even Josephine had been told of his incredible luck at the last auction he had attended. How long ago! But the packet of old papers had justified his negligible speculation.

He read the first few sentences of the manuscript under his hand, presumably a letter addressed to an Italian officer of police:

It was about the year 1832. One day a young American presented himself at my house with an introduction from his fellow countryman, the famous novelist Fenimore Cooper . . . His name was Edgar Poe. From the outset I realized that I had to deal with a remarkable man. Two or three remarks which he made on my furniture, the things I had about me, the way my articles of everyday use were strewn about the room, and on my moral and intellectual characteristics, impressed me with their accuracy and truth. On the very first day of our acquaintance I freely proffered him my friendship and asked for his . . . At this time I had a little house all to myself in the Rue de l' Ouest. I offered to let Edgar Poe have two rooms for the duration of his stay in Paris . . .

The bells over the door tinkled musically and Papa Ponsard looked up with a start. A spasm of fear crossed his face. But it was only young Valentin Nadaud, who had run in from next door to look upon that unique item, Josephine Joly.

"Hello, Papa Ponsard," cried Valentin, and then almost reverently he added, for he had seen the book, "*Mon Dieu!* You are cataloguing the *Zadig!*"

"Good day to you, young man," said Papa Ponsard severely. "And what is it to you, may I ask, if I am cataloguing my *Zadig?*" But he smiled after a moment and continued, "So long as my granddaughter Josephine is not missing from her accustomed place, I imagine you will continue to favor me with your patronage."

"True," said the young man, "true. And how is that charming young woman today? It is all of twenty-four hours since I have seen her."

"I was about to call him to his soup," responded Josephine from the top step, "and I am very well, thank you, very well indeed. You are at liberty to join us if you care to."

"That I am not," said the young man, laughing. "For I have just come from eating my own soup. It was my thought that you would have finished. You are late today, are you not?"

"Just a little. But Grandfather was cataloguing his *Zadig* and I could not interrupt him. We shall be through before long."

"Before long," murmured the old man, climbing down from his

perch. "Yes, we shall all be through before long." He peered again for a moment into his open drawer and read:

Poe had one curious idiosyncrasy: he liked the night better than the day. Indeed, his love of darkness amounted almost to a passion. But the Goddess of Night could not always afford him her shade . . . so he contrived a substitute. As soon as day began to break he hermetically sealed up the windows of his room and lit a number of candles. In the midst of this pale illumination he worked or read, or suffered his thoughts to wander in the insubstantial regions of reverie; or else he fell asleep . . . But as soon as the clock told him the real darkness had come, he would come in for me and take me out with him . . .

Papa Ponsard shuffled across the room and laid a hand on Valentin's shoulder. "And mind you, Valentin, if Monsieur Gebhart comes while I am out of the shop, you are to say to him that I am—that I am—"

"That he is eating his cheese soup and will return in a few minutes," said Josephine from the doorway. "But he will not come today."

"Trust me," said Valentin. "I shall say and do exactly the right thing, whatever that may be. Perhaps it will occur to me to tickle his ribs with this dagger which I see before me." And he picked up a paper knife of curious design and tried the blunt edge with his thumb.

"Kind Heaven!" cried the old man. "Would you ruin us all?"

"Your cheese soup, Grandfather!" said Josephine firmly. "Valentin is only fooling with you."

Which was true, for Valentin, left alone in the shop, cast aside the stiletto and looked around him for matters of greater interest. He was an impatient young man and he was very much in love. He was really only a boy.

So the *Zadig* was being catalogued at last! How often he had heard it threatened. And what matter, after all, since the catalogue was never to be printed and sent forth? It was merely another indication, another milestone passed, in the tragedy of Papa Ponsard. Just to have reached the point where he was willing to catalogue the book was an adumbration of the end. Poor Papa Ponsard! Valentin felt genuinely sorry for him. But he felt sorrier for Papa Ponsard's granddaughter and sorrier still for himself.

He approached the desk with some curiosity; but it was not the *Zadig* that engaged his attention nor yet the secret manuscript, for Papa had closed the drawer. He read the last scratchy item in the ledger with interest, perhaps with some sense of its pathos. He read it with a little gesture of impatience. The *Zadig* was worth little more than was being asked for it. Valentin had made private inquiry of the matter himself.

Something impish smiled inside him; he plucked the old man's quill from the inkhorn and poised it above the page. With a swift glance toward the top step, the pedestal of his Josephine, he added another cipher to the widely spaced figures that stood beside the description of the book, then hastily laid down the pen.

The price of the delightful *Zadig* stood now at 400000 francs.

Then, as the bells tinkled above the door, Valentin wheeled sharply and looked into the eyes of Monsieur Gebhart, who stood within the aperture. He had really come. What an evil-looking thing a landlord was, to be sure!

Valentin nervously recited his lesson, "He is eating his cheese soup and will return in a few minutes."

"I shall wait," said Monsieur Gebhart, not pleasantly; but a moment later his eyes had narrowed and his smile was cold, for he had recognized this hanger-on. For an instant he had thought the old man had been able to afford a clerk. "Young man," said Monsieur Gebhart sternly, "I have seen you here before. You are the suitor for his granddaughter's hand. You know his business. Tell me, is he able to pay?"

"I—I—I am afraid not," replied Valentin sadly.

"And you? You are not prepared to help him?"

"I am sorry," answered Valentin, "but I have nothing." He drew a long breath and continued, "I am sure, Monsieur Gebhart, that all he requires is a little time."

"He has had already more than a little time," said Monsieur Gebhart, "and I have another tenant for the shop. I am sorry for him, of course, and for the girl."

But he did not look particularly sorry, thought Valentin. Suddenly the boy's eyes were on the paper knife. He glanced quickly away. Now was his time—now or never! But he knew at once it would be never. Such things occurred only in books and in the films.

"I am sorry too," said Valentin, and for a fleeting moment his eyes rested again on the stiletto. "And now I think I must run to my own job while it is left to me." He repeated the message, "He is eating his cheese soup and will return in a few minutes."

"I shall wait," said Monsieur Gebhart for the second time.

Then the little bells over the door jingled less happily as Valentin Nadaud hurried back to his place in the shop next door, for he could not bear to wait and see Papa Ponsard and Josephine thrust into the street. He had no doubt that it would happen just that way. He had often seen it in the films, and he had read about it in books.

Monsieur Gebhart, left alone in the shop, wandered idly to the high desk and stood for a moment looking out at the hurrying feet that passed along the sidewalk above. His eyes fell casually on the glorious *Zadig*, paused there for an instant, and looked away again. Monsieur Gebhart was not interested in books. But in the next instant his glance was on the open ledger, and *that* was a book with whose uses he was well acquainted.

His eyes widened behind his horn-rimmed lenses. The last line in the ledger had caught his attention: *"I have seen only one other copy of this book in fourteen years."* Immediately above he saw the hiero-glyphic that now read *"400000 fr."*

"The old rascal!" murmured Monsieur Gebhart incredulously.

Then for several minutes he thought furiously and with, as it seemed to him, truly remarkable clarity.

It was obvious, of course, that he was being fooled, that he had been fooled for months on end. This cunning old devil Ponsard, pretending poverty, was actually possessed of books of extraordi-nary value which, no doubt, he was selling at fabulous prices. 400,000 francs! And the debt to him—Anatole Gebhart—his rent—was a beggarly 30,000.

Or was it possible that Papa Ponsard did not know the full value of his own books? It was a new thought and for a moment it staggered Monsieur Gebhart. He considered its possibilities. A book worth 400,000 francs to Papa Ponsard might to another dealer be worth an even larger sum. But even at 400,000 one could not lose—not for a book of which the old devil had not seen another copy in fourteen years! There must be no doubt, mused Monsieur Gebhart, that there were in the world books of astonish-ing rarity and value. Vaguely he recalled the headlines of the newspapers after an important sale at the auctioneer's. And once there had been a paragraph about an American . . . and a book . . . What was it the fool had paid for a single volume? Perhaps as much as 1,000,000 francs!

With an oath Monsieur Gebhart brought his fist down on the desk so that the ink jumped in the horn. Then a slow smile crossed his face and again his brain functioned with its customary shrewd-ness. When the door at the top of the steps opened to admit Papa Ponsard, Monsieur Gebhart was seated comfortably in a chair, with crossed knees, in a spot remote from the high desk and the telltale ledger. There was even a kindly smile on his face.

Papa Ponsard, however, was dismayed. *"Mon Dieu!"* he cried. "I knew it! It is Monsieur Gebhart!"

Josephine's face was pale as she came forward. Immediately she began to explain. "We are sorry to have kept you waiting. We thought we heard the bells, Monsieur Gebhart, but we supposed it to be Valentin—Monsieur Nadaud—leaving the shop. And when we heard them again we thought it was Monsieur Nadaud returning."

Monsieur Gebhart was affable and magnanimous. "And no one else ever opens your door and rings your bells?" he questioned them archly.

His pleasantry shocked them. They stared in horror at this new evidence of his wickedness. It was Josephine who answered. "Alas, no one else, Monsieur!"

"That is a great pity," smiled Monsieur Gebhart. "Come then, since my visit has so upset you, let us get to business—since the sooner that is over the sooner I shall depart. I must suppose, Papa Ponsard, that you are ready to pay the money that you owe me."

But Papa Ponsard had collapsed into a chair. Suddenly he struggled to his feet. He shuffled toward a nail driven into the wall, upon which hung his incredible hat.

"My coat, Josephine!" he panted. "My best coat, darling. There may still be time."

"Mother of God, Papa Ponsard! What is it that you would do?" cried his granddaughter. "Where is it you would go?"

"To Ricardou, my pet, my good friend Ricardou. He alone can save us now. I shall ask a little loan—just enough to get us by. If he has it, I am sure he will give it to me. Only wait a little, Monsieur Gebhart, and I think I can promise you . . ."

But Monsieur Gebhart interrupted with a cry of "Fiddlesticks!" Then he gripped himself and contrived a little smile. "My dear Papa Ponsard," he said suavely, "surely I have heard you speak of your good friend Ricardou before. Already twice you have been to Ricardou while I waited, and once, unless I am mistaken, you returned with a hundred francs, which *he* had borrowed from a friend of *his*. No, no, let us put aside all thought of Ricardou. Come now, I am not inclined to be harsh, however gruff I may have seemed when I was here before. The fact is, since we last talked together I have become interested in books—in *all* books, I may say. In a small way I have become the strange thing you call, I believe, a collector."

Papa Ponsard's mouth opened and closed without sound; he seemed to have lost his voice.

"Why should it surprise you? Only in a small way, of course. Yes, I think I may now call myself a collector, Papa Ponsard, and it is my fondest wish to own one of the fine volumes you have in your shop. I refer, of course, to your lovely *Zadig*."

"My *Zadig!*"

"The *Zadig!*" cried Josephine, and laid her hand against her breast.

"In the circumstances you must allow me to name my own figure, however," continued Monsieur Gebhart. "You have much to thank me for, Papa Ponsard. You are lucky that you have had a roof over your head these several months past. Very well, then, you owe me thirty thousand francs. I wipe out that debt! I hand you this receipt for it, which I have written here at your desk while you guzzled your cheese soup. There, that is done. But the *Zadig* is mine for three hundred thousand francs."

"Three hundred thousand francs!" Papa Ponsard screamed the words. "You offer me three hundred thousand francs for my *Zadig?*"

Monsieur Gebhart shrugged. "I shall not go a sou higher," he said coldly. "You must take it or leave it."

It was at this point that Josephine Joly, with what is supposed to be a woman's intuition, reached the conclusion that Monsieur Gebhart had gone mad. However, it was a madness that spelled happiness for herself and Papa Ponsard. She spoke quickly.

"We accept your offer, Monsieur Gebhart," she said. "It is a book he has always valued and naturally he is loath to part with it—but it is yours."

"Then our business is concluded when I have paid you the money," said Monsieur Gebhart. "Fortunately, I have the amount with me. You will, of course, give me a bill of sale for the volume?—signed paid in full."

"Of course," answered Josephine. "I have often made them out for Papa Ponsard. I will give it to you at once."

Papa Ponsard, slumped in his chair, continued to stare blindly at the slip of paper in his hand—a receipt for thirty thousand francs back rental that he had never paid.

When the little bells above the door had jingled happily at the departure of Monsieur Gebhart and the *Zadig* was irrevocably gone, Papa Ponsard tottered to his old desk and peered into its drawer. After a moment he continued to read the manuscript it concealed:

In these nocturnal rambles I could not help remarking with wonder and admiration (although his rich endowment of ideas should have prepared me for it) the extraordinary faculty of analysis exhibited by Edgar Poe. He seemed to delight in giving it play and neglected no opportunity of indulging himself in that pleasure ... He would remark with a smile of proud satisfaction that for him man had an open window where his heart was; and as a rule he accompanied that assertion with an immediate demonstration which, having me for its object, could leave no doubt in my mind about Edgar's power of divination ...

That was all. What a pity the manuscript was incomplete! At least two pages appeared to be missing. But how fortunate that he had been able to identify the handwriting. That flowing script, that unmistakable manner! The signature was missing, to be sure, but it was photographed upon his mind as if the dashing syllables *Alexandre Dumas* were under his eyes. This was a treasure that no Monsieur Gebhart, no rich American, would ever take from him.

Papa Ponsard returned to his chair. A little helplessly, Josephine too sat down; the strain on her also had been considerable.

There she still sat when Valentin Nadaud entered hurriedly amid a perfect ecstasy of bells.

"He has gone?" asked the boy anxiously. "You are still here?"

"He is gone," answered Josephine, "and we are still here." And she told him what had happened.

"Mon Dieu!" cried Valentin, understanding. "But when he comes to sell it?"

"It was his own offer," said Josephine sharply. "What do you mean? What are you thinking, Valentin?"

"I am thinking that now you are rich, I must wait a little longer." said Valentin sadly.

EDITORS' POSTSCRIPT: *Try to find those books today! And at Papa Ponsard's original prices! Ah, the snows of yester-year . . .*

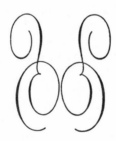

HELP WANTED, MALE

BY REX STOUT

When Rex Stout's last novel, *A Family Affair*, was published just before his death, *The New Yorker* wrote: "Mr. Stout, almost incredibly, will be eighty-nine years old in December, and this is the forty-sixth Nero Wolfe adventure with which he has entertained us, but there is not the slightest hint here of a diminished vigor or a flagging inventiveness." He was born in Noblesville, Indiana, on December 1, 1886, and died in Brewster, N.Y., on October 27, 1975. The first Nero Wolfe novel was published when Mr. Stout was forty-eight.

HE PAID US a visit the day he stopped the bullet.

Ben Jensen was a publisher, a politician, and, in my opinion, a dope. I had had a sneaking idea that he would have gone ahead and bought the inside Army dope that Captain Root had offered to sell him if he had been able to figure out a way of using it without any risk of losing a hunk of hide. But he had played it safe and had cooperated with Nero Wolfe like a good little boy. That had been a couple of months before.

Now, early on a Tuesday morning, he phoned to say he wanted to see Wolfe. When I told him that Wolfe would be occupied with the orchids, as usual, until eleven o'clock, he fussed a little and made a date for eleven sharp. He arrived five minutes ahead of time, and I escorted him into the office and invited him to deposit his big, bony frame in the red leather chair.

After he sat down he asked me, "Don't I remember you? Aren't you Major Goodwin?"

"Yep."

"You're not in uniform."

"I was just noticing," I said, "that you need a haircut. At your age, with your gray hair, it looks better trimmed. More distinguished. Shall we continue with the personal remarks?"

There was the clang of Wolfe's personal elevator out in the hall, and a moment later Wolfe entered, exchanged greetings with the caller and got himself, all of his two hundred and sixty-some pounds lowered into his personal chair behind his desk.

Ben Jensen said, "Something I wanted to show you—got it in the mail this morning," and took an envelope from his pocket and stood up to hand it across. Wolfe glanced at the envelope, removed a piece of paper from it and glanced at that, and passed them along to me. The envelope was addressed to Ben Jensen, neatly hand-printed in ink. The piece of paper had been clipped from something, all four edges, with scissors or a sharp knife, and it had printed on it, not by hand, in large, black type:

YOU ARE ABOUT TO DIE—
AND I WILL WATCH YOU DIE!

Wolfe murmured, "Well, sir?"

"I can tell you," I put in, "free for nothing, where this came from."

Jensen snapped at me, "You mean who sent it?"

"Oh, no. For that I would charge. It was clipped from an ad for a movie called *Meeting at Dawn*. The movie of the century. I saw the ad last week in *The American Magazine*. I suppose it's in all the magazines. If you could find—"

Wolfe made a noise at me and murmured again at the fidgeting Jensen, "Well, sir?"

"What am I going to do?" Jensen demanded.

"I'm sure I don't know. Have you any notion who sent it?"

"No. None at all." Jensen sounded grieved. "Damn it, I don't like it. It's not just the usual junk from an anonymous crank. Look at it! It's direct and to the point. I think someone's going to try to kill me, and I don't know who or why or when or how. I suppose tracing it is out of the question, but I want some protection. I want to buy it from you."

I put up a hand to cover a yawn. I knew there would be nothing doing—no case, no fee, no excitement. In the years I had been living in Nero Wolfe's house on West 35th Street, acting as goad, prod, lever, irritant, and chief assistant in the detective business, I had heard him tell at least fifty scared people, of all conditions and ages, that if someone had determined to kill them and was going to be stubborn about it, he would probably succeed.

On occasion, when the bank balance was doing a dive, he had furnished Cather or Durkin or Panzer or Keems as a bodyguard at a 100 percent markup, but now they were all very busy fighting Japs, and anyhow we had just deposited a five-figure check from a certain client.

Jensen got sore, naturally, but Wolfe only murmured at him that he might succeed in interesting the police, or that we would be glad to give him a list of reliable detective agencies which would provide companions for his movements as long as he remained alive—at sixty bucks for twenty-four hours. Jensen said that wasn't it, he wanted to hire Wolfe's brains. Wolfe merely made a face and shook his head. Then Jensen wanted to know what about Goodwin? Wolfe said that Major Goodwin was an officer in the United States Army.

"He's not in uniform," Jensen growled.

Wolfe was patient. "Officers in Military Intelligence on special assignments," he explained, "have freedoms. Major Goodwin's special assignment is to assist me in various projects entrusted to me by the Army. For which I am not paid. I have little time now for my private business. I think, Mr. Jensen, you should move and act with reasonable precaution for awhile. For example, in licking the flaps of envelopes—such things as that. Examine the strip of mucilage. Nothing is easier than to remove mucilage from an envelope flap and replace it with a mixture containing a deadly poison. Any door you open, anywhere, stand to one side and fling the door wide with a push or a pull before crossing the sill. Things like that."

"Good God," Jensen muttered.

Wolfe nodded. "That's how it is. But keep in mind that this fellow has severely restricted himself, if he's not a liar. He says he will watch you die. That greatly limits him in method and technique. He or she has to be there when it happens. So I advise prudence and a decent vigilance. Use your brains, but give up the idea of renting mine. No panic is called for. . . . Archie, how many people have threatened to take my life in the past ten years?"

I pursed my lips. "Oh, maybe twenty-two."

"Pfui." He scowled at me. "At least a hundred. And I am not dead yet, Mr. Jensen."

Jensen pocketed his clipping and envelope and departed, no better off than when he came except for the valuable advice about licking envelopes and opening doors. I felt kind of sorry for him and took the trouble to wish him good luck as I escorted him to the front door and let him out to the street, and even used some breath to tell him that if he decided to try an agency, Cornwall & Mayer had the best men.

Then I went back to the office and stood in front of Wolfe's desk, facing him, and pulled my shoulders back and expanded my chest. I took that attitude because I had some news to break to him and thought it might help to look as much like an army officer as possible.

"I have an appointment," I said, "at nine o'clock Thursday morning, in Washington, with General Carpenter."

Wolfe's brows went up a millimeter. "Indeed?"

"Yes, sir. At my request. I wish to take an ocean trip. I want to get a look at a Jap. I would like to catch one, if it can be done without much risk, and pinch him and make some remarks to him. I have thought up a crushing remark to make to a Jap and would like to use it."

"Nonsense." Wolfe was placid. "Your three requests to be sent overseas have been denied."

"Yeah, I know." I kept my chest out. "But that was just colonels and old Fife. Carpenter will see my point. I admit you're a great detective, the best orchid-grower in New York, a champion eater and beer-drinker, and a genius. But I've been working for you a hundred years—anyhow, a lot of years—and this is a hell of a way to spend a war. I'm going to see General Carpenter and lay it out. Of course he'll phone you. I appeal to your love of country, your vanity, your finer instincts what there is of them, and your dislike of Japs. If you tell Carpenter it would be impossible for you to get along without me, I'll put pieces of gristle in your crabmeat and sugar in your beer."

Wolfe opened his eyes and glared at me. The mere suggestion of sugar in his beer made him speechless.

That was Tuesday. The next morning, Wednesday, the papers headlined the murder of Ben Jensen on the front page. Eating breakfast in the kitchen with Fritz, as usual, I was only halfway through the report in the *Times* when the doorbell rang, and when I answered it I found on the stoop our old friend, Inspector Cramer, of the homicide squad.

Nero Wolfe said, "Not interested, not involved, and not curious."

He was a sight, as he always was when propped up in bed with his breakfast tray. The custom was for Fritz, his chef, to deliver the tray to his room on the second floor at eight o'clock. It was now 8:15, and already down the gullet were the peaches and cream, most of the bacon, and two thirds of the eggs, not to mention coffee and the green tomato jam. The black silk coverlet was folded back, and you had to look to tell where the yellow percale sheet ended and the yellow pajamas began. Few people except Fritz and me ever got to see him like that, but he had stretched a point for Inspector Cramer, who knew that from nine to eleven he would be up in the plant-rooms with the orchids, and unavailable.

"In the past dozen years," Cramer said in his ordinary growl, without any particular feeling, "you have told me, I suppose, in round figures, ten million lies."

The commas were chews on his unlighted cigar. He looked the way he always did when he had been working all night—peevish and put upon but under control, all except his hair, which had forgotten where the part went.

Wolfe, who was hard to rile at breakfast, swallowed toast and jam and then coffee, ignoring the insult.

Cramer said, "He came to see you yesterday morning, twelve hours before he was killed. You don't deny that."

"And I have told you what for," Wolfe said politely. "He had received that threat and said he wanted to hire my brains. I declined to work for him and he went away. That was all."

"Why did you decline to work for him? What had he done to you?"

"Nothing." Wolfe poured coffee. "I don't do that kind of work. A man whose life is threatened anonymously is either in no danger at all, or his danger is so acute and so ubiquitous that his position is hopeless. My only previous association with Mr. Jensen was in connection with an attempt by an army captain named Root to sell him inside army information for political purposes. Together we got the necessary evidence, and Captain Root was court-martialed.

25

Mr. Jensen was impressed, so he said, by my handling of that case. I suppose that was why he came to me when he decided that he wanted help."

"Did he think the threat came from someone connected with Captain Root?"

"No. Root wasn't mentioned. He said he had no idea who intended to kill him."

Cramer humphed. "That's what he told Tim Cornwall, too. Cornwall thinks you passed because you knew or suspected it was too hot to handle. Naturally, Cornwall is bitter. He has lost his best man."

"Indeed," Wolfe said mildly. "If that was his best man . . ."

"So Cornwall says," Cramer insisted, "and he's dead. Name of Doyle; been in the game twenty years, with a good record. The picture as we've got it doesn't necessarily condemn him. Jensen went to Cornwall & Mayer yesterday about noon, and Cornwall assigned Doyle as a guard.

"We've traced all their movements—nothing special. In the evening Doyle went along to a meeting at a midtown club. They left the club at eleven-twenty, and apparently went straight home, on the subway or bus, to the apartment house where Jensen lived on Seventy-third Street near Madison. It was eleven-forty-five when they were found dead on the sidewalk at the entrance to the apartment house. Both shot in the heart with a thirty-eight, Doyle from behind and Jensen from the front. We have the bullets. No powder marks. No nothing."

Wolfe murmured sarcastically, "Mr. Cornwall's best man."

"Nuts," Cramer objected to the sarcasm. "He was shot in the back. There's a narrow passage ten paces away where the guy could have hid. Or the shots could have come from a passing car, or from across the street. We haven't found anybody who heard the shots. The doorman was in the basement stoking the water heater, the excuse for that being that they're short of men like everybody else. The elevator man was on his way to the tenth floor with a passenger, a tenant. The bodies were discovered by two women on their way home from a movie. It must have happened not more than a minute before they came by, but they had just got off a Madison Avenue bus at the corner."

Wolfe got out of bed, which was an operation deserving an audience. He glanced at the clock on the bed table. It was 8:35.

"I know, I know," Cramer growled. "You've got to get dressed and get upstairs to your horticulture. . . . The tenant going up in the elevator was a prominent doctor who barely knew Jensen by sight. The two women who found the bodies are Seventh Avenue models who never heard of Jensen. The elevator man has worked there over twenty years without displaying a grudge, and Jensen was a generous tipper and popular with the bunch. The doorman is a fat nitwit who was hired two weeks ago only because of the manpower situation and doesn't know the tenants by name.

"Beyond those, all we have is the population of New York City and the guests who arrive and depart daily and nightly. That's why I came to you, and for the lord's sake give me what you've got. You can see that I need it."

"Mr. Cramer." The mountain of yellow pajamas moved. "I repeat. I am not interested, not involved, and not curious." Wolfe headed for the bathroom.

Exit Cramer—mad.

Back in the office there was the morning mail. I was getting toward the bottom of the stack without encountering anything startling or promising when I slit another envelope, and there it was.

I stared at it. I picked up the envelope and stared at that. I don't often talk to myself, but I said, loud enough for me to hear, "My goodness." Then I left the rest of the mail for later and went and mounted the three flights to the plant-rooms on the roof. Proceeding through the first three departments, past everything from rows of generating flasks to Cattleya hybrids covered with blooms, I found Wolfe in the potting-room, with Theodore Horstmann, the orchid nurse, examining a crate of sphagnum that had just arrived.

"Well?" he demanded, with no sign of friendliness. The general idea was that when he was up there I interrupted him at my peril.

"I suppose," I said carelessly, "that I shouldn't have bothered you, but I ran across something in the mail that I thought you'd find amusing," and I put them on the bench before him, side by side: the envelope with his name and address printed on it by hand, in ink, and the piece of paper that had been clipped from something with scissors or a sharp knife, reading in large, black type, printed, but not by hand:

YOU ARE ABOUT TO DIE—
AND I WILL WATCH YOU DIE!

"It sure is a coincidence," I remarked, grinning at him.

Wolfe said without any perceptible quiver, "I'll look over the mail at eleven o'clock as usual."

It was the grand manner, all right. Seeing he was impervious, I retrieved the exhibits without a word, returned to the office, and busied myself with the chores.

It was eleven on the dot when he came down, and began the routine. Not until Fritz had brought the beer and he had irrigated his interior did he lean back in his chair, let his eyes go half shut, and observe, "You will, of course, postpone your trip to Washington."

I let my frank, open countenance betray surprise. "I can't. I have an appointment with a Lieutenant General. Anyhow, why?" I indicated the envelope and clipping on his desk. "That tomfoolery? No panic is called for. I doubt the urgency of your peril. A man planning a murder doesn't spend his energy clipping pieces out of adver—"

"You are going to Washington?"

"Yes, sir. I have a date. Of course, I could phone Carpenter and tell him your nerves are a little shaky on account of an anony—"

"When do you leave?"

"I have a seat on the six o'clock train."

"Very well. Then we have the day. Your notebook."

Wolfe leaned forward to pour beer and drink, and then leaned back again. "I offer a comment on your jocosity. When Mr. Jensen called here yesterday and showed us that thing, we had no inkling of the character of the person who had sent it. It might have been merely the attempt of a coward to upset his digestion.

"However, we no longer enjoy that ignorance. This person not only promptly killed Mr. Jensen, with wit equal to his determination, but also killed Mr. Doyle, a stranger, whose presence could not have been foreseen. We now know that this person is cold-blooded, ruthless, quick to decide and to act, and an egomaniac."

"Yes, sir. I agree. If you go to bed and stay there until I get back from Washington, letting no one but Fritz enter the room, I may not be able to control my tongue when with you, but actually I will understand and I won't tell anybody. You need a rest, anyway. And don't lick any envelopes."

"Bah." Wolfe wiggled a finger at me. "That thing was not sent to you. Presumably you are not on the agenda."

"Yes, sir."

"And this person is dangerous and requires attention."

"I agree."

Wolfe shut his eyes. "Very well. Take notes as needed. . . . It may be assumed, if this person means business with me as he did with Mr. Jensen, that this is connected with the case of Captain Root. I had no other association with Mr. Jensen. . . . Learn the whereabouts of Captain Root."

"The court-martial gave him three years in the cooler."

"I know it. Is he there? Also, what about that young woman, his fiancée, who raised such a ruction about it? Her name is Jane Geer." Wolfe's eyes half opened for an instant. "You have a habit of knowing how to locate personable young women without delay. Have you seen that one recently?"

"Oh," I said offhand, "I sort of struck up an acquaintance with her. I guess I can get in touch with her. But I doubt—"

"Do so. I want to see her. . . . Excuse me for interrupting, but you have a train to catch. . . . Also, inform Inspector Cramer of this development and suggest that he investigate Captain Root's background, his relatives and intimates, anyone besides Miss Geer who might thirst for vengeance at his disgrace. I'll do that. If Captain Root is in prison, arrange with General Fife to bring him here. I want to have a talk with him. . . . Where is the clipping received yesterday by Mr. Jensen? Ask Mr. Cornwall and Mr. Cramer. There is the possibility that this is not another one like it, but the same one."

I shook my head. "No, sir. This one is clipped closer to the printing at the upper right."

"I noticed that, but ask, anyway. Inspect the chain bolts on the doors and test the night gong in your room. Fritz will sleep in your room tonight. I shall speak to Fritz and Theodore. All of this can easily be attended to by telephone except Miss Geer, and that is your problem. When will you return from Washington?"

"I should be able to catch a noon train back—my appointment's at nine. Getting here around five." I added earnestly, "If I can clear it with Carpenter to cross the ocean, I will, of course, arrange not to leave until this ad-clipper has been attended to."

"Don't hurry back on my account. Or alter your plans. You receive a salary from the Government." Wolfe's tone was dry, sharp, and icy. He went on with it: "Please get General Fife on the phone. We'll begin by learning about Captain Root."

The program went smoothly, all except the Jane Geer number. If it hadn't been for her I'd have been able to make the six o'clock train with hours to spare. Fife reported back on Root in thirty minutes, to the effect Root was in the clink on government property down in Maryland, and would be transported to New York without delay for an interview with Wolfe.

Cornwall said he had turned the clipping and envelope Jensen had received over to Inspector Cramer, and Cramer verified it and said he had it. When I had explained the situation, Cramer emitted a hoarse chuckle, and said offensively, "So Wolfe is not interested, involved, or curious." I knew Wolfe would have a visit from him. Not pleasant.

On Jane Geer the luck was low. When, before noon, I phoned the advertising agency she worked for, I was told that she was somewhere on Long Island admiring some client's product for which she was to produce copy. When I finally did get her after four o'clock, she went willful on me, presumably because she regarded my phoning five times in one day as evidence that my primal impulses had been aroused and I was beginning to pant. She would not come to Nero Wolfe's place unless I bought her a cocktail first. So I met her a little after five at the Stork Club.

She had put in a full day's work, but, looking at her, you might have thought she had come straight from an afternoon nap.

She darted her brown eyes at me. "Let me," she said, "see your right forefinger."

I poked it at her. She rubbed its tip gently with the tip of her own. "I wondered if it had a callus. After dialing my number five times in less than five hours."

She sipped her Tom Collins, bending her head to get her lips to the straw. A strand of her hair slipped forward over an eye and a cheek, and I reached across and used the same finger to put it back in place.

"I took that liberty," I told her, "because I wish to have an unobstructed view of your lovely phiz. I want to see if you turn pale."

"Overwhelmed by you so near?"

"No, I know that reaction—I correct for it. Anyhow, I doubt if I'm magnetic right now, because I'm sore at you for making me miss a train."

"I didn't phone you this time. You phoned me."

"Okay." I drank. "You said on the phone that you still don't like Nero Wolfe and you wouldn't go to see him unless you knew what for, and maybe not even then. So this is what for: He wants to ask you whether you intend to kill him yourself or hire the same gang that you got to kill Jensen and Doyle."

"Mercy." She looked my face over. "You'd better put your humor on a diet. It's taking on weight."

I shook my head. "Ordinarily, I would enjoy playing catch with you, as you are aware, but I can't miss all the trains. Because Wolfe's life has been threatened in the same manner as Jensen's was, the supposition is that Jensen was murdered for revenge, for what he did to Captain Root. Because of the cutting remarks you made when Root was trapped, and your general attitude, there is a tendency to want to know what you have been doing lately."

"Nero Wolfe seriously thinks I—did that? Or had it done?"

"I didn't say so. He wants to discuss it."

Her eyes flashed. Her tone took on an edge: "It is also extremely corny. And the police. Have you kindly arranged that when Wolfe finishes with me I proceed to headquarters?"

"Listen, Tiger-eyes." She let me cut her off, which was a pleasant surprise. "Have you noticed me sneaking up on you from behind? If so, draw it for me. I have explained a situation. Your name has not been mentioned to the police, though they have consulted us.

But since the police are onto the Root angle they are apt to get a steer in your direction without us, and it wouldn't hurt if Wolfe had already satisfied himself that you wouldn't kill a fly."

"By what process?" She was scornful. "I suppose he asks me if I ever committed murder, and I smile and say no, and he apologizes and gives me an orchid."

"Not quite. He's a genius. He asks you questions like do you bait your own hook when you go fishing, and you reveal yourself without knowing it."

"It sounds fascinating." Her eyes suddenly changed. "I wonder," she said.

"What is it?—and we'll both wonder."

"Sure." Her eyes had changed more. "This wouldn't by any chance be a climax you've been working up to? You, with a thousand girls and women, so that you have to issue ration books so many minutes to a coupon, and yet finding so much time for me? Leading up to this idiotic frame—"

"Turn that one off," I broke in, "or I'll begin to get suspicious, myself. You know darned well why I have found time for you, having a mirror as you do. I have been experimenting to test my emotional reaction to form, color, touch, and various perfumes, and I have been deeply grateful for your cooperation. I thank you—but that is all."

"Ha, ha." She stood up, her eyes not softening nor her tone melting. "I am going to see Nero Wolfe. I welcome an opportunity to reveal myself to Nero Wolfe. Do I go or are you taking me?"

I took her. I paid the check and we went out and got a taxi.

But she didn't get to see Wolfe.

Since chain-bolt orders were in effect, my key wouldn't let us in and I had to ring the doorbell for Fritz. I had just pushed the button, when who should appear, mounting the steps to join us on the stoop, but the army officer that they use for a model when they want to do a picture conveying the impression that masculine comeliness will win the war. I admit he was handsome; I admitted it to myself right then, when I first saw him. He looked preoccupied and concentrated, but, even so, he found time for a glance at Jane.

At that moment the door swung open and I spoke to Fritz: "Okay, thanks. Is Mr. Wolfe in the office?"

"No, he's up in his room."

"All right; I'll take it." Fritz departed, and I maneuvered into position to dominate the scene, on the doorsill facing out. I spoke to the masculine model: "Yes, Major? This is Nero Wolfe's place."

"I know it is." He had a baritone voice that suited him to a T. "I want to see him. My name is Emil Jensen. I am the son of Ben Jensen, who was killed last night."

31

"Oh." There wasn't much resemblance, but that's nature's look-out. I have enough to do. "Mr. Wolfe has an appointment. It would be handy if I could tell him what you want."

"I want to—consult him. If you don't mind. I'd rather tell him." He smiled to take the sting off. Probably Psychological Warfare Branch.

"I'll see. Come on in."

I made room for Jane, and he followed her. After attending to the bolt I escorted them to the office, invited them to sit, and went to the phone on my desk and buzzed Wolfe's room.

"Yes?" Wolfe's voice came.

"Archie. Miss Geer is here. Also, Major Emil Jensen just arrived. He is the son of Ben Jensen and prefers to tell you what he wants to consult you about."

"Give them both my regrets. I am engaged and can see no one."

"Engaged for how long?"

"Indefinitely. I can make no appointments for this week."

"But you may remember—"

"Archie! Tell them that please." The line died.

So I told them that. They were not pleased. The Lord knows what kind of performance Jane would have put on if she hadn't been restrained by the presence of a stranger; as it was, she didn't have to fumble around for pointed remarks. Jensen wasn't indignant, but he sure was stubborn. During an extended conversation that got nowhere, I noticed a gradual increase in their inclination to cast sympathetic glances at each other.

I thought it might help matters along, meaning that they might clear out sooner if I changed the subject, so I said emphatically, "Miss Geer, this is Major Jensen."

He got to his feet, bowed to her like a man who knows how to bow, and told her, "How do you do? It looks as if it's hopeless, at least for this evening, for both of us. I'll have to hunt a taxi, and it would be a pleasure if you'll let me drop you."

So they left together. Going down the stoop, which I admit was moderately steep, he indicated not obtrusively that he had an arm there, and she rested her fingers in the bend of it to steady herself. That alone showed astonishing progress in almost no time at all, for she was by no means a born clinger.

Oh, well, I was a major too. I shrugged indifferently as I shut the door. Then I sought Wolfe's room, knocked, and was invited in.

Standing in the doorway to his bathroom, facing me, his old-fashioned razor in his hand, all lathered up, he demanded brusquely, "What time is it?"

"Six-thirty."

"When is the next train?"

32

"Seven o'clock. But what the hell, apparently there is going to be work to do. I can put it off to next week."

"No. It's on your mind. Get that train."

I tried one more stab. "My motive is selfish. If, while I am sitting talking to Carpenter in the morning, word comes that you have been killed, or even temporarily disabled, he'll blame me and I won't stand a chance. So for purely selfish reasons—"

"Confound it!" he barked. "You'll miss that train! I have no intention of getting killed. Get out of here!"

I faded. . . .

After the war I intended to run for Congress and put through laws about generals. I have a theory that generals should be rubbed liberally with neat's-foot oil before being taken out and shot. Though I doubt if I would have bothered with the oil in the case of General Carpenter that morning if I had had a free hand.

I was a major. So I sat and said yessir yessir yessir, while he told me that he had given me the appointment only because he thought I wanted to discuss something of importance, and that I would stay where I was put, and shut my trap about it. When it was all over, he observed that since I was in Washington I might as well confer with the staff on various cases, finished and unfinished, and I would report immediately to Colonel Dickey.

I doubt if I made a good impression, considering my state of mind. They kept me around, conferring, all day Thursday and most of Friday. I phoned Wolfe that I was detained. By explaining the situation on 35th Street I could have got permission to beat it back to New York, but I wasn't going to give that collection of brass headgear an excuse to giggle around that Nero Wolfe didn't have brains enough to keep on breathing, in his own house, without me there to look after him. Wolfe would have had my scalp.

But I was tempted to hop a plane when, late Thursday evening, I saw the ad in the *Star*. I had been too busy all day to take more than a glance at the New York papers I'd been following for news of the Jensen case. I was alone in my hotel room when it caught my eye, bordered and spaced to make a spot:

WANTED, A MAN
weighing about 260–270, around 5 ft. 11; 45–55 years old, medium in coloring, waist not over 48, capable of easy and normal movement. Temporary. Hazardous. $100 a day. Send photo with letter. Box 292 Star.

I read it through four times, stared at it disapprovingly for an additional two minutes, and then reached for the phone and put in a New York call. I got Fritz Brenner on the phone, and he assured me Wolfe was all right.

Getting ready for bed, I tried to figure out in what manner, if I

33

were making preparations to kill Nero Wolfe, I could make use of an assistant, hired on a temporary basis at a hundred bucks a day, who was a physical counterpart of Wolfe. The two schemes I devised weren't very satisfactory, and the one I hit on after I got my head on the pillow was even worse, so I flipped the switch on the nervous system and let the muscles quit. . . .

In the morning I finished conferring and made tracks for New York.

Arriving at Wolfe's house on 35th Street a little before eleven, I gave the button three short pushes as usual, and in a moment there were footsteps, and the curtain was pulled aside and Fritz was peering at me through the glass panel. Satisfied, he let me in.

I saw Wolfe was in the office, since the door to it was open and the light shining through, so I breezed down the hall and on in.

"I am a fug—" I began, and stopped. Wolfe's chair behind his desk, his own chair and no one else's under any circumstances, was occupied by the appropriate mass of matter in comparatively human shape—in other words, by a big, fat man—but it wasn't Nero Wolfe. I had never seen him before.

Fritz, who had stayed to bolt the door, came at me from behind, talking. The occupant of the chair neither moved nor spoke, but merely leered at me. Fritz was telling me that Mr. Wolfe was up in his room.

The specimen in the chair said in a husky croak, "I suppose you're Goodwin. Archie. Have a good trip?"

I stared at him. In a way I wished I was back at the Pentagon, and in another way I wished I had come sooner.

He said, "Fritz, bring me another highball."

Fritz said, "Yes, sir."

He said, "Have a good trip, Archie?"

That was énough of that. I marched out to the hall and up a flight, went to Wolfe's door and tapped on it, and called, "Archie!" Wolfe's voice told me to come in.

He was seated in his number two chair, under the light, reading a book. He was fully dressed, and there was nothing in his appearance to indicate that he had lost his mind.

I did not intend to give him the satisfaction of sitting there smirking and enjoying fireworks. "Well," I said casually, "I got back. If you're sleepy we can wait till morning for conversation."

"I'm not sleepy." He closed the book, with a finger inserted at his page. "Are you going overseas?"

"You know damn well I'm not." I sat down. "We can discuss that at some future date when I'm out of the Army. It's a relief to find you all alive and well around here. It's very interesting down in Washington. Everybody on their toes."

"No doubt. Did you stop in the office downstairs?"

"I did. So you put that ad in the *Star* yourself. How do you pay him—cash every day? Did you figure out the deductions for income tax and social security? I sat down at my desk and began to report to him. I thought it was you. Until he ordered Fritz to bring him a highball, and I know you hate highballs. Deduction. It reminds me of the time your daughter from Yugoslavia showed up—"

"Archie. Shut up."

Wolfe put the book down and shifted in his chair, with the routine grunts. When the new equilibrium was established he said, "You will find details about him on a slip of paper in the drawer of your desk. He is a retired architect named H. H. Hackett, out of funds, and an unsurpassed nincompoop with the manners of a wart hog. I chose him, from those answering the advertisement, because his appearance and build were the most suitable and he is sufficiently an ass to be willing to risk his life for a hundred dollars a day."

"If he keeps on calling me 'Archie' the risk will become—"

"If you please." Wolfe wiggled a finger at me. "Do you think the idea of him sitting there in my chair is agreeable to me? He may be dead tomorrow or the next day. I told him that. This afternoon he went to Mr. Ditson's place in a taxicab to look at orchids, and came back ostentatiously carrying two plants. Tomorrow afternoon you will drive him somewhere and bring him back, and again in the evening. Dressed for the street, wearing my hat and lightweight coat, carrying my stick, he would deceive anyone except you."

"Yes, sir. But why couldn't you just stay in the house? You do, anyway. And be careful who gets in. Until . . ."

"Until what?"

"Until the bird that killed Jensen is caught."

"Bah!" He glared at me. "By whom? By Mr. Cramer? What do you suppose he is doing now? Pfui! Major Jensen, Mr. Jensen's son, arriving home on leave from Europe five days ago, learned that during his absence his father had sued his mother for divorce. The father and son quarreled, which was not unique. But Mr. Cramer has a hundred men trying to collect evidence that will convict Major Jensen of killing his father! Utterly intolerable asininity. For what motive could Major Jensen have for killing me?"

"Well, now." My eyebrows were up. "I wouldn't just toss it in the wastebasket. What if the major figured that sending you the same kind of message he sent his father would make everybody react the way you are doing?"

Wolfe shook his head. "He didn't. Unless he's a born fool. He would have known that merely sending me that thing would be inadequate, that he would have to follow it up by making good on the threat; and he hasn't killed me, and I doubt if he intends to. General Fife has looked up his record for me. Mr. Cramer is wasting his time, his men's energy, and the money of the people of New York. I am handicapped. The men I have used and can trust have gone to war. You bounce around thinking only of yourself, deserting me. I am confined to this room, left to my own devices, with a vindictive, bloodthirsty maniac waiting an opportunity to kill me."

He sure was piling it on. But I knew better than to contribute a note of skepticism when he was in one of his romantic moods, having been fired for that once; and, besides, I wouldn't have signed an affidavit that he was exaggerating the situation. So I only asked him, "What about Captain Root? Did they bring him?"

"Yes. He was here today and I talked with him. He has been in that prison for over a month and asserts that this cannot possibly be connected with him or his. He says Miss Geer has not communicated with him for six weeks or more. His mother is teaching school at Danforth, Ohio; that has been verified by Mr. Cramer; she is there. His father, who formerly ran a filling station at Danforth, abandoned wife and son ten years ago, and is said to be working in a war plant in Oklahoma. Wife and son prefer not to discuss him. No brother or sister. According to Captain Root, there is no one on earth who would conceivably undertake a ride on the subway, let alone multiple murder, to avenge him."

"He might just possibly be right."

"Nonsense. There was no other slightest connection between Mr. Jensen and me. I've asked General Fife to keep Root in New York and to request the prison authorities to look over his effects there if he has any."

"When you get an idea in your head—"

"I never do. As you mean it. I react to stimuli. In this instance I am reacting in the only way open to me. The person who shot Mr. Jensen and Mr. Doyle is bold to the point of rashness. He can probably be tempted to proceed with his program." . . .

I went up to my room.

The gong was a dingus under my bed. The custom was that when I retired at night I turned a switch, and if anyone put his foot down in the hall within ten feet of Wolfe's door the gong gonged. It had been installed on account of a certain occurrence some years previously, when Wolfe had got a knife stuck in him. The thing had never gone off except when we tested it, and in my opinion never would but I never failed to switch it on, because if Wolfe had stepped into the hall some night and the gong hadn't sounded it would have caused discussion.

This night, with a stranger in the house, I was glad it was there.

In the morning breakfast was all over the place. Afterward I spent an hour up in the plant-rooms with Wolfe.

We got to details. Jane Geer was making a nuisance of herself. I understood now, of course, why Wolfe had refused to see her Wednesday evening. After sending me to get her he had conceived the strategy of hiring a double, and he didn't want her to get a look at the real Nero Wolfe, because if she did she would be less likely to be deceived by the counterfeit and go to work on him.

She had phoned several times, insisting on seeing him, and had come to the house Friday morning and argued for five minutes with Fritz through the three-inch crack which the chain bolt permitted the door to open to. Now Wolfe had an idea for one of his elaborate charades. I was to phone her to come to see Wolfe at six o'clock that afternoon. When she came I was to take her in to Hackett. Wolfe would coach Hackett for the interview.

I looked skeptical.

Wolfe said, "It will give her a chance to kill Mr. Hackett."

I snorted. "With me right there to tell her when to cease firing."

"I admit it is unlikely, but it will give me an opportunity to see her and hear her. I shall be at the hole."

So that was really the idea. He would be in the passage, a sort of alcove, at the kitchen end of the downstairs hall, looking through into the office by means of the square hole in the wall. The hole was camouflaged on the office side by a picture that was transparent one way. He loved to have an excuse to use it.

Major Jensen had phoned once and been told that Wolfe was engaged; apparently he wasn't as persistent as Jane.

When I got down to the office Hackett was there in Wolfe's chair, eating cookies and getting crumbs on the desk.

From the phone on my desk I got Jane Geer at her office. "Archie," I told her.

She snapped, "Archie who?"

"Oh, come, come. We haven't sicked the police onto you, have we? Nero Wolfe wants to see you."

"He does? Ha, ha. He doesn't act like it."

"He has reformed. I showed him a lock of your hair. I showed him a picture of Elsa Maxwell and told him it was you. This time he won't let me come after you."

"Neither will I."

"Okay. Be here at six o'clock and you will be received. Six o'clock today P.M. Will you?"

She admitted that she would.

I made a couple of other calls and did some miscellaneous chores. But I found that my jaw was getting clamped tighter and tighter on account of an irritating noise. Finally I spoke to the occupant of Wolfe's chair: "What kind of cookies are those?"

"Gingersnaps." Evidently the husky croak was his normal voice.

"I didn't know we had any."

"We didn't. I asked Fritz. He doesn't seem to know about gingersnaps, so I walked over to Ninth Avenue and got some."

"When? This morning?"

"Just a little while ago."

I turned to my phone, buzzed the plant-rooms, got Wolfe, and told him, "Mr. Hackett is sitting in your chair eating gingersnaps. Just a little while ago he walked to Ninth Avenue and bought them. If he pops in and out of the house whenever he sees fit, what are we getting for our hundred bucks?"

Wolfe spoke to the point. I hung up and turned to Hackett and spoke to the point. He was not to leave the house except as instructed by Wolfe or me. He seemed unimpressed.

"All right," he said; "if that's the bargain I'll keep it. But there's two sides to a bargain. I was to be paid daily in advance, and I haven't been paid for today. A hundred dollars net."

I took five twenties from the expense wallet and forked it over.

"I must say," he commented, folding the bills neatly and stuffing them in his waistband pocket, "this is a large return for a small effort. I am aware that I may earn it—ah, suddenly and unexpectedly." He leaned toward me. "Though I may tell you confidentially, Archie, that I expect nothing to happen. I am sanguine by nature."

"Yeah," I told him, "me too."

I opened the drawer of my desk, the middle one on the right, where I kept armament, got out the shoulder holster and put it on, and selected the gun that was my property—the other two belonged to Wolfe. There were only three cartridges in it, so I pulled the drawer open farther to get to the ammunition compartment, and filled the cylinder.

As I shoved the gun into the holster I happened to glance at Hackett, and saw that he had a new face. The line of his lips was tight, and his eyes looked startled, wary.

"It hadn't occurred to me before," he said, and his voice had changed too. "This Mr. Wolfe is quite an article, and you're his man. I am doing this with the understanding that someone may mistake me for Mr. Wolfe and try to kill me, but I have only his word for it that this is actually the situation. If it's more complicated than that, and the intention is for you to shoot me yourself, I want to say emphatically that that would not be fair."

I grinned at him sympathetically, trying to make up for my blunder, realizing that I should not have dressed for the occasion in

38

his presence. The sight of the gun, a real gun and real cartridges, had scared him stiff.

"Listen," I told him earnestly; "you said a minute ago that you expect nothing to happen. You may be right. I'm inclined to agree with you. But in case somebody does undertake to perform, I am wearing this little number"—I patted under my arm where the gun was—"for two purposes: first, to keep you from getting hurt; and, second, if you do get hurt, to hurt him worse."

It seemed to satisfy him, for his eyes got less concentrated, but he didn't resume with the gingersnaps. At least, I had accomplished that much.

To tell the truth, by the time the afternoon was over and I had him back in the house again, a little after five-thirty, I had to maintain a firm hold on such details as gingersnaps and his calling me "Archie" to keep from admiring him. During that extended expedition we made stops at the Metropolitan Museum of Art, the Botanical Gardens, and three or four stores. He occupied the rear seat, of course, because Wolfe always did, and the mirror showed me that he sat back comfortably, taking in the sights, a lot more imperturbable than Wolfe, himself, ever was in a car.

When we made one of our stops and Hackett got out to cross the sidewalk, he was okay. He didn't hurry or dodge or jerk or weave, but just walked. In Wolfe's hat and coat and stick, he might even have fooled me. I had to hand it to him, in spite of the fact that the whole show struck me as the biggest bust Wolfe had ever concocted.

Back in the house, I left Hackett in the office and went to the kitchen, where Wolfe was sitting at the big table drinking beer.

I reported: "They tried to get him from the top of the Palisades with a howitzer, but missed him. He was a little bruised on his left elbow from the revolving door at Rusterman's but otherwise unhurt."

Wolfe grunted. "How did he behave?"

"Okay."

Wolfe grunted again. "After dark we may more reasonably expect results. I repeat what I told you at noon; you will take an active part in the interview with Miss Geer, but you will restrain yourself. If you permit yourself to get fanciful, there is no telling what the effect may be on Mr. Hackett. As you know, his instructions are precise, but his discipline is questionable. See that she speaks up, so I can hear her. Seat her at the corner of my desk farthest from you, so I will have a good view of her face."

"Yes, sir."

But, as it turned out, I wasn't able to obey orders. It was then nearly six o'clock. When the doorbell rang, a few minutes later, and I went to answer it, glancing in at the office on my way down the hall to make sure that Hackett didn't have his feet up on the desk, I opened the door, to find that Miss Geer hadn't ventured alone on the streets of the great city, after all. Major Emil Jensen was there with her.

"Well," I said brightly, "two on one hook?"

Jensen said hello. Jane volunteered, "Major Jensen decided to come on the spur of the moment. We were having cocktails." She looked me up and down; it was true that I was blocking the way. "May we come in?"

Certainly I could have told Jensen we had only one extra chair so he had better go for a walk, but if there was going to be anything accomplished by having either of those two get the idea that Hackett was Nero Wolfe, I would have picked him for the experiment rather than her. On the other hand, with Hackett primed only for her, it would have been crowding our luck to confront him with both of them, and, anyway, I couldn't take such a chance on my own hook. I needed advice from headquarters. So I decided to herd them into the front room, ask them to wait, and go consult Wolfe.

"Sure," I said hospitably; "enter." I had got them seated, and was headed for the hall before noticing an unfortunate fact: The door from the front room to the office was standing open. That was careless of me, but I hadn't expected complications. If they moved across, as they naturally would, Hackett, sitting in the office, would be in plain sight. But what the hell, that was what he was there for. So I kept going, down the hall to the turn into the alcove at the far end, found Wolfe there ready to take position at the peephole, and muttered to him:

"She brought an outrider along. Major Jensen. I put them in the front room. The door into the office is open. Well?"

He scowled at me. He whispered, "Confound it. Return to the front room by way of the office, closing that door as you go. Tell Major Jensen to wait, that I wish to speak with Miss Geer privately. Take her to the office by way of the hall, and when you—"

Somebody fired a gun.

At least, that's what it sounded like, and the sound didn't come from outdoors. The walls and the air vibrated. Judging by the noise, I might have fired it myself, but I hadn't. I moved. In three jumps I was at the door to the office. Hackett was sitting there, looking startled and speechless. I dashed through to the front room. Jensen and Jane were there, on their feet, she off to the right and he to the left, both also startled and speechless, staring at each other. Their hands were empty, except for Jane's bag. I might have been inclined to let it go for Hackett biting a gingersnap if it hadn't been for the smell. I knew that smell.

I snapped at Jensen, "Well?"

"Well yourself." He had transferred the stare to me. "What the hell was it?"

"Did you fire a gun?"

"No. Did you?"

I pivoted to Jane. "Did you?"

"You—you idiot," she stammered, trying not to tremble. "Why would I fire a gun?"

"Let me see the one in your hand," Jensen demanded.

I looked at my hand and was surprised to see a gun in it. I must have snatched it from the holster automatically en route. "Not it," I said. I poked the muzzle to within an inch of Jensen's nose. "Was it?"

He sniffed. "No."

I said, "But a gun was fired inside here. Do you smell it?"

"Certainly I smell it."

"Okay. Let's join Mr. Wolfe and discuss it. Through there." I indicated the door to the office with a flourish of the gun.

Jane started jabbering about a put-up job, but I followed Jensen into the other room.

"This is Mr. Nero Wolfe," I said. "Sit down." I was using my best judgment, and figured I was playing it right, because Wolfe was nowhere in sight. I had to decide what to do with them while I found the gun and maybe the bullet.

Jane was still trying to jabber, but she stopped when Jensen blurted, "Wolfe has blood on his head!"

I glanced at Hackett. He was standing up behind the desk, leaning forward with his hand on the desk, staring wildly at the three of us. Blood dribbled down the side of his neck.

I took in breath and yelled, "Fritz!"

He appeared instantly, probably having been standing by in the hall, and when he came I handed him my gun. "If anybody reaches for a handkerchief, shoot."

"Those instructions," Jensen said sharply, "are dangerous if he—"

"He's all right."

"I would like you to search me." Jensen stuck his hands toward the ceiling.

"That," I said, "is more like it," and crossed to him and explored him from neck to ankles, invited him to relax in a chair, and turned to Jane. She darted me a look of lofty disgust.

I remarked, "If you refuse to stand inspection and then you

41

happen to make a gesture and Fritz shoots you in the tummy, don't blame me."

She darted more looks, but took it. I felt her over not quite as comprehensively as I had Jensen, took her bag and glanced in it, and returned it to her, and then stepped around Wolfe's desk to examine Hackett. After Jensen had announced the blood, he had put his hand up to feel and was staring at the red on his fingers with his big jaw hanging open.

"My head?" he croaked. "Is it my head?"

The exhibition he was making of himself was no help to Nero Wolfe's reputation for intrepidity.

After a brief look I told him distinctly, "No, sir. Nothing but a nick in the upper outside corner of your ear."

"I am not—hurt?"

I could have murdered him. Instead, I told Fritz, standing there with my gun, that unnecessary movements were still forbidden, and took Hackett to the bathroom in the far corner and shut the door behind us. While I showed him the ear in the mirror and dabbed on some iodine and taped on a bandage, I told him to stay in there until his nerves calmed down and then rejoin us, act detached and superior, and let me do the talking.

As I reappeared in the office, Jane shot at me, "Did you search *him?*"

I ignored her and circled around Wolfe's desk for a look at the back of the chair. The head-rest was upholstered with brown leather; and about eight inches from the top and a foot from the side edge, a spot that would naturally have been on a line behind Hackett's left ear as he sat, there was a hole in the leather. I looked behind, and there was another hole on the rear side. I looked at the wall back of the chair and found still another hole, torn into the plaster.

From the bottom drawer of my desk I got a screwdriver and hammer, and started chiseling, ran against a stud, and went to work with the point of my knife. When I finally turned around I held a small object between my thumb and finger. As I did so, Hackett emerged from the bathroom.

"Bullet," I said informatively. "Thirty-eight. Passed through Mr. Wolfe's ear and the back of his chair, and ruined the wall."

Jane sputtered. Jensen sat and gazed at me with narrowed eyes. Hackett shuddered.

"It could be," Jensen said coldly, "that Wolfe fired that bullet himself."

"Yeah?" I returned his gaze. "Mr. Wolfe would be glad to let you inspect his face for powder marks."

"He washed them off in the bathroom," Jane snapped.

"They don't wash off." . . . I continued to Jensen, "I'll lend you a magnifying glass. You can examine the chair, too."

By gum, he took me up. He nodded and rose, and I got the glass from Wolfe's desk, the big one. First he went over the chair, the portion in the neighborhood of the bullet hole, and then crossed to Hackett and gave his face and ear a look. Hackett stood still with his lips compressed and his eyes straight ahead. Jensen gave me back the glass and returned to his seat.

I asked him, "Did Mr. Wolfe shoot himself in the ear?"

"No," he admitted. "Not unless he had the gun wrapped."

"Sure." My tone cut slices off of him. "He tied a pillow around it, held it at arm's length, pointing it at his ear, and pulled the trigger. How would you like to try demonstrating it? Keeping the bullet within an inch of your frontal lobe?"

He never stopped gazing at me. "I am," he declared, "being completely objective. With some difficulty."

"If I understand what happened—" Hackett began, but I cut him off.

"Excuse me, sir. The bullet helps, but the gun would help still more. Let's be objective, too. We might possibly find the object in the front room." I moved, touching his elbow to take him along. "Fritz, see that they stay put."

"I," said Jensen, getting up, "would like to be present—"

"The hell you would." I wheeled on him. My voice may have gone up a notch. "Sit down, brother. I am trying not to fly off the handle. Whose house is this, anyway, with bullets zipping around?"

He had another remark to contribute, and so did Jane, but I disregarded them and wangled Hackett ahead of me into the front room and shut the soundproof door.

"It seems incredible to me," Hackett said, choosing his words carefully, "that one of them could have shot at me from in here, through the open door, without me seeing anything."

"You said that before, in the bathroom. You also said you didn't remember whether your eyes were open or shut, or where you were looking, when you heard the shot."

I moved my face to within fourteen inches of his. "See here. If you are suspecting that I shot at you, or that Wolfe did, you have got fleas or other insects playing tag in your brain and should have it attended to. One thing alone: The way the bullet went, straight past your ear and into the chair-back, it had to come from in front, the general direction of that door and this room. It couldn't have come from the door in the hall or anywhere else, because we haven't got a gun that shoots a curve. Now, you will sit down and keep still."

He grumbled, but obeyed. I surveyed the field. On the assump-

43

tion that the gun had been fired in that room, I adopted the theory that either it was still there or it had been transported or propelled without. As for transportation, I had got there not more than five seconds after the shot and found them there staring at each other. As for propulsion, the windows were closed and the Venetian blinds down. I preferred the first alternative.

I began to search, but I had the curious feeling that I probably wouldn't find the gun, no matter how thoroughly I looked; I have never understood why.

If it was a hunch, it was a bad day for hunches, because when I came to the big vase on the table between the windows and peeked into it and saw something white, and stuck my hand in, I felt the gun. Getting it by the trigger guard, I lifted it out. Judging by smell, it had been fired recently, but of course it had had time to cool off. It was an old Granville thirty-eight, next door to rusty. The white object I had seen was an ordinary cotton handkerchief, man's size, with a tear in it through which the butt of the gun protruded. With proper care about touching, I opened the cylinder and found there were five loaded cartridges and one shell.

Hackett was there beside me, trying to say things. I got brusque with him:

"Yes, it's a gun, recently fired, and not mine or Wolfe's. Is it yours? No? Good. Okay, keep your shirt on. We're going back in there, and there will be sufficient employment for my brain without interference from you. Do not try to help me. If this ends as it ought to, you'll get an extra hundred. Agreed?"

I'll be damned if he didn't say, "Two hundred. I was shot at. I came within an inch of getting killed."

I told him he'd have to talk the second hundred out of Wolfe, and opened the door to the office and followed him through. He detoured around Jane Geer and went and sat in the chair he had just escaped being a corpse in. I swiveled my own chair to face it out.

Jensen demanded sharply, "What have you got there?"

"This," I said cheerfully, "is a veteran revolver, a Granville thirty-eight, which has been fired not too long ago." I lowered it onto my desk. "Fritz, give me back my gun."

He brought it. I kept it in my hand.

"Thank you. I found this other affair in the vase on the table in there, dressed in a handkerchief. Five unused cartridges and one used. It's a stranger here. Never saw it before. It appears to put the finishing touch on a critical situation."

Jane exploded. She called me an unspeakable rat. She said she wanted a lawyer and intended to go to one immediately. She called Hackett three or four things. She said it was the dirtiest frame-up in

44

history. "Now," she told Hackett, "I know damned well you framed Captain Root! I let that skunk Goodwin talk me out of it! But you won't get away with it this time!"

Hackett was trying to talk back to her, making his voice louder and louder, and when she stopped for breath he could be heard: ". . . will not tolerate it! You come here and try to kill me! You nearly do kill me! Then you abuse me about a Captain Root, and I have never heard of Captain Root!" He was putting real feeling into it; apparently he had either forgotten that he was supposed to be Nero Wolfe, or had got the notion, in all the excitement, that he really was Nero Wolfe. He was proceeding, "Young lady, listen to me! I will not—"

She turned and made for the door. I was immediately on my feet and after her, but halfway across the room I put on the brake, because the doorway had suddenly filled up with a self-propelled massive substance and she couldn't get through. She stopped, goggle-eyed, and then fell back a couple of paces.

The massive substance advanced, halted, and used its mouth: "How do you do? I am Nero Wolfe."

He did it well, at top form, and it was quite an effect. Nobody made a chirp. He moved forward, and Jane retreated again.

Wolfe stopped at the corner of his desk and wiggled a finger at Hackett. "Take another chair, sir, if you please?"

Hackett sidled out, without a word, and went to the red leather chair. Wolfe leaned over to peer at the hole in the back of his own chair, and then at the hole in the plaster, grunted, and got himself seated.

"This," Jensen said, "makes it a farce."

Jane snapped, "I'm going," and headed for the door, but I had been expecting that, and with only two steps had her by the arm with a good grip and was prepared to give her the twist if she went thorny on me. Jensen sprang to his feet with both of his hands fists. Evidently in the brief space of forty-eight hours it had developed to the point where the sight of another man laying hands on his Jane started his adrenalin spurting in torrents.

"Stop it!" Wolfe's voice was a whip. It turned us into a group of statuary. "Miss Geer, you may leave shortly, if you still want to, after I have said something. Mr. Jensen, sit down. Archie, go to your desk, but be ready to use the gun. One of them is a murderer."

"That's a lie!" Jensen was visibly breathing. "And who the hell are you?"

"I introduced myself, sir. That gentleman is my temporary employee. When my life was threatened I hired him to impersonate me."

Jane spat at him, "You fat coward!"

45

He shook his head. "No, Miss Geer, It is no great distinction not to be a coward, but I can claim it. Not cowardice. Conceit convinced me that only I could catch the person daring and witty enough to kill me. I wished to be alive to do so."

He turned abruptly to me: "Archie, get Inspector Cramer on the phone."

Jane and Jensen both started talking at once, with vehemence.

Wolfe cut them off: "If you please! In a moment I shall offer you an alternative: the police or me. Meanwhile, Mr. Cramer can help." He glanced at Hackett. "If you want to get away from this uproar, there is your room upstairs . . ."

"I think I'll stay here," Hackett declared. "I'm a little interested in this myself, since I nearly got killed."

"Cramer on," I told Wolfe.

He lifted his phone from the cradle. "How do you do, sir? . . . No. . . . No, I have a request to make. If you'll send a man here right away, I'll give him a revolver and a bullet. First, examine the revolver for fingerprints and send me copies. Second, trace the revolver if possible. Third, fire a bullet from it and compare it both with the bullet I am sending you and with the bullets that killed Mr. Jensen and Mr. Doyle. Let me know the results. That's all. . . . No. . . . Confound it, no! If you come yourself you will be handed the package at the door and not admitted. I'm busy."

As he hung up I said, "Does Cramer get the handkerchief, too?"

"Let me see it."

I handed the gun to him, with its butt still protruding through the tear in the handkerchief. Wolfe frowned as he saw that the handkerchief had no laundry mark or any other mark and was a species that could be bought in almost any dry-goods store.

"We'll keep the handkerchief," Wolfe said.

Jensen demanded, "What the devil was it doing there?"

Wolfe's eyes went shut. He was, of course, tasting Jensen's expression, tone of voice, and mental longitude and latitude, to try to decide whether innocent curiosity was indicated or a camouflage for guilt. He always shut his eyes when he tasted. In a moment they opened again halfway.

"If a man has recently shot a gun," he said, "and has had no opportunity to wash, an examination of his hand will furnish incontestable proof. You probably know that. One of you, the one who fired that shot, certainly does. The handkerchief protected the hand. Under a microscope it would be found to contain many minute particles of explosives and other residue. The fact that it is a man's handkerchief doesn't help. Major Jensen would naturally possess a man's handkerchief. Miss Geer could buy or borrow one."

"You asked me to stay while you said something," Jane snapped.

She and Jensen were back in their chairs. "You haven't said anything yet. Where were *you* when the shot was fired?"

"Pfui." Wolfe sighed. "Fritz, pack the gun and bullet in a carton, carefully with tissue paper, and give it to the man when he comes. First, bring me beer. Do any of you want beer?"

Evidently no one did.

"Very well, Miss Geer. To assume, or pretend to assume, some elaborate hocus-pocus by the inmates of this house is inane. At the moment the shot was fired, I was standing near the kitchen talking with Mr. Goodwin. Since then I have been at a spot from which part of this room can be seen and voices heard."

His eyes went to Jensen and back to Jane. "One of you two people is apt to make a mistake, and I want to prevent it if possible. I have not yet asked you where you were and what you were doing at the instant the shot was fired. Before I do so I want to say this, that even with the information at hand it is demonstrable that the shot came from the direction of that door to the front room, which was standing open. Mr. Hackett could not have fired it; you, Mr. Jensen, satisfied yourself of that. Mr. Brenner was in the kitchen. Mr. Goodwin and I were together. I warn you—one of you—that this is sufficiently provable to satisfy a jury in a murder trial.

"Now, what if you both assert that at the instant you heard the shot you were together, close together perhaps, looking at each other? For the one who fired the gun that would be a blessing, indeed. For the other it might be disastrous in the end, for when the truth is disclosed, as it will be, the question of complicity will arise. . . . How long have you two known each other?"

Jane's teeth were holding her lower lip. She removed them. "I met him day before yesterday. Here."

"Indeed. Is that correct, Mr. Jensen?"

"Yes."

Wolfe's brows were up. "Hardly long enough to form an attachment to warrant any of the more costly forms of sacrifice. Unless the spark was exceptionally hot, not long enough to weld you into collusion for murder. I hope you understand, Miss Geer, that all that is wanted here is the truth. Where were you and what were you doing when you heard the shot?"

"I was standing by the piano. I had put my bag on the piano and was opening it."

"Which way were you facing?"

"Toward the window."

"Were you looking at Mr. Jensen?"

"Not at the moment, no."

"Thank you." Wolfe's eyes moved. "Mr. Jensen?"

"I was in the doorway to the hall, looking down the hall and

47

wondering where Goodwin had gone to. For no particular reason. I was not at that moment looking at Miss Geer."

Wolfe poured beer, which Fritz had brought. "Now we are ready to decide something." He took them both in. "Miss Geer, you said you wanted to go to a lawyer, heaven protect you. But it would not be sensible to permit either of you to walk out of here, to move and act at your own will and discretion. Since that bullet was intended for me, I reject the notion utterly. On the other hand, we can't proceed intelligently until I get a report from Mr. Cramer. There is time to be passed."

Wolfe heaved a sigh. "Archie, take them to the front room and stay there till I send for you. Fritz will answer the bell."

Two hours of stony silence grow tiresome.

I appreciated the break in the monotony when, a little before nine, I heard the doorbell, and Fritz came in. He said, "Archie, Mr. Wolfe wants you in the office. Inspector Cramer is there with Sergeant Stebbins. I am to stay here."

If the situation in the front room had been unjovial, the one in the office was absolutely grim. One glance at Wolfe was enough to see that he was in a state of uncontrollable fury, because his forefinger was making the same circle, over and over, on the surface of his desk. Hackett was not in the room, but Sergeant Purley Stebbins was standing by the wall, looking official. Inspector Cramer was in the red leather chair, with his face about the color of the chair.

Wolfe tapped a piece of paper on his desk. "Look at this, Archie."

I went and looked. It was a search warrant.

Wowie! I was surprised that Cramer was still alive, or Wolfe, either.

Cramer growled, holding himself in, "I'll try to forget what you just said, Wolfe. It was totally uncalled for. Damn it, you have given me a run-around too many times. There I was with that gun. A bullet fired from it matched the bullet you sent me and also the two that killed Jensen and Doyle. That's the gun, and you sent it to me. All right; then you've got a client, and when you've got a client you keep him right in your pocket. I would have been a fool to come here and start begging you. I've begged you before."

He started to get up. "We're going to search this house."

"If you do you'll never catch the murderer of Mr. Jensen and Mr. Doyle."

Cramer dropped back in the chair. "I won't?"

"No, sir."

"You'll prevent me?"

"Bah!" Wolfe was disgusted. "Next you'll be warning me formally that obstruction of justice is a crime. I didn't say that the

48

murderer wouldn't be caught, I said you wouldn't catch him. Because I already have."

Cramer said, "The hell you have."

"Yes, sir. Your report on the gun and bullets settles it. But I confess the matter is a little complicated, and I do give you a formal warning: You are not equipped to handle it. I am." Wolfe shoved the warrant across the desk. "Tear that thing up."

Cramer shook his head. "You see, Wolfe, I know you. Lord, don't I know you! But I'm willing to have a talk before I execute it."

"No, sir." Wolfe was murmuring again: "I will not submit to duress. I would even prefer to deal with District Attorney Skinner. Tear it up, or proceed to execute it."

That was a dirty threat. Cramer's opinion of Skinner was that he was one of the defects of our democratic system of government. Cramer looked at the warrant, at Wolfe, at me, and back at the warrant. Then he picked it up and tore.

"Can the gun be traced?" Wolfe said.

"No. The number's gone. It dates from about nineteen-ten. And there are no prints on it that are worth anything. Nothing but smudges."

Wolfe nodded. "Naturally. A much simpler technique than wiping it clean or going around in gloves. . . . The murderer is in this house."

"I suspected he was. Is he your client?"

"The main complication," Wolfe said, in his purring tone, "is this: There are a man and a woman in that front room. Granting that one of them is the murderer, which one?"

Cramer frowned at him. "You didn't say anything about granting. You said that you have caught the murderer."

"So I have. He or she is in there, under guard. I suppose I'll have to tell you what happened, if I expect you to start your army of men digging, and it looks as though that's the only way to go about it. I have no army. To begin with, when I received that threat, I hired a man who resembles me—"

Purley Stebbins nearly bit the end of his tongue off, trying to get it all in his notebook.

Wolfe finished. Cramer sat scowling. Wolfe purred, "Well, sir, there's the problem. I doubt if it can be solved with what we have, or what is available on the premises. You'll have to get your men started."

"I wish," Cramer growled, "I knew how much dressing you put on that."

"Not any. I have only one concern in this. I have no client. I withheld nothing and added nothing."

"Maybe." Cramer straightened up like a man of action. "Okay,

49

we'll proceed on that basis and find out. First of all I want to ask them some questions."

"I suppose you do." Wolfe detested sitting and listening to someone else ask questions. "You are handicapped, of course, by your official status. Which one do you want first?"

Cramer stood up. "I've got to see that room before I talk to either of them. I want to see where things are. Especially that vase."

Jane was seated on the piano bench. Jensen was on the sofa, but arose as we entered. Fritz was standing by a window.

Wolfe said, "This is Inspector Cramer, Miss Geer."

She didn't make a sound or move a muscle.

Wolfe said, "I believe you've met the inspector, Mr. Jensen."

"Yes, I have." Jensen's voice had gone unused so long it squeaked, and he cleared his throat. "So the agreement not to call in the police was a farce, too." He was bitter.

"There was no such agreement. I said that Mr. Cramer couldn't be kept out of it indefinitely. The bullet that was fired at me—at Mr. Hackett—came from the gun that was found in that vase," Wolfe pointed at it—"and so did those that killed your father and Mr. Doyle. So the field has become—ah, restricted."

"I insist," Jane put in, in a voice with no resemblance to any I had ever heard her use before, "on my right to consult a lawyer."

"Just a minute, now," Cramer told her in the tone he thought was soothing. "We're going to talk this over, but wait till I look around a little."

He proceeded to inspect things, and so did Sergeant Stebbins. They considered distances, and the positions of various objects. Then there was this detail: From what segment of that room could a gun send a bullet through the hole in Wolfe's chair and the one in the wall? They were working on that together when Wolfe turned to Fritz and asked him, "What happened to the other cushion?"

Fritz was taken aback. "Other cushion?"

"There were six velvet cushions on that sofa. Now there are only five. Did you remove it?"

"No, sir." Fritz gazed at the sofa and counted. "That's right. They've been rearranged to take up the space. I don't understand it. They were all here yesterday."

"Are you sure of that?"

"Yes, sir. Positive."

"Look for it. Archie, help him."

It seemed like an odd moment to send out a general alarm for a sofa cushion, but since I had nothing else to do at the moment I obliged.

I finally told Wolfe, "It's gone. It isn't in here."

He muttered at me, "I see it isn't."

I stared at him. There was an expression on his face that I knew well. It wasn't exactly excitement, though it always stirred excitement in me. His neck was rigid, as if to prevent any movement of the head, so as not to disturb the brain, his eyes were half shut and not seeing anything, and his lips were moving, pushing out, then relaxing, then pushing out again.

Suddenly he turned and spoke: "Mr. Cramer! Please leave Mr. Stebbins in here with Miss Geer and Mr. Jensen. You can stay here, too, or come with me, as you prefer. Fritz and Archie, come." He headed for the office.

Cramer, knowing Wolfe's tones of voice almost as well as I did, came with us.

Wolfe waited until he was in his chair before he spoke: "I want to know if that cushion is on the premises. Search the house from the cellar up—except the south room; Mr. Hackett is in there lying down. Start in here."

Cramer barked, "What the hell is all this about?"

"I'll give you an explanation," Wolfe told him, "when I have one. I'm going to sit here and work, now, and must not be disturbed."

He leaned back and closed his eyes, and his lips started moving. Cramer slid farther back in his chair, crossed his legs, and got out a cigar and sank his teeth in it.

Half an hour had passed while I searched the office, when I heard Wolfe let out a grunt. I nearly toppled off the stepladder turning to look at him. He was in motion. He picked up his wastebasket, which was kept at the far corner of his desk, inspected it, shook his head, put it down again, and began opening the drawers of his desk. The first two, the one at the top and the one in the middle, apparently didn't get him anything, but when he yanked out the double-depth one at the bottom, as far as it would go, he looked in, bent over closer to see better, then closed the drawer and announced, "I've found it."

In those three little words there was at least two tons of self-satisfaction and smirk.

We all goggled at him.

He looked at me: "Archie. Get down off that thing, and don't fall. Look in your desk and see if one of my guns has been fired."

I stepped down and went and opened the armament drawer. The first one I picked up was innocent. I tried the second with a sniff and a look, and reported, "Yes, sir. There were six cartridges, and now there are five. Same as the cushions. The shell is here."

"Tchah! The confounded ass! . . . Tell Miss Geer and Mr. Jensen that they may come in here if they care to hear what happened, or they may go home or anywhere else. We don't need them. Take

Mr. Stebbins with you upstairs and bring Mr. Hackett down here. Use caution, and search him with great care. He is an extremely dangerous man."

Naturally, Jane and Jensen voted for joining the throng in the office, and their pose during the balloting was significant. They stood facing each other, with Jensen's right hand on Jane's left shoulder, and Jane's right hand, or perhaps just the fingers, on Jensen's left forearm. I left it to them to find the way to the office alone, told Purley Stebbins what our job was, and took him upstairs with me.

It was approximately ten minutes later that we delivered our cargo in the office. Even though Mr. Hackett staged one of the most convincing demonstrations of unwillingness to cooperate that I have ever encountered.

We got him to the office in one piece, nothing really wrong with any of us that surgical gauze wouldn't fix. We propped him in a chair.

I said, "He was reluctant."

I'll say one thing for Wolfe—I've never seen him gloat over a guy about to get it. He was contemplating Hackett more as an extraordinary object that deserved study.

I said, "Purley thinks he knows him."

Purley, as was proper, spoke to his superior: "I swear, Inspector, I'm sure I've seen him somewhere, but I can't remember."

Wolfe nodded. "A uniform makes a difference. I suggest that he was in uniform."

"Uniform?" Purley scowled. "Army?"

Wolfe shook his head. "Mr. Cramer told me Wednesday morning that the doorman on duty at the apartment house at the time Mr. Jensen and Mr. Doyle were killed was a fat nitwit who had been hired two weeks ago and didn't know the tenants by name, and also that he claimed to have been in the basement stoking the water heater at the moment the murders were committed. A phone call would tell us whether he is still working there."

"He isn't," Cramer growled. "He left Wednesday afternoon because he didn't like a place where people were murdered. I never saw him. Some of my men did."

"Yeah," Purley said, gazing at Hackett's face. "By God, it's him."

"He is," Wolfe declared, "a remarkable combination of fool and genius. He came to New York determined to kill Mr. Jensen and me. By the way, Mr. Hackett, you look a little dazed. Can you hear what I'm saying?"

Hackett made no sound.

"I guess you can," Wolfe went on. "This will interest you. I requested Military Intelligence to have an examination made of the effects of Captain Root at the prison in Maryland. A few minutes ago I phoned for a report, and got it. Captain Root was lying when he stated that he was not in communication with his father and had not been for years. There are several letters from his father among his belongings, dated in the past two months, and they make it evident that his father, whose name is Thomas Root, regards him as a scion to be proud of. To the point of mania."

Wolfe wiggled a finger at Hackett. "I offer the conjecture that you are in a position to know whether that is correct or not. Is it?"

"One more day," Hackett said in his husky croak. His hands were twitching. "One more day," he repeated.

Wolfe nodded. "I know. One more day and you would have killed me, with the suspicion centered on Miss Geer or Mr. Jensen, or both, on account of your flummery here this afternoon. And you would have disappeared."

Jensen popped up. "You haven't explained the flummery."

"I shall, Mr. Jensen." Wolfe got more comfortable in his chair. "But first that performance Tuesday evening."

He was keeping his eyes on Hackett. "That was a masterpiece. You decided to kill Mr. Jensen first, which was lucky for me, and, since all apartment house service staffs are short-handed, got a job there as doorman with no difficulty. All you had to do was await an opportunity, with no passers-by or other onlookers. It came the day after you mailed the threat, an ideal situation in every respect except the presence of the man he had hired to guard him.

"Arriving at the entrance to the apartment house, naturally they would have no suspicion of the doorman in uniform. Mr. Jensen probably nodded and spoke to you. With no one else in sight, and the elevator man ascending with a passenger, it was too good an opportunity to lose. Muffling the revolver with some piece of cloth, you shot Mr. Doyle in the back, and when Mr. Jensen whirled at the sound you shot him in the front, and skedaddled for the stairs to the basement and started stoking the water heater. I imagine the first thing you fed it was the cloth with which you had muffled the gun."

Wolfe moved his eyes. "Does that rattle anywhere, Mr. Cramer?"

"It sounds tight from here," Cramer said.

"That's good. Because it is for those murders that Mr. Hackett—or Mr. Root, I suppose I should say—must be convicted. He can't be electrocuted for hacking a little gash in his own ear." Wolfe's eyes moved again, to me. "Archie, did you find any tools in his pockets?"

"Only a boy scout's dream," I told him. "One of those knives with scissors, awl, nail file . . ."

"Let the police have it to look for traces of blood. Just the sort of thing Mr. Cramer does best."

"The comedy can wait," Cramer growled. "I'll take it as is for Tuesday night and go on from there."

Wolfe heaved a sigh. "You're rushing past the most interesting point of all: Mr. Hackett's answering my advertisement for a man. Was he sufficiently acute to realize that its specifications were roughly a description of me, suspect that I was the advertiser, and proceed to take advantage of it to approach me? Or was it merely that he was short of funds and attracted by the money offered?

"Actually, I am sure that he saw it as precisely the kind of opportunity I meant it to be—an opportunity to kill Nero Wolfe. Nor was my insertion of the advertisement a mere shot in the dark. I was very sure we were dealing with a dangerous killer and a bold ingenious personality.

"Accordingly, Archie, when, after you had left to meet Miss Geer, I looked out the window and saw this fellow pass by, and saw him again three times in the next three hours in the vicinity of the house, it occurred to me that a lion is much safer in a cage even if you have to be in the cage with him. I thought the advertisement should provide proper enticement for a character who had shown complete disregard for danger in his previous attempt at murder. . . .

"In any event, having answered the advertisement and received a message from me, he was, of course, delighted, and doubly delighted when he was hired.

"Now, from the moment he got in here, Mr. Root was concocting schemes, rejecting, considering, revising; and no doubt relishing the situation enormously. The device of the handkerchief to protect a hand firing a gun was no doubt a part of one of those schemes.

"This morning he learned that Miss Geer was to call on me at six o'clock, and he was to impersonate me. After lunch, in here alone, he got a cushion from the sofa in there, wrapped his revolver in it, and fired a bullet through the back of this chair into the wall.

"He stuffed the cushion into the rear compartment of the bottom right-hand drawer of this desk, then put the gun in his pocket."

"If the hole had been seen, the bullet would have been found," Cramer muttered.

"I have already pronounced him," Wolfe said testily, "an unsurpassable fool. Even so, he knew that Archie would be out with him the rest of the afternoon, and I would be in my room. I had made a remark which informed him that I would not sit in that chair again until he was permanently out of it. At six o'clock Miss Geer arrived, unexpectedly accompanied by Mr. Jensen. They were shown into the front room, and that door was open. Mr. Root's brain moved swiftly, and so did the rest of him. He got one of my guns from Archie's desk, returned to this chair, opened the drawer where he had put the cushion, fired a shot into the cushion, dropped the gun in, and shut the drawer."

Wolfe sighed again. "Archie came dashing in, cast a glance at Mr. Root seated here, and went on to the front room. Mr. Root grasped the opportunity to do two things: return my gun to the drawer of Archie's desk, and use a blade of his knife, I would guess the awl, to tear a gash in the corner of his ear. That, of course, improved the situation for him. What improved it vastly more was the chance that came soon after, when Archie took him to the bathroom and left him there. He might have found another chance, but that was perfect. He entered the front room from the bathroom, put his own gun, handkerchief attached, in the vase, and returned to the bathroom, and later rejoined the others here.

"It was by no means utterly preposterous if I had not noticed the absence of that cushion. Since this desk sits flush with the floor, no sign of the bullet fired into the bottom drawer would be visible unless the drawer was opened, and why should it be? It was unlikely that Archie would have occasion to find that one of my guns in his desk had been fired, and what if he did? Mr. Root knows how to handle a gun without leaving fingerprints, which is simple."

Cramer slowly nodded. "I'm not objecting. I'll buy it. But you must admit you've described quite a few things you can't prove."

"I don't have to. Neither do you. As I said before, Mr. Root will be put on trial for the murder of Mr. Jensen and Mr. Doyle, not for his antics here in my house."

Cramer stood up. "Let's go, Mr. Root."

Back in the office, Wolfe, in his own chair with only one bullet hole that could easily be repaired, and with three bottles of beer on a tray in front of him, was leaning back, the picture of a man at peace.

He murmured at me, "Archie, remind me in the morning to telephone Mr. Viscardi about that tarragon."

"Yes, sir." I sat down. "And if I may, sir, I would like to offer a man-eating tiger weighing around two hundred and sixty pounds capable of easy and normal movement. We could station him behind the big cabinet, and when you enter he could leap on you from the rear."

It didn't faze him. He was enjoying the feel of his chair and I doubt if he heard me.

MUM IS
THE WORD

BY ELLERY QUEEN

Ellery Queen is the pseudonym of the late Manfred B.
Lee (b. January 11, 1905; d. April 3, 1971) and his cousin
Frederic Dannay (b. October 20, 1905). Ellery Queen is
also the name of their fictional detective, who has appeared in 33 novels, 78 short stories and novelettes, and
more than 300 radio plays, as well as in the movies, on
stage and in television. *Ellery Queen's Mystery Magazine*,
now in its 35th year of continuous publication, is edited
by Frederic Dannay and considered the finest periodical
of its kind in the world.

December 31, 1964 THE BIRTHDAY of the new year and the old man became a fact at midnight. The double anniversary was celebrated in the high-ceilinged drawing room of Godfrey Mumford's house in Wrightsville with certain overtones not in the tradition. Indeed, in accepting the offerings of his family and his friend, old Godfrey would have been well advised to recall the warning against gift-bearing Greeks (although there had never been a Greek in Wrightsville, at least none of Godfrey's acquaintance; the nearest to one had been Andy Birobatyan, the florist who was of Armenian descent; Andy had shared the celebrated Mumford green thumb until the usual act of God had severed it).

The first Greek to come forward with her gift was Ellen Mumford Nash. Having gone through three American husbands, Godfrey's daughter had just returned from England, where she was in the fifth year of a record run with number four, an Egyptologist connected with the British Museum—the prodigal daughter home for a visit, her nostrils flaring as if she smelled something unpleasant.

Nevertheless, Ellen said sweetly to her father, "Much happiness, darling. I do hope you find these useful."

As it developed, the hope was extravagant. Her gift to him was a gold-plated cigarette case and lighter. Godfrey Mumford had given up smoking in 1952.

Christopher's turn came next. A little less than 30 years before, Christopher had followed Ellen into the world by a little less than 30 minutes. (Their father had never allowed himself to be embittered by the fact that their birth had killed their mother, although he had had occasional reason to reflect on the poor exchange.)

Ellen, observing her twin over the champagne they were all sharing, was amused by his performance. How well he did the loving-son bit! With such talent it seemed remarkable that dear Chris had never risen above summer stock and walk-ons off Broadway. The reason, of course, was that he had never worked very hard at his chosen profession; but then he had never worked very hard at anything.

"A real swinger of a birthday, father," Christopher was saying with passionate fondness. "And a hundred more to come."

"I'll settle for one at a time, son. Thanks very much.' Godfrey's hair was gray but still vigorous; his big body tended toward gauntness now, but after 70 years he carried himself straight as a dancer.

He was examining a silver-handled walking stick. "It's really handsome."

Christopher sidled stage right, smiling sincerely; and Godfrey set the stick aside and turned to the middle-aged woman standing by. She was small, on the dumpling side; the hands holding the gift had the stub nails and rough skin of habitual housework. Her face under the snowy hair lay quiet as a New England winter garden.

"You shouldn't have gone to all this trouble, Mum," the old man protested, "with the work you have to do around here."

"Goodness, Godfrey, it was no trouble. I wish it could have been more."

"I'm trying to remember the last time I had a hand-knit sweater." Godfrey's voice was gruff as he fingered it. "It's just what I need to wear in the greenhouse these days. When on earth did you find the time?"

The sun came through to shine on the garden. "It's not very elegant, Godfrey, but it will keep you warm."

It was 28 years since Margaret Caswell had come to Wrightsville to nurse her sister Louise—Godfrey's wife—in Louise's fatal illness. In that time she had brought into the world a child of her own, buried her husband, become "Mum" to the three children growing up in the household—Godfrey's two and her one—and planned (she had recently figured it out) more than 30,000 meals. Well, Godfrey Mumford had earned her devotion; he had been a second father to her child.

She sometimes felt that Godfrey loved her Joanne more than his own twins; she felt it now, in the drawing room. For Godfrey was holding in his hands a leather desk set decorated with gold-leaf chrysanthemums, and his shrewd blue eyes were glittering like January ice. The set was the gift of Joanne, who was watchimg him with a smile.

"You're uncanny, Jo," Godfrey said. "It's taking advantage of an old man. This is beautiful."

Jo's smile turned to laughter. "With most men it's supposed to be done with steak and potatoes. You're a pushover for chrysanthemums. It's very simple."

"I suppose people think *I'm* very simple. A senile delinquent," Godfrey said softly.

A frail little man with a heavy crop of eyebrows above very bright eyes hooted at this. He was Godfrey Mumford's oldest friend, Wolcott Thorp, who had formerly taught anthropology at Merrimac University in Connhaven. For the past few years Thorp had been serving as curator of the Merrimac University Museum, where he had been developing his special interest, the cultural anthropology of West Africa.

"I'll contribute to your delinquency, too," Wolcott Thorp chuckled. "Here's something, Godfrey, that will help you waste your declining years."

"Why, it's a first edition of an Eighteenth Century work on mums!" Godfrey devoured the title page. "Wolcott, this is magnificent."

The old man clutched the tome. Only Jo Caswell sensed the weariness in his big body. To Wrightsville and the horticultural world he was the breeder of the celebrated Mumford's Majestic Mum, a double bloom on a single stem; he was a member of the Chrysanthemum Society of America and of chrysanthemum clubs in England, France, and Japan; his correspondence with fellow breeders and aficionados encompassed the globe. To Jo he was a gentle, kind, and troubled man, and he was dear to her heart.

"I'm grateful for all these kindnesses," Godfrey Mumford said. "It's a pity my response has to be to give you bad news. It's the wrong occasion, but I don't know when I'll have you all together under this roof again. Forgive me for what I'm about to tell you."

His daughter Ellen had an instinct for the quality and degree of trouble. By the flare of her nostrils she had sensed that what was coming was bad news indeed.

"Father—" she began.

But her father stopped her. "Let me tell this without interruption, Ellen. It's hard enough . . . When I retired in 1954, my estate was worth about five million dollars; the distribution in my will was based on that figure. Since that time, as you all know, I've pretty well neglected everything else in experimenting with the blending and hybridizing of mums."

Godfrey paused, took a deep breath. "I recently found out that I'm a fool. Or maybe it was fated. Anyway, the result is the same."

He glanced at the old book in his hands as if surprised to find it still there. Then he set it carefully on the coffee table and sat down on the crewel-fringed couch.

"I had put all my financial affairs in the hands of Truslow Addison's law firm. Where I made my mistake was in sticking with the status quo when Tru died and his son took over the practice. I should have known better. You remember, Christopher, what a wild youngster Tru Junior was—"

"Yes," said Christopher Mumford. "Father, you don't mean—"

"I'm afraid so," the old man said. "After young Tru died in that auto accident last May, the affairs of the law firm were found to be like a basket of broken eggs. You couldn't even make an omelet of them. Some of the funds in his trust he had simply gambled away; the rest vanished because of bad business judgment, stupid speculations, investments without rhyme or reason . . ."

His voice trailed away, and after a while the silence was cracked by the voice of Ellen Mumford Nash. Her slim and elegant figure was stiff with outrage.

"Are you saying, father, that you're without a *shilling*?"

Behind her Christopher made an abrupt move, extending his arm in a sort of forensic gesture, as if he were trying to argue away a legal point that threatened his whole case.

"You're joking, father. It can't be that bad. There's got to be something left out of so much loot."

"Hear me out," his father said heavily. "By liquidating assets I've managed to pay off all the creditors. This house and the property are mortgaged; there's not very much equity. I have an old annuity that will let Mum and Joanne and me live here decently, but on my death the income from it stops. I'll have to cut down my mums operation—"

Ellen broke in, bitter as the cold outside. "Damn your mums! If you'd stuck to growing seeds, the way you started, father, none of this would have happened. Left without a farthing! After all these years."

Godfrey had gone pale at her curse; otherwise his face showed nothing. He had apparently prepared himself well for the ordeal. "Your brother was right in one respect, Ellen. There is something valuable left—something that no one's known about. I want to show it to you."

Mumford rose and went over to the wall behind him. He pushed aside an oil painting of a vaseful of chrysanthemums, exposing a square-doored wall safe. His silent audience heard the faint clicking—more like a swishing—of a dial. He removed something, shut the door of the safe, and came back.

Ellen's breath came out in a whinny.

Her father's hand was holding up a magnificent pendant.

"You'll recall," the old man said, "that on my retirement I took a trip to the Far East to bone up on Oriental mums. Well, while I was in Japan I managed to get my hands on this beauty. I paid nowhere near what it's worth, although it cost me a lot of money. How could I pass this up? There are records authenticating it as a royal gift from the Emperor Komei, father of Meiji. It's known as the Imperial Pendant."

The gold links of the chain were exquisitely carved in the shape of tiny, intricate chyrsanthemums; the pendant itself was a chrysanthemum, with an enormous diamond in the center surrounded by sixteen diamond petals. The superb gems, deep yellow in color, gathered the light in the room and cast it back in a shattering explosion.

"These stones are perfectly matched. The Emperor's agents

searched the world to find enough of these rare yellow diamonds to complete the pendant. As a group, they're unique."

Ellen Nash's eyes, as hard as the gems, became slitted. She had never heard of Emperor Komei or the Imperial Pendant, but she was not invulnerable to beauty, especially when it had a high market value.

"Father, that must be worth a fortune."

"Believe it or not, it's been appraised at a million dollars." There was an arpeggio of gasps; and the warmth in Godfrey Mumford's voice expired, as if his pleasure had been chilled suddenly. "Well, you've seen it, so I'll put it back in the safe."

"For God's sake, father," cried Christopher, "not in a dinky little home safe! Why don't you put it in a bank vault?"

"Because I like to take it out every once in a while and look at it, son. I've had it here for a long time, and no one's stolen it yet. By the way, I'm the only one who knows the combination of the safe. I suppose I ought to leave a record of it, in case anything happens to me."

"I should think so!" said Ellen.

Godfrey's expression did not change. "I'll take care of it, Ellen."

He returned to the wall safe. When he faced them again, the painting hung in place and his hands were empty.

"So there's what's left of my estate," he said. "A piece of historic jewelry worth a million dollars." His fine face saddened now, as if he had reached the limit of self-discipline. "Wolcott, my old will included a bequest to you of a hundred thousand dollars to finance that expedition to West Africa you've always talked about."

"I know, Godfrey, I know," said Thorp.

"Now, when I die, I'm afraid your legacy will be only one-fifth that."

Wolcott Thorp made a face. "I'm getting too old for expeditions. Do we have to talk about these things?"

He said this in a mutter, as if the whole subject were painful to him. Godfrey Mumford turned mercifully to Margaret Caswell.

"Mum, I originally planned a bequest to you and Joanne of a quarter of a million dollar trust fund. Well, I'm not going to make you suffer for my mistake after giving me half your lifetime, at least any more than I can help. The inheritance tax will cut down the pie, but my new will takes ample care of you in a revised trust. I wanted you and Jo to know that."

He turned to Ellen and Christopher. "What's left, of course, will go to you children share and share alike. It isn't what I'd planned, and I know it won't be what you expected, but you'll have to make the best of it. I'm sorry."

"So," said Ellen with a little snap of her jaws, "am I."

"Oh, shut up, Ellen," her brother said.

And there was a silence.

It was broken by Joanne. "Well! Shall we drink a toast to the birthday boy?" And she made for the rest of the champagne she had ordered from Dunc MacLean in the Square (which was round), in High Village, leaving behind her a definitely dismal New Year's Eve party.

January 1, 1965 Christopher Mumford was suffering from an unfamiliar malady—some sort of malfunction of the glands, as he diagnosed it. His mood had changed overnight. He gulped a mouthful of air as cold and clean and heady as Joanne's night-before champagne, and blew it out with a happy snort, like a horse. Even the thought of his many creditors failed to depress him.

"What a scrumbumptious day!" he exulted. "What an absolutely virgin way to start the year! Let's mosey on up to the woods beyond the greenhouse. I'll race you, Jo—what do you say?"

Joanne giggled. "Don't be a chump. You'd fall flat on your tunkus after twenty yards. You're in pitiful physical condition, Chris, and you know it. Dissipated, is what."

"You're right, of course. As dissipated as father's estate," said Christopher cheerfully.

"You could still repair the damage."

"Gyms make me dizzy. No, it's hopeless."

"Nothing is hopeless unless you make it so."

"Beware! Little Coz is mounting her pulpit! I warn you, Jo, for some ridiculous reason I'm higher than the Mahoganies this morning. You simply can't spoil it."

"I don't want to. I *like* to see you happy. It's such a welcome change."

"Right again. In pursuance whereof, and since New Year's Day is the time for resolutions, I hereby resolve to restrict my coffin nail intake, ration my poison-slupping, and consort only with incorruptible virgins, starting with you."

"How do you know I'm, well, incorruptible?"

"By me you are," said Christopher. "I ought to know. I've tried enough times."

"And that's a fact," said Jo in a rather grim tone. But then she laughed, and he laughed, too.

They skirted the big glasshouse, whose panes cast into the hard bright air a fireworks of sparks, and went on across a carpet of dead grass toward a noble stand of evergreens.

Christopher was happily conscious of Joanne beside him. Her stride was long and free, a no-nonsense sort of locomotion that managed to emphasize her secondary sex characteristics, which were notable. And not even the wool stockings and the thick-soled walking shoes could spoil as captivating a pair of legs as his connoisseur's eye had ever studied.

"You implied that I'm different when I'm happy," Christopher said.

"You certainly are."

"Well, I've been feeling different this morning, and I couldn't figure it. Now I can. I'm not different—I'm the same old rounder I've always been. What I am is, I'm responding to a fresh stimulus. You, Cousin. It's you who spell the difference."

"Thank you, sir," said Jo.

"Oh, before this I've gone through the battlefield maneuvers with you, but I didn't actually *notice* you. You know what I mean?"

"I'm getting a clue," said Jo warily.

"But now I *am*. I mean I'm noticing *you*, Cousin. In the aggregate, as it were, not merely here and there. Am I communicating? What does it mean?"

"It means you're bored, and you've decided to make a little time to while away your boredom."

"Not at all. Suddenly you've turned into a marvelously desirable piece of goods."

"And you're the susceptible buyer."

"Not the way you mean. You forget that I make my way boardstreading. I'm used to desirable women—the theater is lousy with them. So much so that I've been in danger of turning monk."

"Then why are you tickling my hand?"

"Because I've decided against celibacy. With your permission I'll go further. I'll put my arm around you."

"Permission denied. I've been through *that* maneuver before with you, and it leads to a major battle. We'll sit here on this log for a while and rest. Then we'll go back."

They sat. It was cold. They sat closer—for warmth, Joanne told herself.

"Gosh, it's wonderful," breathed Christopher in little puffs, like smoke.

"What's wonderful?"

"How things change. When we were kids I thought you were the world's biggest stinker."

"I couldn't stand you, either. There are times when I still can't. Like last night."

"Last night? Why, I was a model of deportment!"

"You don't know your father well, do you?"

"Father? As well as anybody."

"Your gift to him didn't show it. Nor Ellen's—Uncle Godfrey hasn't smoked in years. And you gave him a cane, for heaven's sake! Don't you realize Uncle Godfrey's too proud to use a cane? He'd never admit dependence that way."

Christopher Mumford had to admit to himself that her indictment was justified. He had bought the walking stick (on credit) without any real consideration of his father's needs or wants.

"You're right," he sighed. "What with handling father's correspondence and puttering around after him in the greenhouse, you've come to know him better than his own children."

They went on sitting on the log and holding hands. Jo had to hold his hands very firmly.

January 3 Breakfast was not a ritual at the Mumford's, but a certain deference was customarily shown to the head of the house. Family and guests, barring illness or improbably late hours the night before, were encouraged to present themselves promptly at 9:00, which was the time Godfrey Mumford invariably appeared.

Christopher, still floating in his euphoria, came downstairs a good 20 minutes ahead of schedule. He was astonished to find his distaff counterpart in the breakfast room before him. Ellen, the one member of the family traditionally AWOL from the morning meal, on this morning was lounging in a spot of sunshine with a cup of Margaret Caswell's rich coffee in her hand.

"I knew it, I knew it," Christopher said. "A day for miracles. Imagine finding you on your feet at this proletarian hour."

Ellen glared at him through the aromatic steam. "What makes you so cheerful of late? It's disgusting."

"Something rare has entered my life. As the ecclesiastical arm puts it, I have been uplifted in spirit."

Ellen sniffed. "You?" Confessing to a tardy conversion? It would be too simply dreary."

"Hell, no, nothing so primitive." Chris spread himself over a chair and inhaled deeply of the delicious smells from the kitchen. "Although God knows neither of us has much to be cheerful about, I grant you."

"That's why I was hoping to catch you alone before breakfast." Ellen's tone expressed her resentment of the radical recourse forced upon her. "You may not realize it, Chris, but you've been pretty slimy lately. Is the sisterly eye mistaken, or aren't you being awfully attentive to our litte country cousin? You aren't casting her for a role in some dirty drama you're working on, are you?"

"Don't be foul," said Christopher shortly. "And Jo's no yokel. Just because she hasn't had the advantage of living in London and acquiring a vocabulary of British clichés—"

"Bless my soul and whiskers." The saccharine in Ellen's smile was chemically combined with acid. "Lord Ironpants has suddenly developed a tender spot."

"Never *mind*. Just what did you want to talk about?"

"Father's performance the other night. What did you think of it?"

"Top hole, pip-pip, stiff upper, and all that."

"Do you suppose he was telling the whole truth?"

"Father? Of course. You know father isn't capable of a deliberate deception."

"I wonder," said Ellen thoughtfully.

"Don't be silly. He was giving it to us straight."

"Aren't you being terribly indifferent to it all? In my opinion, it's no trifle having your inheritance reduced from millions to thousands by your father's stupidity and the venality of some crooked solicitor. There must be *something* we can do about it."

"Sure—grin and bear it. It isn't as if we'll have to go on relief, Ellen. There ought to be several hundred thou' at least to be divided between us after taxes. In the parlance of Wrightsville, that ain't hay."

"It 'ain't' five million, either. Honestly, I'm so furious with father I could spit!"

Christopher grinned. Ellen's rage made her almost human. "Chin up, old girl," he said, not unfondly. "It's the Empiah tradition, y'know."

"Oh, go to hell! I don't know why I bother to discuss anything with you."

Jo Caswell entered the breakfast room at that moment, looking lusciously slim and young in a heather wool dress, and bringing in with her, Christopher was prepared to swear, a personal escort of sunshine. He immediately quit the natural variety for Jo's peculiar radiance; and Ellen, finding herself a crowd, withdrew disdainfully to the other end of the table.

Jo's mother, starchily aproned, appeared in the doorway from the kitchen. "Is Godfrey down?"

"Not yet, Mum," Jo said.

"That's funny. It's a quarter past nine by the kitchen clock. He's always on time."

Ellen snapped, "Obviously, he's sometimes not."

Worry lines were showing between Mum's faded eyes. "In all the years I've been here, your father's never been late for his breakfast except when he was ill."

"Oh, for goodness' sake, Mum," said Jo, "he's probably gone out to the greenhouse and lost track of the time. It isn't as if it were two in the afternoon."

But Mum Caswell shook her head stubbornly. "I'm going to look in his room."

"What a bloody bore." Ellen's impatience turned nasty. "What about my breakfast? Am I expected to get it myself?"

"Perish the thought!" said Christopher, anticipating Jo.

Nevertheless, Mum hurried out. Ellen brandished her empty coffee cup, ready to behead the peasant who had failed to refill it. Christopher appeased his hunger by devouring Joanne, who was trying valiantly not to let her dislike for Ellen show.

Silence poured.

Until the cry from upstairs.

It was a cry raucous with urgency and terror. And then it became a shriek, and the shriek repeated itself.

Joanne bolted for the doorway and vanished, Christopher at her heels. Ellen trailed behind, her face a curious study in dread and hope.

She came on the others midway up the staircase. Her aunt was clinging to the banister, her dumpling features the color of old dough. She managed a jerky thumb-up gesture, and Jo and Christopher sprang past her and disappeared in the upstairs hall. In a moment Jo was back alone, running down the stairs, past her mother, past Ellen.

"I've got to phone the doctor," Jo panted. "Ellen, please take care of mother."

"But what's the matter?" demanded Ellen. "Is it father? Has something happened to him?"

"Yes . . ." Jo flew for the phone. Ellen, ascending with an arm around Margaret Caswell's waist, heard the dial clacking, and then Joanne's urgent voice: "Dr. Farnham? Jo Caswell at the Mumford place. Uncle Godfrey's had a stroke, I think. Can you come right away?"

Dr. Conklin Farnham took the stairs two at a time. Mum, still dough-faced but recovered from the first shock, had insisted on returning to her brother-in-law's bedside; the doctor found her there. Christopher and Ellen, acting like trespassers, hung about in the hall outside their father's room, Joanne with them. They waited without words.

When Dr. Farnham emerged, his shoulders elevated in a chilling shrug. "He's had a stroke, all right. He's paralyzed."

"Poor pop," said Christopher. He had not called his father that in twenty years. "What's the prognosis, Doctor?"

"It depends on a number of things, most of them unpredictable."

"Any chance of a recovery from the paralysis, Dr. Farnham?" Joanne asked in a tight voice.

"The paralysis will gradually lift, but just how soon or how completely I can't say. It all depends on the extent of the damage. He ought to be in the hospital, but we're absolutely jammed just now, not a bed available, even in the wards. And I'd rather not risk the long jaunt up to Connhaven on these winter roads. So it looks like a home job, at least for now. He'll need nurses—"

"How about me?" asked Margaret Caswell, materializing in the doorway.

"Well." The doctor seemed doubtful. "I know you've done your share of patient-care, Mrs. Caswell, but in a case like this . . . Although it's true we haven't got an R.N. available right now, either . . ."

"I've taken care of Godfrey for over a quarter of a century," Mum Caswell said, with the obstinacy she showed in all matters pertaining to Godfrey Mumford. "I can take care of him now."

January 4-5 The first 48 hours after a cerebral thrombosis, Dr. Farnham told them, were the critical ones, which was all Mum had to hear. For the next two days and nights she neither took her clothes off nor slept; nor was there anything Joanne could do or say to move her from Godfrey Mumford's bedside, not even for ten minutes.

When the crisis was over, and the patient had survived—and was even making, according to the doctor, a sensational recovery—Jo and Ellen were finally able to pry Mum out of the sickroom and get her to lie down for a few hours. She fell asleep smiling triumphantly, as if she had scored a hand-to-hand victory over the Grim Reaper.

Wolcott Thorp, apprised by Christopher of the stroke, drove down from Connhaven on the night of the fifth, looking like a miniature Russian in his old-fashioned greatcoat and astrakhan hat.

"Godfrey's all right, isn't he? He's going to live?"

They reassured him; and he sank into a chair in the foyer, beside the little table with the silver salver on it. "All my old friends are going," he mumbled. He was so pale that Joanne got him some brandy. "And those of us who survive feel guilty and overjoyed at the same time. What swine people are . . ."

It was some time before he was able to go upstairs and look in on the patient, who was being tended again by Margaret Caswell. For ten minutes Thorp chattered to his friend with desperate animation, as Godfrey stared helplessly back at him; until, clearing his throat repeatedly as if he himself had developed a paralysis, Thorp allowed Mum to shoo him out.

"It's too much to have to watch," Thorp told Jo and the twins downstairs. "I'm too big a coward to sit there while he struggles with that paralysis. The way he tried to talk! I'm going home."

"But you can't, Uncle Wolcott," said Jo, giving him the courtesy title she had used since childhood. "It's started to snow, and the report on the radio is that it's going to be a heavy one. I'm not going to let you take that long drive back over slippery roads. The plows won't even have had time to go over them."

"But Joanne," said the old curator weakly, "I have a huge day tomorrow at the Museum. And really, I'd rather—"

"I don't *care* what you'd rather. You're not leaving this house tonight, and that's that."

"Jo's right, you know," Christopher put in. "Anyway, Uncle Wolcott, you don't stand a chance. This is the new Joanne. Look at that chin, will you?"

"You look at it," said his sister Ellen. "Oh, hell, why did I ever come home? Who's for a snack?"

January 6   The snow had fallen through half the night. From the kitchen window Christopher could look out across the white earth, an old bed with fresh sheets, past the glasshouse to the woods, where the conifers stood green among the sleeping nudes.

From behind him came a rattle of pans and the homely hiss of bacon; all around him, creeping like woodsmoke, lay warmth. Making the sounds and evoking the smells was Joanne; when her mother had turned nurse, Jo had taken over the housekeeping and cooking chores. Chris had promptly given himself the KP assignment for breakfast.

It was not a morning for fantasy; the day was too clear, the smells too real—it should have happened on a black night, with wind tearing at the house to an accompaniment of creaks. But, as Jo and Chris later agreed over clutched hands, perhaps that was what made it so creepy—the dreadful nightmare striking on a crisp morning to the smell of frying bacon.

For at the very instant that Christopher turned away from the window with a wisecrack about to part his lips—at the very instant that he opened his mouth—he screamed. Or so it seemed. But it was a fantastic coincidence of timing. The scream was hysterically feminine and originated upstairs. It was repeated and repeated in a wild fusillade.

Jo stood fixed at the kitchen range with the long fork in her hand; and then she cried, "*Mother!*" and flung the fork down and ran for the doorway as if the kitchen had burst into flames. And Chris ran after her.

In the hallway stood Wolcott Thorp, one leg raised like an elderly stork, caught in the act of putting on his galoshes in preparation for his return to Connhaven. The curator was gaping at the staircase. At the top of the flight sagged Margaret Caswell, hanging on to the banister with one hand, while her other hand clawed at her throat.

And as she saw Jo and Christopher, Mum screeched. "He's dead, he's dead," and began to topple, ever so slowly, as in a film, so that Joanne, streaking past old Thorp, was able to catch her just before she could tumble. And Christopher followed, bounding up the stairs. He collided with his sister on the landing.

"What is it?" yelled Ellen; she was in a hastily donned robe. "What in God's name has happened now?"

"It must be father." Christopher dodged around her, shouting over his shoulder, "Come on, Ellen! I may need help."

In the hall below, activated at last, Wolcott Thorp hopped for the phone, one unhooked galosh flapping. He found Dr. Farnham's number jotted on a pad for ready reference and dialed it. The doctor, located at Wrightsville General Hospital where he was making his morning rounds, would come at once. Thorp hung up, stared for a moment at the telephone, then dialed Operator.

"Operator," he said, swallowing. "Get me the police."

Chief of Police Anselm Newby cradled the phone cautiously, as if it might respond to rougher treatment by snapping at him, like a dog. He inclined his almost delicate frame over his desk and fixed bleak eyes, of an inorganic blue, on his visitor. The visitor, relaxing on the back of his neck, had the sudden feeling that he was unwelcome, which was ridiculous.

"Ellery," said Chief Newby, "why the hell don't you stay in New York?"

Ellery slid erect, blinking. "I beg your pardon?"

"Where you belong," said the Chief in a rancorous tone. "Go home, will you?"

A manifest injustice. Home, thought Ellery, is where the heart is, and for many years he had had a special coronary weakness for Wrightsville. He had arrived in town only yesterday on one of his spur-of-the-moment visits; and, of course, the very first thing this morning he had sought out the Chief in police headquarters at the County Court House Building.

"What," Ellery inquired, "brings this on? Here we were, wallowing in remembrance of things past, warm as a pair of tea cosies. In a moment I become *persona non grata*. It's obviously the telephone call. What's happened?"

"Damn it, Ellery, every time you come to Wrightsville a major crime is committed."

Ellery sighed. It was not the first time he had been so indicted.

69

Before Newby's tenure there had been the salty old Yankee, Chief Dakin, with his sorrowful accusations. It's a continuing curse, he thought, that's what it is.

"Who is it this time?"

"They've just found Godfrey Mumford. That was a friend of his, Wolcott Thorp, on the phone, to notify me of Mumford's murder."

"Old Mumford? The Chrysanthemum King?"

"That's the one. I suppose there's nothing I can do but invite you along. Are you available?"

Mr. Q, rising slowly, was available, if with reluctance. His Wrightsville triumphs invariably left an aftertaste of ashes.

"Let's go," said Wrightsville's perennial hoodoo.

Christopher, dressed for the snow, blundered on Joanne on his way to the front door. She was crouched on the second step of the staircase, hugging her knees. Jo had not cried, but her eyes were pink with pain.

"You need fresh air," prescribed Christopher. "How about it?"

"No, Chris. I don't feel like it."

"I'm just trundling around the house."

"What for?"

"Come see."

He held out his hand. After a moment she took it and pulled herself up. "I'll get my things on."

Hand in hand they trudged around the house, leaving a double perimeter of footprints in the deep snow. Eventually they came back to where they had started.

"Did you notice?" Christopher asked darkly.

"Notice? What?"

"The snow."

"I could hardly not notice it," said Joanne. "I got some in the top of one of my boots."

"Tracks."

"What?"

"There aren't any."

"There are, too," said Jo. "A double set. We just made them."

"Exactly."

"Oh, stop talking like a character in a book," Jo said crossly. "What are you driving at?"

"*We* left a double set of footprints," said Christopher. "Just now. But nobody else left any. Where are the tracks of the murderer?"

"Oh," said Jo; and it was a chilled, even a tremulous "Oh"—like a little icicle preparing to fall to bits.

70

They stood there looking at each other, Jo shivering, like a scared and forlorn child.

He opened his arms. She crept into them.

It was Ellen who answered the door. She had used the short wait to recover her poise; she had, so to speak, raised the Union Jack. Chief Anselm Newby stepped in, followed by Ellery.

"You're the Chief Constable," Ellen said. "The last time I was in Wrightsville, Dakin was Constable."

Newby received this intelligence with a displeasure that even Ellen Nash recognized. In Anse Newby's glossary, constables were exceedingly small potatoes, found in tiny, dying New England villages.

"Chief of Police," he corrected her. Professionally he used a quiet voice, with an occasional whiplash overtone. He evidently felt that this was such an occasion, for his correction flicked out at her, leaving a visible mark. "The name is Newby. This is Ellery Queen, and he's not a constable either. Who are you?"

"Mrs. Nash—Ellen Mumford Nash, Mr. Mumford's daughter," said Ellen hastily. "I've been visiting over the holidays from England." This last she uttered in a defiant, even arrogant, tone, as if invoking the never-setting sun. It made Newby examine her with his mineral eyes.

The tension Ellery detected under the woman's gloss was clearly shared by the group huddled in the entrance hall behind her. His glance sorted them out with the automatic ease of much practice. The handsome young fellow was obviously the brother of the constable-oriented Anglophile, and he was (just as obviously) feeling proprietary about the grave and lovely girl whose elbow he gripped. Ellery became aware of a familiar pang. What quality in Wrightsville is this, he thought, that it must cast in every murder melodrama at least one ingenue with a special talent for touching the heart?

His glance passed on to the the snow-haired lady, fallen in with exhaustion; and to the little elderly gentleman with the jungle eyebrows and the musty aura of old things, undoubtedly the Wolcott Thorp who had announced the finding of the body to Anse Newby over the phone. Newby, it appeared, knew Thorp; they shook hands, Thorp absently, as if his thoughts were elsewhere— upstairs, in fact, as indeed they were.

When the Chief introduced Ellery, it turned out that some of them had heard of him. He would have preferred anonymity. But this was almost always the toe he stubbed in stumbling over a skeleton in some Wrightsville closet.

"Rodge and Joan Fowler were talking about you only a few weeks ago," Joanne murmured. "To listen to them, Mr. Queen, you're a cross between a bulldog and a bloodhound when it comes to—things like this. You remember, Chris, how they raved."

"I certainly do," Christopher said gloomily. He said nothing more, and Ellery looked at him. But all Ellery said was, "Oh, you know the Fowlers?" Then he was being introduced to Ellen.

"*That* Queen," said Ellen. Ellery could have sworn, from the way her nostrils flared, that he was giving off unsocial odors. And *she* said nothing more.

"Well," the Chief of Police said in a rubbing-the-hands tone of voice, "where's the body? And did anybody notify a doctor?"

"I did, just before I telephoned you," Wolcott Thorp said. "He's waiting in Godfrey's bedroom."

"Before we go up," suggested Ellery—and they all started—"would you people mind telling us how the body was found, and so on? To fill us in."

They told their stories in detail up to the point of the call to headquarters.

Newby nodded. "That's clear enough. Let's go."

So they went upstairs, Margaret Caswell leading the way, followed by Newby and Ellery, with the others straggling behind.

The old man was lying on the floor beside his bed. He lay on his back, his eyes fixed in the disconcerting stare of death. The front of his pajama coat was clotted with the seepage from the knife wound in his chest. There had been very little bleeding. A black-handled knife trimmed in what looked like nickel protruded from the region of his heart.

"Hello, Conk," Ellery said to the doctor, but looking at the corpse.

"Ellery," Dr. Farnham exclaimed. "When did you get to town?"

"Last night. Just in time, as usual." Ellery was still looking at the dead man. "How's Molly?"

"Blooming—"

"Never mind Old Home Week," said Newby irritably. "What's your educated guess, Doctor, as to the time he got it?"

"Between four and five a.m., I'd say. A good spell after the snow stopped, if that's what you're thinking of."

"Speaking of the snow," said Ellery, looking up. "Who made that double set of tracks around the house I noticed on driving up?"

"Joanne and I," said Christopher from between his teeth.

"Oh? When did you make them, Mr. Mumford?"

"This morning."

"You and Miss Caswell walked all around the house?"

"Yes."

"Did you notice any tracks in the snow other than those you and

72

Miss Caswell were making?" After a moment Ellery said, "Mr. Mumford?"

"No."

"Not anywhere around the house?"

"No!"

"Thank you," Ellery said. "I could remark that that's very helpful, but I can understand that you ladies and gentlemen may have a different point of view. It means no one entered or left the house after the snow stopped falling. It means the murder was committed by someone *in the house*—someone, moreover, who's still here."

"That's what it means, all right," said Chief Newby with undisguised satisfaction. He was inching carefully about the room, his bleak glance putting a touch of frost on everything.

"That was intelligent of you, Chris," Ellen Nash said viciously. "So now we're all under suspicion. What a bloody farce!"

"You've got the wrong category, I'm afraid," her brother said morosely. "As one of us, I suppose, is going to find out."

There was a dreary moment. Jo's fresh face held a look of complete incredulity, as if the full meaning of the trackless snow had just now struck home. Ellen was staring over at her recumbent father, her expression saying that it was all his fault. Margaret Caswell leaned against the door, her lips moving without a sound. Christopher took out a pack of cigarettes, held it awkwardly for a moment, then put it back in his pocket. Wolcott Thorp mumbled something about the absolute impossibility of it all; his tone said he wished he were back in his museum among the relics of the legitimately dead.

"The knife," Ellery said. He was looking down again at Godfrey Mumford's torso. "The fact that the killer left it behind, Newby, undoubtedly means that it's useless as a clue. If it had any fingerprints on it, they probably were wiped off."

"We'll dust the room and knife for prints, anyway," said the Chief. "Don't any of you come any further than that doorway . . . Not that it's going to do us any good, as you say, Ellery. You people—I take it you've all been in this bedroom in the last day or so at one time or another?" He shrugged at their nods.

"By the way," Ellery said, "I haven't seen one of these old-fashioned jackknives in years. Does anyone recognize it? Mrs. Caswell?"

"It's Godfrey's," Mum said stiffly. "He kept it on the writing desk there. It was one of his prized possessions. He'd had it from childhood."

"He never carried it around with him?"

"I've never seen it anywhere but on his desk. He was very sentimental about it . . . He used it as a letter opener."

73

"I have a boyhood artifact or two myself that I'm inclined to treasure. Did everyone know this, Mrs. Caswell?"

"Everyone in the household—" She stopped with a squeak of her breath—like, Ellery thought, a screech of brakes. But he pretended not to notice. Instead, he knelt to pick something up from the floor beside the body.

"What's that?" demanded Chief Newby.

"It's a memo pad," Dr. Farnham said unexpectedly. "It was kept on the night table at my suggestion for notations of temperature, time of medications, and so on. It apparently fell off the table when Mr. Mumford toppled from the bed; he must have jostled the table. When I got here the pad was lying on the body. I threw it aside in making my examination."

"Then it doesn't mean anything," the Chief began; but Ellery, back on his feet, staring at the top sheet of the pad, said, "I disagree. Unless . . . Conk, did Mr. Mumford regain any mobility since his stroke?"

"Quite a bit," replied Dr. Farnham. "He was making a far better and faster recovery than I expected."

"Then this pad explains why he fell out of bed in the first place, Newby—why, with that knife wound, he didn't simply die where he lay after being struck."

"How do you figure that? You know how they'll thrash around sometimes when they're dying. What does the pad have to do with it?"

"The pad," said Ellery, "has this to do with it: after his murderer left him, thinking he was dead, Godfrey Mumford somehow found the strength to raise himself to a sitting position, reach over to the night table, pick up the pencil and pad—you'll find the pencil under the bed, along with the top sheet of the pad containing the medical notations, where they must have fallen when he dropped them—and blockprinted a message. The dying message, Newby, on this pad."

"What dying message?" Newby pounced. "Let me see that! Had he recovered enough from the paralysis, Doc, to be able to *write?*"

"With considerable effort, Chief, yes."

The dead man's message consisted of one word, and Newby pronounced it again, like a contestant in a spelling bee.

"MUM," he read. "Capital M, capital U, capital M—MUM."

In the silence, fantasy crept. It made no sense of the normal sort at all.

MUM.

"What on earth could Godfrey have meant?" Wolcott Thorp exclaimed. "What a queer thing to write when he was dying!"

"Queer, Mr. Thorp," Ellery said, "is the exact word."

74

"I don't think so," said the Chief with a grin. "It won't do, Ellery. I don't say I always believe what's in front of my nose, but if there's a simple explanation, why duck it? Everybody in town knows that Mrs. Caswell hére is called Mum, and has been for over twenty-five years. If Godfrey meant to name his killer, then it's a cinch this thing on the pad refers to her. No embroidery, Ellery—it's open and shut."

"What—what *rot!*" Joanne cried, jumping to her mother's side. "Mother *loved* Uncle Godfrey. You know what you are, Chief Newby? You're a—you're a nitwit! Isn't he, Mr. Queen?"

"I would like to think about it," said Mr. Queen, staring at the pad.

January 9   It is a fact that must be recorded, at whatever peril to his reputation, that Mr. Queen had achieved in Wrightsville the status of a professional house guest. In more than two decades he had proved a miserably meager source of revenue to the Hollis Hotel. No sooner did he check in, it seemed, than he was checking out again. Let it be said in his defense that this was not the result of parsimony. It was simply because of his flair for entangling himself in Wrightsville's private lives and, as a consequence, being invited to Wrightville's relevant private homes.

The invitation to move over to the Mumfords' was extended by an unhilarious Christopher at the iron plea of Joanne. Jo's motive was transparent enough; Ellery was not sufficiently vain to suppose it had anything to do with moonlight and roses. With Chief Newby breathing down her mother's neck, Jo had sensed an ally; she wanted Ellery not only on her side morally, but physically at hand.

Which explains why, on the morning of January ninth, Ellery settled his account at the checkout desk of the Hollis and, lugging his suitcases like ballast on either side, tacked briskly toward the northwest arc of the Square. Crossing Upper Dade Street, he luffed past the Wrightsville National Bank, Town Hall, and the Our Boys Memorial at the entrance to Memorial Park, and finally made the side entrance of the County Court House Building. In the police headquarters he paused long enough to register his change of address with Chief Newby, who received the announcement with an unenthusiastic nod.

"Any luck with the fingerprinting, by the way?" Ellery asked.

"All kinds of it. We found *everybody's* fingerprints in the bedroom. But not a one on the jackknife. Wiped clean, all right." Newby scowled. "Who'd have thought a nice little housekeeper like Mum Caswell would have the know-how to remove her prints or wear gloves?"

75

"If you're so certain she killed Mumford, why don't you make the pinch?"

"On what evidence? That MUM message?" The Chief threw up his hands. "Imagine the corned-beef hash a defense lawyer would make of *that* in court. Ellery, find something for me in that house, will you?"

"I'll do my best," said Ellery. "Although it may not turn out to be for you."

"What do you mean?"

"I'm concerned with the truth, Anse. You're merely concerned with the facts," said Ellery.

And he left—before Newby could reply.

Ellery commandeered a taxicab driven, to his surprise, by someone he did not recognize, and was trundled off (after circling the Square) back up broad-bottomed State Street to the oldest part of town, where the houses were black-shuttered pre-Colonials well set back on rolling lawns in the shade of centuries-old trees. And soon he was ringing the chimes-doorbell of the Mumford mansion.

It was the day after Mumford's funeral, and the big house was still haunted. The old man's presence seemed to linger in the sight and scent of his precious chrysanthemums, which in lesser greenhouses bore their blooms from late August to December.

Joanne let him in with a glad little cry.

She established him in a tall-ceilinged bedroom upstairs with a tester bed and a beautiful Duncan Phyfe highboy that he instantaneously coveted. But he was made melancholy by the vase of two-headed mums that Jo had set on the night table, and he soon descended in search of fleshlier company.

He found Jo, Ellen, and Christopher in the library, and it became clear at once that the exercise of his peculiar gifts, at least as far as Ellen Nash was concerned, was her charge for his lodging.

"I'm not going to dignify for one moment the absurd conclusion that one of us murdered father," Ellen said. "He was done in by some maniac, or tramp or something—"

"The snow," her brother said damply.

"To hell with the snow! What I'm interested in is that father left a million dollars' worth of pendant in his wall safe, and I want that safe opened."

"Pendant?" said Ellery. "What pendant?"

So Christopher told him all about the New Year's Eve party, and what Godfrey Mumford had told them, and how he had exhibited the Imperial Pendant to them and then returned it to the safe.

"And he also told us," Christopher concluded, "that he was the only one who knew the safe combination. He said he was going to make a note of the combination for us. But we haven't looked for it yet."

"I have," said Ellen, "and I can't find it. So that your stay here won't be a complete waste of time, Mr. Queen, why not show us how Superman detects? A little thing like finding a safe combination should barely test your reputation."

"Do we have to worry about the pendant *now?*" asked Jo.

"It shouldn't take too long, Miss Caswell," said Ellery. To himself he was saying: maybe a million dollars' worth of jewelry has something to do with where Godfrey's boyhood knife had finally rested.

Searches were Ellery's forte, but this one defeated him. Trailed by relatives of the deceased, he squandered the rest of the morning looking in obvious places. But unlike Poe's purloined letter, the combination of the safe was nowhere to be found.

They took time out for lunch and an inventory of the unlikelier places, and the afternoon passed in exhausting this inventory. Then time out again, and over dinner a round-table discussion of other possibilities, however remote. Mr. Queen's fame as a sleuth clearly underwent reappraisal by at least one conferee present. And Mr. Queen himself grew visibly more quiet.

After dinner Ellen returned to the search of the files she had already ransacked once. Ellery, reminding himself bravely in the face of his failure that there was, after all, more than one way to flay a kitty, took Christopher aside.

"I'm prompted," Ellery announced, "to go directly to the source of the problem—namely, to the safe itself. Can you show me where the blamed thing is?"

"What do you have in mind?" asked Christopher. "Nitro?"

"Nothing so common. A bit of fiddling with the dial, à la Jimmy Valentine."

"Who's he?"

Ellery said sadly, "Never mind."

Christopher led him to the drawing room and, turning on the lights went to the chrysanthemum painting on the wall and pushed it aside. Ellery began to flex his fingers like a violin virtuoso before a recital.

He studied the thing. The safe door was about ten inches square and in the middle was a rotating dial about six inches in diameter. Etched into the circumference of the dial were 26 evenly spaced notches numbered in sequence from 1 to 26. Around the dial Ellery saw a narrow immovable ring or collar in the top of which was set a single unnumbered notch—the notch used for aligning the numbers of the combination when opening the safe.

In the center of the dial was a bulky knob, about half the diameter of the dial itself, and on the knob was etched the manufacturer's trademark—an outline of the god of metal-working, Vulcan; around the rim of the knob appeared the manufacturer's name and address:VULCAN SAFE & LOCK COMPANY, INC., NEW HAVEN, CONN.

The safe door was locked. Ellery duly fiddled with the dial, ear cocked à la Jimmy Valentine. Nothing happened—at least, to the safe door. What did happen was the entrance into the drawing room of Ellen, in a sort of half excitement, trailed by a disdainful Joanne.

"Ah, the ladies," said Ellery, trying to cover up his chagrin. "And have you found the combination to this stubborn little brute?"

"No," Ellen said, "but we've found this. Maybe it'll tell you something."

Ellery took the sheet of paper. It was a bill of sale for the wall safe.

"Dated nine years ago." He pinched his nose, which was itching. "Must have been ordered just after he got back from that trip to the Orient you told me about, when he acquired the Imperial Pendant. Especially ordered, then, to be the repository of the pendant. Invoice tallies—same name and address of manufacturer; terse description, 'Wall safe per order.'"

"That's it," said Christopher. "No doubt about it."

"Is it important, Mr. Queen?" asked Jo, in spite of herself.

"It could be mighty important, Miss Caswell. While I have fiddled and burned, you may have discovered a treasure."

"Then you have better eyes than I," said Ellen. "Anyway, where do we go from here?"

"Patience, Mrs. Nash. Chris, I want you to take a trip to New Haven. Check out the safe company and learn everything you can about this particular model—details of the original order, any special instructions accompanying the order—and, yes, check the price, which seems very high to me. Also, the Vulcan Company may have the combination on file, which would simplify matters. If they don't, hire one of their experts to come back with you, in case we have to force the safe.

"Meanwhile, you girls keep searching for a record of the combination. Cover every room in the house. Not excluding the greenhouse."

January 11   Christopher's return taxi from the Wrightsville airport produced a clamor. Jo flew into the foyer from the direction of the kitchen, followed by Mum; Ellen descended from upstairs in jumps. Ellery, a lonely stag, was meandering among the red spruce and birch outside; and Joanne, booted and mackinawed, was dispatched to fetch him.

Assembled in the drawing room, they saw from Christopher's expression that he was no courier of good news.

"Briefly," Christopher told them, "the Vulcan Safe and Lock Company, Inc. no longer exists. The plant and all its files were destroyed by a fire in 1958. The firm never went back into business. Fellow sufferers, I return to your bosoms with nothing—not a clue, not a record of anything connected with the purchase of the safe."

"The high price," Ellery asked, frowning. "Did you remember to check the price?"

"Right. I did. And you were. Right, I mean. The price father paid was just about twice what safes of similar size and type were bringing the year he ordered it. It's funny that father would let himself be skinned that way. He may have been careless about his lawyer, but he was a good enough businessman, after all, to have made millions in packaged seeds before he went chrysanthemum-happy."

"There was nothing wrong with your father's business sense, Chris," said Ellery. "Nothing at all." And his eyes promptly went into hiding.

Ellen, who held a more cynical view of her late sire, was clearly of the opinion that the father's simplicity had been passed on to his son. "Didn't you at least bring back a safe expert to open the bloody thing?"

"No, but I got in touch with another New Haven safe outfit, and they'll send a man up as soon as I phone them."

"Then do it. Put through a trunk call right now. What kind of fool are you?"

Christopher's ears had turned a lovely magenta. "And you, sister mine, you're a greedy little devil. You're so hot to lay your hands on that pendant that you've lost the few decent instincts you used to have. You've waited this long, can't you wait another couple of days? Father's hardly settled in his grave."

"Please," murmured Mum.

"Please!" cried Jo.

His reflections disturbed by the sibling colloquy, Ellery roused himself. "It may not be necessary to call in anybody. Your father left a dying message—MUM. Chief Newby is positive that Godfrey was leaving a clue to his killer's identity—Mum Caswell here. But if Godfrey meant to identify his murderer, why did he choose to write MUM? MUM can mean a great many different things, which I shan't go into now; but, as an identification, it's an ambiguity. Had he wanted to accuse Mrs. Caswell, he could simply have written down her initials, MC. If he'd meant to accuse Joanne or Mr. Thorp—JC or WT. One of his children? 'Son' or 'daughter'

—or *their* initials. Any one of which would have been specific and unmistakable.

"I choose to proceed, then," Ellery went on, "on the assumption that Godfrey, in writing MUM, did not mean his killer.

"Now. What had he promised to leave for you? The combination of the safe containing the only considerable asset in his estate. So his dying message may have been meant to be the safe combination. If so, the theory can be tested."

Going to the painting, he pushed it aside. Entranced, they trooped after him.

"Study this dial for a moment," Ellery said. "What do you see? Twenty-six numbered notches. And what does twenty-six suggest? *The number of letters in the alphabet!*

"So let's translate M-U-M into numbers. M is the thirteenth letter of the alphabet, U the twenty-first. Safe Combination: 13-21-13. Now first we twirl the dial a few revolutions—to clear the action, so to speak. Then we turn to 13 and set it directly under the alignment notch—there. Next we turn the dial to the right—we'll try that direction first—and align the 21. And now to the left—usually the directions alternate—back to 13."

Ellery paused. The crucial instant was at hand. There was no movement behind him, not even a breath.

He took hold of the knob and pulled, gently.

The thick, heavy door of the safe swung open.

A shout of triumph went up—and died as if guillotined.

The safe was empty. Utterly. No pendant, no jewel box, not even a scrap of paper.

Later that day, true to his commitment, Ellery visited Anse Newby at police headquarters and reported the opening of the safe, including its emptiness.

"So what have you accomplished?" the Chief growled. "Somebody killed the old man, opened the safe, swiped the pendant. That doesn't knock my theory over. It just gives us the motive."

"You think so?" Ellery squeezed his lower lip. "I don't. According to everyone's testimony, Godfrey told them he was the only one who knew the combination. Did one of them figure out the M-U-M combination before I did and beat me to the safe? Possible, but I consider it unlikely, if you'll pardon the self-puff. It takes experienced follow-through thinking to make the jump from M-U-M to 13-21-13."

"All right, try this," argued Newby. "Somebody sneaked downstairs in the middle of that night and got lucky."

"I don't believe in that sort of luck. Anyway, it would call on one of them to be a mighty good actor."

"One of them is an actor."

"But I gather, not a good one."

"Or maybe she—"

"Let's keep it a neutral 'he'."

"—maybe he forced old Godfrey to tell him the combination before sinking the knife into him."

"Even less likely. Everyone knew that Godfrey's paralysis included his speaking apparatus, which even in a good recovery is usually the last to come back, if it comes back at all. Certainly no one could bank on the old man's being able to talk suddenly. Did the killer order Godfrey to write the combination down, under threat of the knife? Even so, Godfrey would have been a fool to do it; his daughter notwithstanding, he seems to have been very far from a fool. He'd have known he was a goner the moment he wrote it.

"I'll admit," scowled Ellery, "that all these unlikelihoods don't make for exclusive conclusions. But they do accumulate a certain mass, and the weight of them convinces me that the killer put Mumford out of his misery simply to hurry up the inheritance of the pendant, not to steal it; that the killer then left, and Mumford wrote M-U-M on his own."

"You talk all-fired pretty," said Chief Newby with a grin. "There's only one thing."

"And that is?"

"If the killer didn't swipe the pendant, where is it?"

"That," Ellery nodded morosely, "is Bingo."

"I don't mean to high-hat my betters," twanged Newby, "but you have to admit you've got a tendency to bypass the obvious. All right, you hit on M-U-M as Godfrey's 13-21-13 safe combination. But why does that have to have anything to do with his reason for writing MUM on the pad? He was a bug on mums, so it was natural for him to use M-U-M as the combination. But he could have meant something entirely different when he wrote M-U-M on the pad. I still say he was fingering his murderer. And when you have a suspect around who's actually known as M-U-M, and called Mum, what more do you want?"

"Mum Caswell isn't the only obvious referent."

"Come again?"

Ellery's reasoning organ, needled by a phrase Newby had used, was busy with its embroidery.

"A bug on mums, you say. My point is, it's absolutely bizarre and incredible that MUM should have been his dying message. MUM is the symbol of the man who wrote it. He was a famous horticulturist specializing in mums. Everything about the man said MUM, from the flowers in his greenhouse to the oil paintings and prints and sculptures and intaglios and jewelry and Lord knows what else of

81

them throughout the place. MUM was Mumford's trademark: a mum on his stationery, as I've taken the trouble to check; also on his wallet, and on his car, and in wrought iron over the front entrance. The moldings and doorknobs are all decorated with carved mums. And did you notice that his shirts sport an embroidered mum instead of his monogram? Also, if you'll pardon me, there's the irony of the knife that took his life, Godfrey's boyhood knife. How many times, allow me to wonder, did little Goddie Mumford play *mum*blety-peg with it?"

At this terminal extravagance—this spacecraft leap into whimsy—the Chief could not avoid a groan. Ellery rose, undismayed.

"It's that kind of case, Newby. And by the way, there's one line of investigation I haven't followed through yet. The search for that safe combination sidetracked me. I'll look into it tomorrow morning."

January 12   Having strained his prerogatives as a houseguest by arranging to borrow one of the Mumford's cars, Ellery came downstairs the next morning before anyone else was up; and as he was passing the table in the foyer something caught his eye. There was a letter on the silver salver.

Being the world's nosiest noonan, Mr. Q paused to look it over. The dime-store envelope was unstamped, unpostmarked, and addressed in a childishly disguised scrawl.

The envelope read: *To Ellery.*

He was surprised and delighted—surprised because the letter was so totally unexpected, delighted because he was in great need of a new point of inquiry. He tore open the envelope and removed from it a sheet of cheap notepaper.

The handwriting of the message was similarly disguised:

12/1/65

Mum's the word. If you tell what you know I'll kill you, too.

There was no signature.

Was this a new development? Hardly. All it did was obfuscate the mystification. The letter was from a not too uncommon type—the garrulous murderer; but what was he, Ellery, supposed to "know"? Whatever it was, he ardently wished he knew it.

He began to chew on the problem. After a while he began to look more cheerful. Obviously, his supposed knowledge was dangerous to the murderer. A yeast was therefore at work in the brew. Fear— the killer's fear—might produce a heady potion on which the killer would choke.

Ellery slipped the letter into his pocket and left the house.

He drove the station wagon to Connhaven, where he made for the Merrimac campus. Here he sought out the university museum. In the main office of the tomblike building he found waiting for him—he had telephoned ahead for the appointment—Wolcott Thorp.

"You have me all atwitter, Mr. Queen." The curator touched Ellery's hand with his papery paw. "And not entirely at ease. I assume you're working on poor Godfrey's murder. Why me?"

"You're a suspect," Ellery pointed out.

"Of course!" And Thorp hastened to add, "Aren't we all? If I'm acting guilty, it's human nature."

"That's the trouble, or one of them." Ellery smiled. "I'm familiar with the psychology of guilt by confrontation, even of the innocent. But that's not what I'm here for, so stop worrying. A museum to me is what the circus is to small boys. Do you have time to show me around yours?"

"Oh, yes!" Thorp began to beam.

"I'm curious about your particular field. It's West Africa, isn't it?"

The beam became sheer sunshine. "My friend," said Wolcott Thorp, "come with me! No, this way . . ."

For the next hour Ellery was the beneficiary of the man's genuine erudition. Ellery's interest was by no means simulated. He had a deep-rooted feeling for antiquity and anthropology (what was it but detection of a different kind?), and he was fascinated by the artifacts Thorp showed him from what had been western Sudan and the district of Kayes on the Senegal—idols and tutelary gods, fetishes, masks, charms, headdresses of pompons used by the Mandingos to ward off the powers of evil.

Happily inundated with information, Ellery finally interrupted the curator's flow long enough to ask for a sheet of paper on which to make notes. The curator obliged with a piece of museum stationery; and Ellery, preparing to notate, forced himself back from the dark tribalisms of Africa.

The inscription on the museum letterhead was arranged in two lines. The top line was simply the initials of the museum; the line below spelled out the full name: Merrimac University Museum.

The top line . . . MUM.

Thorp had excused himself for a moment; and folding the paper, clean of unnoted notes, Ellery took from his pocket the anonymous letter he had picked up from the salver that morning. He was about to insert the museum letterhead into the envelope when his attention was caught by the envelope's scrawled salutation.

To Ellery.

No, that was wrong!

To was correct enough, as he had read it, but not *Ellery*. The final letter had a long tail on it; this tail had been the cause of his mistaken reading. On re-examination the *ry* was not an *ry* at all; it was a straggle-tailed *n*.

To Ellen.

It was Ellen who knew something dangerous to the killer.

It was Ellen who was being threatened.

Wolcott Thorp, returning, was astounded to see his visitor clap a hand to his head, jam a letter into his pocket, and dart out without so much as a fare-thee-well.

Crouched over the wheel of the station wagon, Ellery roared back to Wrightsville and the Mumford house; cursing every impediment that forced him to slacken speed. He left the car in the driveway and clattered past an alarmed Margaret Caswell and up the stairs in the longest leaps his long legs could manage.

He burst into Ellen's room.

Ellen, propped up on a chaise longue by a picture window in some flowing garment that might have been designed for a painting by Gainsborough, was sipping hot chocolate from what could only have been—even in his agitation Ellery noticed it—a bone-china mustache cup.

"Am I supposed to be flattered, Mr. Queen," asked Ellen in a her-Ladyship-is-not-amused sort of voice, "by your boorish intrusion?"

"Beg pardon," panted Ellery. "I thought you might be dead."

Her Wedgwood eyes blued further. She set the antique cup down on an end table. "Did you say *dead?*"

He extended the anonymous letter. "Read this."

"What is it?"

"It's for you. I found it on the salver this morning and opened it by mistake, thinking it was addressed to me. I'm thankful I did. And you may be, too, before we're finished."

She took the letter and read it swiftly. The paper slipped from her hand, struck the edge of the chaise, and fluttered to the floor.

"What does it mean?" she whispered. "I don't understand."

"I think you do." Ellery stooped over her. "You know something dangerous to your father's murderer, and your father's murderer knows you know it. Ellen, tell me what it is, for the sake of your own safety. Think! What do you know that would explain a threat like this?"

He read in her eyes the immediate qualification of her terror. A slyness crept into them, and the lids slid halfway down.

"I don't know what you're talking about."

"It's foolhardy of you to hold it back. We have a murderer on our hands and he's getting edgy. Tell me, Ellen."

"There's nothing to tell. I know nothing." She turned away. "Now will you please leave? I'm not exactly dressed for entertaining."

Ellery retrieved the note and left, damning all idiots. In addition to his other commitments he would now have to undertake the thankless task of acting as the woman's watchdog.

What was Ellen concealing?

Christopher, sighting the pale sun over the top of a pine, recited the opening lines of *Snowbound*.

"Whittier," he explained. "I still have a childish fondness for the old boy."

Joanne laughed, a sound of sleigh bells. "Delivered like a pro. Bravo."

"Not really. A pro gets fairly steady employment."

"You could, too, if you tried. Really tried."

"You think so?"

"I know so."

"You know something? So do I. But only when I'm with you."

"I'm glad."

"Enough to cleave to my bosom?"

"I don't quite know," said Joanne cautiously, "how to take that, Chris."

"Take it as an interim proposal. I don't want to tie you up in knots until I've made it all the way. You make me feel life-size, Jo. I suppose what I'm trying to say is that I need you."

Jo smiled, but inside. She slipped a little mittened hand into his glove, and they strolled toward the pines and the pale sun.

Wolcott Thorp came down from the university and Chief Newby drove over from headquarters after dinner, both at Ellery's invitation.

"What's up?" Newby asked Ellery, aside. "Have you come up with something?"

"Have you?" asked Ellery.

"Not a damn thing. I'm not the Wizard of Oz, the way you're supposed to be. No miracles yet?"

"No miracles, I'm afraid."

"Then what's cooking tonight?"

"A mess. I'm going to fling it at them, and see who runs for the mop—if any."

They joined the others in the drawing room.

"I've taken the liberty of asking Chief Newby to drop by," Ellery

85

began, "because we need, I think, to redefine our position. Especially in reference to the dying message.

"When Chief Newby and I first found M-U-M on the scene, we made the natural assumption that Godfrey Mumford had left it as a clue to his killer's identity. Further thought compromised this theory, at least as far as I was concerned. The clue had so many possible interpretations that I shifted to the theory that it meant the safe combination. That worked out fine but accomplished nothing. I opened the safe, and the safe proved to be empty."

Ellery paused, seeming to wing far off. But his vision was in focus, and he could see nothing in their faces but attentiveness and bafflement.

"Now, after thinking it over again, I've changed my mind again," he went on. "If Godfrey had wanted to leave the combination, all he had to write down was 13-21-13. It would have been almost as easy to write as M-U-M, and there would have been no chance of its being misunderstood. So now I've gone back to the original theory, which Newby has never abandoned—namely, that the message points to the murderer's identity. If so, to whom?"

He paused again; and most of his captive audience waited in varying stages of nervousness for revelation.

"The Chief," said Ellery, with a side-glance at Mrs. Caswell, who alone seemed unmoved, "is convinced of that identity. And, of course, from a strictly logical point of view, it is certainly possible."

"It is certainly *stuff*," said Mum; then pulled her head back in like a turtle.

"If it's stuff, Mrs. Caswell," smiled Ellery, "what's coming is pure moonshine. Yet—who knows? I'm not going to turn my back on a theory simply because it sounds like something out of Lewis Carroll. Bear with me.

"From the beginning this case has exhibited a remarkable series of what I have to call, for want of a more elegant term, 'doubles.'

"For example, there have been at least four 'doubles' connected with the murdered man: Godfrey had developed a famous chrysanthemum with a *double* blossom on one stem; the party he gave was to celebrate a *double* event, New Year's Eve and his seventieth birthday; his wall safe cost about *double* what it should have cost; and his children, Ellen and Christopher, are twins—another *double*.

"Further, let's not overlook the most significant *double* in the case: the double mystery of who killed Godfrey and what happened to the Imperial Pendant.

"What's more, we can go on through a great many more doubles. Because, if you interpret the dying message as a clue to the killer, each of you has at least two connections with MUM.

86

"For instance, Ellen." Ellen gave a visible start. "One, her maiden name was Mumford—first syllable, *Mum*. Second, she's married to an Egyptologist. Egyptology connotes pyramids, the Sphinx—and *mum*mies."

Ellen reacted with a double sort of sound, like a jeer crossed with a neigh. "Rubbish! Nonsense!"

"It is, isn't it? Yet this thing gets curiouser and curiouser. Take Christopher. Again, the first syllable of *Mum*ford. And second, Chris, your profession."

"My profession?" asked Christopher, puzzled. "I'm an actor."

"And what are other words for actor? Player, performer, thespian, trouper . . . *mum*mer."

Christopher's handsome face reddened; he seemed torn between the impulse to laugh and the need to fume. As a compromise he simply threw up his hands.

Chief Newby was looking embarrassed. "Are you serious, Ellery?"

"Why, I don't know whether I am or not," said Ellery gravely. "I'm just trying it on for size. You're next, Mr. Thorp."

The elderly curator immediately looked frightened. "I? How do I fit in?"

"First, the initials of the museum as they appear on your stationery: Merrimac University Museum—M-U-M. Second, your special interest in the culture of West Africa and its artifacts: fetishes, masks, charms, talismans—oh, and pompons."

"I fail," said Thorp coldly, "to see the connection."

"The pompon is a variety of chrysanthe*mum*. And if you want still another cross-reference, Mr. Thorp, there's a phrase to describe your special field. Surely you know it?"

Here Thorp's erudition was apparently wanting. He shook his head.

"*Mum*bo jumbo," Ellery solemnly told him.

Thorp looked astonished. Then he chuckled. "How true. In fact, the very words come from the language of the Klassonke, a Mandingo tribe. What a quaint coincidence!"

"Yes," said Ellery; and the way he said it re-established the mood the museum man's laughter was shattering. "And Mrs. Caswell. I remind you again that Chief Newby has all along thought the dying message points to you. *Mum* Caswell."

Margaret Caswell's features took on the slightest pallor. "I hardly think this is the time to be playing games, Mr. Queen. But—all right, I'll play, too. You said that each of us has at least two connections with Godfrey's word on that pad. What's the other one of mine?"

Ellery's tone was positively apologetic. "I've noticed that you're

87

fond of beer, Mrs. Caswell, particularly German beer. One of the best-known of the German beers is called *mum*.

And this at last brought Joanne to her feet, her little hands clenched. Her anger gave her a charming dimension.

"At first this was plain ridiculous," stormed Jo. "Now it's—it's criminally asinine! Are you purposely making fun of us? And if I may ask a silly question—and no doubt I'll get a pair of silly answers—what are *my* two connections with MUM?"

"There," mourned Ellery, "you have me, Jo. I haven't been able to spot one connection, let alone two."

"Quite amusing, I'm sure," Ellen said. "Meanwhile, we're neglecting the important thing. What happened to the pendant?"

All Christopher's dissatisfaction with the Queen performance burst out at finding a target he felt free to attack. "*Important* thing," he cried. "I can't make head or tail of what's going on here, but don't you consider it important to find out who killed father, Ellen? Aren't you concerned with anything but that damned pendant? You make me feel like a ghoul!"

"Don't flatter yourself," Ellen said to her twin. "You're nothing so impressive as a ghoul, Chris. What you are is a bloody ass."

He turned his back on his sister; and regal as a Borgia, she stalked from the room. From the stairway her complaint came to them distinctly: "You'd think father would have installed a lift instead of making us climb these antediluvian stairs."

"Yes, your Majesty!" yelled Christopher.

While Mr. Q murmured to Chief Newby, "Ellery in Blunderland. Through the Magnifying Glass . . ."

"What are you," snarled the Chief of Police, grabbing his coat and hat, "a nut or something?"

January 13   The one morning of the week when Ellen could be relied on to come down for breakfast was Sunday. Invariably she descended to a kipper and a slice of dry toast (except on communion days), after which, trailing High Church clouds of glory, she strode off to join her Anglican co-worshipers.

It was therefore a matter of remark that on this particular Sunday morning she failed to appear.

It was especially remarkable to Ellery, who had been barred by the proprieties from passing the night guarding her bedside. Enlisting Margaret Caswell's chaperonage, he rushed upstairs, kicked open the unlocked door, and dashed in.

Ellen was still in bed. He listened frantically to her breathing; he took her pulse; he shook her, shouting in her ear. Then he damned her perversity and the unlocked door, which was an example of it.

"Phone Conk Farnham!" he bellowed at Mrs. Caswell.

There followed a scene of chaos, not without its absurdity, like an old Mack Sennett comedy. Its climax came when, for the umpteenth time in ten days, Dr. Farnham arrived on the run with his little black bag. It was surely Conk's opinion, thought Ellery, that he was hopelessly trapped in the antics of a houseful of lunatics.

"Sleeping pills," the doctor said. "Slight overdose. No need for treatment; she didn't take enough. She'll come out of it by herself soon—in fact, she's coming out of it now."

"This must be it on the night table," Ellery mumbled.

"What?"

"The medium of the pills."

A cup of scummy cold chocolate sat there, almost full.

"That's it all right," said Dr. Farnham, after tasting it. "It's loaded. If she'd swallowed the whole cupful, Ellery, she'd have been done for."

"When will she be able to talk?"

"As soon as she's all the way out."

Ellery snapped his fingers. "Excuse me, Conk!" he said, and dashed past Mrs. Caswell and tore down the stairs. In the breakfast room, silent and glum, sat Jo and Chris and Wolcott Thorp.

"How's Ellen?" Chris asked, half rising.

"Sit down. She's all right. This time. Now we can start worrying about next time."

"Next time?"

"Somebody slipped a lethal overdose of sleeping pills in her hot chocolate before she went to bed last night—unless you're prepared to argue that Ellen is the type who would attempt suicide, which in my book she definitely is not. Anyway, she took only a few sips, thereby surviving. But whoever tried to kill her may try another time, and my guess is the time will be sooner than later. So let's not dawdle. Who knows who prepared the hot chocolate last night?"

"I do," said Joanne. "She prepared it herself. I was in the kitchen with her."

"All the time she was fixing it?"

"No, I left before she did."

"Anyone else in the kitchen at the time, or near it?"

"Not I," said Christopher promptly wiping his brow, which for some reason was damp. "If I ever give way to one of my homicidal impulses toward Ellen, I'll use something sure, like cyanide."

But no one smiled.

"You, Mr. Thorp?" asked Ellery, fixing the curator with a glittering eye.

"Not I," said the little man, stuttering.

"Had anyone gone up to bed?"

89

"I don't think so," said Jo, her eyes worried. "No, I'm sure no one had. It was just after we finished that crazy farce of yours in the drawing room—when Ellen pranced out, I mean. A few minutes later she came downstairs again to prepare her chocolate. All the rest of us were still here. Don't you remember?"

"No, because I was seeing Chief Newby out, and we talked outside for a few minutes before he drove off. Unfortunately I share the general weakness of being unable to be in two places at the same time. Did Ellen go directly upstairs with her chocolate?"

"I can answer that," said Christopher. "I'd gone to the library to lick my wounds, and Ellen came in for a book to read in bed, she said. She wasn't there more than two or three minutes. She took one of yours, if I'm not mistaken."

"Maybe that's why she fell asleep so soon," said Jo with a little snap-crackle-pop in her voice.

"Even that," said Ellery with a bow, "is not impossible. In any event, she must have left her cup standing in the kitchen for those two or three minutes."

"I guess so," said Christopher. "It would also seem that we were all milling around, with opportunity to dodge into the kitchen and tamper with it, allowing for a healthy lie or two. Take your pick, Mr. Queen. In my own defense I can only say I didn't do it."

"Nor," stuttered little Wolcott Thorp, "did I."

"It looks," said Jo, "as if you'll have to make the most of what you have."

"Which," snapped Ellery, "is precious little."

And he left them to go back upstairs, where he found Dr. Farnham preparing to depart. Ellen was awake, propped up against the headboard, looking not hung over at all. What she did look like was hostile and furtive.

Ellery went to work.

But his most tried techniques, running from the sympathetic plea to the horrendous warning, failed to budge her. Her brush with death seemed to have left her only the more doggedly crouched over whatever secret she was concealing.

The most Ellery could pry out of her was the admission that she had bought sleeping pills herself from a local "chemist," on the prescription of another doctor in town whom she did not name. Finally, slipping down in the bed, she turned her face to the wall and refused to answer any more of his questions whatsoever.

Checkmated, Ellery withdrew, leaving Mrs. Caswell on guard.

Someone else, he thought, was at the moment sharing his frustration. The agent of the sleeping pills.

* * *

The dinner conversation had gaps. Ellery pushed the food around on his plate. Ellen attempted a show of Empire fortitude, but the attempt was sorry, and he suspected that she had come down to the dinner table only because of the creepy isolation of her bedroom.

Margaret Caswell sat in a tense posture that suggested listening, as for the baying of bloodhounds. Christopher and Joanne sought reassurance in eloquent eye examination of each other. Wolcott Thorp tried to stimulate a discussion of some recent Fulah acquisitions by the museum, but no one listened even politely, and he too fell under the spell of the pervasive gloom.

They were about to leave the dinner table when the doorbell rang with an angry chime. Ellery leaped to life.

"Chief Newby," he said. "I'll let him in, if no one minds. Please go to the drawing room—all of you. We're going to get on with this lethal nonsense and make something of it if it takes all night."

He hurried to the front door. Newby hurled his hat and overcoat on a tapestried chair but pointedly failed to remove his overshoes, as if announcing that at the first sound of jabberwocky he intended to exit.

They joined the others in the drawing room, and Newby said, "All right, Ellery, get on with it."

"Let's begin," Ellery said, "with a fact. The fact that you, Ellen, are in imminent danger. What we don't know, and must know, is why. It's something only you can tell us, and I suggest you do so before it's too late. I remind you that the murderer of your father is here in this room, listening and watching."

Four pairs of eyes shifted from Ellen immediately, but they came right back again.

Ellen's lips remained drawn at the corners, like a scar. "I told you—I don't know what you're talking about."

"You're afraid, of course. But do you think you're going to buy immunity with silence? A murderer needs to sleep at night, too, and his best assurance of peace of mind is your permanent removal. So talk while you still can."

"It's my job to warn you, Mrs. Nash," Chief Newby put in sourly, "that if you're holding back evidence, you're committing a crime. How much trouble do you want to be in?"

But Ellen fixed her eyes on the fists in her lap.

"All right," said Ellery, and his tone was so odd that even Ellen stirred. "If you won't talk, I will.

"Let's start all over again. What did Godfrey mean by writing M-U-M? Ignore what I've said before about it. I've now come to a final conclusion.

"A man clear-headed enough to leave a dying message is clear-headed enough to avoid ambiguity. Since MUM involved most of you—and in more ways than one, far fetched as most of them are—then I have to conclude that Godfrey did not intend MUM to indicate the identity of his murderer.

"Consequently, once more I have to go back to what Godfrey did promise to leave you—the combination of his safe."

"But you went through all that," exploded Newby. "And it washed out—the safe was empty."

"Not a complete washout, Newby. I translated MUM into numbers because of the twenty-six numbers on the dial, and that proved correct as far as it went. But what if it didn't go far enough? Remember the doubles? One was that the safe cost Godfrey about double what it should have. *What if there was a good, solid, practical reason for that double cost?* Suppose there's more to that safe than meets the eye—*some feature that cost the extra money.* Double cost . . . *how about double safe?*"

That brought their mouths open, and he continued swiftly. "If it was a double safe, there would be *two* combinations. One would work by the numbers 13-21-13, as it does, and would open the orthodox safe. The other combination would open another safe!—which obviously must be contained *within* the safe, making an inner, smaller safe. And suppose—since that's the word Godfrey wrote down just before he died—suppose that not only is MUM the combination for the outer safe, but MUM is also the combination for the inner safe. One MUM translating into numbers, the second remaining exactly what it is—*a word of three letters.*"

"But there aren't any letters on the dial," protested Newby.

"Right. But remember what's etched on the rim of the knob? The name and address of the manufacturer: VULCAN SAFE & LOCK COMPANY, INC., NEW HAVEN, CONN. And you'll note that, contained in those words, are an M and a U!

"Shall we try it?"

Ellery went over to the oil painting and slid it to one side. He revolved the dial a few times, then turned it until the M of COMPANY lay directly under the alignment notch; then he turned right to the U of VULCAN, aligning that, then left, back to the M of COMPANY.

He pulled on the knob.

The safe door did not swing open. Instead, the knob came out in his hand! And behind the knob, within the thickness of the safe door, where the tumblers and mechanism lay, appeared a small compartment—a safe within a safe. And in the compartment, flashing like a minor sun surrounded by sixteen glowing planets, was the Imperial Pendant.

"Alagazam," Ellery said softly, holding it aloft so that the light from the old-fashioned crystal chandelier blazed from the pendant in a thousand coruscations. "When Mr. Mumford put the necklace away, his back must have been to you, and it was a broad back. It was into the knob-safe that he put this, not into the regular one. That's why he probably never bothered to put the pendant in a bank vault, Christopher. Even if someone tried to burgle this safe, could he dream that the real safe was behind the knob? It was, if you'll excuse the pun, very safe indeed. Here, Newby, I imagine you'd better take charge of this until the will is probated and certain other matters are cleared up."

And Ellery tossed the pendant to Newby, while the others' heads moved in unison, like the heads of spectators at a tennis match.

"Q.E.D.," said Ellery. "Only half of our mystery is solved. It remains only to solve the other half.

"Who killed Godfrey Mumford?"

He faced them with such fierceness that they all shrank back.

"I've known since yesterday morning who the murderer is," Ellery said. "There wasn't a chance, by the way, that he'd take off—not so long as the pendant was missing. It was the finding of the pendant that was holding me up, too.

"I want you all to look at this letter from the murderer to Ellen. Examine it carefully."

He took it from his pocket and handed it to Chief Newby, who looked it over, scowled, and passed it on.

12/1/65

Mum's the word. If you tell what you know I'll kill you, too.

When it came back to him from Thorp, the last to read it, Ellery could detect nothing but blankness on any face.

"You don't see it?"

"Come on, Ellery," Newby rasped. "So I'm as blind as the rest and you've got the eyes of a chicken hawk. What's the point?"

"The point is the date."

"The date?"

"The date at the top. *12/1/65*."

"Why, that's wrong," said Jo suddenly. "It's January, not December."

"Correct. The letter was left on the salver the morning of January twelfth—*1/12/65*. The writer reversed the numerals for the month and day. Why? In the United States we write the month numeral first, always, *then* the day numeral. *It's in England that they do it the opposite way.*

"Who in this household has been living in England for years? Who uses the Anglicism 'trunk call' for 'long distance'? Who says

93

'lift' for 'elevator', 'Chief Constable' for 'Chief of Police', 'chemist' instead of 'druggist' or 'pharmacist'?

"Ellen, of course. Ellen, who wrote this 'threatening' letter to herself."

Ellen was glaring at Ellery as if he had turned into a monster from outer space. "No, I didn't!"

But Ellery ignored her. "And why should Ellen have written a threatening letter to herself? Well, what was the effect the letter produced? It made her look as though she were next in line to be murdered—by implication, therefore, innocent of the killing of Godfrey.

"This was doubly indicated by the clumsy poisoning attempt on herself—an evident phony. She never meant to drink more than a few sips. The whole hot chocolate episode was designed to make that 'threat' look good."

Now his eyes found Ellen's and locked.

"Why should you want to make yourself look innocent, Ellen? The innocent don't have to *make* themselves look innocent. Only the guilty—"

"Are you accusing *me*?" Ellen shrieked. "Of stabbing my own father to death?" She looked about wildly. "Chris, Jo—you can't believe—*Mum*!"

But Ellery drove ahead without mercy. "The clue points directly to you, Ellen, and only to you. Of course, if you've anything to say that puts a different complexion on all this, I advise you to say it now."

Ellery kept her gaze pinned down like a butterfly specimen. She began to tremble. And as she did so, he suddenly said in the kindest of voices, "Don't be afraid any more, Ellen. You see, I know what you know. All I want you to do is to speak out, to tell us what you know."

And she did, her story rushing out. "I was up the night father was murdered—couldn't sleep for some reason. It was long past midnight. While I was in the upstairs hall, on my way down to the kitchen for a snack . . . I happened to see somebody sneak out of father's room. I was sure he saw me. I was afraid to tell . . ."

"And who was it you saw, Ellen?"

"It was . . . it was . . ." And her arm shot out—" . . . it was Wolcott Thorp!"

Ellery went early to his room, packed his suitcases, and slipped like the Arab silently away, leaving behind a bread-and-butter note. He did not check back in to the Hollis, the savor having gone out of Wrightsville; but he had a couple of hours to kill before plane time, and he killed them, appropriately, at police headquarters.

94

"Ellery!" Chief Newby greeted him, rising and seizing his hand. "I was hoping you'd drop in. I never did get to thank you properly. That was a slick scene you put on last night. You told a real whopper."

"I may have told," said Ellery soberly, "several."

"You said you knew what Ellen knew."

"Oh, that. Yes, of course. But I had to get her to talk; I was reasonably certain that was what she was holding back. And that letter business—"

"Did you really think she wrote that letter?"

"Not for a moment. Except for psychos, murderers don't admit their killings—even in disguised handwritings—at a time when they're not even suspected. And Ellen's Britishness was so blatant that anyone could have used the British dating system to frame her. So although I knew she hadn't written that threatening letter to herself, I accused her of it last night to frighten her into putting the finger on Thorp.

"Thorp, of course, was the one who wrote the letter. He counted on my spotting the Anglicism and pinning it on Ellen for the reason I gave—that double whammy about if-she-wants-us-to-think-she's-innocent-she-must-be-guilty. And if I hadn't spotted it, he could always have called it to my attention.

"It may even be that Thorp originally designed the frame-up letter to be used by him in the event Ellen did talk and accused him of what she'd seen. The trouble was, even when Ellen kept her mouth shut, Thorp had second thoughts. That poisoned chocolate business wasn't an attempt on Ellen's part to make herself look innocent, as I mendaciously suggested last night in putting the pressure on her; it was a genuine attempt by Thorp to shut her mouth before she could open it. He expected us—if it had succeeded—to accept it as a suicide-confession."

"Incidentally," said the Chief, "you said you knew it was Thorp—"

"A slight exaggeration. I had reason to suspect Thorp, but I had no proof—not an iota; and I was afraid another attack on Ellen might succeed."

"But why," asked the Chief, "would a man like Thorp murder his best friend in cold blood? He's confessed to the killing, but we haven't been able to get a word out of him about the motive. It certainly can't be that measly twenty thousand Godfrey was leaving him."

Ellery sighed. "The collector breed are a strange lot, Newby. In spite of what he told Godfrey, Thorp probably didn't consider himself too old to go on that expedition to West Africa; he must have been waiting desperately for years for what he thought was going to be a hundred thousand dollars to finance the trip. When he learned that Godfrey's carelessness had caused it to shrink to only one-fifth of that, he flipped. That expedition was the dream of his life. Is there anyone we can come to hate more than the loved one who disappoints and frustrates us?"

Newby held up his hand as Ellery rose. "Wait a minute! What made you suspect Thorp in the first place? It must be something fancy I missed."

Ellery did not display pride. His Wrightsville triumphs too often felt like defeats. Perhaps it was because he loved the old town, and it had been his lot to clean up her filth.

"Nothing fancy, Newby. The dreariest kind of slip on Thorp's part. When you and I first went to the house, they told us in detail what had gone on at the discovery of the body. The line of previous action was very clear. Margaret Caswell rushed out of Godfrey's bedroom, crying out that the old man was—mark the word—*dead*. They all rushed upstairs except Thorp, who went to the downstairs phone, called Dr. Farnham, then called you here at headquarters. And what did Thorp tell you? That Mumford had been found, not merely dead, but *murdered*. Why should Thorp have leaped to the conclusion that the old man's death was unnatural *unless he already knew it?*

"You know, Newby," Ellery said with a half smile that apologized in advance. "Wolcott Thorp would have been far, far better off if he'd followed his own advice and—forgive me—kept mum."

THE CASE
OF THE CRYING SWALLOW

BY ERLE STANLEY GARDNER

Erle Stanley Gardner, who was born on July 17, 1889, had sales of 200 million copies of his books in America alone when he died in 1970. His total output is said to be 120 books, but it would not be surprising if this were an underestimate. His Perry Mason stories began in 1932 with *The Case of the Velvet Claws*. He achieved later success with his Donald Lam-Bertha Cool series, which he wrote under one of his many pen-names, A. A. Fair.

PERRY MASON, TILTED BACK IN HIS walnut desk chair, was studying a recent decision of the State Supreme Court when Della Street, his secretary, opened the door from the outer office, advanced to the desk, and quietly laid ten crisp one-hundred-dollar bills on the blotter.

Mason, too engrossed to notice what she was doing, continued his reading.

Della Street said, "A client sends his card."

Mason straightened in the swivel chair and for the first time caught sight of the money which Della Street had so neatly spread out.

"He said his name was Mr. Cash," Della Street explained. "Then he handed me ten one-hundred-dollar bills and said these were his cards."

Mason grinned. "What does Mr. Cash look like?"

"He's a floor walker."

Mason raised his eyebrows. "A *floorwalker?*"

"No, no, not a department-store floorwalker! I mean that he's a floor *walker*, the same as you are. He paces the floor when he's worried. He's doing a carpet marathon out there right now. He's distinguished-looking, has a slight limp, is deeply tanned, and . . . and I've seen him somewhere before. Oh, now I have it. I've seen his picture!"

"Give."

"Major Claude L. Winnett, polo player, yachtsman, millionaire playboy. When the war came, he quit being a playboy and became an aviator, bagged a whole flock of German planes and then was captured, liberated last fall, discharged because of his wound, returned to his doting mother and . . ."

Mason nodded. "I remember reading about the chap. He got a citation or something. Didn't he get married?"

"About four or five weeks ago," Della Street said. "That was where I first saw his picture—in the paper. Then again last week a reporter for the society supplement paid a visit to the Winnett home—one of the old-time country estates with stables of polo ponies, riding trails, hedges, private golf course . . ."

"Show him in," Mason said. "But let him know first that you've placed him. It may save time."

Major Winnett, lean, fit, bronzed, and nervous, followed Della Street into the office. The excitement and anxiety of his manner were more noticeable than his slight limp. A well-modulated voice and patrician bearing made his surrender to emotion all the more impressive.

"Mr. Mason," he said as soon as he was in the room, "I had intended to keep my identity a secret and ask you to represent another person. Now that your secretary has recognized me, I'll put my cards on the table. My wife has disappeared. She needs your help. She's in trouble of some sort."

"Tell me about it," Mason said.

Major Winnett reached into his pocket, took out a piece of letter paper, and handed it to Mason.

The lawyer opened the letter, read:

"Claude, my darling, there are some things that I can't drag *you* into. I thought I had a way out, but I guess I didn't. Our happiness was such a beautiful thing. But beautiful things are always fragile. Don't worry about anything. I am responsible, and I am not going to let you suffer because of what you have done for me. Goodbye, my darling.—MARCIA"

"What does she mean by saying she's responsible and not letting you suffer because of what you have done for her?" Mason asked.

Major Winnett's manner was uneasy. "My marriage was not exactly in accordance with the wishes of my mother. I went ahead with it despite her objections."

"Spoken objections?"

"Certainly not."

"Yet your wife knew of them?"

"Women feel many things without the necessity of words, Mr. Mason. I want you to find her and straighten things out for her."

"And then report to you?"

"Certainly."

Mason shook his head.

For a moment there was silence, broken only by the faint rumble of traffic and the breathing of Mason's client. Then Major Winnett said, "Very well. Do it your way."

"When did your wife leave?"

"Last night. I found this note on the dresser about midnight. I thought she had previously retired."

"Is there any reason why your wife would have been vulnerable to what we might call an outside influence?"

"Absolutely not—if you mean blackmail."

"Then tell me why your wife wasn't free to come to you with her troubles."

"I don't know, unless it's on account of my mother."

"What about her?"

"My mother is a very unusual person. When my father died, a

dozen years ago, mother stepped in and took charge. She is living in a bygone era. She has old-fashioned ideas."

"The proprieties?" Mason asked.

"Not so much the proprieties as . . . well, class distinctions, the aristocracy of wealth and that sort of thing. I think she would have been more happy if I had married someone more in our own set."

"Who, for instance?"

"Oh, I didn't say any particular person," Major Winnett said hastily.

"I know you didn't. That's why I'm asking you."

"Well, perhaps Daphne Rexford."

"You think this caused your wife to leave?"

"No, no. Not directly. My mother has accepted Marcia into the family. Whatever may have been Mother's ideas about the marriage, Marcia is now one of us—a Winnett."

"Then suppose you tell me what you mean when you say 'not directly.'"

"Marcia would have done anything rather than subject me to any notoriety because she knew how my mother felt about that. You see, Mr. Mason, we live in a large, rather old-fashioned estate surrounded by hedges, with our private bridle paths, high wire fences, locked gates, no-trespassing signs, and all the rest. The more the world moves in a way that meets with the disapproval of my mother, the more she tries to shut that part of the world out from her life."

"Anything unusual happen within the last few days?" Mason asked.

"A burglar entered our house Tuesday night."

"Take anything?" Mason asked.

"My wife's jewelry, valued at perhaps twenty-five or thirty thousand dollars, although I don't suppose a person could get that for it. It had been insured for fifteen thousand dollars."

"Had been?" Mason asked.

"Yes, my wife canceled the insurance. As it happened, only the day before the burglary."

Major Winnett glanced almost appealingly at the lawyer.

"Canceled her insurance," Mason said, "and then twenty-four hours later the burglary took place?"

"Yes."

"And you fail to see any connection between those two facts?"

"I am certain there is none," Major Winnett said hastily. "My wife's reasoning was absolutely sound. She had carried this insurance policy and paid high premiums on it while she was living in apartments and hotels because she wanted to keep her jewelry with her and wanted to wear it. But when she married me and came to live in Vista del Mar, it seemed hardly necessary to continue paying high premiums."

"Tell me more about that burglary and why you didn't report it to the police."

"How did you know we didn't report it to the police?"

"Your facial expression," Mason said dryly.

"That was purely on account of the fact that my mother . . . well, you know, the newspaper notoriety and . . ."

"Tell me about the burglary," Mason said.

Major Winnett spoke with the rhythm of a man who is carefully choosing his words. "I am a sound sleeper, Mr. Mason. My wife is not. On Tuesday night I was awakened by the sound of my wife's scream."

"What time?"

"I didn't look at my watch at the time but I did look at it a few minutes later and as nearly as I can place the time, it was around quarter to one."

"How long had you been in bed?"

"We retired about eleven."

"And you slept until your wife screamed?"

"Well, I have, in the back of my consciousness, a vague recollection of a swallow crying."

Mason raised his eyebrows.

"You are, of course, familiar," Major Winnett went on hastily, "with the famed swallows of the Mission of San Juan Capistrano?"

Mason nodded.

"The nesting place of those swallows is not confined to the Mission. They get more publicity at the Mission because they leave on a certain day and return on a certain day. I believe that the time of their return can be predicted almost to the hour. A very unusual sense of keeping a calendar. How they are able to return year after year . . ."

"And you have some of those swallows at your house?" Mason interrupted.

"Yes. They are a nuisance. Their nests are built out of mud and are fastened to the eaves. Our gardener knocks them down as soon as he detects the birds building, but in case one of them eludes his vigilance and the nest is built, then we don't disturb it, because the birds lay eggs very soon after the nests are built."

"Go on," Mason said.

"Well, this particular swallow's nest was located in a very unfortunate place. The main residence at Vista del Mar is a large Spanish-type house with the tile roofs and a white exterior. My bedroom is on the second floor with a projecting balcony. The tile projects out over the balcony and the birds had made their nest in such a place that if a man climbed over the balcony rail, he'd be within a few feet of the nest."

"And a man did climb over that rail?"

"Evidently that is what happened. We found a ladder that had been placed against the side of the house. The intruder had climbed up the ladder. In doing so, he disturbed the swallows. They have a peculiar throaty chirp."

"I either heard it or dreamed that I did. My wife doesn't remember it, and she is a much lighter sleeper than I am, but I don't think I was mistaken."

"Then you went back to sleep?"

"Apparently I did. I remember hearing the protestations of the swallows and, while I was aroused from a sound slumber, I didn't thoroughly waken. I dozed off again and was soon in a deep sleep from which I was awakened by my wife's scream."

"She saw the burglar?"

"She was aroused by some noise in the room. She saw this man standing at her dresser. At first she thought I had gone to the dresser for some purpose and she started to speak to me. Then she looked over and saw that I was in my bed . . ."

"There was enough light for that?"

"Yes. The moon was giving some light."

"What happened?"

"The man heard the motion—some sound of the bedsprings, I guess. He darted out to the balcony. My wife screamed and that awakened me, but it took me a few seconds to get oriented, to realize where I was and what was happening. By that time the man had made his escape."

"And you think the swallows were crying because the man disturbed them?"

"That's right. When he entered the building, he must have climbed over the balcony rail and touched the nest."

"When did your wife cancel the insurance?"

"Monday afternoon."

Mason toyed with his lead pencil, asked abruptly, "What happened Monday morning?"

"We all four breakfasted together."

"Who's the fourth?"

"Helen Custer, my mother's nurse."

"Your mother isn't well?"

"She has a bad heart. Her physician feels it's advisable to have a nurse in the house."

"She's been with you long?"

"For three years. We consider her very much one of the family."

"You breakfasted and then what?"

"I wrote letters. My mother . . . I didn't know exactly where she *did* go. Marcia went riding."

"Where?"

"Heavens, I don't know. One of our bridle paths."

Mason said, "I believe it rained Sunday night, didn't it?"

Major Winnett looked at him curiously. "What," he asked, "does that have to do with it?"

"Skip it," Mason said. "What happened next?"

"Nothing. My wife returned about eleven."

"When did she tell you she was going to cancel the insurance?"

"That was just before lunch. She telephoned to the insurance company, then she wrote them a letter confirming her action."

"Did you notice anything unusual in your wife's manner?"

"Nothing." Major Winnett said it so swiftly that it seemed the answer had been poised on his tongue, waiting merely for Mason's question.

Mason said, "Well, it's ten thirty. I want to get Paul Drake of the Drake Detective Agency. We'll make a start out at your place and go on from there. I'll leave here about eleven. Does your mother know your wife has left?"

Major Winnett cleared his throat. "I told her my wife was visiting friends."

"How will you account for us?" Mason asked.

"How many will there be?"

"My secretary Miss Street, Paul Drake the detective, myself, and perhaps one of Mr. Drake's assistants."

Major Winnett said, "I'm working on a mining deal. I can explain to my mother that you're giving me some advice in connection with that. Your detective wouldn't mind posing as a mining expert?"

"Not at all."

"You'll come to the house and . . . will you want to stay there?"

Mason nodded. "I think we'd better. And I'll want photographs and a description of your wife."

Major Winnett took an envelope from his inside pocket, extracted nearly a dozen photographs. "I brought these along. They're snapshots. She's twenty-five, redheaded, bluish gray eyes, five feet two, a hundred and fifteen, and as nearly as I can tell from checking the clothes that are left in the closet, she's wearing a checkered suit, sort of a gray plaid. It's the one that she's wearing in this picture."

Mason studied the photographs, then reached for the envelope. "All right," he said, "we'll be out. You can go on ahead and see that all necessary arrangements are made."

The city of Silver Strand Beach lay in a sheltered cove on the leeside of a peninsula. The Winnett estate dominated this peninsu-

la, its wire fences with forbidding *No Trespassing* signs stretching for
some two and a half miles. The Spanish-type house, perched on the
summit some five hundred feet above the ocean, commanded a
view in all directions.

Mason's car swept around the last curve in the graveled driveway, came to a stop in front of the imposing house as he said to Paul
Drake, "I think the cancellation of that insurance policy is, perhaps,
the first indication of what she had in mind, Paul. And I think that
may have some connection with the horseback ride she took Monday morning."

Paul Drake's professionally lugubrious face didn't change expression in the least. "Anything to go on, Perry?"

"It rained Sunday night," Mason said. "It hasn't rained since. If
you could find the path she took, it's quite possible you might be
able to track her horse."

"For the love of Pete, do I have to ride a horse?"

"Sure. Tell the groom you'd like to ride. Ask him about some of
the bridle paths."

"I can't see anything from a horse," Drake complained. "When a
horse trots, I bounce. When I bounce, I see double."

"After you get out of sight of the house, you can lead the horse,"
Mason suggested.

"How about me?" Della asked.

"Try and get acquainted with the nurse," Mason suggested, "and
take a look around."

Major Winnett himself answered Mason's ring, and the swift
efficiency with which he installed them in rooms, introduced them
to his mother, and Helen Custer, the nurse, showed that he had
already made his preliminary explanations.

While Drake departed for the stables, after having expressed his
spurious enthusiasm for horseflesh, Major Winnett took Mason on
a tour of inspection.

Once they were alone in the upper corridors, Major Winnett
asked quickly and in a low voice, "Is there anything in particular
you want to see?"

"I'd like to get familiar with the entire house," Mason said guard-
edly. "But you might begin by showing me your room."

Major Winnett's room was on the south side. Glass doors opened
on the balcony, from which the ocean could be seen shimmering in
the sunlight.

"That's the swallow's nest?" Mason asked, indicating a gourd-like
projection of mud which extended from the tiles just above the
balcony.

"Yes. You can see that a person climbing a ladder . . ."

"Was the ladder already there?" Mason asked.

"Yes. The handyman had been doing some work on a pane of glass on the side of the bedroom. He had left the ladder in position that night because he intended to finish it the next morning. Damn careless of him."

"In that case," Mason said, "your thief was an opportunist, since he didn't bring his own ladder."

"Yes, I suppose so."

"One who was, moreover, apparently familiar with the house. How about your servants?"

"You can't ever tell," Major Winnett said. "Particularly these days. But I *think* they're all right. Mother pays good wages and most of the help have been with her for some time. However, she *is* rather strict and there is a certain turnover."

"You own virtually all the land on this peninsula?"

"Quite a bit of it, but not all. In a moment we'll go up to the observation tower and I can show you around from there. Generally, we take in about three-fourths of the peninsula. There is a strip out on the end where the county maintains a public camp ground."

"The public can reach that camp without crossing your estate?"

"Yes. Our line runs along by the grove of trees—beautiful oaks that offer a place for picnics. Picnickers are always scattering papers and plates around. We try to persuade them to go on down to the public camp grounds on the end of the peninsula."

"So anyone who came out here at night would have been a trespasser?"

"Definitely."

"And having taken that risk, must have had some specific objective in mind, and would, therefore, if he were at all prudent, have arranged some manner of reaching his objective?"

"Yes, I suppose so."

"Therefore," Mason went on, "your burglar must either have been someone who knew that the ladder was here, or else it was an inside job."

"But how could anyone have known the ladder was here?"

Mason said, "If you can see the camp and the picnic grounds from here, it is quite possible that someone in the camp or picnic grounds could see the house."

"Yes, the house is quite a landmark. You can see it for miles."

"And perhaps a man, looking up here about dusk and noticing that a ladder had been left in place, would have decided it might be worthwhile to climb that ladder."

"Yes, I suppose so. However, Mr. Mason, I can't see that there is the slightest connection between the theft of my wife's jewelry and her disappearance."

"Probably not," Mason said.

They finished their tour with a trip up a flight of stairs to the place which Major Winnett described as "the tower."

Here was a belfry-like room, fifteen feet square, with plate glass windows on all sides. In the center, a pair of eighteen-power binoculars attached to a swivel on a tripod could be turned and locked in any position.

"In times past," Major Winnett explained, "when there was more merchant shipping up and down the coast, we used to enjoy looking the boats over. You see, these binoculars can be swung in any direction. Now I'll point them toward town and . . ."

"Just a minute," Mason warned sharply, as Major Winnett reached for the binoculars. "They seem to be pointed toward that grove of trees. If you don't mind, I'd like to look through them."

Mason looked through the powerful prismatic binoculars. The right eye showed a shaded spot under the clump of big live oaks where the road crossed a mesa before dipping down through a little canyon to again come into view as it swung out toward the picnic and camping grounds on the extreme tip of the promontory.

"There's no central focusing screw," Major Winnett explained. "You have to adjust each eyepiece individually. Perhaps . . ."

"Yes, so I see," Mason said, removing his eyes from the binoculars.

"Here is what I mean," Major Winnett went on. "You simply screw this eyepiece . . ."

Mason courteously but firmly arrested the Major's hand. "Just a moment, Major," he said. "I want to look at that right eyepiece."

"Someone must have been tampering with it. It's way out of proper adjustment," the Major said.

"The left eyepiece is at zero adjustment. I take it that means a perfectly normal eye," Mason said, "whereas, on this right eyepiece, there is an adjustment of negative five. I take it those graduations are made so that a person can remember his own individual adjustment and adjust the binoculars readily."

"I suppose so. The figures represent diopters."

"And an adjustment of negative five certainly blurs the entire . . ."

"That can't be an adjustment," the Major interposed. "Someone has idly turned that eyepiece."

"I see your point," Mason said and promptly turned the eyepiece back to zero. "There," he announced, "that's better."

It was now possible to make out details in what had before been merely a patch of shadow.

Mason swung the binoculars to the picnic ground and could see quite plainly the masonry barbecue pits, the tables and chairs. Beyond them, through the trees, he caught a glimpse of the ocean.

"A beach down there?" he asked.

"Not a beach, but a very fine place for surf fishing."

Mason swung the binoculars once more toward the clump of trees and the wide place in the road. "And you say people picnic there?"

"Occasionally, yes."

"From that point," Mason said, "one could see the house quite plainly with binoculars."

Mason waited until he saw Major Winnett leave the house, walking toward the stables. Then the lawyer quietly opened the door of his room, walked down the corridor to Winnett's bedroom, crossed the balcony and climbed to the rail.

The entrance of the swallow's nest was too small to accommodate the lawyer's hand but he enlarged the entrance by chipping away bits of the dried mud with his thumb and forefinger.

From inside the nest came faint rustlings. An immature beak pushed against Mason's finger.

The parent swallows cried protests as they swooped in swift, stabbing circles around the lawyer's head, but Mason, working rapidly, enlarged the opening so that he could insert his hand into the nest. He felt soft down-covered bodies. Below them his groping fingers encountered only the concave surface of the nest.

A frown of annoyance crossed the lawyer's face. He continued groping, however, gently moving the young birds to one side. Then the frown faded as the tips of his fingers struck a hard metallic object.

As the lawyer managed to remove this object, sunlight scintillated an emerald and diamond brooch into brilliance.

Mason swiftly pocketed the jewelry, drew back from the fierce rushes of the swallows. He dropped to the floor of the balcony and returned to the bedroom.

Back in the bedroom he made a swift, thorough search of various places where small objects might be concealed. A sole leather gun case in the back of a closet contained an expensive shotgun. Mason looked through the barrels. Both were plugged with oiled rags at breach and muzzle.

Mason's knife extracted one of the rags. He tilted the barrels, and jewelry cascaded out into his palm—rings, earrings, brooches, a diamond and emerald necklace.

Mason replaced the jewelry, inserted the rag once more, put the barrels back in the leather case, and returned the case to the closet.

Preparing to leave the room, he listened for a few moments at the bedroom door, then boldly opened it and stepped out, retracing his steps toward his own room.

He was halfway down the corridor when Mrs. Victoria Winnett appeared at an intersecting corridor and moved toward Mason with stately dignity and a calm purpose.

"Were you looking for something, Mr. Mason?" she asked.

The lawyer's smile was disarming. "Just getting acquainted with the house."

Victoria Winnett was the conventional composite of a bygone era. There were pouches beneath her eyes, sagging lines in her face, but the painstakingly careful manner in which every strand of hair had been carefully coiffed, her face massaged, powdered, and rouged, indicated the emphasis she placed on appearance; and there was a stately dignity about her manner which, as Della Street subsequently remarked, reminded one of an ocean liner moving sedately up to its pier.

Had she carefully rehearsed her entrance and been grooming herself for hours to convey just the right impression of dignified rebuke, Mrs. Victoria Winnett would not have needed to change so much as a word. "I think my *son* wanted to show you around," she said as she fell into step at Mason's side.

"Oh, he's done that already," Mason said with breezy informality. "I was just looking the place over."

"You're Mr. *Perry* Mason?"

"That's right."

"I had gathered from what I read about your cases that you specialize mostly in trial work."

"I do."

"*Murder* trials?"

"Oh, I handle lots of other cases. The murder cases get the most publicity."

"I see," she said in the tone of one who doesn't see at all.

"Nice place you have here," the lawyer went on. "I am very much interested in that observation cubicle on top of the house."

"It was my husband's idea. He liked to sit up there. Didn't I hear the swallows crying out there?"

"I thought *I* heard them too," Mason said.

She looked at him sharply. "We try to keep them from nesting here but occasionally the gardener fails to see a nest until it is completed; then we don't disturb the nest until after the young birds have hatched. They're noisy and talkative. You can hear them quite early in the mornings. I trust they won't disturb you. Are you a sound sleeper, Mr. Mason?"

They had paused at the head of the stairs. Mrs. Winnett apparently did not intend to go down, so Mason, standing poised on the upper stair, used strategy to terminate the interview.

"My friend, Drake, is looking over the horses, and if you'll pardon me I'll join him."

He flashed her a smile and ran swiftly down the stairs.

In the patio Della Street caught Perry Mason's eye, gave him a significant signal, and moved casually over to the driveway where she climbed into the car and sat down.

Mason walked over. "I think Paul Drake has something," he said. "I'm going down and look him up. He's just coming in on the bridle path. What have you got?"

"I can tell you something about the nurse, chief."

"What?"

"In the first place, if a woman's intuition counts for anything, she's in love with the Major—one of those hopeless affairs where she worships him from a distance. In the second place, I think she has a gambling habit of some sort."

"Races?"

"I don't know. I was up in the cupola just after you were. There was a pad of paper in the drawer of the little table up there. At first it looked completely blank. Then I tilted it so the light struck it at an angle and could see that someone had written on the top sheet with a hard enough pencil to have made an imprint on the sheet underneath. Then the top sheet had been torn off."

"Good girl! What was on the sheet of paper?"

"Evidently some gambling figures. I won't bother to show you the original at this time but here's a copy that I worked out. It reads like this: *These numbers* on the first line, then down below that, *called;* then down below that a space and 5"5936; down below that 6"8102; down below that 7"9835; down below that 8"5280; down below that 9"2460; down below that 10"1320."

"Anything else?" Mason asked.

"Then a line and below the line, the figure 49"37817. That looks like some sort of a lottery to me. I learned Mrs. Winnett has been up in the cupola lately and since *she'd* hardly be a gambler, I assume the nurse must have written down the figures."

Mason said thoughtfully, "Notice the last three numbers, Della, 5280, 2640, 1320. Does that sequence mean something to you?"

"No, why?"

Mason said, "5280 feet in a mile."

"Oh, yes, I get that."

"The next number, 2640 feet, is a half mile, and the last number, 1320 feet, is a quarter mile."

"Oh, yes, I see now. Then that double mark means inches, doesn't it?"

"It's an abbreviation of inches, yes. What does this nurse seem like, Della? Remember, I only barely met her."

"Despite her muddy complexion, straight hair, and glasses, her eyes are really beautiful. You should see them light up when the Major's name comes up. My own opinion is this nurse could be good-looking. Then Mrs. Winnett would fire her. So she keeps herself looking plain and unattractive so she can be near the Major."

"Look here," Mason said, "if you've noticed that within an hour and a half, how about Mrs. Victoria Winnett? Doesn't she know?"

"I think she does."

"And hasn't fired the nurse?"

"No. I think she doesn't mind if the nurse worships the ground the Major walks on but doesn't presume to raise her eyes to look at him, if you get what I mean."

"I get it," Mason said thoughtfully, "and I don't like it. Wait, here comes Paul now."

Drake, walking stiffly, joined them.

"Find anything, Paul?" Mason asked.

"I found something," Drake conceded, "but I don't know what it is."

"What does it look like, Paul?"

"In the first place," Drake said, "you can easily follow her tracks. She took the lower bridle path. After the first quarter mile there's only one set of tracks going and coming. They were made when the ground was soft and they go down to a road and a gate that's locked. I didn't have a key but I could see where the horse's tracks went through the gate and down onto the road, so I tied up my horse and managed to squeeze through the fence."

"Any tracks around those trees, Paul?"

"An automobile had been parked there," Drake said. "There must have been two automobiles. That's the only way I can figure it out but I still can't figure the tracks right."

"How come?"

Drake took a small thin book from his pocket. "This is a little pocket book which gives the tread designs of all makes of tires. Now an automobile was in there that had some fairly new tires. One of the wheels was worn too much to identify but I identified the track of a right front wheel. Then the track of the other front wheel and the other rear wheel and . . . well, there I bogged down, Perry."

"What do you mean?"

"Of course, you have to understand it's a little difficult trying to get those tracks all fitted into the proper sequence. They . . ."

"What are you getting at?" Mason said.

"Hang it, Perry, I got *three* wheels."

"And the fourth was worn smooth?"

"Not that—what I mean is, Perry, I got three wheels *on a single side*."

Mason frowned at the detective. "*Three* wheels on a side?"

"Three wheels on a side," Paul Drake insisted doggedly.

Mason said rather excitedly, "Paul, did you notice a circular spot in the ground, perhaps eight or ten inches in diameter?"

"How the deuce did you know that spot was there?" Drake demanded, his face showing bewilderment.

Mason said, "It was made by the bottom part of a bucket, Paul. And the three tracks on each side were all right. That's the way it should be."

"I don't get it."

"A house trailer," Mason explained. "An automobile and a house trailer were parked under the trees. The waste water from a trailer sink is carried out through a drain to the outside. A bucket is placed there to catch the water as it runs off."

"That's it, all right," Drake admitted.

Mason said, "It now begins to look as though Marcia Winnett kept an appointment on Monday with someone in a house trailer. And that seems to have been very much a turning point in her life."

Drake nodded. "On Monday—that's a cold trail, Perry."

"It's the only one we have," Mason pointed out.

Mason, studying the tire tracks, said, "It was an automobile and a house trailer, Paul. The round place which marks the location of the spout bucket can be taken as being approximately in the middle of the trailer. You can see over here the mark of an auxiliary wheel attached to the front of the trailer to carry part of the weight while the trailer was parked. That enables us to estimate the length of the trailer."

Drake said, "The trailer must have been backed in between these trees, Perry."

Mason started prowling along the edge of the fence. "Took some clever handling to get it in there. Let's look around for garbage. If the trailer remained here overnight, there are probably some tin cans, potato peelings, stuff of that sort."

Mason, Della Street, and Drake separated, covering the ground carefully.

Abruptly Della said, "Chief, don't look too suddenly, but casually take a peek at the big house on the hill. I think I saw someone moving in the glassed-in observation tower."

"I rather expected as much," Mason said, without even looking up. "However, it's something we can't help."

Drake exclaimed, "Here it is, Perry, some tin cans and garbage."

Mason moved over to where Drake was standing. Here the water from the winter rains, rushing down the ditch at the side of the road, had eddied around one of the roots of the big live oak and formed a cave which extended some three feet back under the roots of the tree.

Mason, squatting on his heels, used two dry sticks to rake out the articles.

There were three cans which had been flattened under pressure, some peelings from onions and potatoes, waxed paper which had been wrapped around a loaf of bread, an empty glass container bearing a syrup label, and a crumpled paper bag.

Mason carefully segregated the items with his sticks. As he did so, he kept up a running fire of conversation.

"That flattening of the cans is the trick of an old outdoor man," he said.

"Why flatten them?" Della inquired.

"Animals get their heads stuck in cans sometimes," Mason said. "Moreover, cans take up less room when they're flattened and require a smaller hole when they're buried. This little garbage pit tells quite a story. The occupant of the trailer must have been a man. Notice the canned beans, a can of chili con carne, potatoes, bread, onions—no tomato peelings, no lettuce leaves, no carrots, no fresh vegetables at all. A woman would have had a more balanced diet. These are the smallest cans obtainable and . . . hello, what's this?"

Mason had pulled apart the paper bag as he talked. Now he brought out a small oblong slip of paper on which figures had been stamped in purple ink.

Della Street said, "That's a cash register receipt from one of the cash-and-carry grocery stores."

Mason picked up the receipt. "And a very interesting one," he said. "The man bought fifteen dollars and ninety-four cents' worth of merchandise. There's a date on the back of the slip and this other figure refers to the time. The groceries were bought at five minutes past eight on Saturday morning. It begins to look, Paul, as though this is where you take over."

"What do you want me to do?" Drake asked.

Mason said, "Get a room in the hotel at Silver Strand Beach. Open up something of an office there. Get men on the job—lots of men. Have your men buy groceries. See if the printing on the slip from any cash register matches this. If it does, try and find out something about the single, sun-bronzed man who purchased fifteen dollars and ninety-four cents' worth of groceries at five minutes past eight on Saturday morning. A sale of that size to a man just a few minutes after the store opened might possibly have attracted attention."

"Okay," Drake said. "Anything else?"

"Lots else," Mason said, "Della, where's the copy you made of the numbers you found in the observation tower?"

Della ran to the glove compartment and brought back the slip of paper.

Drake looked at it, said, "What is it, Perry?"

"Stuff Della found in the observation tower. What do you make of it?"

"Some sort of dimensions," Drake said. "Here's this number 8 inches and 5280 feet, 9 inches and a half a mile, 10 inches and quarter of a mile. What's the idea, Perry, why should the inches run 5, 6, 7, 8, 9, 10, and . . .?"

"Suppose they aren't inches?" Mason said. "Suppose they're ditto marks."

"Well, it could be."

"Then what?" Mason asked.

Drake said, "Then the numbers could have something to do with a lottery of some sort."

"Add them up," Mason said.

"The total is already here," Drake said, "49″37817."

Mason handed him a pencil.

Della Street, leaning over Drake's shoulder, was the first to get it. "Chief," she exclaimed, "the total isn't correct."

"I knew it wasn't," Mason said. "I didn't know just how much it was off, however. Let's find out."

Della Street said, "The total is . . . Wait a minute, Paul, I'll get it . . . 45″33113, but the total that's *marked* there is 49″37817."

"Subtract them," Mason said. "What do you get?"

Della Street's skillful fingers guided the pencil as she hastily wrote down numbers, performed the subtraction. "4″4704," she said.

Mason nodded. "I think," he said, "when we get this case solved, we'll find the important figure is the one that *isn't* there. Bear that figure in mind, Paul. It may turn up later."

Perry Mason took the steep stairs to the observation tower two at a time.

There was no one in the cupola. The binoculars, however, had once more been swung so that they were pointing to the grove of trees where the trailer had been parked. Mason placed his eyes to the binoculars. The left eye showed a clear vision, the right was blurred.

Mason bent over to study the adjustment on the right lens, saw it was set once more at negative five, then he changed the focus on the binoculars.

As he did so, he heard motion behind him and straightened abruptly.

Mrs. Victoria Winnett was standing in the doorway. At her side was a slender brunette in riding clothes whose face showed startled surprise. Mrs. Winnett's face showed no expression whatever.

"I hardly expected to find *you* here," Mrs. Winnett said to Mason, and then turning to the young woman at her side said, "Miss Rexford, permit me to present Mr. Perry Mason, the lawyer."

Daphne Rexford favored Mason with a smile which went only as far as her lips. Her eyes showed an emotion which might have been merely nervousness, might have been panic.

Mason acknowledged the introduction, then said, "I'm fascinated with the view you get from here, Mrs. Winnett."

"My late husband spent much of his time here. The place does hold something of a fascination. Daphne loves it."

"You're here frequently?" Mason asked Daphne Rexford.

"Yes, I study birds."

"I see."

"But," she went on hastily, "since you're here, I'll postpone my bird study until some other time."

"On the contrary," Mason said, "I was just leaving. I wanted to get the lay of the land."

"He's working with Claude on a mining deal," Mrs. Winnett hastened to explain to Daphne Rexford. "There's a mining engineer with him. And Mr. Mason has his secretary. You'll meet them if you're over for dinner tonight."

"Oh, thank you, but I . . . I don't think I can make it for dinner tonight. If Claude's going to be busy . . . Where's Marcia?"

"Visiting friends," Mrs. Winnett said dryly. "*Please* come."

"Well, I . . . I should . . ."

Mason said as she hesitated, "Well, I must go down and hunt up my client. After all, I must earn my fee, you know."

"I feel quite sure you will," Mrs. Winnett said with a certain subtle significance. "Come, Daphne, dear. Draw up a chair. What was it you were saying about swallows?"

Daphne said hurriedly, "Oh, there's a meadow lark! I think there must be a nest down by that bush."

Mason quietly closed the door, walked down the stairs . . .

Major Winnett was in the drawing room. He looked up as Mason crossed toward the patio. "What luck?" he asked.

"Progress," Mason said.

Major Winnett's lips tightened. "Can't you do better than that? Or are you just running around in circles?"

114

"A good hound always runs around in circles to pick up a scent."

"Then you haven't anything definite yet?"

"I didn't say that."

"You intimated it."

Mason slid his right hand down into his trousers pocket, abruptly withdrew the diamond and emerald brooch he had taken from the swallow's nest.

"Seen this before?" he asked, extending his hand.

Major Winnett stiffened for a moment to rigid immobility. "It looks. . .Mr. Mason, that certainly is similar to a brooch my wife had."

"One that was stolen?"

"I believe so, yes."

"Thank you," Mason said and slipped the brooch back into his pocket.

"May I ask where you got that?" Claude Winnett asked excitedly.

"Not yet," Mason told him.

The telephone rang sharply. Major Winnett moved over to the library extension, picked up the receiver, said, "Hello," then turned to Mason. "It's for you."

Mason took the telephone. Drake's voice said, "We've got something, Perry."

"What?"

"That oblong slip of paper from the cash register. We've located the store. The girl who was on duty remembers our party. We've got a good description now. With that to go on, we had no trouble picking up his trail in a trailer camp. He registered under the name of Harry Drummond."

"There now?" Mason asked.

"Not now. He pulled out early yesterday morning. I've got men covering every trailer camp anywhere near here. We should pick him up soon. We have the license number and everything. And here's a funny one, Perry. There's a Jane looking for him."

"You mean . . . ?"

"No, not the one we're interested in, another one. She's brunette, snaky, young and tall, and she was asking the cashier about him earlier in the day. Had a good description. Wanted to know if such a man had been in."

"Are you located there in the hotel?"

"Yes. I've fixed up an office here and have half a dozen men out on the job, with more coming in all the time."

Mason said, "I'll be right up."

"Okay, be looking for you."

Mason heard the click at the other end of the line but did not immediately hang up. He stood holding the receiver, frowning at the carpet.

Abruptly he heard another sharp click and the telephone bell in the library extension gave a little tinkle.

Mason dropped the receiver into place, turned to Major Winnett. "I take it," he said, "you have several extensions on the phone?"

"Four," Major Winnet said. "No, there's five. There's one up in the observation tower. I almost forgot about that."

"Thank you," Mason said, and then added after a moment, "so did I."

Paul Drake was talking on the phone when Mason entered the suite of rooms Drake was using for headquarters. In an adjoining room Della Street, a list of numbers at her elbow, was putting through a steady succession of calls.

"Come in, Perry," Drake said, hanging up the receiver. "I was trying to get you. We're getting results fast."

"Shoot."

"Our party is a man thirty-eight years old, bronzed, wears cowboy boots, a five-gallon hat, leather jacket, Pendleton trousers, rather chunky, and has a wide, firm mouth. The license number of his automobile is 4E4705. He's driving a Buick automobile and has quite an elaborate house trailer painted green on the outside with aluminum paint on the roof. Up until Saturday morning he was in the Strand Trailer Camp. He left Saturday, showed up again late Monday night, pulled out again Wednesday morning, and hasn't been seen since."

"How did you get it?" Mason asked.

"Just a lot of leg work."

"What are you doing now?"

"I've got operatives scattered around with automobiles covering every trailer camp, every possible parking place for a house trailer anywhere in this part of the country. We're working in a constantly widening circle and should turn up something soon."

Mason took out his notebook. "The number is 4E4705?"

"That's right."

"Then our mysterious observer in the observation tower made a mistake in addition. Remember, we were looking for a number 4"4704. The first number must have been 4E4705 and ditto marks were beneath the E. The real total then should have been . . ."

He was interrupted by a quick staccato knock on the door.

Mason exchanged glances with Drake. The detective left the desk, crossed over, and opened the door.

The woman who stood on the threshold was twenty-seven or twenty-eight, a tall brunette with flashing black eyes, high cheekbones, and an active, slender figure. A red brimless hat perched well back on her head emphasized the glossy darkness of her hair and harmonized with the red of her carefully made-up lips.

She smiled at Paul Drake, a stage smile which showed even, white teeth. "Are *you* Mr. Drake?" she asked, looking from him to Mason.

Drake nodded.

"May I come in?"

Drake wordlessly stood to one side.

His visitor entered the room, nodded to Perry Mason, and said, "I'm *Mrs.* Drummond."

Drake started to glance at Mason, then caught himself in time, and managed to put only casual interest in his voice. "I'm Mr. Drake," he said, "and this is Mr. Mason. Is there something in particular, Mrs. Drummond?"

"You're looking for my husband."

Drake merely raised his eyebrows.

"At the Strand Trailer Camp," she went on nervously. And *I'm* looking for him *too.* I wonder if we can't sort of pool information?"

Mason interposed suavely. "*Your* husband, and you're looking for him, Mrs. Drummond?"

"Yes," she said, her large dark eyes appraising the lawyer.

"How long since you've seen him?" Mason asked.

"Two months."

"Perhaps if you want us to *pool* information, you'd better tell us a little more about the circumstances and how you happened to know we were looking for him."

She said, "I'd been at the Silver Strand Trailer Camp earlier in the day. The man promised me that he'd let me know if my husband returned. When your detectives appeared and started asking questions, he took the license number of their car, found out it belonged to the Drake Detective Agency, and . . ." She laughed nervously and said, "And that is where I started to do a little detective work on my own. Are you looking for him for the same reason I am?"

Mason smiled gravely. "That brings up the question of why you're looking for him."

She gave an indignant toss of her head. "After all, I have nothing to conceal. We were married a little over a year ago. It didn't click. Harry is an outdoor man. He's always chasing around on the trail of some mining deal or some cattle ranch. I don't like that sort of life and . . . well, about two months ago we separated. I sued for divorce."

"Have you got it yet?"

"Not yet. We had an understanding about a property settlement. When my lawyer sent my husband the papers, he sent them back with an insulting note and said he wouldn't pay me a red cent and that if I tried to get tough about it, he'd show that I didn't have any rights whatever."

"Why?"

"I don't know."

"And you want to find out just what he means by that?" Mason asked.

"That's right. And now suppose you tell me what *you* want him for. Has he done something?"

"Is he the type that would?" Mason asked.

"He's been in trouble before."

"What sort of trouble?"

"A mining swindle."

Drake glanced inquiringly at Mason.

"Where are you located?" Mason asked Mrs. Drummond.

"I'm right here at the hotel. And don't think they're the ones who told me about Mr. Drake's being here," she added hastily. "I found that out by . . . in another way."

"You spoke of *pooling* information," Mason said suggestively.

She laughed and said, "Well, what I meant was if you find him, will you let me know? And if I find him, I could let you know. After all, he shouldn't be difficult to locate with that trailer, but I want to catch him before he can get out of the state. If I can find out where he is, I have—some papers to serve."

"You have a car?" Mason asked.

She nodded, then added, "That is one thing I salvaged out of our marriage. I made him buy me a car, and that's one of the reasons I want to see him. The car's still in his name. He agreed to let me have it as part of the property settlement, but in his letter to my lawyer he said he could even take the car away from me if I tried to make trouble. Do either of you gentlemen have any idea what he meant by that?"

Mason shook his head and so did Drake.

"Perhaps," Mason suggested, "we might work out something. You see, even if your assumption is correct that we are looking for your husband, we would be representing some client and would naturally have to discuss things with that client."

"Is it because of something he's done?" she asked apprehensively. "Is he in more trouble? Will it mean all his money will go for lawyers again, just like it did before?"

"I'm sure I couldn't tell you," Mason said.

"That means you won't. Look, I'm in Room 613. Why don't you ask your *client* to come and see me?"

"Will you be there all evening?" Drake asked.

"Well . . ." She hesitated. "I'll be in and out. I'll . . . I'll tell you what I'll do. I'll keep in touch with the hotel and if there are any messages, I'll be where I can come right back."

She flashed them a smile, moved toward the door with quick grace, then almost as an afterthought, turned and gave them her hand, glancing curiously through the open door of the adjoining room to where Della Street was seated at the telephone. Then she gave Mason another smile as the lawyer held the door open for her, and left the room, walking with quick nervous steps.

Mason closed the door, cocked a quizzical eyebrow at Paul Drake.

"The guy's wise," Drake said. "That means we haven't much time, Perry."

"You think he was watching his back trail?"

Drake nodded. "She's an alert little moll who knows her way around. This man Drummond has done something that he's trying to cover up. He left her to watch. She hypnotized the man who runs the trailer camp and then when my man showed up in an agency car . . ."

"But how about her asking questions at the cash-and-carry, Paul?"

Drake snapped his fingers. "Shucks, there's nothing to *that*. That's the way she builds up a background for herself. After all, she . . ."

The telephone interrupted. Drake picked up the receiver, said, "Drake talking . . . Okay, let's have it . . . When? . . . Where? . . . Okay, stay on the job . . . We'll be right down."

Drake hung up the receiver, said, "Well, that's it. We've got him located."

"Where?"

"Little down-at-the-heel trailer camp in a eucalyptus grove about three miles from here. Not much of a place—auto court cabins in front and trailer space in the rear. The conveniences aren't too good and it's patronized mostly by people who want to save two bits a day on the regular parking rate. The chief advantage is lots of elbow room. The grove consists of several acres and if a man wants to walk far enough to the bath and shower, he can pick his own parking place for the trailer."

"Any details?" Mason asked.

"One of my men just located it. The trailer came in yesterday night. The man who runs the place was busy selling gasoline at the time, and the driver of the car called out that he'd come back and register later. He tossed the man a silver dollar and the man told him to park any place he wanted to where he could find a plug for his electric connection."

Mason said, "Let's go. Della, you stay here and run the place. We'll telephone you in half an hour or so."

They drove down to the trailer camp in Mason's car. Drake's operative, lounging casually in the door of one of the auto cabins, gave the detective a surreptitious signal, and pointed toward the adjoining cabin.

Registering simply as "P. Drake," the detective rented the vacant cabin, then settled down with Perry Mason. A few moments later, Drake's operative came across to join them.

"Ever met Pete Brady?" Drake asked Mason.

Mason shook hands, said, "I've seen him once or twice before around your office."

"Glad to know you," Brady said to Mason, and then to Drake, "I'm not certain but what the guy who runs the place is getting suspicious. I asked too many questions."

"What's the dope?"

"The trailer's out there attached to the car. So far, I haven't had a glimpse of the man who is in it, but it's the license number of the car we want—4E4705."

"Let's take a look around," Mason said.

"You'll have to take it easy," Brady warned.

"How about the gag of buying a trailer," Drake asked. "Have you used that?"

Brady shook his head.

"We'll try that," Drake said. "You can wait here for awhile. What's the guy's name who runs the place?"

"Elmo, Sidney Elmo."

"Did he see you come over here?"

"No. I waited until he was selling gas."

"Okay. Stick around. I'll go tell the bird that we heard one of the trailers here was for sale. He won't know anything about it. That gives us an opportunity to go sauntering around looking them over."

Five minutes later when Drake returned, Mason joined him and they walked slowly out past the line of somewhat dilapidated cabins into the eucalyptus grove. The ground was still moist from the rain and the drippings of the trees.

"There's the outfit," Drake said. "What do we do? Go right up and knock and ask him if it's for sale?"

Mason said, "Let's try one of the other trailers first. We can talk loud enough so our voices will carry over here."

"Good idea," Drake said.

"Take this one," Mason said.

The two walked over to the small homemade trailer Mason had indicated. It was parked about a hundred feet from the green trailer. Electric lights showed a well-fleshed woman in her late forties cooking over the stove. On the outside, a man was taking advantage of the failing light to tinker with the bumper on the trailer. There was an Oklahoma license plate on the car.

"This the outfit that's for sale?" Mason asked.

The man looked up and a long thin mouth twisted into a smile. He said with a drawl, "I ain't saying yes, and I ain't saying no. You want to buy?"

"We're looking for a trailer that we heard was for sale here."

"What sort of a trailer?"

"We just heard it was a good one."

"That's the description of this job all right."

Drake interposed, "You're not the man who spoke to the manager of the Strand Trailer Park and said he wanted to sell, are you?"

"Nope. Fact is, I'm not particularly anxious to sell. But if you wanted to buy it, I'd be willing to listen."

"We're looking for a particular trailer that's for sale," Mason explained. "How about that green one over there? Know anything about it?"

"No. It just came in last night."

"Don't suppose you've talked with the people who own it?"

"I ain't seen 'em. They haven't been around all day."

Mason said, "That looks like it. Let's go over there, Paul."

"Take it easy," Mason said as they approached. "Ever use a house trailer, Paul?"

"No. Why?"

"The steady weight of the trailer has a tendency to wear out springs. So most trailers are equipped with an auxiliary wheel which can be screwed into position when the trailer is parked."

"There isn't any here," Drake said.

"That's just the point. Furthermore, no spout bucket has been put out under the spout. And to cap it all, the cord hasn't been connected with the electric outlet."

"What are you getting at, Perry?"

Mason knocked loudly on the trailer. When there was no response, the lawyer tentatively tried the knob.

The door swung open.

There was still enough afternoon light to show the sprawled figure lying in dark silence on the floor. The dark pool eddying out from under the body showed little jagged streaks, but its ominous significance could not possibly be misjudged . . .

Mason entered the trailer, and carefully avoiding the red pool, looked down at the body. Then he bent over, touched the high-heeled cowboy boot, moved it gently back and forth.

"Been dead for some time, Paul. *Rigor mortis* has set in."

"Come on out," Drake begged. "Let's play this one safe and notify the police."

"Just a minute," Mason said. "I . . ." He bent over, and as he did so a shaft of light struck his face.

"What's that?" Drake asked.

Mason moved slightly so that the beam of light struck his eye.

"That," he announced, "is a hole in this trailer, directly in line with the window of that Oklahoma trailer. Light from the window over where the woman is cooking comes through the hole in this trailer. The hole could have been made by a bullet."

"Okay, Perry. Let's notify the police."

Mason said, "First I want to find out a little more about that Oklahoma trailer."

"For the luvva Mike, Perry, have a heart! You're in the clear on this one—so far."

Mason, moving cautiously, left the trailer. He hesitated a moment when he stepped to the ground. Then he carefully polished the doorknob with his handkerchief.

"That's removing evidence," Drake said. "There are other prints there besides yours."

"How do you know?"

"It stands to reason."

"You can't prove it," Mason said. "The murderer probably wiped his fingerprints off the door just as I did."

Mason walked back to the trailer with the Oklahoma license. The man, still bent over the bumper at the rear of the trailer, seemed to be working aimlessly, stalling for time. The position of his head indicated an interest in what had been going on over at the other trailer.

"That the one?" he asked as Mason approached.

"I don't know. No one seems to be home."

"I ain't seen 'em leave. They couldn't go very far without their car."

"Seen any visitors over there?" Mason asked casually.

"Not today. There was a young woman called last night."

"What time?"

"I don't know. We'd gone to bed. Her headlights shone in the window and woke me up when she came. I sat up in bed and looked out the window."

"See her plain?"

"Yeah—a redhead. Checkered suit—trim-looking package."

"She go in?"

"I guess so. She switched off her lights and I went back to sleep. Woke me up again when she left. Her car backfired a couple of times."

Mason glanced at Drake. "I'd like to find these people."

"I think there's only one—a man. He drove in last night and he had quite a bit of trouble backing the trailer around. But what really woke me up was headlights shining in my window. I looked out and seen this woman."

"Remember what sort of car she was driving?"

"It was a rented car."

"How do you know?"

"From the gasoline rationing stamp on the windshield."

"Your wife didn't wake up?"

"No."

"How long have *you* been here?" Mason asked.

"What's it to you?"

"Nothing."

"I thought not," the man said, suddenly suspicious, and then after a moment added, "You're asking a lot of questions."

"Sorry," Mason said.

The man hesitated a moment, then, by way of dismissal, turned back to the bumper.

Mason glanced at Paul Drake. Silently the two walked away.

"Okay, Paul," Mason said in a low voice. "Get Della on the phone. Tell her to put operatives on every drive-yourself car agency within a radius of fifty miles and see if we can find where the woman rented the car. When we spot the place, I'll handle the rest of it."

"I don't like it," Drake said.

"I don't like it myself," Mason told him. "The young woman who called there last night was Marcia Winnett."

"And her car backfired," Drake said dryly.

Mason met his eyes. "Her car backfired, Paul. And in case it ever becomes necessary, remember that the only person who heard it said it *was* a backfire."

Drake nodded gloomily. "Not that *that* will do any good, Perry."

"It keeps us in the clear, Paul. You don't rush to the police to report that someone's car backfired."

"When you've discovered a body, you do."

"Who knows we've discovered any body?"

"I do."

Mason laughed. "Back to the hotel, Paul. We'll try and trace that car. And just to be on the safe side, we'll see where Mrs. Drummond was last night."

The last task Mason had given Paul Drake turned out to be simple. Mrs. Drummond had been trying to locate her husband in the nearby trailer camps all the evening before, and she had arranged with a police officer who was off duty to accompany her.

Locating the rented car in which the girl in the checkered suit went to the trailer camp was another matter.

Despite all Drake's efficiency, it was nearing eight o'clock when his detectives uncovered the lead Mason wanted. A man who operated a car rental agency in one of the coast cities, some twenty-five miles from Silver Strand Beach, had rented a car to a young woman who wore a checkered suit and who answered the description of Marcia Winnett.

Drake looked up from the telephone. "Want my man to try and pick up the trail from there or do you want to do it, Perry?"

Mason said, "I'll do it, Paul. And just to be on the safe side, let your man think that isn't the trail we want."

"Okay," Drake said, and then into the telephone, "Describe her, Sam. Uh huh . . . uh huh, well, that's not the one. Keep working. Cover those other agencies."

Drake hung up the phone. "Want me to come along, Perry?"

"Della and I'll handle it," Mason said. "Start calling your men in. Let them feel it turned out to be a false lead. And you'd better start checking on Mrs. Drummond, Paul. I wouldn't like to have her show up right now."

Drake nodded, said solicitously, "Watch your step, Perry."

"I'm watching it. Come on, Della."

The man who operated the car rental agency which had furnished a car to Marcia Winnett was not particularly communicative. It took diplomacy to get him in the mood to talk. Even then he confined his information to bare essentials.

He had never seen his customer before. She gave her name as Edith Bascom. She said her mother had died and it was necessary for her to use a car in connection with handling the estate. She was registered at the local hotel.

"Do you check on these stories?" Mason asked. "Or do you just rent cars?"

"Sometimes we just rent cars. Sometimes we check."

"What did you do in this case?"

"Cars are scarce now," the man said. "We checked."

"How?"

The man picked up a daily paper dated the day before and indicated the obituary column. Mason followed the man's finger to the stereotyped announcement of the death of Mrs. Shirley Bascom and the statement that funeral arrangements would be private.

Mason said, "I guess that covers it all right."

"What's your interest in it?"

"I'm a lawyer."

"I see. Well, she's okay. Rather upset on account of her mother's death, but a nice girl. You'll find her in the Palace Hotel, two blocks down the street."

It was but a matter of routine for Mason and his secretary to get the number of the room assigned to Edith Bascom. Two minutes later Mason was knocking on the door.

There was no answer. Mason tried the knob. The door was locked.

Mason made a swift survey of the hall, stooped, and held out his hands. "Step on my hands, Della. Take a quick look through the transom."

She braced herself with a hand on his shoulder, caught the lower ledge of the transom, and peered through.

Mason, steadying her, felt her body stiffen. Then she was scrambling to get down.

"Chief," she said in an ominous whisper, "she's stretched out on the bed. She's . . . terribly still."

"Lights on?"

"No, but the shade is up and there's enough light coming in from the electric sign in front to make out the form on the bed."

Mason said, "There's a spring lock on the door . . . Better take another look, Della. See if she's breathing . . . hold it. Here comes a chambermaid."

The chambermaid who wearily approached was aroused only momentarily from the lethargy of overwork by the bill Mason pushed into her palm.

"My wife and I seem to have left our key downstairs. If you could let us in, it would save us a trip down . . ."

"It's against the rules," she said, then added tonelessly, "but I guess it's okay." She produced her passkey and clicked back the latch on the door.

Mason boldly pushed open the door, stood aside for Della to enter, then followed her into the dimly lighted room, and closed the door behind him.

Della Street crossed over to the woman lying on the bed and groped for her pulse.

"She's alive!" Della Street said.

"The lights," Mason said crisply. "Pull the shades first."

Della Street jerked down the shades, ran over and switched on the light.

Mason glanced at the bottle of sleeping tablets by the side of the bed, picked up the newspaper on the floor, glanced at it.

"She must have taken them yesterday," Della said.

"This afternoon," Mason interrupted curtly. "This is a late edition of the afternoon paper."

He dropped the paper, shook the sleeper, said, "Towels, Della. Cold water. Fast."

Della Street grabbed towels, turned on the cold water in the bathroom. Mason slapped Marcia Winnett with cold towels until the eyelids flickered open.

"What is it?" she asked thickly. Mason said to Della Street, "Run

125

down to the drug store, Della. Get an emetic. Have room service send up some black coffee."

"How about a doctor?"

"Not if we can avoid it. Let's hope she hasn't had the tablets down long enough to get the full effects."

Marcia Winnett tried to say something but the words were unintelligible. She dropped back against Mason's shoulder.

Thirty minutes later Mason and Della Street assisted Marcia Winnett from the bathroom. There was a dead, lackluster look about her eyes but she could talk now, and the coffee was beginning to take effect.

Mason said, "Concentrate on what I'm telling you. I'm a lawyer. I'm retained to represent you."

"By whom?"

"Your husband."

"No, no, he mustn't . . . he can't . . ."

Mason said, "I'm *your* lawyer. Your husband retained me to help you. I don't have to tell him anything."

She sighed wearily, said, "Let me go. It's better this way."

Mason shook her once more into wakefulness. "You went riding Monday morning. You talked with a man in a trailer. He made demands on you. You had to have money and have it at once. You didn't dare to ask your husband for it."

Mason waited for an answer. She made none. Her eyelids drooped and raised as if by a conscious effort.

Mason said, "You went back to the house. You canceled the insurance on your jewelry because you were too conscientious to stick the insurance company. You arranged to have some repairs made to a window on the side of your bedroom so that a ladder would be handy. You got up in the night, went out to the balcony, and dumped your jewelry into the swallow's nest. Then you started screaming."

Her face might have been a mask.

Mason went on, "You had waited until Tuesday to stage the burglary. You knew that it would be too obvious if it happened Monday night, the day you had canceled the insurance. Wednesday morning you found an opportunity to get most of the jewelry out of the swallow's nest. There was one piece you overlooked. Now then, suppose you tell me what happened after that."

She said, with the drowsy calm of one who discusses a distant event, "I wanted to kill him. I can't remember whether I did or not."

"Did you shoot him?"

"I can't remember a thing that happened after I left the house."

Mason glanced at Della Street, said, "If I'm going to help you, I have to know what hold that man had on you."

"His name is Harry Drummond. He was my first husband."

"You were divorced?"

"I *thought* I was divorced. There were reasons why *I* couldn't go to Nevada. From time to time he sent me reports of how things were coming. Twice he asked for more money. Then he wrote me the divorce had been granted. He was lying. He'd gambled the money away. There never had been a divorce."

"When did you find this out?"

"Monday morning," she said. "He was clever. He'd kept in touch with me. He knew I rode down along that bridle path. He parked his trailer there. Mrs. Victoria Winnett doesn't like to have people camp there, so I rode down to ask whoever was in the trailer to please move on to the public camp grounds."

"You had no idea who was in the trailer?"

"Not until Harry opened the door and said, 'Hello, Marcia. I thought it was about time you were showing up.'"

"What did he want?"

"Money."

"And he threatened you with—what?"

"The one weapon Claude couldn't stand—notoriety."

"So you promised to get him money?"

"I promised to get him my jewelry. He had to have money at once. He said someone was putting screws on him for cash."

"You were to meet him there when?"

"Wednesday morning."

"So you manipulated this fake burglary on Tuesday night after canceling your insurance on Monday. Then you took him the jewelry. Did he ask you how you had managed to get your hands on the jewelry?"

"Yes. I told him the whole story. I told him it was all right to pawn it because the Winnetts wouldn't report the burglary to the police."

"And then what happened?"

"I can't remember."

"What can't you remember?"

"I can't remember a thing from the time . . . from the time Harry took the jewelry. He made some sneering remark, and I remember becoming very angry and then . . . then my mind went entirely blank."

"Did you have a revolver with you when you went down to the trailer Wednesday morning?" Mason asked.

"Yes."

"Where did you get it?"

"From a bureau drawer."

"Whose gun was it?"

127

"I don't know. I think it was . . . Mrs. Winnett's gun—pearl-handled. I thought I might need some protection. It was a crazy idea, but I took it along."

"Where is that gun now?"

"I don't know. I tell you I can't remember a thing that happened after I gave him the jewelry and he made that sneering remark."

"Did he make some further demands on you? Did he tell you to meet him at an isolated trailer park last night?"

"I don't know. I can't remember."

"*Did* you meet him there?"

"I can't remember."

"Did you," Mason asked, "rent an automobile from a drive-yourself agency about two blocks down the street?"

Her forehead puckered into a frown. "I seem to have a faint recollection of doing something like that, but I . . . " She shook her head. "No, I can't remember."

Mason said impatiently, "Why don't you come clean? You were clever enough to read the obituary notices and pretend to be the daughter of a woman who had just died. I'm trying to help you. At least tell me what I'm up against."

"I don't know. I can't remember."

Mason motioned toward the bottle of sleeping tablets. "And you thought you could take this way out and it would help?"

"I don't know. I guess I must have been . . . Perhaps I hadn't been sleeping at all and I just took too large a dose. I can't remember."

Mason turned to Della Street. "Willing to take a chance, Della?"

She nodded. "Anything you say, chief."

Mason said, "Put her in a car. Take her into Los Angeles. See that there's plenty of money in her purse. Take her to a *private* hospital. Under no circumstances give *your* name or address. Put on the rush act. Tell the first nurse you meet that this woman accosted you on the street and asked you to help her find out who she was. That you think it's a racket of some sort, but that she seems to have money and if she needs any assistance, the hospital is the place where she should get it. Then get out of there fast."

Della nodded.

Mason turned to Marcia Winnett. "You heard what I said?"

"Yes . . . I . . . you mustn't take chances for me. I know that I must have killed him. I *think* it was in self-defense. I can't remember."

"I know," Mason said gently. "Don't worry about it. Remember you're a widow now. Don't get your memory back, and the next time you see me remember I'm a stranger. I'm going to try to help you. Get started, Della. Drive with the window open. Let her get lots of cold air. Get her to a hospital."

"How'll *you* get back?" Della asked.

"I'll have one of Drake's men pick me up."

The gravel on the driveway caused the wheels to slide as Mason slammed on the brakes. The car skidded at a sharp angle and Mason didn't even bother to straighten it out. He snapped off the lights and the ignition, leaped out and headed up the steps of the Winnett mansion, pushed open the door, and strode into the drawing room unannounced.

Mrs. Victoria Winnett and Daphne Rexford were lingering over liqueurs, talking in low voices.

Mrs. Winnett's smile was distantly friendly. *"Really,* Mr. Mason," she said, "you're rather late—for dinner."

The lawyer merely nodded, glanced at Daphne Rexford.

Mrs. Winnett reached for the bell. "I presume I can get you something," she said. "But after this, if you don't mind . . ."

"Let the food go," Mason said. "I want to talk with you."

The finger which had been touching the bell remained motionless. She said, *"Really,* Mr. Mason," in a voice that indicated a polite rebuke.

Daphne Rexford hurriedly arose. "If you'll excuse me, I have a telephone call to make."

"Sit down, my dear. After all, I can't permit this human tornado to come bursting in on our tête-à-tête with . . ."

Mason caught Daphne Rexford's eye, jerked his head.

She made a feeble attempt at a smile and left the room.

"Really, Mr. Mason," Mrs. Winnett said, her voice now quite cold. "My attachment to my son is such that I am willing to make all allowances for his friends. Even so . . ."

She let her unfinished sentence carry its own meaning.

Mason drew up a chair and sat down. "Where's the Major?"

"He was called out about twenty minutes ago."

"You're fond of Daphne Rexford, aren't you?"

"Of course."

"Was she in the observation tower Monday?"

"Really, Mr. Mason, I'm not on the witness stand."

"You're going to be," Mason said.

"I'm afraid you've been drinking."

"If you think this is a joke," Mason said, "just keep on stalling. Time is precious. The officers may be out here any minute."

"Officers?"

"Officers. Cops. Detectives. Plainclothes men. Newspaper photographers. Walking around here with their hats on, throwing cigarettes on the rugs, taking flashlight pictures with captions like *Society Leader Insists on Innocence*."

That last did it. Mason saw her wince.

"You're a good poker player, but you can't bluff now. This is a showdown, Mrs. Winnett."

"Just what do you want?"

"To know all that you know."

She took a quick breath. "I know some trouble has developed between Marcia and Claude. I think that Marcia has left him. I hope she has."

"Why?"

"Because I don't feel that they are destined to be happy together."

"No, I mean why has she left him?"

"I don't know."

"Make a guess."

"I can't."

"You know something about what happened on Monday?"

"On *Monday*? No."

"Was Daphne in the cupola on Monday?"

"I think she was."

"Did she come to you and tell you anything about what she saw either Monday or Wednesday?"

"Mr. Mason, you're being impertinent!"

Mason said, "You found out something about Marcia. You thought she had involved the family's good name, and took it on yourself to try and avoid notoriety. Your attempt backfired. I'm trying to find out just how badly it backfired."

"You can't prove any of these things you're saying, Mr. Mason."

"That," Mason said, "is only because I haven't the facilities at my command that the police have. The police may prove it."

"They won't," she said coldly. "I have told you absolutely everything I know."

Mason pushed back his chair, started for the door which led to the patio, then abruptly whirled, tiptoed swiftly back to the drawing room door, and jerked it open.

Daphne Rexford, plainly embarrassed, tried to pretend she had just been approaching the door. "Heavens," she said laughing, "I thought we were going to have a collision, Mr. Mason. You seem in a hurry." She tried to push easily on past him.

Mason barred her way. "You were listening."

"Mr. Mason, how *dare* you say anything like that?"

"Come in," Mason said. "Let's have it out. Let's . . . no, on second thought, I think I'll talk with you alone. Come on."

Mason took her arm. She drew back.

Mrs. Winnett said, "Mr. Mason is completely overstepping the prerogatives of a guest. I dislike to ask him to leave in my son's absence, but . . ."

Mason said to Daphne Rexford, "Police are going to be swarming over the place before midnight. Do you want to talk to me or do you want to talk to them?"

Daphne Rexford said over her shoulder to Mrs. Winnett, "Good heavens, Victoria, let's humor the man! I'll be back in a few minutes."

Without waiting for an answer from Victoria Winnett, she smiled disarmingly at Mason and moved away from the drawing room. "Come on, where do you want to talk?"

"Over here's good enough," Mason said, stopping in a corner of the library.

Daphne Rexford stood facing him. "What," she asked in a low voice, "are the police going to be investigating?"

Mason met her eyes. "Murder."

"Who . . . who was killed?"

"Let's talk first about what *you* know," Mason said. "You're the one who has the trick right eye. Mrs. Winnett has been covering up for you."

"I'm afraid I don't know what you mean."

"Whenever you look through the binoculars," Mason explained, "you have to move the right eyepiece in order to see clearly, don't you?"

"What if I do?"

Mason said, "*You* were the one who was watching Marcia on Monday. What did you see?"

"Nothing. I . . ."

"Were you here Monday? Were you in the observation cupola?"

"I believe I was."

"You're over here quite a bit?"

"Yes. Victoria and I are very good friends. She's an older woman, of course, but I like her. I like what she stands for and . . ."

"And like to be near Major Winnett and see as much of him as you can?"

"Certainly not," she said indignantly.

"We'll let it go at that for the time being," Mason said. "Now, about Monday, what did you see?"

"Nothing. I . . ."

"You were up in the tower?"

"Yes. I go there quite frequently. I study birds, and I write poetry. I can get inspiration up there . . ."

"And keep an eye on Major Winnett's wife when she's around the grounds, I suppose?"

"Mr. Mason, that's unfair."

"All right. You saw her Monday. *What* did you see?"

"I . . . nothing."

Mason said, "You saw her go into that orange trailer that was parked down in the trees . . ."

"It wasn't orange. It was green."

Mason grinned at her.

"All right," she said. "Don't think you're trapping me. I just happened to notice Marcia riding, and then I saw a house trailer parked in the trees."

"Did you see her go in?"

"I saw her tie up her horse and walk over toward the trailer. I wasn't interested. I returned to the poetry I was writing."

"How long was she in there?"

"I don't know."

"Why did you watch her?"

"I didn't watch her. I was looking at birds."

"You had a pencil and a pad of paper up there with you?"

"Yes, of course. I told you I write poetry. One doesn't write on the walls, Mr. Mason. I keep pencil and paper in the drawer of the table up there."

"You used the binoculars to get the license number of the automobile. You marked it down?"

"No."

"When were you up there last?"

"Why . . . why, today."

"Do you go up there every day?"

"Not every day, but quite frequently."

"Have you been up every day this week?"

"I . . . I guess I have. Yes."

The telephone rang a sharp, strident summons.

Mason waited, listening, heard the butler answer it. Then the butler walked with unhurried dignity across the library to the drawing room, said something to Mrs. Winnett. She went to the telephone.

Mason heard her say, "Hello, Claude darling . . . Yes, dear . . . he's here; I'm afraid, Claude, that there has been some misunderstanding. Mr. Mason's activities are hardly such as one would connect with a mining matter. He has shown quite an interest in what Marcia . . ."

Mason walked over, gently pushed her aside, took the receiver from her hand, and said into the telephone, "Okay, Major, I've got it now. Get out here at once."

Major Winnett's voice was harsh with anger. "Just what do you mean, Mr. Mason?"

Mason said, "Your mother is trying to protect somebody. Daphne Rexford is trying to protect somebody. There's only one person I can think of whom they'd both go to such lengths to protect. That's you. If you get out here fast, we *may* be able to beat the police to it."

"What do you mean?"

"You know damn well what I mean," Mason said and hung up.

Major Winnett's limp was more noticeable as he moved across the drawing room to confront Perry Mason. "I don't know exactly what's been going on here," he said angrily, "but as far as I'm concerned, our relationship is ended."

Mason said, "Sit down."

"I'm waiting to drive you to town, Mason, in case you don't have a car. If you do, I'll go with you to your room and you can pack up."

Mason said, "As nearly as I can put things together, you had previously discovered the trailer parked down in the trees. You were suspicious. You went up to the observation tower and saw Marcia go to the trailer and then later on saw the car and trailer go away. You took down the license number of the car. You looked up the man who owned that car. After that you kept a pretty close watch on what was going on.

"You didn't say anything when Marcia canceled the insurance on her jewelry and then had such an opportune burglary. You were very careful not to call the police because you knew the police would tab it as an inside job. You let your wife think it was because your mother didn't want any notoriety but you got the jewelry and hid it in that twelve-gauge shotgun. After that you kept a pretty good watch on your wife. Where did you get the jewelry?"

"Mason," Winnett said coldly. "If you don't leave this house at once, I'm going to call the servants and have you put out."

Mason brushed aside Major Winnett's angry statement with a gesture. "You'll have to hire more servants, then," he said, and then went on. "When the trailer came back on Wednesday and Marcia went down there the second time, you decided to investigate. When you got down there, you found you had a fight on your hands. You killed Harry Drummond. Then you locked up the trailer, came back to the house and waited until dark. Then you took the trailer with its evidence of murder, drove to a camp . . ."

"Mason, watch what you're saying. By heaven, I'll throw you out myself!"

"Parked the trailer," Mason went on smoothly, "got out, and went home. Then you felt it would add an artistic touch to have two shots fired so the *time* of the killing could be definitely fixed. You went back, sneaked into the trailer park, stood in the dark *outside* the trailer, and fired two shots in the air.

"You didn't realize that Marcia had been following you, and when she heard those shots she naturally thought you had killed Drummond out of jealousy, decided that she loved you too much to let you take the rap, and skipped out. That's the reason you didn't go to a detective agency to get someone to try to find your wife. You wanted a lawyer who specialized in murder cases—*because you knew there was going to be a murder case.*"

Major Winnett snapped his fingers. "A lot of half-baked theories!"

"You see," Mason continued, "you made a couple of fatal mistakes. One of them was that the first shot you fired missed Drummond and went clean through the trailer, leaving a hole in the double walls that clearly shows the direction taken by the bullet. When you parked that trailer in the automobile camp under the eucalyptus trees, it was dark and you didn't take the precaution of noticing where a bullet fired under such circumstances would have hit. That was a mistake, Major. As it happened, the hole in the trailer was lined up absolutely with the window of an adjoining trailer.

"At first the police will think the shot *might* have been fired from the other trailer. Then they'll make a more careful investigation and find that the direction of the bullet was the other way. Then they'll *know* that the murder wasn't committed at the trailer park. There's another little thing you hadn't thought of. At the time you moved the trailer, the body had been dead for some time but the pool of blood hadn't entirely coagulated. Near the center of the pool there was blood that was still liquid. It spread around when the trailer swayed from side to side in going over irregularities in the road. That is what gives the pool of clotted blood the peculiar appearance of having little jagged streamers flowing from it."

Major Winnett was silent and motionless. His eyes were fixed on Mason with cold concentration.

"So," Mason went on, "you knew that when police started to investigate, they would find the dead man had been Marcia's first husband. You knew they would then start looking for her. When they found that she had skipped out, you knew what would happen. And so you came to me."

Major Winnett cleared his throat. "You made a statement that Marcia had followed me. Do you have any evidence to back that up?"

Mason said, "It's a logical deduction from . . ."

"That's where you're wrong. Come to my room, I want to talk with you."

Mason said, "You haven't much time. The police have found the body. They're going to be out here looking for Marcia as soon as they have completed an identification and checked up on the man's history."

"All right," Winnett said, "come with me. Mother, you and Daphne pretend you haven't heard any of this. I'll talk with you later."

Major Winnett led the way to his room, opened a portable bar, took out a bottle of whiskey.

Mason refused with a gesture, then when Winnett had poured out a drink, the lawyer reached over and poured half of that drink back into the bottle. "Just enough to give yourself a bracer," he warned, "not enough to give you a letdown afterwards. You're going to be talking with the police pretty soon. Start talking with me now."

Winnett said, "I didn't know Marcia went to visit the man in the trailer on Monday. I did know that Marcia went to the trailer on Wednesday."

"*How* did you know?"

"I was watching her."

"Why were you watching her?"

"Someone told me she had been to the trailer on Monday."

"Who?"

"My mother."

"What did you do?"

"After she left the trailer on Wednesday, I went down there to see who was in the trailer and find out why my wife was having a rendezvous."

"What did you find?"

"I found the man dead. I found Marcia's jewelry spread out on a table in front of him. I realized what must have happened. I saw that one shot had gone into the man's heart. One had apparently gone past his head and into the wall of the trailer."

"All right," Mason said, "it's your story. What did you do then?"

"I took Marcia's jewelry and locked up the trailer. I came home. I waited until after dark, then moved the trailer to a trailer camp I knew of, where I parked it. I got out and left the trailer and walked to where I had parked my own car earlier in the day. I had driven home before I realized that I could completely throw the police off the scent by making it appear as if the murder had been committed late that night in the trailer camp. So I returned, stood near the trailer, fired two shots into the air, then ran to my car and came back home. I thought Marcia was in bed. But when, after a couple of hours, I went up, I found she wasn't there, that she had left that note. That's why I came to you. I needed your help. That's the truth, so help me."

Mason said, "You wrote down the license number of that automobile. Later on you tried to cover it up by adding some words and some figures. . . ."

"Mr. Mason, I swear I did not."

"Who did then?"

"I don't know."

"Someone wrote down the license number of the car," Mason said, "4E4705, then tried to camouflage it by working in a number of other figures and writing at the top *These numbers called*—but a mistake was made in the addition. I . . . wait a minute . . ."

Mason stood motionless, his eyes lidded with concentration.

"Perhaps," Major Winnett suggested, "it was . . ."

Mason motioned him to silence, then after a moment he picked up the telephone, dialed the hotel where Drake had established an office, and when he had Drake on the line, said, "Hello, Paul, Perry talking. I think I've got it. There was no mistake in addition."

"I don't get it," Drake said, "the total should be 49″37818. Actually it's 49″37817."

"And that figure is right," Mason said. "The number we want is 4E4704."

"But the license number was 4E4705."

Mason said, "What happens when you have two cars? You are given license numbers in numerical order. Look up license number 4E4704. You can start your search in Room 613 there at the hotel."

Mason slammed the telephone receiver and nodded to Major Winnett. "We've got one more chance. It's slim. The next time you go to a lawyer, don't be so smart. Tell him the truth. Where's your mother's room?"

"In the other wing at the far end of the corridor."

"And the nurse's room?" Mason asked. "That must be a communicating room?"

"It is."

Mason said, "Let's go."

Helen Custer, answering their knock, seemed somewhat flustered. "Why, good evening, I, ah . . ."

Mason pushed his way into the room. Major Winnett hesitated a moment, then followed. Mason kicked the door shut.

"Police are on their way out here," Mason said to the nurse.

"The police? What for?"

"To arrest you."

"For what?"

Mason said, "That's up to you."

"What do you mean?"

Mason said, "Playing it one way, it's blackmail. Playing it the other way, it's being an accessory after the fact on a murder charge. You'd better take the rap for blackmail."

"I . . . I . . . why, *what* are you talking about?"

Mason said, "I've practiced law long enough to know that a man should never torture clues to make them point in the direction he thinks they should go. When that column of figures added up to 49E37817 and I thought it should have been 49E37818, I assumed a mistake had been made in the addition. It wasn't a mistake. You marked down the number *Cal* 4E4704. You wanted to preserve that number but you didn't want anyone to think that it had any significance, so you added the words at the top. *These numbers* and then inserted *led* after the *Cal*, so that made it read, *These numbers called.* Then you added other numbers and then you totaled the sum. Now, you probably have less than five minutes to tell us why you wrote down 4E4704."

She glanced from Mason to Major Winnett. There was dismay in her eyes. "What makes you—"

Mason took out his watch, said, "If the police get here first, you'll be an accessory after the fact. If you use your head, you *may* be able to get by with a rap for attempted blackmail."

"I . . . I . . . oh, Mr. Mason. I can't . . ."

Mason watched the hands ticking off the seconds.

"All right," she blurted. "It was yesterday morning. I was looking for Mrs. Victoria Winnett. I thought she was up in the observation tower. I went up there. She wasn't there. The binoculars were adjusted so that they pointed down to that grove of trees. I just happened to look through them and saw the trailer. A light coupé was parked beside the big Buick that was attached to the trailer. A man and a woman were having a struggle of some sort. The man tried to strike her and the woman reached into her blouse. I saw the flash of a gun, then another flash. The man staggered back and the woman calmly closed the door of the trailer, got in her car, and drove away.

"Through the binoculars I got a look at the number of her automobile. It was Cal 4E4704. I wrote it down on a piece of paper, intending to tell the police. Then . . . well, then I . . . thought . . ."

"What did you do with the piece of paper?" Mason asked.

"I didn't want that number to seem too conspicuous, so I wrote down other things, just as you said."

"The first number you wrote on a single sheet of paper that was on the table and not on the pad. When you wrote the rest of it, you had placed the paper on the pad."

"I . . . I guess I did."

Mason pointed to the telephone. "Ring up police headquarters," he said, "tell them what you saw. Tell them that it has been bothering you, that you thought you should have reported it to the police but Mrs. Winnett is so opposed to any form of publicity that you didn't know just what to do; that tonight you asked Mrs. Winnett about it and she told you to telephone the police at once; that the reason you didn't do so before was because the trailer was gone when you looked again and you supposed that the man hadn't been hurt and had driven the trailer away."

"If I do that," she said, "then I . . ."

"Then you stand about one chance in ten of beating the rap all around," Mason said grimly. "Don't do it, and you're stuck. What did you do—actually?"

"I looked up the license number. I found that the car was registered in the name of a Mrs. Harry Drummond. I located her and while I wasn't crude or anything . . . I wanted to open a beauty shop . . . well, she agreed to finance me."

Once more Mason pointed to the telephone. "Get police headquarters. Come on, Major. Let's go."

Out in the corridor Major Winnett said, "But how about my wife, Mason? How about my wife? That's the thing that bothers me—"

"And it damned well should bother you," Mason said. "She must have seen you driving the trailer Wednesday night and followed you to the place where you parked it. She went in, found Drummond dead, and thought you had been trying to avenge the family's good name. You can see now what happened. She gave Drummond money to get a divorce. He told her he'd secured one. She married again. Drummond made the mistake of also marrying again. When the blowoff came, his second wife threatened to prosecute him for bigamy unless he gave her money. The only way he had to get money was to put the pressure on Marcia. She was too conscientious to ask you for money or to try and stick the insurance company for money, so she staged a fake burglary, cached her jewelry in the swallow's nest, then turned over the jewelry to him. When the second Mrs. Drummond came for her money, all her husband had to offer her was jewelry. She thought it was hot. That started a fight and she shot him."

"But how am I going to explain—about moving the body?" Major Winnett asked.

"You're not going to explain one damn thing," Mason said. "What do you think you have a lawyer for? Get in my car. Let the nurse put the police on a hot trail."

It was nearing midnight when Perry Mason and Paul Drake walked into metropolitan police headquarters with a description of Marcia Winnett and a series of photographs.

Of course," Mason explained to Sergeant Dorset, "the Major doesn't want any publicity. She had a spell of amnesia several years ago. He's afraid it *may* have returned."

Sergeant Dorset frowned at a memo on his desk. "We've picked up a woman who answers that description—amnesia—a hospital telephoned in the report. How does it happen *you're* mixed up in the case, Mason?"

"I handle the Winnetts' business."

"The county teletype says a man named Drummond was murdered. Mrs. Winnett's nurse saw it all, phoned in a report. She had the license number of the murder car, Drummond's wife."

"Indeed," Mason said, his voice showing courteous interest, but nothing else. "May we take a look at this amnesia case now? The Major is very anxious."

"And," Dorset went on, "when the county officers picked up Drummond's wife, she swore that not only was the killing in self-defense, but that the nurse had been blackmailing her. The nurse called her a liar. Mrs. Drummond's confession puts her in a poor position to claim blackmail. I understand the county is so pleased with having cracked the murder case they're washing their hands of all the rest of it."

Mason glared at Sergeant Dorset. "Will you kindly tell me what all this has to do with Major Winnett's wife?"

Dorset sighed. "I wish to hell I knew," he said, and then added significantly, "but I'll bet a hundred to one we never find out."

Mason said, "Come down to earth. That murder case is county. The sheriff's office wouldn't like a city detective sticking his nose in."

Dorset nodded. "And by the way you've arranged it, the amnesia case is city and the county men won't mess around with *that*."

He regarded the lawyer with a scowling respect.

Mason said very positively, "I don't see what the murder has to do with all this if the sheriff's office has a solution and a confession. But one thing I do know is that if you have Major Winnett's wife here, she's suffering from a nervous ailment and if you make it worse with a lot of fool notions, you'll wish you hadn't. Do I get her now, or do I get a *habeas corpus?*"

"Hell, you get her now," Dorset said disgustedly. "I can't help feeling that if I knew everything you'd been doing in the last twelve hours I'd get a promotion and if I try to find out, I'll be back pounding pavements. Damn it!"

He picked up the telephone, said into the transmitter, "Send that amnesia case number eighty-four on the night bulletin up to my office."

THE HOUSE IN GOBLIN WOOD

BY CARTER DICKSON

John Dickson Carr (b. November 30, 1906), who also writes as Carter Dickson and Carr Dickson, is master of the locked-room mystery. He was influenced by Poe and Chesterton and his Dr. Gideon Fell is a very Chestertonian figure. Carr himself is often mistaken as British, but though he lived for some years in England he was born in Pennsylvania and now resides in South Carolina. Among his best-received books are *The Crooked Hinge*, *The Judas Window* and *The Hollow Man*. Since 1969 he has written the monthly book-review column for *Ellery Queen's Mystery Magazine*.

In Pall Mall, that hot July afternoon three years before the war, an open saloon car was drawn up to the curb just opposite the Senior Conservatives' Club.

And in the car sat two conspirators.

It was the drowsy post-lunch hour among the clubs, where only the sun remained brilliant. The Rag lay somnolent; the Atheneum slept outright. But these two conspirators, a dark-haired young man in his early thirties and a fair-haired girl perhaps half a dozen years younger, never moved. They stared intently at the Gothic-like front of the Senior Conservatives'.

"Look here, Eve," muttered the young man, and punched at the steering wheel. "Do you think this is going to work?"

"I don't know," the fair-haired girl confessed. "He absolutely *loathes* picnics."

"Anyway, we've probably missed him."

"Why so?"

"He can't have taken as long over lunch as that!" her companion protested, looking at a wrist-watch. The young man was rather shocked. "It's a quarter to four! Even if . . ."

"Bill! There! Look there!"

Their patience was rewarded by an inspiring sight.

Out of the portals of the Senior Conservatives' Club, in awful majesty, marched a large, stout, barrel-shaped gentleman in a white linen suit.

His corporation preceded him like the figurehead of a man-of-war. His shell-rimmed spectacles were pulled down on a broad nose, all being shaded by a Panama hat. At the top of the stone steps he surveyed the street with a lordly sneer.

"Sir Henry!" called the girl.

"Hey?" said Sir Henry Merrivale.

"I'm Eve Drayton. Don't you remember me? You knew my father!"

"Oh, ah," said the great man.

"We've been waiting here a terribly long time," Eve pleaded. "Couldn't you see us for just five minutes?—The thing to do," she whispered to her companion, "is to keep him in a good humor. Just keep him in a good humor!"

As a matter of fact, H.M. was in a good humor, having just triumphed over the Home Secretary in an argument. But not even his own mother could have guessed it. Majestically, with the same lordly sneer, he began in grandeur to descend the steps of the Senior Conservatives'. He did this, in fact, until his foot encountered an unnoticed object lying some three feet from the bottom.

It was a banana skin.

"Oh, dear!" said the girl.

Now it must be stated with regret that in the old days certain urchins, of what were then called the "lower orders," had a habit of placing such objects on the steps in the hope that some eminent statesman would take a toss on his way to Whitehall. This was a venial but deplorable practice, probably accounting for what Mr. Gladstone said in 1882.

In any case, it accounted for what Sir Henry Merrivale said now.

From the pavement, where H.M. landed in a seated position, arose in H.M.'s bellowing voice such a torrent of profanity, such a flood of invective and vile obscenities, as has seldom before blasted the holy calm of Pall Mall. It brought the hall-porter hurrying down the steps, and Eve Drayton flying out of the car.

Heads were now appearing at the windows of the Atheneum across the street.

"Is it all right?" cried the girl, with concern in her blue eyes. "Are you hurt?"

H.M. merely looked at her. His hat had fallen off, disclosing a large bald head; and he merely sat on the pavement and looked at her.

"Anyway, H.M., get up! Please get up!"

"Yes, sir," begged the hall-porter, "for heaven's sake get up!"

"Get up?" bellowed H.M., in a voice audible as far as St. James' Street. "Burn it all, how *can* I get up?"

"But why not?"

"My behind's out of joint," said H.M. simply. "I'm hurt awful bad. I'm probably goin' to have spinal dislocation for the rest of my life."

"But, sir, people are looking!"

H.M. explained what these people could do. He eyed Eve Drayton with a glare of indescribable malignancy over his spectacles.

"I suppose, my wench, *you're* responsible for this?"

Eve regarded him in consternation.

"You don't mean the banana skin?" she cried.

"Oh, yes, I do," said H.M., folding his arms like a prosecuting counsel.

"But we—we only wanted to invite you to a picnic!"

H.M. closed his eyes.

"That's fine," he said in a hollow voice. "All the same, don't you think it'd have been a subtler kind of hint just to pour mayonnaise over my head or shove ants down the back of my neck? Oh, lord love a duck!"

"I didn't mean that! I meant . . ."

"Let me help you up, sir," interposed the calm, reassuring voice of the dark-haired and blue-chinned young man who had been with Eve in the car.

"So you want to help too, hey? And who are *you?*"

"I'm awfully sorry!" said Eve. "I should have introduced you! This is my *fiancé*. Dr. William Sage."

H.M.'s face turned purple.

"I'm glad to see," he observed, "you had the uncommon decency to bring along a doctor. I appreciate that, I do. And the car's there, I suppose, to assist with the examination when I take off my pants?"

The hall-porter uttered a cry of horror.

Bill Sage, either from jumpiness and nerves or from sheer inability to keep a straight face, laughed loudly.

"I keep telling Eve a dozen times a day," he said, "that I'm not to be called 'doctor.' I happen to be a surgeon—"

(Here H.M. really did look alarmed.)

"—but I don't think we need operate. Nor, in my opinion," Bill gravely addressed the hall-porter, "will it be necessary to remove Sir Henry's trousers in front of the Senior Conservatives' Club."

"Thank you very much, sir."

"We had an infernal nerve to come here," the young man confessed to H.M. "But I honestly think, Sir Henry, you'd be more comfortable in the car. What about it? Let me give you a hand up?"

Yet even ten minutes later, when H.M. sat glowering in the back of the car and two heads were craned round towards him, peace was not restored.

"All right!" said Eve. Her pretty, rather stolid face was flushed; her mouth looked miserable. "If you won't come to the picnic, you won't. But I did believe you might do it to oblige me."

"Well . . . now!" muttered the great man uncomfortably.

"And I did think, too, you'd be interested in the other person who was coming with us. But Vicky's—difficult. She won't come either, if you don't."

"Oh? And who's this other guest?"

"Vicky Adams."

H.M.'s hand, which had been lifted for an oratorical gesture, dropped to his side.

"Vicky Adams? That's not the gal who . . .?"

"Yes!" Eve nodded. "They say it was one of the great mysteries, twenty years ago, that the police failed to solve."

"It was, my wench," H.M. agreed somberly. "It was."

"And now Vicky's grown up. And we thought if you of all people

143

went along, and spoke to her nicely, she'd tell us what really happened on that night."

H.M.'s small, sharp eyes fixed disconcertingly on Eve.

"I say, my wench. What's your interest in all this?"

"Oh, reasons." Eve glanced quickly at Bill Sage, who was again punching moodily at the steering wheel, and checked herself. "Anyway, what difference does it make now? If you won't go with us . . ."

H.M. assumed a martyred air.

"I never said I *wasn't* goin' with you, did I?" he demanded. (This was inaccurate, but no matter.) "Even after you practically made a cripple of me, I never said I *wasn't* goin'?" His manner grew flurried and hasty. "But I got to leave now," he added apologetically. "I got to get back to my office."

"We'll drive you there, H.M."

"No, no, no," said the practical cripple, getting out of the car with surprising celerity. "Walkin' is good for my stomach if it's not so good for my behind. I'm a forgivin' man. You pick me up at my house tomorrow morning. G'bye."

And he lumbered off in the direction of the Haymarket.

It needed no close observer to see that H.M. was deeply abstracted. He remained so abstracted, indeed, as to be nearly murdered by a taxi at the Admiralty Arch; and he was halfway down Whitehall before a familiar voice stopped him.

"Afternoon, Sir Henry!"

Burly, urbane, buttoned up in blue serge, with his bowler hat and his boiled blue eye, stood Chief Inspector Masters.

"Bit odd," the Chief Inspector remarked affably, "to see you taking a constitutional on a day like this. And how are you, sir?"

"Awful," said H.M. instantly. "But that's not the point. Masters, you crawlin' snake! You're the very man I wanted to see."

Few things startled the Chief Inspector. This one did.

"You," he repeated, "wanted to see *me?*"

"Uh-huh."

"And what about?"

"Masters, do you remember the Victoria Adams case about twenty years ago?"

The Chief Inspector's manner suddenly changed and grew wary.

"Victoria Adams case?" he ruminated. "No, sir, I can't say I do."

"Son, you're lyin'! You were sergeant to old Chief Inspector Rutherford in those days, and well I remember it!"

Masters stood on his dignity.

"That's as may be, sir. But twenty years ago . . ."

"A little girl of twelve or thirteen, the child of very wealthy parents, disappeared one night out of a country cottage with all the doors and windows locked on the inside. A week later, while everybody was havin' screaming hysterics, the child reappeared again: through the locks and bolts, tucked up in her bed as usual. And to this day nobody's ever known what really happened."

There was a silence, while Masters shut his jaws hard.

"This family, the Adamses," persisted H.M., "owned the cottage, down Aylesbury way, on the edge of Goblin Wood, opposite the lake. Or was it?"

"Oh, ah," growled Masters. "It was."

H.M. looked at him curiously.

"They used the cottage as a base for bathin' in summer, and ice-skatin' in winter. It was black winter when the child vanished, and the place was all locked up inside against drafts. They say her old man nearly went loopy when he found her there a week later, lying asleep under the lamp. But all she'd say, when they asked her where she'd been, was, '*I don't know*.'"

Again there was a silence, while red buses thundered through the traffic press of Whitehall.

"You've got to admit, Masters, there was a flaming public rumpus. I say: did you ever read Barrie's *Mary Rose?*"

"No."

"Well, it was a situation straight out of Barrie. Some people, y'see, said that Vicky Adams was a child of faërie who'd been spirited away by the pixies . . ."

Whereupon Masters exploded.

He removed his bowler hat and made remarks about pixies, in detail, which could not have been bettered by H.M. himself.

"I know, son, I know." H.M. was soothing. Then his big voice sharpened. "Now tell me. Was all this talk strictly true?"

"What talk?"

"Locked windows? Bolted doors? No attic-trap? No cellar? Solid walls and floor?"

"Yes, sir," answered Masters, regaining his dignity with a powerful effort, "I'm bound to admit it *was* true."

"Then there wasn't any jiggery-pokery about the cottage?"

"In your eye there wasn't," said Masters.

"How d'ye mean?"

"Listen, sir." Masters lowered his voice. "Before the Adamses took over that place, it was a hideout for Chuck Randall. At that time he was the swellest of the swell mob; we lagged him a couple of years later. Do you think Chuck wouldn't have rigged up some gadget for a getaway? Just so! Only . . ."

"Well? Hey?"

"We couldn't find it," grunted Masters.

"And I'll bet that pleased old Chief Inspector Rutherford?"

"I tell you straight: he was fair up the pole. Especially as the kid herself was a pretty kid, all big eyes and dark hair. You couldn't help trusting her story."

"Yes," said H.M. "That's what worries me."

"Worries you?"

"Oh, my son!" said H.M. dismally. "Here's Vicky Adams, the spoiled daughter of dotin' parents. She's supposed to be 'odd' and 'fey'. She's even encouraged to be. During her adolescence, the most impressionable time of her life, she gets wrapped round with the gauze of a mystery that people talk about even yet. What's that woman like now, Masters? What's that woman like now?"

"Dear Sir Henry!" murmured Miss Vicky Adams in her softest voice.

She said this just as William Sage's car, with Bill and Eve Drayton in the front seat, and Vicky and H.M. in the back seat, turned off the main road. Behind them lay the smoky-red roofs of Aylesbury, against a brightness of late afternoon. The car turned down a side road, a damp tunnel of greenery, and into another road which was little more than a lane between hedgerows.

H.M.—though cheered by three good-sized picnic hampers from Fortnum & Mason, their wickerwork lids bulging with a feast—did not seem happy. Nobody in that car was happy, with the possible exception of Miss Adams herself.

Vicky, unlike Eve, was small and dark and vivacious. Her large light-brown eyes, with very black lashes, could be arch and coy; or they could be dreamily intense. The late Sir James Barrie might have called her a sprite. Those of more sober views would have recognized a different quality: she had an inordinate sex-appeal, which was as palpable as a physical touch to any male within yards. And despite her smallness, Vicky had a full voice like Eve's. All these qualities she used even in so simple a matter as giving traffic directions.

"First right," she would say, leaning forward to put her hands on Bill Sage's shoulders. "Then straight on until the next traffic light. Ah, clever boy!"

"Not at all, not at all!" Bill would disclaim, with red ears and rather an erratic style of driving.

"Oh, yes, you are!" And Vicky would twist the lobe of his ear, playfully, before sitting back again.

(Eve Drayton did not say anything. She did not even turn round. Yet the atmosphere, even of that quiet English picnic-party, had already become a trifle hysterical.)

"Dear Sir Henry!" murmured Vicky, as they turned down into

the deep lane between the hedgerows. "I do wish you wouldn't be so materialistic! I do, really. Haven't you the tiniest bit of spirituality in your nature?"

"Me?" said H.M. in astonishment. "I got a very lofty spiritual nature. But what I want just now, my wench, is grub.—Oi!"

Bill Sage glanced round.

"By that speedometer," H.M. pointed, "we've now come forty-six miles and a bit. We didn't even leave town until people of decency and sanity were having their tea. Where are we *going*?"

"But didn't you know?" asked Vicky, with wide-open eyes. "We're going to the cottage where I had such a dreadful experience when I was a child."

"Was it such a dreadful experience, Vicky dear?" inquired Eve.

Vicky's eyes seemed far away.

"I don't remember, really. I was only a child, you see. I didn't understand. I hadn't developed the power for myself then."

"What power?" H.M. asked sharply.

"To dematerialize," said Vicky. "Of course."

In that warm sun-dusted lane, between the hawthorn hedges, the car jolted over a rut. Crockery rattled.

"Uh-huh. I see," observed H.M. without inflection. "And where do you go, my wench, when you dematerialize?"

"Into a strange country. Through a little door. You wouldn't understand. Oh, you *are* such Philistines!" moaned Vicky. Then, with a sudden change of mood, she leaned forward and her whole physical allurement flowed again towards Bill Sage. "*You* wouldn't like me to disappear, would you, Bill?"

(Easy! Easy!)

"Only," said Bill, with a sort of wild gallantry, "if you promised to reappear again straightaway."

"Oh, I should have to do that." Vicky sat back. She was trembling. "The power wouldn't be strong enough. But even a poor little thing like me might be able to teach you a lesson. Look there!"

And she pointed ahead.

On their left, as the lane widened, stretched the ten-acre gloom of what is fancifully known as Goblin Wood. On their right lay a small lake, on private property and therefore deserted.

The cottage—set well back into a clearing of the wood so as to face the road, screened from it by a line of beeches—was in fact a bungalow of rough-hewn stone, with a slate roof. Across the front of it ran a wooden porch. It had a seedy air, like the long yellow-green grass of its front lawn. Bill parked the car at the side of the road, since there was no driveway.

"It's a bit lonely, ain't it?" demanded H.M. His voice boomed out against that utter stillness, under the hot sun.

"Oh, yes!" breathed Vicky. She jumped out of the car in a whirl of skirts. "That's why *they* were able to come and take me. When I was a child."

"They?"

"Dear Sir Henry! Do I need to explain?"

Then Vicky looked at Bill.

"I must apologize," she said, "for the state the house is in. I haven't been out here for months and months. There's a modern bathroom, I'm glad to say. Only paraffin lamps, of course. But then," a dreamy smile flashed across her face, "you won't need lamps, will you? Unless . . ."

"You mean," said Bill, who was taking a black case out of the car, "unless you disappear again?"

"Yes, Bill. And promise me you won't be frightened when I do."

The young man uttered a ringing oath which was shushed by Sir Henry Merrivale, who austerely said he disapproved of profanity. Eve Drayton was very quiet.

"But in the meantime," Vicky said wistfully, "let's forget it all, shall we? Let's laugh and dance and sing and pretend we're children! And surely our guest must be even more hungry by this time?"

It was in this emotional state that they sat down to their picnic.

H.M., if the truth must be told, did not fare too badly. Instead of sitting on some hummock of ground, they dragged a table and chairs to the shaded porch. All spoke in strained voices. But no word of controversy was said. It was only afterwards, when the cloth was cleared, the furniture and hampers pushed indoors, the empty bottles flung away, that danger tapped a warning.

From under the porch Vicky fished out two half-rotted deck-chairs, which she set up in the long grass of the lawn. These were to be occupied by Eve and H.M., while Vicky took Bill Sage to inspect a plum tree of some remarkable quality she did not specify.

Eve sat down without comment. H.M., who was smoking a black cigar opposite her, waited some time before he spoke.

"Y' know," he said, taking the cigar out of his mouth, "you're behaving remarkably well."

"Yes." Eve laughed. "Aren't I?"

"Are you pretty well acquainted with this Adams gal?"

"I'm her first cousin," Eve answered simply. "Now that her parents are dead, I'm the only relative she's got. I know *all* about her."

From far across the lawn floated two voices saying something about wild strawberries. Eve, her fair hair and fair complexion vivid against the dark line of Goblin Wood, clenched her hands on her knees.

"You see, H.M.," she hesitated, "there was another reason why I invited you here. I—I don't quite know how to approach it."

"I'm the old man," said H.M., tapping himself impressively on the chest. "You tell me."

"Eve, darling!" interposed Vicky's voice, crying across the ragged lawn. "Coo-ee! Eve!"

"Yes, dear?"

"I've just remembered," cried Vicky, "that I haven't shown Bill over the cottage! You don't mind if I steal him away from you for a little while?"

"No, dear! Of course not!"

It was H.M., sitting so as to face the bungalow, who saw Vicky and Bill go in. He saw Vicky's wistful smile as she closed the door after them. Eve did not even look round. The sun was declining, making fiery chinks through the thickness of Goblin Wood behind the cottage.

"I won't let her have him," Eve suddenly cried. "I won't! I won't! I won't!"

"Does she want him, my wench? Or, which is more to the point, does he want her?"

"He never has," Eve said with emphasis. "Not really. And he never will."

H.M., motionless, puffed out cigar smoke.

"Vicky's a faker," said Eve. "Does that sound catty?"

"Not necessarily. I was just thinkin' the same thing myself."

"I'm patient," said Eve. Her blue eyes were fixed. "I'm terribly, terribly patient. I can wait for years for what I want. Bill's not making much money now, and I haven't got a bean. But Bill's got great talent under that easy-going manner of his. He *must* have the right girl to help him. If only . . ."

"If only the elfin sprite would let him alone. Hey?"

"Vicky acts like that," said Eve, "towards practically every man she ever meets. That's why she never married. She says it leaves her soul free to commune with other souls. This occultism—"

Then it all poured out, the family story of the Adamses. This repressed girl spoke at length, spoke as perhaps she had never spoken before. Vicky Adams, the child who wanted to attract attention, her father Uncle Fred and her mother Aunt Margaret seemed to walk in vividness as the shadows gathered.

"I was too young to know her at the time of the 'disappearance,' of course. But, oh, I knew her afterwards! And I thought . . ."

"Well?"

"If I could get *you* here," said Eve, "I thought she'd try to show off with some game. And then you'd expose her. And Bill would see what an awful faker she is. But it's hopeless! It's hopeless!"

149

"Looky here," observed H.M., who was smoking his third cigar. He sat up. "Doesn't it strike you those two are being a rummy-awful long time just in lookin' through a little bungalow?"

Eve, roused out of a dream, stared back at him. She sprang to her feet. She was not now, you could guess, thinking of any disappearance.

"Excuse me a moment," she said curtly.

Eve hurried across to the cottage, went up on the porch, and opened the front door. H.M. heard her heels rap down the length of the small passage inside. She marched straight back again, closed the front door, and rejoined H.M.

"All the doors of the rooms are shut," she announced in a high voice. "I really don't think I ought to disturb them."

"Easy, my wench!"

"I have absolutely no interest," declared Eve, with the tears coming into her eyes, "in what happens to either of them now. Shall we take the car and go back to town without them?"

H.M. threw away his cigar, got up, and seized her by the shoulders.

"I'm the old man," he said, leering like an ogre. "Will you listen to me?"

"No!"

"If I'm any reader of the human dial," persisted H.M., "that young feller's no more gone on Vicky Adams than I am. He was scared, my wench. Scared." Doubt, indecision crossed H.M.'s face. "I dunno what he's scared of. Burn me, I don't! But . . ."

"Hoy!" called the voice of Bill Sage.

It did not come from the direction of the cottage.

They were surrounded on three sides by Goblin Wood, now blurred with twilight. From the north side the voice bawled at them, followed by crackling in dry undergrowth. Bill, his hair and sports coat and flannels more than a little dirty, regarded them with a face of bitterness.

"Here are her blasted wild strawberries," he announced, extending his hand. "Three of 'em. The fruitful (excuse me) result of three quarters of an hour's hard labor. I absolutely refuse to chase 'em in the dark."

For a moment Eve Drayton's mouth moved without speech.

"Then you weren't . . . in the cottage all this time?"

"In the cottage?" Bill glanced at it. "I was in that cottage," he said, "about five minutes. Vicky had a woman's whim. She wanted some wild strawberries out of what she called the 'forest.'"

"Wait a minute, son!" said H.M. very sharply. "You didn't come out that front door. Nobody did."

"No! I went out the back door! It opens straight on the wood."

"Yes. And what happened then?"

"Well, I went to look for these damned . . ."

"No, no! What did *she* do?"

"Vicky? She locked and bolted the back door on the inside. I remember her grinning at me through the glass panel. She—"

Bill stopped short. His eyes widened, and then narrowed, as though at the impact of an idea. All three of them turned to look at the rough-stone cottage.

"By the way," said Bill. He cleared his throat vigorously. "By the way, have you seen Vicky since then?"

"No."

"This couldn't be . . .?"

"It could be, son," said H.M. "We'd all better go in there and have a look."

They hesitated for a moment on the porch. A warm, moist fragrance breathed up from the ground after sunset. In half an hour it would be completely dark.

Bill Sage threw open the front door and shouted Vicky's name. That sound seemed to penetrate, reverberating, through every room. The intense heat and stuffiness of the cottage, where no window had been raised in months, blew out at them. But nobody answered.

"Get inside," snapped H.M. "And stop yowlin'." The Old Maestro was nervous. "I'm dead sure she didn't get out by the front door; but we'll just make certain there's no slippin' out now."

Stumbling over the table and chairs they had used on the porch, he fastened the front door. They were in a narrow passage, once handsome with parquet floor and pine-paneled walls, leading to a door with a glass panel at the rear. H.M. lumbered forward to inspect this door and found it locked and bolted, as Bill had said.

Goblin Wood grew darker.

Keeping well together, they searched the cottage. It was not large, having two good-sized rooms on one side of the passage, and two small rooms on the other side, so as to make space for bathroom and kitchenette. H.M., raising fogs of dust, ransacked every inch where a person could possibly hide.

And all the windows were locked on the inside. And the chimney-flues were too narrow to admit anybody.

And Vicky Adams wasn't there.

"Oh, my eye!" breathed Sir Henry Merrivale.

They had gathered, by what idiotic impulse not even H.M. could have said, just outside the open door of the bathroom. A bath-tap dripped monotonously. The last light through a frosted-glass window showed three faces hung there as though disembodied.

"Bill," said Eve in an unsteady voice, "this is a trick. Oh, I've longed for her to be exposed! This is a trick!"

"Then where is she?"

"H.M. can tell us! Can't you, H.M.?"

"Well . . . now," muttered the great man.

Across H.M.'s Panama hat was a large black handprint, made there when he had pressed down the hat after investigating a chimney. He glowered under it.

"Son," he said to Bill, "there's just one question I want you to answer in all this hokey-pokey. When you went out pickin' wild strawberries, will you swear Vicky Adams didn't go with you?"

"As God is my judge, she didn't," returned Bill, with fervency and obvious truth. "Besides, how the devil could she? Look at the lock and bolt on the back door!"

H.M. made two more violent black handprints on his hat.

He lumbered forward, his head down, two or three paces in the narrow passage. His foot half-skidded on something that had been lying there unnoticed, and he picked it up. It was a large, square section of thin, waterproof oilskin, jagged at one corner.

"Have you found anything?" demanded Bill in a strained voice.

"No. Not to make any sense, that is. But just a minute!"

At the rear of the passage, on the left-hand side, was the bedroom from which Vicky Adams had vanished as a child. Though H.M. had searched this room once before, he opened the door again.

It was almost dark in Goblin Wood.

He saw dimly a room of twenty years before: a room of flounces, of lace curtains, of once-polished mahogany, its mirrors glimmering against white-papered walls. H.M. seemed especially interested in the windows.

He ran his hands carefully round the frame of each, even climbing laboriously up on a chair to examine the tops. He borrowed a box of matches from Bill; and the little spurts of light, following the rasp of the match, rasped against nerves as well. The hope died out of his face, and his companions saw it.

"H.M.," Bill said for the dozenth time, "where is she?"

"Son," replied H.M. despondently, "I don't know."

"Let's get out of here," Eve said abruptly. Her voice was a small scream. "I kn-know it's all a trick! I know Vicky's a faker! But let's get out of here. For God's sake let's get out of here!"

"As a matter of fact," Bill cleared his throat, "I agree. Anyway, we won't hear from Vicky until tomorrow morning."

"*Oh, yes, you will,*" whispered Vicky's voice out of the darkness.

Eve screamed.

They lighted a lamp.

But there was nobody there.

Their retreat from the cottage, it must be admitted, was not very dignified.

How they stumbled down that ragged lawn in the dark, how they piled rugs and picnic-hampers into the car, how they eventually found the main road again, is best left undescribed.

Sir Henry Merrivale has since sneered at this—"a bit of a goosy feeling; nothin' much,"—and it is true that he has no nerves to speak of. But he can be worried, badly worried; and that he was worried on this occasion may be deduced from what happened later.

H.M., after dropping in at Claridge's for a modest late supper of lobster and *Pêche Melba*, returned to his house in Brook Street and slept a hideous sleep. It was three o'clock in the morning, even before the summer dawn, when the ringing of the bedside telephone roused him.

What he heard sent his blood pressure soaring.

"Dear Sir Henry!" crooned a familiar and sprite-like voice.

H.M. was himself again, full of gall and bile. He switched on the bedside lamp and put on his spectacles with care, so as adequately to address the 'phone.

"Have I got the honor," he said with dangerous politeness, "of addressin' Miss Vicky Adams?"

"Oh, yes!"

"I sincerely trust," said H.M., "you've been havin' a good time? Are you materialized yet?"

"Oh, yes!"

"Where are you now?"

"I'm afraid," there was coy laughter in the voice, "that must be a little secret for a day or two. I want to teach you a really *good* lesson. Blessings, dear."

And she hung up the receiver.

H.M. did not say anything. He climbed out of bed. He stalked up and down the room, his corporation majestic under an old-fashioned night-shirt stretching to his heels. Then, since he himself had been waked up at three o'clock in the morning, the obvious course was to wake up somebody else; so he dialed the home number of Chief Inspector Masters.

"No, sir," retorted Masters grimly, after coughing the frog out of his throat, "I do *not* mind you ringing up. Not a bit of it!" He spoke with a certain pleasure. "Because I've got a bit of news for you."

H.M. eyed the 'phone suspiciously.

"Masters, are you trying to do me in the eye again?"

"It's what you always try to do to me, isn't it?"

"All right, all right!" growled H.M. "What's the news?"

"Do you remember mentioning the Vicky Adams case yesterday?"

"Sort of. Yes."

"Oh, ah! Well, I had a word or two round among our people. I was tipped the wink to go and see a certain solicitor. He was old Mr. Fred Adams's solicitor before Mr. Adams died about six or seven years ago."

Here Masters's voice grew triumphant.

"I always said, Sir Henry, that Chuck Randall had planted some gadget in that cottage for a quick getaway. And I was right. The gadget was . . ."

"You were quite right, Masters. The gadget was a trick window."

The telephone, so to speak, gave a start.

"What's that?"

"A trick window." H.M. spoke patiently. "You press a spring. And the whole frame of the window, two leaves locked together, slides down between the walls far enough so you can climb over. Then you push it back up again."

"How in lum's name do you know that?"

"Oh, my son! They used to build windows like it in country houses during the persecution of Catholic priests. It was a good enough *second* guess. Only . . . it won't work."

Masters seemed annoyed. "It won't work now," Masters agreed. "And do you know why?"

"I can guess. Tell me."

"Because, just before Mr. Adams died, he discovered how his darling daughter had flummoxed him. He never told anybody except his lawyer. He took a handful of four-inch nails, and sealed up the top of that frame so tight an orangoutang couldn't move it, and painted 'em over so they wouldn't be noticed."

"Uh-huh. You can notice 'em now."

"I doubt if the young lady herself ever knew. But, by George!" Masters said savagely. "I'd like to see anybody try the same game now!"

"You would, hey? Then will it interest you to know that the same gal has just disappeared out of the same house AGAIN?"

H.M. began a long narrative of the facts, but he had to break off because the telephone was raving.

"Honest, Masters," H.M. said seriously, "I'm not joking. She didn't get out through that window. But she did get out. You'd better meet me," he gave directions, "tomorrow morning. In the meantime, son, sleep well."

It was, therefore, a worn-faced Masters who went into the Visitors' Room at the Senior Conservatives' Club just before lunch on the following day.

The Visitors' Room is a dark sepulchral place, opening on an air-well, where the visitor is surrounded by pictures of dyspeptic-looking gentlemen with beards. It has a pervading mustiness of wood and leather. Though whiskey and soda stood on the table, H.M. sat in a leather chair far away from it, ruffling his hands across his bald head.

"Now, Masters, keep your shirt on!" he warned. "This business may be rummy. But it's not a police matter—yet."

"I know it's not a police matter," Masters said grimly. "All the same, I've had a word with the Superintendent at Aylesbury."

"Fowler?"

"You know him?"

"Sure. I know everybody. Is he going to keep an eye out?"

"He's going to have a look at that ruddy cottage. I've asked for any telephone calls to be put through here. In the meantime, sir—"

It was at this point, as though diabolically inspired, that the telephone rang. H.M. reached it before Masters.

"It's the old man," he said, unconsciously assuming a stance of grandeur. "Yes, yes! Masters is here, but he's drunk. You tell me first. What's that?"

The telephone talked thinly.

"Sure I looked in the kitchen cupboard," bellowed H.M. "Though I didn't honestly expect to find Vicky Adams hidin' there. What's that? Say it again! Plates? Cups that had been . . ."

An almost frightening change had come over H.M.'s expression. He stood motionless. All the posturing went out of him. He was not even listening to the voice that still talked thinly, while his eyes and his brain moved to put together facts. At length (though the voice still talked) he hung up the receiver.

H.M. blundered back to the center table, where he drew out a chair and sat down.

"Masters," he said very quietly, "I've come close to makin' the silliest mistake of my life."

He cleared his throat.

"I shouldn't have made it, son. I really shouldn't. But don't yell at me for cuttin' off Fowler. I can tell you now how Vicky Adams disappeared. And she said one true thing when she said she was going into a strange country."

"How do you mean?"

"She's dead," answered H.M.

The word fell with heavy weight into that dingy room, where the bearded faces looked down.

"Y'see," H.M. went on blankly, "a lot of us were right when we thought Vicky Adams was a faker. She was. To attract attention to herself, she played that trick on her family with the hocused window. She's lived and traded on it ever since. That's what sent me straight in the wrong direction. I was on the alert for some *trick* Vicky Adams might play. So it never occurred to me that this elegant pair of beauties, Miss Eve Drayton and Mr. William Sage, were deliberately conspirin' to murder *her*."

Masters got slowly to his feet.

"Did you say . . . murder?"

"Oh, yes."

Again H.M. cleared his throat.

"It was all arranged beforehand for me to be a witness. They knew Vicky Adams couldn't resist a challenge to disappear, especially as Vicky always believed she could get out by the trick window. They wanted Vicky to *say* she was goin' to disappear. They never knew anything about the trick window, Masters. But they knew their own plan very well.

"Eve Drayton even told me the motive. She hated Vicky, of course. But that wasn't the main point. She was Vicky Adams's only relative; she'd inherit an awful big scoopful of money. Eve said she could be patient. (And, burn me, how her eyes meant it when she said that!) Rather than risk any slightest suspicion of murder, she was willing to wait seven years until a disappeared person can be presumed dead.

"Our Eve, I think, was the fiery drivin' force of that conspiracy. She was only scared part of the time. Sage was scared all of the time. But it was Sage who did the real dirty work. He lured Vicky Adams into that cottage, while Eve kept me in close conversation on the lawn . . ."

H.M. paused.

Intolerably vivid in the mind of Chief Inspector Masters, who had seen it years before, rose the picture of the rough-stone bungalow against the darkling wood.

"Masters," said H.M., "why should a bath-tap be dripping in a house that hadn't been occupied for months?"

"Well?"

"Sage, y'see is a surgeon. I saw him take his black case of instruments out of the car. He took Vicky Adams into that house. In the bathroom he stabbed her, he stripped her, and *he dismembered her body in the bath tub.* —Easy, son!"

"Go, on," said Masters without moving.

"The head, the torso, the folded arms and legs, were wrapped up in three large square pieces of thin transparent oilskin. Each was sewed up with coarse thread so the blood wouldn't drip. Last night

I found one of the oilskin pieces he'd ruined when his needle slipped at the corner. Then he walked out of the house, with the back door still standin' unlocked, to get his wild-strawberry alibi."

"Sage went out of there," shouted Masters, "leaving the body in the house?"

"Oh, yes," agreed H.M.

"But where did he leave it?"

H.M. ignored this.

"In the meantime, son, what about Eve Drayton? At the end of the arranged three quarters of an hour, she indicated there was hanky-panky between her *fiancé* and Vicky Adams. She flew into the house. But what did she do?

"She walked to the back of the passage. I heard her. *There she simply locked and bolted the back door.* And then she marched out to join me with tears in her eyes. And these two beauties were ready for investigation."

"Investigation?" said Masters. *"With that body still in the house?"*

"Oh, yes."

Masters lifted both fists.

"It must have given young Sage a shock," said H.M., "when I found that piece of waterproof oilskin he'd washed but dropped. Anyway, these two had only two more bits of hokey-pokey. The 'vanished' gal had to speak—to show she was still alive. If you'd been there, son, you'd have noticed that Eve Drayton's got a voice just like Vicky Adams's. If somebody speaks in a dark room, carefully imitatin' a coy tone she never uses herself, the illusion's goin' to be pretty good. The same goes for a telephone.

"It was finished, Masters. All that had to be done was remove the body from the house, and get it far away from there . . .'

"But that's just what I'm asking you, sir! Where was the body all this time? And who in blazes *did* remove the body from the house?"

"All of us did," answered H.M.

"What's that?"

"Masters," said H.M., "aren't you forgettin' the picnic hampers?"

And now, the Chief Inspector saw, H.M. was as white as a ghost. His next words took Masters like a blow between the eyes.

"Three good-sized wickerwork hampers, with lids. After our big meal on the porch, those hampers were shoved inside the house where Sage could get at 'em. He had to leave most of the used crockery behind, in a kitchen cupboard. But three wickerwork hampers from a picnic, and three butchers' parcels to go inside 'em. I carried one down to the car myself. It felt a bit funny . . ."

H.M. stretched out his hand, not steadily, towards the whiskey.

"Y'know," he said, "I'll always wonder if I was carrying the—head."

A ROUTINE NIGHT'S WORK

BY GEORGE HARMON COXE

George Harmon Coxe was born on April 23, 1901, in Olean, New York, and spent his youth there and in nearby Elmira, where Frederic Dannay (Ellery Queen) also spent his childhood. After a year at Purdue and another at Cornell, he worked five years with newspapers in California, Florida and New York and did advertising work for a New England printer for five more. Since then he has devoted himself to writing. His first novel, *Murder with Pictures*, was published in 1935. He is a past president of the Mystery Writers of America.

CARL BRODERICK, FIRST-GRADE detective attached to Homicide, eased the police sedan to a stop at the side of the Riverway and said, "It ought to be about here."

He cut the motor and snapped on his parking lights. When he opened the door and got out, Wally Grant, columnist deluxe for the *Gazette*, opened the other door to join him. They stood at the side of the road for a moment letting their eyes become accustomed to the darkness that stretched across the quarter-mile void between the road and the river. Then Broderick started along the weed-strewn stretch of turf that extended to the embankment.

Neither man spoke until they reached the edge of the steeply sloping gravel bluff overhanging the brief shoreline of the river, and then Grant said dryly, "Pretty, huh?"

Overhead the night sky was overcast and sullen, the clouds low-hung as though compressing the humid air into a heavy vacuum that dispelled all breeze. The river, a half mile wide here, was sleek and black and restless, its flat sheen broken by the shimmer of reflected lights from the city on its opposite bank and from the long arc of lamps that dotted the Raleigh Bridge a mile or more to the left.

Thirty feet from the shore, the red and green riding lights of a police launch hung motionless above the water and made the hull an obscure blotch. At the river's edge a vague figure crunched gravel under restless feet until Broderick said,

"Hey, how do you get down?"

A flashlight stabbed the darkness, focusing on the detective's face. A thick voice boomed,

"Hello, Brodie. Slide."

Broderick grunted and jumped stiff-legged. His heels hit the slope halfway down and he slid the remaining distance, filling his shoes with sand and fine gravel. As he recovered his balance, Grant smacked into him, knocking him into the harbor policeman who cursed once and said,

"You bring the M.E.?"

Broderick said, "No. Let's take the flash."

He swiveled the beam across the launch and the uniformed figure lounging on the cushioned seat behind the wheel, then dipped it to the water's edge. One end of a long pole about two inches in diameter lay on the beach. About eight feet of this pole was out of water. He knew what was on the other end, but he could not see it—just the section of pole and the black oily surface of the river.

The policeman, a burly figure in hip boots, said, "We got her down at the Bayside Club. Her coat caught on a nail in the float. The searchlight picked her up."

Broderick stood there silently, a straight stiff figure staring sightlessly at the spot where the pole disappeared in the water. His neat blue suit and his compact leanness made him look taller than his even six feet, and the reflected light made his tawny rectangular face a somber brown mask beneath the lightweight gray felt. A passing mood brought on by imagination and the dank smell of the river pressed in upon him, bringing with it an unusual sense of depression. Grant broke into this mood before it could grow:

"Well, when do we start?" the columnist wanted to know.

"When the Medical Examiner gets here."

"Hell, I thought it would be short and snappy."

"Did I ask you to come? Why don't you go write that column?"

"It's written—for tomorrow," Grant said wearily. "Anyway, I need a change, and you amuse me. Only I don't know yet why a homicide man has to check up on every suicide by drowning."

"How do you know it's suicide? You haven't seen her."

"It'll be suicide."

Broderick turned off the flashlight and sighed. "Probably. I told you it was routine. The Captain just wanted it checked and I'm the sort of guy that does checking and—"

"Checking," Grant cut in, "to see she hadn't got a bullet in her or her head bashed in. The department's getting jumpy and you're afraid you'll get another one you can't solve."

"Yeah," snorted Broderick. "And it's you newspaper guys—" His voice trailed off and he turned away, reaching for a cigarette.

There was more than a little truth in what Grant said. Captain Sharkey, head of the Homicide Squad, was plenty jumpy. Ten days ago a young woman, identified after an exhaustive investigation as Ruth Jackson, an unemployed entertainer, had been picked up in a vacant lot with her skull crushed.

The murder broke on a night that had been unusually barren of important stories and the newspapers had seized the morsel gleefully. The work of a madman, they said, someone temporarily crazed when the girl resisted him. They warned the city's parents, decried the police department for the outrage.

And for the police it was the Homicide Squad that bore the brunt of the attack that came from the Mayor via the District Attorney, the Commissioner, and the Superintendent. So Broderick was here to make sure that this death was routine business.

Grant moved up to him behind the dull glow of a cigarette-end as Broderick glanced out across that black water and again felt the heaviness of that depressing mood.

"It's a tough way to go," he said finally.

"Why?" asked Grant.

"I don't know. The river bothers me. Gettin' hauled out of the water don't appeal to me. Something futile, hopeless about it. The end of the road for somebody that's been kicked around until—"

"I might make a paragraph out of it sometime," Grant said.

"Out of what?"

"You. The human side of a cop." Grant's snort was faintly mocking. "It's the sentiment in you."

"Sentiment?" scoffed Broderick, matching the columnist's tone. "Me? Why, at heart I'm a softie."

"At heart you're an ice cube," scoffed Grant.

When the Examiner's physician and two ambulance attendants arrived, they pulled her out and placed her on the gravel shore.

She might have been anywhere between thirty and thirty-five, and her figure had the rather heavy solidness that often comes at that age. She wore a sodden linen suit and a shabby-looking dark coat; there was no hat and her dark hair was matted and tangled about her forehead and nape. In the glare of two flashlights her face was curiously pale and mottled, and the lipstick she had used was permanently waterproof. Yet for all its deathlike significance there was about the face something of peace and resignation.

The Examiner's man rose after a cursory examination.

"Not a mark on her that I can see. Of course I'll check that later." He sucked his lips audibly. "She hasn't been in long either."

"How long?" asked Broderick flatly.

"Well,—I'm speaking comparatively," the doctor said. "Two or three hours. Maybe five. But no longer than that."

"Probably wouldn't've got her," the harbor cop offered, "if the current hadn't pushed her against that float so that her coat caught."

"You through?" the Examiner's man asked Broderick.

"I want to look at her clothes."

"I'll shove off then." The doctor jerked a thumb toward the two ambulance men. "They'll take care of her when you finish."

While the policeman held the flashlight, Broderick went to one knee and made a thorough search. When he finished and stood up he said thoughtfully, "That's funny. Not a damn thing but a label in the coat. And that looks so old it won't do much good. No jewelry, nothing in any of the pockets."

There was one other thing that bothered him. The woman's face was vaguely familiar. He had seen it before—someplace. Not recently but—he turned to Grant.

The columnist was staring down at the dead woman, and Broderick realizing now that Grant had not spoken since the arrival of the Examiner's man, wondered why.

He knew Grant well, had known him when he was a reporter and before he inherited a column the *Gazette* had developed. Since then Grant had built up a feature that had become enormously popular; but for all of this he remained a smart reporter who got around and seemed to know everyone and everything.

His dry sardonic speech, his bored and nonchalant manner, was largely a defensive pose which was apparently meant to say, "Just because I peddle sentiment is no reason why I have to be that way myself." Right now the veneer of his manner was raised. He stood there, a trim-figured fellow, immaculately dressed in a dark suit and a black evening felt, keenly interested, held, almost transfixed, by the dead woman's face.

Broderick said, "I'm glad I brought you. You know her, huh?"

"Alma Morgan," Grant said.

Broderick repeated the name softly. It meant something, struck a responsive chord, but still it eluded him. He could not place the woman and after a moment said so. The announcement apparently snapped Grant's reverie. When he spoke again his voice was caustic.

"Certainly you can't place her—you're only a cop."

"You know where she lives?"

"No. But she's got a husband. An ex-husband. Lou Tandy. He might know."

Broderick took off his hat and ran a hand over a forehead and hairline that were damp. "He runs the Club doesn't he?"

"He fronts for it."

"Also I hear he's a theatrical booker."

"For any cheap act you can name. You want a trio for a club date, see Lou Tandy. Need a dancer, a singer, a piano player, a stripper? Call Lou."

"He was questioned in the Bradford case," Broderick said thoughtfully, "because the girl used to hang around the club sometimes, but nothing came of it. What about this one?"

"The last I heard she was working as cashier down at Enriquo's. Before that—" Grant broke off, seemed to shrug in the darkness. "For a while—that was some years back—she hit some of the best spots in the East, then—"

Broderick reached out and took the columnist by the arm.

"Let's see if we can find out where she lived. You can tell me about it in the car."

Wally Grant took up his tale as soon as the police sedan got under way, and his story became something of a soliloquy, the speech that of a man recapturing memories and talking to himself.

"She started right here when I was a cub reporter on the old *Eagle*, and she went up fast. A dancer. She made a couple of musical comedies and had some real good dates in Florida. Then, for some damn reason, she married Lou Tandy."

Grant grunted softly. "It's things like that you can't figure. He was her manager and he was a heel from 'way back. I guess he was a smoothie and at that time—that's eight or nine years ago—he had ideas. He wanted to put on his own shows. Tried to build them around her. They flopped because she couldn't carry them alone and he wouldn't spend for the talent to back her up.

"They sort of dropped from sight for a while, then I heard he left her out on the West Coast. When I saw her again she was all through as a dancer. She'd put on too much weight and she didn't seem to have any more ambition."

Grant shifted in the seat, slouching down with feet stretched out and his chin on his chest.

"When she finally woke up she got her divorce. She tried to come back in the small time but she never really made it. I guess she got pushed around until the racket licked her. She's been working for Enriquo for over a year.

"Swell, huh? After Broadway." Grant muttered something under his breath, then added, "But the river. It just goes to show you—" He broke off suddenly, pushed erect. "But why all the sudden interest?" he said. "Why all this checking up? It's not your job now. Anybody'd think it was homicide."

"I'm wondering," Broderick murmured.

"Wondering? About what? She couldn't take it any longer, so she jumped—that's all. Not a mark on her."

"And no identification either," said Broderick. "Nothing in her pockets, no cards or purse or money—nothing. That ain't the way most suicides go. Most of 'em leave a note. When they don't, they don't bother about going unidentified—unless they've got something to cover up. From what you say she didn't have anything to cover up but failure and that's excusable and—"

"A moralist, huh?"

"—anyway, there's lots of easier ways than this. A woman might want to call it off, but damn few of 'em would get steamed up about Potter's Field, or maybe no burial at all . . . I don't say it's homicide," Brokerick added wearily, "but until I get more dope it could be. And anything that could be is my job." He grunted resignedly and lapsed into silence.

He did not, he told himself, think this was really murder. On the

163

face of it the death was suicide, pure and simple. Lack of identification bothered him but was by no means conclusive. His argument with Grant was merely the outlet for a stubborn irritation at the columnist's cocksure manner.

"Anyway," the detective added flatly, "the skipper said check, so I check." He glanced out the window, saw that they had crossed the bridge and were approaching the avenue. "If this bores you—"

"It bores me," Grant cut in, "but so would a nightclub."

Enriquo's was closed but light showed at the edges of the shutters and Broderick's second knock brought the proprietor to the door. When he recognized Grant he opened up immediately.

"Ahh, Mr. Grant. Come in, come in. We are closed, as you can see, but if you would like a drink—"

"No, thanks," Grant said. "How's the chicken caneloni these days?"

"Superb as always. But you do not come to see for yourself."

Grant said he would make a note of it. He introduced Broderick, then spoke of Alma Morgan, asking if she still worked as cashier.

"Until last Saturday, yes," Enriquo said.

"Did she quit?" Broderick asked.

"It is hard to say." Enriquo tipped his head and half closed one eye. "There was a man. I think maybe Alma is in love. She say she may marry this man and she give me notice and I tell her to take some time off to be sure."

He went on to tell how the man had come for dinner one night, then returned night after night, at first stopping only to talk to Alma and then as the friendship progressed, returning to meet her when she quit work.

"What's his name?" Broderick asked.

Enriquo frowned and finally shook his head. "I am sorry. I have heard the name but I cannot recall it now. A funny name. Short."

"Well, what does he look like?"

"Medium tall." Enriquo held his palms apart. "Sort of broad. Maybe forty, with much color in face, like he work outside, not in city . . . Has something happened to Alma?"

Grant opened his mouth but Broderick cut him off. "Just checking some things. You got her address?"

"Sure." Enriquo stepped behind the desk and read it off.

Broderick made a note of it. He thanked Enriquo, nodded to Grant, and said he would be back some evening to try the chicken caneloni.

"You do that," Enriquo said. "And if you see Alma you tell her we miss her."

A taxi was parked at the curb halfway to the corner in the quiet darkness of Stephan Street, and the police car angled in front of it to stop a few feet beyond, opposite a squarish, three-story house with a towered, antiquated form of architecture that was apparent even in the darkness.

Broderick took a quick glance at the taxi and the dozing driver, making a mental note of the license number before starting up the high stone steps that led to an open vestibule, Grant at his heels, A glass-framed sign hanging at the edge of the outer door said: ROOMS. The inner door was unlocked and they stepped into the cool, musty air that hung in the high-ceilinged hall. After one glance around Broderick stepped back to the vestibule and pushed the bell button, setting up a jangling metallic vibration that came from some unseen spot deep down the hall adjacent to the stairs.

The landlady, a spare, gaunt figure with a hatchet face and wearing a faded blue wrapper, was fully two minutes in answering the bell, and when she did arrive she was in a snapping, irritable frame of mind.

Broderick said he was sorry to disturb her, and asked if Alma Morgan lived there.

"No, she don't," the landlady said. "She did."

"Until when?"

"Until today. I got a note from her. Her brother brought it—and the rent she owed me. It said for me to let him pack her things."

"Where was she going?"

"She didn't say. Just said she had a job and wouldn't have time to get her things."

"When'd you get the note?"

"About an hour and a half ago—round ten-thirty."

"An hour and—" wheezed the columnist.

"Yes. And don't stand there and ask me anything else because that's all I know and I'm up at five-thirty and I need my sleep." The woman folded the wrapper tighter, spun about, and started down the hall.

Broderick asked how to get to Alma Morgan's former room and the landlady called directions without turning or slowing down. When he started up the stairs, with Grant crowding at his heels, he said,

"How does it look now?"

"Screwy," said Grant. "But the hour and a half don't mean anything. She could have written the note before."

"Quite a while before," said Broderick.

Alma Morgan's room was the last one on the right in the second-floor hall, and Broderick, realizing now that he should have taken the precaution of asking for the key, tried the knob. When it turned easily, he pushed into a room that was already lighted and not as empty as he had expected.

Near the opposite wall a man knelt beside a black hatbox and a bulky suitcase. He was nattily dressed in gray flannel and his hat was pushed back from a swart, smooth face. Apparently startled by the sudden entrance as he attempted to strap up the suitcase, his black eyes widened, then narrowed quickly as his body tensed.

Broderick swept the room with a glance and found it discouraging. A furnished place. Soiled slipcovers on the two overstuffed pieces, the rest of the cheap furniture worn and scarred. His glance jerked back to the kneeling man and as he moved across the threshold, he felt Grant at his side and heard the door click shut.

"You the guy that brought the note?" Broderick asked.

"Yeah."

"Her brother."

"Her brother," the fellow said, his voice challenging and insolent.

"Where was she going?"

"To Chicago. She's already gone. And who the hell are you?"

Broderick's lean face had fashioned a fixed smile that was grimly amused. He knew definitely, although he could not yet reason it out, that there was something more than simple suicide. His hand moved backward at his side as he said.

"Chicago. And you're her brother?"

He never touched the gun. Not that he was slow; he wasn't. But the other man had a certain professional finesse born of long experience, and he had prepared for possible emergencies by taking out his gun beforehand. It lay hidden by the suitcase, but Broderick did not see it until it flashed into sight.

"Forget it!"

Broderick's hand dropped back to his side. "Okay," he said easily.

The dark face warped into a smile and he stood up, tall and thin in his well-pressed flannels. Backing around to one side, he waved his automatic toward the suitcase.

"Strap it up!"

Broderick came forward and strapped the bag.

"Now, take off your belts, both of you," and when Broderick and Grant obeyed, he spoke to the detective. "Lie down—on your belly."

Broderick's face stiffened and he hesitated a moment, his smoky-blue eyes hard and shiny.

"Or do I park you down that way permanently?"

Broderick got down on his knees and stretched out. The swart

166

man made Grant strap his wrists and ankles. When this was finished, the gunman pulled down the window curtains, twisted them, and tied up the columnist.

He had just finished when a soft knock came at the door. Cursing softly, he moved quickly across the room. He scowled, his black eyes swiveling nervously. When the knock came again, he threw open the door and jumped back, his gun ready.

The man who stood in the opening stared wide-eyed at the gun, his body suddenly stiff and immobile until the gunman ordered him into the room, then closed and locked the door. The newcomer saw Broderick and Grant and some of the color crept back into his face.

Stocky, of medium height, and dressed in a conservative dark suit, he was completely nondescript in appearance, his squarish face ordinary enough except for a noticeable tan. To Broderick, craning his neck to get a better view, he fitted exactly the description Enriquo had given.

"Well," he breathed finally. "What—what's all this?" He took off a felt hat that sat squarely on his head, revealing hair that was merely hair-colored and lusterless. "I thought—isn't Alma here?"

"She's gone," the gunman said.

"Gone?"

"You heard me."

The stocky man turned his hat brim around, eyed the automatic a moment, then continued in a serious, apologetic monotone that matched his manner.

"She wouldn't go without telling me."

"Why not? Who are you—where do you fit?"

"Rudd," the man said slowly. "Thomas Rudd. Alma and I—we had a date."

"At twelve o'clock at night, huh?" cut in Grant.

"But this was a special occasion. She said she had to see some people and make a decision. She said she'd be back before twelve and if everything worked out all right—"

"Shut up!"

The swart man looked suddenly harried and uncertain. His free hand drew into a fist at his side; then he turned and stepped to a telephone stand near an inner doorway. Dialing a number, he waited impatiently, finally said,

"This is Max. Yes. Sure. Only get a load of this. A couple of johnnies walk in on me before I finish. One of 'em looks like a cop . . . Yeah. I got 'em tied up. Only wait—another guy just walked in on us. Name's Rudd. I was thinkin' he might be the guy . . . Yeah. Okay, I just wanted to be sure."

Max hung up and spoke to Rudd. "Come on, you."

Rudd's "Me?" was sheer surprise.

"Yes, you! I need company. Grab those bags."

"But—" sputtered Rudd. "I mean—I—Alma."

Max stepped forward, gun leveled. "Grab the bags!"

Broderick said, "You'd better do what he says. He's getting jumpy."

Rudd tried to smile and failed. He glanced nervously at Broderick and Grant; he finally picked up the two bags and said, "Well—all right." He was still quietly protesting when Max followed him from the room and slammed the door.

When Grant stopped swearing he said, "What a dick you turned out to be."

"Yeah," said Broderick grimly, rolling up against him, "and how does the suicide story look now?"

"It don't."

"Then get your back against mine and undo these straps. I'm gonna find out who put that woman in the river."

When Grant freed Broderick's hands, and he in turn had untied Grant's, the detective stood up and stared morosely about him.

The columnist lit a cigarette. "Now what, Sherlock?"

Broderick ignored the crack and his roving humid gaze fed on a sullen anger that smoldered within him. He was not yet ready to admit defeat, but he would have a hard time explaining this episode and he knew it. With another unsolved case stacked on top of the Ruth Jackson job, the going would be tough for the whole department. And somehow the river, and the cold wet body, haunted him. He was familiar with murder, but not this kind; and something caught in his throat when he remembered the black oiliness of the water and the woman at the end of the pole.

Grant said, "A trance?"—which shattered Broderick's mood and brought him back to the business at hand. Stepping to the telephone, and without lifting the receiver, he began to experiment—to try and reproduce a certain clicking sequence of the dial.

He kept this up for two or three minutes, ignoring Grant's sardonic comments. Finally he said,

"I think I got the first four numbers. It figures P-A for the Parkway exchange, then 7, then either 9 or 0."

"Go on from there."

Broderick pointed to half a dozen scrawled numbers which had been penciled above the telephone stand on the fading pink wallpaper. "Two of these are Parkway numbers. One is 0 and one is 9. It's an even chance."

He dialed headquarters, asked for a connection, then repeated the two numbers. "See if you can check them for me, will you?" he said. "Yeah, I'll hang on."

While he waited he recalled the taxi that had been parked outside, and when he had information about the telephone numbers he gave the license number of the cab.

"It's a Red-and-White," he said. "Check with the dispatcher and have him get the driver on the company radio. If the guy keeps his trip sheet right, we'll know where he went from here . . . Yeah, I'll call you back."

He hung up and glanced at Grant. "One of these numbers is a real estate office. The other's an apartment on Beach Street. I think," he said as he gave his hat brim a tug, "I'll have a go at that apartment house before I get the skipper out of bed."

On the way out Broderick stopped at the doorbell and pushed the button until he roused the landlady. Combating angry protests with curt threats of his own, he learned that the woman had kept the letter brought by Max as a protective measure, in case there was any complaint later. Broderick demanded this evidence and as soon as he and Grant were again in the police sedan, he turned on the dome light and read it.

The note offered little in the way of additional information. It said, in substance, what the irate landlady had already told him. It was neatly written in ink on a sheet of light-gray notepaper with a rough edge suggesting that it had been torn from a larger sheet.

Grant said, "It's a woman's writing."

"Looks like it."

"And she could have written it like I said—earlier today."

"Could have . . . Do you want to guess about this guy Max?"

"That's your job."

"He knew she was dead when he brought that note," Broderick said thoughtfully. "That part's easy to figure. Somebody framed it. They didn't want her identified or traced. With luck her body might've been carried out to sea; the odds were that it wouldn't've been recovered for a week or more. By that time, if it was found, nobody could say how long she had been dead; if we checked back to her room, the landlady'd say she moved and we couldn't prove different. Only the skipper thought I oughta check and—"

"You were lucky enough to have me along," Grant said.

"—the current smacked her against that boat club landing and her coat caught."

"So all we got to do," Grant said, "is find Max, and the guys that killed her, and why, and how—and then prove it." He yawned audibly. "Well, I'll give you credit in my column for trying."

"I'll appreciate that," said Broderick sourly.

The glass inset above the arched doorway of the ordinary-looking gray-brick apartment house on Beach Street read: *The*

Eldorado. The tunnel-like vestibule was at sidewalk level and led to a sunken lobby boasting some potted shrubs, three tapestried chairs, a divan, and a desk which curved around mail cubbyholes and a switchboard.

Literally asleep at the switch, an attendant in an unbuttoned uniform drowsed behind the switchboard. He awoke with a start when Broderick slapped a hard palm down on the desk top, and when he saw the shield and heard the order, he unhooked a chartlike cardboard affair from the side of the switchboard and slid it across the desk.

Broderick let his eyes follow a lean forefinger down the typewritten lines thumbtacked to the board. He heard Grant's choked exclamation, but he paid no attention until he had read every name on the schedule. Then he put the fingernail on a name halfway down the list and said,

"That's her Ex, isn't it? Lou Tandy." He slid the card back. "Anyway, the trip isn't wasted—I wanted to talk with him."

"I'd better announce you, Chief," the employee said hesitantly.

"You'd better not," Broderick said, and there was a level hardness to the tone that brought a corrected reply promptly.

"Yes, s-i-r. I'd better not."

"Don't go popping off with all you know," Broderick told Grant as he pressed the mother-of-pearl button set in the cream-colored doorway of apartment 3-F. "I haven't got any warrant, so to start with this is just a social call."

He turned slightly, cocked an eyebrow at the columnist, and unbuttoned his jacket, loosening the service revolver in its holster. He had to press the buzzer button again before the door opened to frame a plump, round-faced man in a blue-velvet housecoat.

Grant said, "Greetings, Lou."

"Hello, Wally—Broderick." Lou Tandy's chuckle sounded forced. "This looks bad."

Broderick moved forward so that Tandy had to back out of his way, and as he caught a full view of the expensively furnished room he saw that Brad Powell lounged in a club chair near the windows.

Tandy shut the door, sat down on an arm of the sofa, and blinked pale-blue eyes. "What is this?" he asked fliply. "Business or—"

"Business," Broderick said. "We found your wife—ex-wife—in the river."

"Alma?" exclaimed Tandy. "In the river?" He started to laugh, thought better of it. "You're kidding—"

Broderick interrupted, told briefly the story of how and where the body had been found. As he talked, he studied Brad Powell, wondering about his presence.

A nephew by marriage of the city's Number Two alderman, Powell was well set up, as tall as Broderick and heavier, but with a soft, pampered look about him. A loafer who liked bright lights and women, he had held various odd jobs at City Hall, but never for long. More recently he'd been working as Bell Captain at the Carlton House, not the best hotel in the city but one that did a heavy convention business.

"Dead, huh?" Tandy said when Broderick finished his story. "Good God, I never thought—" He broke off to run a puffy hand across a pink, moist face, then stroked his thinning sandy hair.

"She's been down on her luck," he continued thoughtfully. "I've been sending her a monthly check, but I never thought she'd jump in the river and—"

"I didn't say she jumped in," Broderick said quietly. "I said that's where we found her."

Tandy stiffened and his pale eyes narrowed.

"Wait a minute," he said. "Is this supposed to be a gag?"

"Not to me," Broderick answered, "but there are some screwy angles to it." He told about Max and Rudd and the scene at Alma Morgan's room. "That letter doesn't click," he continued in the same even tone. "My hunch is that she was in the river before it was written. I could be wrong, but she hasn't got a brother, and even if she had and he was on the level, why the gun act and—"

"What's this got to do with me?"

"I traced the telephone call Max made," Broderick lied.

"Yeah? Well, it didn't come here. I ain't had a call all evening."

"You don't know anything about it?"

"Hell, no! Why should—"

"Then," said Broderick, moving away from the door, "you hadn't ought to mind if I take a look around."

Tandy stood up quickly. "I mind plenty," he said. "You can't come in here and push me around. If you've got a warrant, produce it. If not—"

The soft note of a buzzer interrupted him. Broderick was nearest the door. He took one quick step and pulled it open.

The girl said, "Oh—" uncertainly, hesitated, took a half step forward. "Isn't Mr. Tandy—" Then she saw him and her face brightened with relief.

She was rather pretty in a superficial way. Her dress was cheaply flashy, her voice a bit shrill. There was something pert and vital about her, though, and she seemed too young for the amount of makeup she carried.

"I—I just wanted to know if you got the baggage all right," she continued eagerly.

171

"Yes," Tandy said briskly. "Sure, it's okay. Now run along. I'm busy."

"That's fine," the girl hurried on innocently. "It would be awful to be stranded without your clothes and I wasn't sure—"

"Shut up!" said Tandy. "And beat it!"

Broderick had tensed when the girl mentioned baggage, and now a solution exploded in his brain in clear-cut detail. He played his hunch before the girl could turn away.

"Alma Morgan's baggage?"

"Yes—"

"I told you—" raged Tandy, striding to the door.

Broderick caught one arm, spun him around. He stepped to the door, then pulled the girl into the room without taking his eyes from Tandy.

"Did you write the letter?" he pressed.

"Why—"

"Did you?"

"Yes."

Tandy's hand flashed to his hip. Grant wheezed a warning, but it was unnecessary. Broderick's right hand whipped out the service revolver before Tandy could draw his gun.

"Leave it!"

Tandy's arm dropped to his side and the detective said, "Get it, Wally—and don't get in front of him." When Grant obeyed, Broderick turned to the thoroughly frightened girl.

"It's okay," he said gently. "Nothing to be scared about. I'm a police officer and there are a couple of things I'd like to get straight. Where was the Morgan woman going?"

"To St. Louis. She had to catch a train and—"

"I thought it was Chicago." Broderick glanced at Tandy, then back at the girl. "What's your name, Miss?"

"Joan Wheeler."

Powell came erect in his chair. "That's enough Joan. You don't have to answer his questions."

Broderick ignored Powell. "Where do you work?"

"The Carlton House," the girl said, unable to take her eyes from the detective's steady gaze. "I'm a waitress in the cocktail lounge."

"Powell asked you to write the letter and sign Alma Morgan's name," Broderick said as things began to add up.

"But they said—I mean—" The girl swallowed and tried again. "I thought I was doing her a favor."

"When did you write it?"

"About ten o'clock."

"Here?"

"Yes."

"When was Alma here last?" he said to Tandy.

"She hasn't been here in a week."

"A fingerprint man will check that too," Broderick said. "If she was here she probably touched something." He glanced at Powell as his mind went on and now he spoke his thoughts aloud.

"The Carlton's a convention hotel and you're the Bell Captain. Married men on the loose for a few days with expense accounts and lots of dough in their pockets. You touted them to the Club and the Jackson girl hung around there on the watch for pickups." He looked at Tandy. "You made sure she got the right sort of customer, huh, Lou?"

When there was no reply he said, "So when a guy got crocked enough, the Jackson dame would go with him to his hotel room and then the 'jealous husband' would muscle in. Max. The jealous husband; maybe with a gun—"

Wally Grant cleared his throat. "The old badger game? I thought that went out with silent movies."

"It's never been out," Broderick said harshly. "Because people don't change. It still works when you set it up right. You just don't hear about it . . . So what happened to the Jackson girl, Lou?" he said. "Did she lose her nerve? How did Alma know about it?"

When he realized there would be no answer he turned again to Grant. "Watch 'em, Wally," and he started for a closed door he had noticed from the moment he stepped into the room. Wary of what might be beyond, he made all his movements with one eye on the panel. Now he threw it open quickly, his trigger finger tense.

He had been prepared to shoot, to take his chances. But he was not prepared for the problem that confronted him.

He said, "Drop it!"

Max said, "Drop it!"

It could have been a tie except for one thing. Max had a little help. His body was shielded by that of Thomas Rudd whom Max held with an arm around the man's neck in a stranglehold that tipped Rudd's head backward.

Max said, "Drop it, cop! I can't miss."

Broderick felt the tension slide swiftly up his spine. For another moment he stood quite still, his mind racing as he figured the odds and found them bad. He backed up a step, Max following, pushing Rudd ahead of him. Broderick thought about Grant and the Wheeler girl and knew he could not gamble with the gun.

"I'm not kidding," Max said. "I'm going to count—"

"Relax," Broderick said. "Let the girl out and I'll drop it."

Lou Tandy liked the idea. "Let her go."

"And have her run to the nearest phone and scream for the cops?" Max shook his head, but his gun was steady.

Powell jumped to his feet. His face was white and sick, and fear showed in his eyes. He wanted only one thing: to get away.

"I'll take her out. I'll keep her with me, Max."

The gunman thought it over; finally he agreed. "Okay. Take her to your place and stay with her until we get there."

Powell blew out his breath and reached for the girl. He spun her roughly toward the door and now, with the fear behind him, his voice got nasty.

"If you'd just kept your stupid mouth shut—"

He grabbed her arm and she whimpered softly. He yanked her through the open door. When it closed, the room was quiet until Grant made a characteristic comment.

"This is the second time tonight Max has topped you, Brodie."

Broderick let his arm swing down. "I've been thinking the same thing," he said.

"Let go of it," Max said.

Broderick dropped the revolver because he could not take a chance with Rudd between them. Max turned to Grant.

"You too."

"You heard him, Wally," Broderick said. "Let it go."

The gun thudded to the carpet and Tandy darted forward to snatch it up and then turn for Broderick's service revolver. In the momentary silence that followed Rudd spoke for the first time.

"I don't understand," he said incredulously. "I don't know why I'm here or where Alma is or—"

"Shut up!" Max tapped him sharply with the gun.

"Let him talk," Broderick said with a casualness he did not feel. "We're not going anywhere right away, are we? What do you do, Rudd?"

"I've got a dairy farm up in Vermont. I came down for a little holiday and I met Alma, so I stayed on. I've got a man handling the farm for me until I get back."

"Enriquo said maybe Alma was going to get married."

"That's what I hoped. When she wouldn't say yes right off, I asked her to come up to Vermont and stay at a hotel a few days and look my place over. She said she would but she had something she had to do first. She said she'd let me know tonight. That's why I—"

Broderick cut him off as he spoke to Tandy. "She knew about the Jackson girl, huh? It has to be that. You were afraid she'd tell Rudd. Did you give her dope first? Did you put her in the river alive?"

"Wait a minute!" Rudd's voice was suddenly ragged. "Put who in the river? What're you talking about?"

"Alma!" Broderick said. "The harbor police fished her out of the river about an hour ago."

"No," said Rudd, his voice tortured. "No!"

"Yes."

Broderick took a breath and now he gambled because he had nothing else left. He made his tone brutal and it was not entirely acting either—his own cold vindictiveness toward those who had put the woman in the river was genuine.

"Ten days ago another girl was picked up in a vacant lot—she had the side of her head bashed in. I think Alma knew something about it and tonight it was her turn. They put her in the river and if we hadn't identified her they might have pulled it off. If the harbor police hadn't been lucky she might never have been found at all."

Rudd's cheekbones showed white through the tan.

"But she said—"

"They murdered her," Broderick said savagely and eased a step toward Max. "She's in the morgue now. On a slab. On a cold—"

Rudd's stocky figure spun toward Max before Broderick finished. He must have known he did not have much chance with the gun in his back. Perhaps he did not consider this; perhaps he did not care. Whatever the reason, he drove his shoulder into the gun just as Max fired.

There was a muffled report and the back of Rudd's jacket lifted to a temporary peak below the shoulder. They hit the floor together and it shook with the impact as the gun was jarred loose from Max's grasp.

Broderick had followed Rudd by a split second. When the gun slid to one side he scooped it up and whirled toward Tandy who had drawn back against the wall. And this time Broderick got an assist.

The columnist had dived for Tandy when the gun went off and now, with Grant practically on top of him, Tandy couldn't decide on a target. Broderick made a snap shot, feeling the welcome slap of the recoil and seeing Tandy's shoulder jerk sideways under the impact of the slug. As Tandy fell against the wall, Grant hit him and Broderick wheeled toward Max.

The gunman had fought clear of Rudd. He was on his knees now, and as Broderick faced him he whipped out a second gun, a tiny automatic that had come from some inside pocket or holster.

Broderick had time to aim and he did, his wrist stiff and the trigger finger steady. When the gun slammed, Max was slapped backward as if someone had struck him. He dropped the automatic, leaned crazily from his knees, and fell.

Broderick turned again to Tandy, who now sat with his back against the wall. Grant had collected both guns and was watching Tandy. It was then that the shot hammered from somewhere behind, and with that Tandy grabbed his chest and started to tip over.

For an instant Broderick stared, shocked and unbelieving. He saw Tandy sag to the floor before he realized what had happened. Then, as he spun about, he saw that Rudd had pushed up to a sitting position on the floor and was just lowering the automatic Max had dropped.

"That was for Alma," Rudd whispered and then the gun slid from his limp fingers.

Broderick stooped to pick up the automatic. He looked at it, and then at the one he had first taken from Max. He glanced over at Grant, who held Broderick's service revolver and the one Tandy had dropped.

"A lot of iron," Grant said dryly.

Broderick nodded and went to the telephone. He said what he had to say and came back to Rudd. For one who had recently been so hard in actions and manner there was a surprising gentleness in the detective's touch as he lifted the limp figure and carried it to the sofa. When he saw that the man's eyes were open he said,

"You'll be okay. It's high and I think it missed the lung."

"I don't care."

"Sure you care. Only this time you were a little out of your class. The Morgan woman was not your kind—"

"I know what she was," Rudd breathed. "She was on the level with me. It would have worked out. She and I were going to—"

The voice trailed off, the eyes closed, and now Broderick swallowed and went over to Grant. Tandy was sitting up, his gaze cloudy and the stain from the two wounds spreading over his chest.

"I won't lie to you, Lou," Broderick said. "I don't know if you'll make it or not. You'd better talk while you've got the chance. Was I right about Ruth Jackson?"

"You had the racket right." Tandy coughed softly. "But it was an accident. She wanted to pull out and she'd been drinking too much. I guess she lost her nerve. We were sitting around my office late one night—she and Max and me. Alma came to see me because I owed her some back alimony. Jackson got ugly. She began screaming and Max clipped her. She fell like a log and the side of her head hit a door stop . . . crushed it. She was dead before we knew it. Had to take her out and leave her."

"Did Alma threaten you?"

"No, but—" he coughed twice and tried again. "It was Max's idea. With Alma here in town he was willing to let it ride because he knew he could always reach her. But if she married Rudd he was afraid she'd talk someday. He wouldn't take the chance. . .She was dead when she hit the river," he said in a voice that could hardly be

176

heard. "I don't know what Max put in her drink, but she was dead."

His head sagged as he finished and he stayed where he was, chin on chest. Broderick stood up and exhaled noisily. He watched Grant rise. He glanced at Tandy and Rudd and Max.

"What a mess," he said wearily.

"For a guy making a routine check on a suicide," Grant said with unaccustomed respect, "you did a hell of a job."

"I did nothing," Broderick said. "Rudd gave us the break."

"The way I write it will be different," Grant said.

"You lay off!" Broderick poked the columnist's chest with a stiff index finger. "You'll wait till the skipper gets here and you'll print just what he says to print."

Grant blinked at the unexpected fierceness in the detective's tone, as though he understood that, in this, Broderick meant just what he said.

"But—you should get a promotion out of this."

"Hah!" Broderick's mouth twisted. "Promotion, hell. I got an idea the skipper's going to be sore at me on account he missed all this because I didn't get him out of bed." He grunted softly and turned away. "I'll be lucky if they don't measure me for a uniform and slap me back in harness again."

MAIGRET'S CHRISTMAS

BY GEORGES SIMENON

Georges Simenon was born Georges Sim in Liège, Belgium, on February 13, 1903. In the year 1928 alone he published forty books. In 1969 he produced his 200th book, 74 of the 200 having been about Inspector Maigret. On his seventieth birthday, in 1973, with *Maigret and Monsieur Charles* (book #214), he formally announced his retirement from writing because of an inner-ear ailment. In his home above Lake Geneva in Switzerland, he is taping his retirement thoughts. "They are not memoirs," he says. "Not literature. Literature, that's finished."

THE ROUTINE NEVER VARIED. When Maigret went to bed he must have muttered his usual, "Tomorrow morning I shall sleep late." And Mme. Maigret, who over the years should have learned to pay no attention to such casual phrases, had taken him at his word this Christmas day.

It was not quite daylight when he heard her stirring cautiously. He forced himself to breathe regularly and deeply as though he were still asleep. It was like a game. She inched toward the edge of the bed with animal stealth, pausing after each movement to make sure she had not awakened him. He waited anxiously for the inevitable finale, the moment when the bedspring, relieved of her weight, would spring back into place with a faint sigh.

She picked up her clothing from the chair and turned the knob of the bathroom door so slowly that it seemed to take an eternity. It was not until she had reached the distant fastness of the kitchen that she resumed her normal movements.

Maigret had fallen asleep again. Not deeply, nor for long. Long enough, however, for a confused and disturbing dream. Waking, he could not remember what it was, but he knew it was disturbing because he still felt vaguely uneasy.

The crack between the window drapes which never quite closed became a strip of pale, hard daylight. He waited a while longer, lying on his back with his eyes open, savoring the fragrance of fresh coffee. Then he heard the apartment door open and close, and he knew that Mme. Maigret was hurrying downstairs to buy him hot *croissants* from the bakery at the corner of the Rue Amelot.

He never ate in the morning. His breakfast consisted of black coffee. But his wife clung to her ritual: on Sundays and holidays he was supposed to lie in bed until midmorning while she went out for *croissants.*

He got up, stepped into his slippers, put on his dressing gown, and drew the curtains. He knew he was doing wrong. His wife would be heartbroken. But while he was willing to make almost any sacrifice to please her, he simply could not stay in bed longer than he felt like it.

It was not snowing. It was nonsense, of course, for a man past 50 to be disappointed because there was no snow on Christmas morning; but then middle-aged people never have as much sense as young folks sometimes imagine.

A dirty, turbid sky hung low over the rooftops. The Boulevard

Richard-Lenoir was completely deserted. The words *Fils et Cie.,
Bonded Warehouses* on the sign above the portecochère across the
street stood out as black as mourning crêpe. The *F*, for some
strange reason, seemed particularly dismal.

He heard his wife moving about in the kitchen again. She came
into the dining room on tiptoe, as though he were still asleep
instead of looking out the window. He glanced at his watch on the
night table. It was only ten past 8.

The night before the Maigrets had gone to the theater. They
would have loved dropping in for a snack at some restaurant, like
everyone else on Christmas Eve, but all tables were reserved for
Réveillon supper. So they had walked home arm in arm, getting in a
few minutes before midnight. Thus they hadn't long to wait before
exchanging presents.

He got a pipe, as usual. Her present was an electric coffee pot,
the latest model that she had wanted so much, and, not to break
with tradition, a dozen finely embroidered handkerchiefs.

Still looking out the window, Maigret absently filled his new pipe.
The shutters were still closed on some of the windows across the
boulevard. Not many people were up. Here and there a light
burned in a window, probably left by children who had leaped out
of bed at the crack of dawn to rush for their presents under the
Christmas tree.

In the quiet Maigret apartment the morning promised to be a
lazy one for just the two of them. Maigret would loiter in his
dressing gown until quite late. He would not even shave. He would
dawdle in the kitchen, talking to his wife while she put the lunch on
the stove. Just the two of them.

He wasn't sad exactly, but his dream—which he couldn't
remember—had left him jumpy. Or perhaps it wasn't his dream.
Perhaps it was Christmas. He had to be extra careful on Christmas
Day, careful of his words, the way Mme. Maigret had been careful
of her movements in getting out of bed. Her nerves, too, were
especially sensitive on Christmas.

Oh, well, why think of all that? He would just be careful to say
nothing untoward. He would be careful not to look out of the
window when the neighborhood children began to appear on the
sidewalks with their Christmas toys.

All the houses in the street had children. Or almost all. The street
would soon echo to the shrill blast of toy horns, the roll of toy
drums, and the crack of toy pistols. The little girls were probably
already cradling their new dolls.

A few years ago he had proposed more or less at random: "Why
don't we take a little trip for Christmas?"

"Where?" she had replied with her infallible common sense.

Where, indeed? Whom would they visit? They had no relatives except her sister who lived too far away. And why spend Christmas in some second-rate country inn, or at a hotel in some strange town?

Oh, well, he'd feel better after he had his coffee. He was never at his best until he'd drunk his first cup of coffee and lit his first pipe.

Just as he was reaching for the knob, the door opened noiselessly and Mme. Maigret appeared carrying a tray. She looked at the empty bed, then turned her disappointed eyes upon her husband. She was on the verge of tears.

"You got up!" She looked as though she had been up for hours herself, every hair in place, a picture of neatness in her crisp clean apron. "And I was so happy about serving your breakfast in bed."

He had tried a hundred times, as subtly as he could, to make her understand that he didn't like eating breakfast in bed. It made him uncomfortable. It made him feel like an invalid or a senile old gaffer. But for Mme. Maigret breakfast in bed was the symbol of leisure and luxury, the ideal way to start Sunday or a holiday.

"Don't you want to go back to bed?"

No, he did not. Decidedly not. He hadn't the courage.

"Then come to breakfast in the kitchen. And Merry Christmas."

"Merry Christmas! . . . You're not angry?"

They were in the dining room. He surveyed the silver tray on a corner of the table, the steaming cup of coffee, the golden-brown *croissants*. He put down his pipe and ate a *croissant* to please his wife, but he remained standing, looking out the window.

"It's snowing."

It wasn't real snow. It was a fine white dust sifting down from the sky, but it reminded Maigret that when he was a small boy he used to stick out his tongue to lick up a few of the tiny flakes.

His gaze focused on the entrance to the building across the street, next door to the warehouse. Two women had just come out, both bareheaded. One of them, a blonde of about 30, had thrown a coat over her shoulders without stopping to slip her arms into the sleeves. The other, a brunette, older and thinner, was hugging a shawl.

The blonde seemed to hesitate, ready to turn back. Her slim little companion was insistent and Maigret had the impression that she was pointing toward his window. The appearance of the concierge in the doorway behind them seemed to tip the scales in favor of the little brunette. The blonde looked back apprehensively, then crossed the street.

"What are you looking at?"

"Nothing . . . two women. . . ."

"What are they doing?"

"I think they're coming here."

The two women had stopped in the middle of the street and were looking up in the direction of the Maigret apartment.

"I hope they're not coming here to bother you on Christmas Day. My housework's not even done." Nobody would have guessed it. There wasn't a speck of dust on any of the polished furniture. "Are you sure they're coming here?"

"We'll soon find out."

To be on the safe side, he went to comb his hair, brush his teeth, and splash a little water on his face. He was still in his room, relighting his pipe, when he heard the doorbell. Mme. Maigret was evidently putting up a strong hedgehog defense, for it was some time before she came for him.

"They insist on speaking to you," she whispered. "They claim it's very important and they need advice. I know one of them."

"Which one?"

"The skinny little one, Mlle. Doncoeur. She lives across the street on the same floor as ours. She's a very nice person and she does embroidery for a firm in the Faubourg Saint-Honoré. I sometimes wonder if she isn't in love with you."

"Why?"

"Because she works near the window, and when you leave the house in the morning she sometimes gets up to watch you go down the street."

"How old is she?"

"Forty-five to fifty. Aren't you getting dressed?"

Doesn't a man have the right to lounge in his dressing gown, even if people come to bother him at 8:30 on Christmas morning? Well, he'd compromise. He'd put his trousers on underneath the robe.

The two women were standing when he walked into the dining room.

"Excuse me, mesdames . . ."

Perhaps Mme. Maigret was right. Mlle. Doncoeur did not blush; she paled, smiled, lost her smile, smiled again. She opened her mouth to speak but said nothing.

The blonde, on the other hand, was perfectly composed. She said with a touch of humor: "Coming here wasn't my idea."

"Would you sit down, please?"

Maigret noticed that the blonde was wearing a housedress under her coat and that her legs were bare. Mlle. Doncoeur was dressed as though for church.

"You perhaps wonder at our boldness in coming to you like this," Mlle. Doncoeur said finally, choosing her words carefully. "Like everyone in the neighborhood, we are honored to have such a distinguished neighbor. . . ." She paused, blushed, and stared at the tray. "We're keeping you from your breakfast."

"I've finished. I'm at your service."

"Something happened in our building last night, or rather this morning, which was so unusual that I felt it was our duty to speak to you about it immediately. Madame Martin did not want to disturb you, but I told her—"

"You also live across the street, Madame Martin?"

"Yes, Monsieur." Madame Martin was obviously unhappy at being forced to take this step. Mlle. Doncoeur, however, was now fully wound up.

"We live on the same floor, just across from your windows." She blushed again, as if she were making a confession. "Monsieur Martin is often out of town, which is natural enough since he is a traveling salesman. For the past two months their little girl has been in bed, as a result of a silly accident. . . ."

Maigret turned politely to the blonde. "You have a daughter?"

"Well, not a daughter exactly. She's our niece. Her mother died two years ago and she's been living with us ever since. The girl broke her leg on the stairs. She should have been up and about after six weeks, but there were complications.

"Your husband is on the road at present?"

"He should be in Bergerac."

"I'm listening, Mlle. Doncoeur."

Mme. Maigret had detoured through the bathroom to regain the kitchen. The clatter of pots and pans had resumed. Maigret stared through the window at the leaden sky.

"I got up early this morning as usual," said Mlle. Doncoeur, "to go to first mass."

"And you did go to church?"

"Yes. I stayed for three masses. I got home about 7:30 and prepared my breakfast. You may have seen the light in my window."

Maigret's gesture indicated he had not been watching.

"I was in a hurry to take a few goodies to Colette. It's very sad for a child to spend Christmas in bed. Colette is Madame Martin's niece."

"How old is she?"

"Seven. Isn't that right, Madame Martin?"

"She'll be seven in January."

"So at 8 o'clock I knocked at the door of their apartment—"

"I wasn't up," the blonde interrupted. "I sometimes sleep rather late."

"As I was saying, I knocked. Madame Martin kept me waiting for a moment while she slipped on her négligée. I had my arms full, and I asked if I could take my presents in to Colette."

Maigret noted that the blonde was making a mental inventory of the apartment, stopping occasionally to dart a sharp, suspicious glance in his direction.

"We opened the door to her room together. . . ."

"The child has a room of her own?"

"Yes. There are two bedrooms in the apartment, a dressing room, a kitchen, and a dining room. But I must tell you—No, I'm getting ahead of myself. We had just opened the door and since the room was dark, Madame Martin had switched on the light . . ."

"Colette was awake?"

"Yes. It was easy to see she'd been awake for some time, waiting. You know how children are on Christmas morning. If she could use her legs, she would certainly have got up long since to see what Father Christmas had brought her. Perhaps another child would have called out. But Colette is already a little lady. She's much older than her age. She thinks a lot."

Now Madame Martin was looking out the window. Maigret tried to guess which apartment was hers. It must be the last one to the right, the one with the two lighted windows.

"I wished her a Merry Christmas," Mlle. Doncoeur continued. "I said to her, and these were my exact words, 'Darling, look what Father Christmas left in my apartment for you.'"

Madame Martin was clasping and unclasping her fingers.

"And do you know what she answered me, without even looking to see what I'd brought? They were only trifles, anyhow. She said, 'I saw him.'

"'Whom did you see?'

"'Father Christmas.'

"'When did you see him?' I asked. 'Where?'

"'Right here, last night. He came to my room.'

"That's exactly what she said, isn't it, Madame Martin? With any other child, we would have smiled. But as I told you, Colette is already a little lady. She doesn't joke. I said, 'How could you see him, since it was dark?'

"'He had a light.'

"'You mean he turned on the electricity?'

"'No. He had a flashlight. Look, Mama Loraine.'

"I must tell you that the little girl calls Madame Martin 'Mama,' which is natural enough, since her own mother is dead and Madame Martin has been taking her place."

The monologue had become a confused buzzing in Maigret's ears. He had not drunk his second cup of coffee and his pipe had gone out. He asked without conviction: "Did she really see someone?"

"Yes, Monsieur l'Inspecteur. And that's why I insisted that Madame Martin come to speak to you. Colette did see someone and she proved it to us. With a sly little smile she threw back the bed-sheet and showed us a magnificent doll . . . a beautiful big doll she was cuddling and which I swear was not in the house yesterday."

"You didn't give your niece a doll, Madame Martin?"

"I was going to give her one, but mine was not nearly as nice. I got it yesterday afternoon at the Galeries, and I was holding it behind me this morning when we came into her room."

"In other words, someone *did* come into your apartment last night?"

"That's not all," said Mlle. Doncoeur quickly; she was not to be stopped. "Colette never tells lies. She's not a child who imagines things. And when we questioned her, she said the man was certainly Father Christmas because he wore a white beard and a bright red coat."

"At what time did she wake up?"

"She doesn't know—sometime during the night. She opened her eyes because she thought she saw a light. And there was a light, shining on the floor near the fireplace."

"I can't understand it," sighed Madame Martin. "Unless my husband has some explanation . . ."

But Mlle. Doncoeur was not to be diverted from her story. It was obvious that she was the one who had questioned the child, just as she was the one who had thought of Maigret. She resumed:

"Colette said, 'Father Christmas was squatting on the floor, and he was bending over, as though he were working at something.'"

"She wasn't frightened?"

"No. She just watched him. This morning she told us he was busy making a hole in the floor. She thought he wanted to go through the floor to visit the people downstairs—that's the Delormes who have a little boy of three—because the chimney was too narrow. The man must have sensed she was watching him, because he got up, came over to the bed, and gave Colette the big doll. Then he put his finger to his lips."

"Did she see him leave?"

"Yes."

"Through the floor?"

"No, by the door."

"Into what room does this door open?"

"Directly into the outside hall. There is another door that opens into the apartment, but the hall door is like a private entrance because the room used to be rented separately."

"Wasn't the door locked?"

"Of course," Madame Martin intervened. "I wouldn't let the child sleep in a room that wasn't locked from the outside."

"Then the door was forced?"

"Probably. I don't know. Mlle. Doncoeur immediately suggested we come to see you."

"Did you find a hole in the floor?"

Madame Martin shrugged wearily, but Mlle. Doncoeur answered for her.

"Not a hole exactly, but you could see that the floor boards had been moved."

"Tell me, Madame Martin, have you any idea what might have been hidden under the flooring?"

"No, Monsieur."

"How long have you lived in this apartment?"

"Since my marriage, five years ago."

"And this room was part of the apartment then?"

"Yes."

"You know who lived there before you?"

"My husband. He's 38. He was 33 when we were married, and he had his own furniture then. He liked to have his own home to come back to when he returned to Paris from the road."

"Do you think he might have wanted to surprise Colette?"

"He is six or seven hundred kilometers from here."

"Where did you say?"

"In Bergerac. His itinerary is planned in advance and he rarely deviates from his schedule."

"For what firm does he travel?"

"He covers the central and southwest territory for Zenith Watches. It's an important line, as you probably know. He has a very good job."

"There isn't a finer man on earth!" exclaimed Mlle. Doncoeur. She blushed, then added, "Except you, Monsieur l'Inspecteur."

"As I understand it then, someone got into your apartment last night disguised as Father Christmas."

"According to the little girl."

"Didn't you hear anything? Is your room far from the little girl's?"

"There's the dining room between us."

"Don't you leave the connecting doors open at night?"

"It isn't necessary. Colette is not afraid, and as a rule she never wakes up. If she wants anything, she has a little bell on her night table."

"Did you go out last night?"

"I did not, Monsieur l'Inspecteur." Madame Martin was annoyed.

"Did you receive visitors?"

"I do not receive visitors while my husband is away."

Maigret glanced at Mlle. Doncoeur whose expression did not change. So Madame Martin was telling the truth.

"Did you go to bed late?"

"I read until midnight. As soon as the radio played *Minuit, Chrétiens,* I went to bed."

"And you heard nothing unusual?"

"Nothing."

"Have you asked the concierge if she clicked the latch to let in any stranger last night?"

"I asked her," Mlle. Doncoeur volunteered. "She says she didn't."

"And you found nothing missing from your apartment this morning, Madame Martin? Nothing disturbed in the dining room?"

"No."

"Who is with the little girl now?"

"No one. She's used to staying alone. I can't be at home all day. I have marketing to do, errands to run. . . ."

"I understand. You told me Colette is an orphan?"

"Her mother is dead."

"So her father is living. Where is he?"

"Her father's name is Paul Martin. He's my husband's brother. As to telling you where he is—"Madame Martin sketched a vague gesture.

"When did you see him last?"

"About a month ago. A little longer. It was around All Saints' Day. He was finishing a novena."

"I beg your pardon?"

"I may as well tell you everything at once," said Madame Martin with a faint smile, "since we seem to be washing our family linen." She glanced reproachfully at Mlle. Doncoeur. "My brother-in-law, especially since he lost his wife, is not quite respectable."

"What do you mean exactly?"

"He drinks. He always drank a little, but he never used to get into trouble. He had a good job with a furniture store in the Faubourg Saint-Antoine. But since the accident . . ."

"The accident to his daughter?"

"No, to his wife. He borrowed a car from a friend one Sunday about three years ago and took his wife and little girl to the country. They had lunch at a roadside inn near Mantesla-Jolie and he drank too much white wine. He sang most of the way back to Paris—until he ran into something near the Bougival bridge. His wife was killed instantly. He cracked his own skull and it's a miracle he's still alive. Colette escaped without a scratch. Paul hasn't been a man since then. We've practically adopted the little girl. He comes to see her occasionally when he's sober. Then he starts over again. . . ."

"Do you know where he lives?"

Another vague gesture. "Everywhere. We've seen him loitering around the Bastille like a beggar. Sometimes he sells papers in the street. I can speak freely in front of Mlle. Doncoeur because unfortunately the whole house knows about him."

"Don't you think he might have dressed up as Father Christmas to call on his daughter?"

"That's what I told Mlle. Doncoeur, but she insisted on coming to see you anyhow."

"Because I see no reason for him to take up the flooring," said Mlle. Doncoeur acidly.

"Or perhaps your husband returned to Paris unexpectedly. . . ."

"It's certainly something of the sort. I'm not at all disturbed. But Mlle. Doncoeur—"

Decidedly Madame Martin had not crossed the boulevard light-heartedly.

"Do you know where your husband might be staying in Bergerac?"

"Yes. At the Hotel de Bordeaux."

"You hadn't thought of telephoning him?"

"We have no phone. There's only one in the house—the people on the second floor, and they hate to be disturbed."

"Would you object to my calling the Hotel de Bordeaux?"

Madame Martin started to nod, then hesitated. "He'll think something terrible has happened."

"You can speak to him yourself."

"He's not used to my phoning him on the road."

"You'd rather he not know what's happening?"

"That's not so. I'll talk to him if you like."

Maigret picked up the phone and placed the call. Ten minutes later he was connected with the Hotel de Bordeaux in Bergerac. He passed the instrument to Madame Martin.

"Hello. . . . Monsieur Martin, please. . . . Yes, Monsieur Jean Martin. . . . No matter. Wake him up."

She put her hand over the mouthpiece. "He's still asleep. They've gone to call him."

Then she retreated into silence, evidently rehearsing the words she was to speak to her husband.

"Hello? . . . Hello, darling. . . . What? . . . Yes, Merry Christmas! . . . Yes, everything's all right. . . . Colette is fine. . . . No, that's not why I phoned. . . . No, no, no! Nothing's wrong. Please don't worry!" She repeated each word separately. "Please . . . don't . . . worry! I just want to tell you about a strange thing that happened last night. Somebody dressed up like Father Christmas and came into Colette's room. . . . No, no! He didn't hurt her. He gave her a big doll. . . . Yes, *doll*! . . . And he did queer things to the floor. He removed two boards which he put back in a hurry. . . . Mlle.

Doncoeur thought I should report it to the police inspector who lives across the street. I'm there now. . . . You don't understand? Neither do I. . . . You want me to put him on?" She passed the instrument to Maigret. "He wants to speak to you."

A warm masculine voice came over the wire, the voice of an anxious, puzzled man.

"Are you sure my wife and the little girl are all right? . . . It's all so incredible! If it were just the doll, I might suspect my brother. Loraine will tell you about him. Loraine is my wife. Ask her. . . . But he wouldn't have removed the flooring. . . . Do you think I'd better come home? I can get a train for Paris at three this afternoon. . . . What? . . . Thank you so much. It's good to know you'll look out for them."

Loraine Martin took back the phone.

"See, darling? The inspector says there's no danger. It would be foolish to break your trip now. It might spoil your chances of being transferred permanently to Paris. . . ."

Mlle. Doncoeur was watching her closely and there was little tenderness in the spinster's eyes.

" . . . I promise to wire you or phone you if there's anything new. . . . She's playing quietly with her new doll. . . . No, I haven't had time yet to give her your present. I'll go right home and do it now."

Madame Martin hung up and declared: "You see." Then, after a pause, "Forgive me for bothering you. It's really not my fault. I'm sure this is all the work of some practical joker . . . unless it's my brother-in-law. When he's been drinking there's no telling what he might do."

"Do you expect to see him today? Don't you think he might want to see his daughter?"

"That depends. If he's been drinking, no. He's very careful never to come around in that condition."

"May I have your permission to come over and talk with Colette a little later?"

"I see no reason why you shouldn't—if you think it worth-while. . . ."

"Thank you, Monsieur Maigret!" exclaimed Mlle. Doncoeur. Her expression was half grateful, half conspiratorial. "She's such an interesting child! You'll see!"

She backed toward the door.

A few minutes later Maigret watched the two women cross the boulevard. Mlle. Doncoeur, close on the heels of Madame Martin, turned to look up at the windows of the Maigret apartment.

Mme. Maigret opened the kitchen door, flooding the dining room with the aroma of browning onions. She asked gently:

"Are you happy?"

He pretended not to understand. Luckily he had been too busy to think much about the middle-aged couple who had nobody to make a fuss over this Christmas morning.

It was time for him to shave and call on Colette.

He was just about to lather his face when he decided to make a phone call. He didn't bother with his dressing gown. Clad only in pajamas, he dropped into the easy chair by the window—*his* chair—and watched the smoke curling up from all the chimney pots while his call went through.

The ringing at the other end—in headquarters at the Quai des Orfèvres—had a different sound from all other rings. It evoked for him the long empty corridors, the vacant offices, the operator stuck with holiday duty at the switchboard. . . . Then he heard the operator call Lucas with the words: "The boss wants you."

He felt a little like one of his wife's friends who could imagine no greater joy—which she experienced daily—than lying in bed all morning, with her windows closed and curtains drawn, and telephoning all her friends, one after the other. By the soft glow of her night-light she managed to maintain a constant state of just having awakened. "What? Ten o'clock already? How's the weather? Is it raining? Have you been out yet? Have you done all your marketing?" And as she established telephonic connection with the hurly-burly of the workaday world, she would sink more and more voluptuously into the warm softness of her bed.

"That you, Chief?"

Maigret, too, felt a need for contact with the working world. He wanted to ask Lucas who was on duty with him, what they were doing, how the shop looked on this Christmas morning.

"Nothing new? Not too busy?"

"Nothing to speak of. Routine. . . ."

"I'd like you to get me some information. You can probably do this by phone. First of all, I want a list of all convicts released from prison the last two or three months."

"Which prison?"

"All prisons. But don't bother with any who haven't served at least five years. Then check and see if any of them has ever lived on Boulevard Richard-Lenoir. Got that?"

"I'm making notes."

Lucas was probably somewhat bewildered but he would never admit it.

"Another thing. I want you to locate a man named Paul Martin, a drunk, no fixed address, who frequently hangs out around the Place de la Bastille. I don't want him arrested. I don't want him molested. I just want to know where he spent Christmas Eve. The commissariats should help you on this one."

190

No use trying. Maigret simply could not reproduce the idle mood of his wife's friend. On the contrary, it embarrassed him to be lolling at home in his pajamas, unshaven, phoning from his favorite easy chair, looking out at a scene of complete peace and quiet in which there was no movement except the smoke curling up from the chimney-pots, while at the other end of the wire good old Lucas had been on duty since six in the morning and was probably already unwrapping his sandwiches.

"That's not quite all, old man. I want you to call Bergerac long distance. There's a traveling salesman by the name of Jean Martin staying at the Hotel de Bordeaux there. No, Jean. It's his brother. I want to know if Jean Martin got a telegram or a phone call from Paris last night or any time yesterday. And while you're about it, find out where he spent Christmas Eve. I think that's all."

"Shall I call you back?"

"Not right away. I've got to go out for a while. I'll call you when I get home."

"Something happen in your neighborhood?"

"I don't know yet. Maybe."

Mme. Maigret came into the bathroom to talk to him while he finished dressing. He did not put on his overcoat. The smoke curling slowly upward from so many chimney pots blended with the gray of the sky and conjured up the image of just as many overheated apartments, cramped rooms in which he would not be invited to make himself at home. He refused to be uncomfortable. He would put on his hat to cross the boulevard, and that was all.

The building across the way was very much like the one he lived in—old but clean, a little dreary, particularly on a drab December morning. He avoided stopping at the concierge's lodge, but noted she watched him with some annoyance. Doors opened silently as he climbed the stairs. He heard whispering, the padding of slippered feet.

Mlle. Doncoeur, who had doubtless been watching for him, was waiting on the fourth floor landing. She was both shy and excited, as if keeping a secret tryst with a lover.

"This way, Monsieur Maigret. She went out a little while ago."

He frowned, and she noted the fact.

"I told her that you were coming and that she had better wait for you, but she said she had not done her marketing yesterday and that there was nothing in the house. She said all the stores would be closed if she waited too long. Come in."

She had opened the door into Madame Martin's dining room, a small, rather dark room which was clean and tidy.

"I'm looking after the little girl until she comes back. I told Colette that you were coming to see her, and she is delighted. I've

191

spoken to her about you. She's only afraid you might take back her doll."

"When did Madame Martin decide to go out?"

"As soon as we came back across the street, she started dressing."

"Did she dress completely?"

"I don't understand."

"I mean, I suppose she dresses differently when she goes downtown than when she merely goes shopping in the neighborhood."

"She was quite dressed up. She put on her hat and gloves. And she carried her shopping bag."

Before going to see Colette, Maigret stepped into the kitchen and glanced at the breakfast dishes.

"Did she eat before you came to see me?"

"No. I didn't give her a chance."

"And when she came back?"

"She just made herself a cup of black coffee. I fixed breakfast for Colette while Madame Martin got dressed."

There was a larder on the ledge of the window looking out on the courtyard. Maigret carefully examined its contents: butter, eggs, vegetables, some cold meat. He found two uncut loaves of fresh bread in the kitchen cupboard. Colette had eaten *croissants* with her hot chocolate.

"How well do you know Madame Martin?"

"We're neighbors, aren't we? And I've seen more of her since Colette has been in bed. She often asks me to keep an eye on the little girl when she goes out."

"Does she go out much?"

"Not very often. Just for her marketing."

Maigret tried to analyze the curious impression he had had on entering the apartment. There was something in the atmosphere that disturbed him, something about the arrangement of the furniture, the special kind of neatness that prevailed, even the smell of the place. As he followed Mlle. Doncoeur into the dining room, he thought he knew what it was.

Madame Martin had told him that her husband had lived in this apartment before their marriage. And even though Madame Martin had lived there for five years, it had remained a bachelor's apartment. He pointed to the two enlarged photographs standing on opposite ends of the mantelpiece.

"Who are they?"

"Monsieur Martin's father and mother."

"Doesn't Madame Martin have photos of her own parents about?"

"I've never heard her speak of them. I suppose she's an orphan."

192

Even the bedroom was without the feminine touch. He opened a closet. Next to the neat rows of masculine clothing, the woman's clothes were hanging, mostly severely tailored suits and conservative dresses. He did not open the bureau drawers but he was sure they did not contain the usual trinkets and knickknacks that women collect.

"Mademoiselle Doncoeur!" called a calm little voice.

"Let's talk to Colette," said Maigret.

The child's room was as austere and cold as the others. The little girl lay in a bed too large for her, her face solemn, her eyes questioning but trusting.

"Are you the inspector, Monsieur?"

"I'm the inspector, my girl. Don't be afraid."

"I'm not afraid. Hasn't Mama Loraine come home yet?"

Maigret pursed his lips. The Martins had practically adopted their niece, yet the child said "Mama Loraine," not just "Mama."

"Do you believe it was Father Christmas who came to see me last night?" Colette asked Maigret.

"I'm sure it was."

"Mama Loraine doesn't believe it. She never believes me."

The girl had a dainty, attractive little face, with very bright eyes that stared at Maigret with level persistence. The plaster cast which sheathed one leg all the way to the hip made a thick bulge under the blankets.

Mlle. Doncoeur hovered in the doorway, evidently anxious to leave the inspector alone with the girl. She said: "I must run home for a moment to make sure my lunch isn't burning."

Maigret sat down beside the bed, wondering how to go about questioning the girl.

"Do you love Mama Loraine very much?" he began.

"Yes, Monsieur." She replied without hesitation and without enthusiasm.

"And your papa?"

"Which one? Because I have two papas, you know—Papa Paul and Papa Jean."

"Has it been a long time since you saw Papa Paul?"

"I don't remember. Perhaps several weeks. He promised to bring me a toy for Christmas, but he hasn't come yet. He must be sick."

"Is he often sick?"

"Yes, often. When he's sick he doesn't come to see me."

"And your Papa Jean?"

"He's away on a trip, but he'll be back for New Year's. Maybe then he'll be appointed to the Paris office and won't have to go away any more. That would make him very happy and me, too."

"Do many of your friends come to see you since you've been in bed?"

"What friends? The girls in school don't know where I live. Or maybe they know but their parents don't let them come alone."

"What about Mama Loraine's friends? Or your papa's?"

"Nobody comes, ever."

"Ever? Are you sure?"

"Only the man to read the gas meter, or for the electricity. I can hear them, because the door is almost always open. I recognize their voices. Once a man came and I didn't recognize his voice. Or twice."

"How long ago was that?"

"The first time was the day after my accident. I remember because the doctor just left."

"Who was it?"

"I didn't see him. He knocked at the other door. I heard him talking and then Mama Loraine came and closed my door. They talked for quite a while but I couldn't hear very well. Afterward Mama Loraine said it was a man who wanted to sell her some insurance. I don't know what that is."

"And he came back?"

"Five or six days ago. It was night and I'd already turned off my light. I wasn't asleep, though. I heard someone knock, and they talked in low voices like the first time. Mademoiselle Doncoeur sometimes comes over in the evening, but I could tell it wasn't she. I thought they were quarreling and I was frightened. I called out, and Mama Loraine came in and said it was the man about the insurance again and I should go to sleep."

"Did he stay long?"

"I don't know. I think I fell asleep."

"And you didn't see him either time?"

"No, but I'd recognized his voice."

"Even though he speaks in low tones?"

"Yes, that's why. When he speaks low it sounds just like a big bumblebee. I can keep the doll, can't I? Mama Loraine bought me two boxes of candy and a little sewing kit. She bought me a doll, too, but it wasn't nearly as big as the doll Father Christmas gave me, because she's not rich. She showed it to me this morning before she left, and then she put it back in the box. I have the big one now, so I won't need the little one and Mama Loraine can take it back to the store."

The apartment was overheated, yet Maigret felt suddenly cold. The building was very much like the one across the street, yet not only did the rooms seem smaller and stuffier, but the whole world seemed smaller and meaner over here.

He bent over the floor near the fireplace. He lifted the loose floor boards, but saw nothing but an empty, dusty cavity smelling of dampness. There were scratches on the planks which indicated they had been forced up with a chisel or some similar instrument.

He examined the outside door and found indications that it had been forced. It was obviously an amateur's work, and luckily for him, the job had been an easy one.

"Father Christmas wasn't angry when he saw you watching him?"

"No, Monsieur. He was busy making a hole in the floor so he could go and see the little boy downstairs."

"Did he speak to you?"

"I think he smiled at me. I'm not sure, though, because of his whiskers. It wasn't very light. But I'm sure he put his finger to his lips so I wouldn't call anybody, because grown-ups aren't supposed to see Father Christmas. Did you ever see him?"

"A very long time ago."

"When you were little?"

Maigret heard footsteps in the hallway. The door opened and Madame Martin came in. She was wearing a gray tailored suit and a small beige hat and carried a brown shopping bag. She was visibly cold, for her skin was taut and very white, yet she must have hurried up the stairs, since there were two pink spots on her cheeks and she was out of breath. Unsmiling, she asked Maigret:

"Has she been a good girl?" Then, as she took off her jacket, "I apologize for making you wait. I had so many things to buy, and I was afraid the stores would all be closed later on."

"Did you meet anyone?"

"What do you mean?"

"Nothing. I was wondering if anyone tried to speak to you."

She had had plenty of time to go much further than the Rue Amelot or the Rue du Chemin-Vert where most of the neighborhood shops were located. She had even had time to go across Paris and back by taxi or the Metro.

Mlle. Doncoeur returned to ask if there was anything she could do. Madame Martin was about to say no when Maigret intervened: "I'd like you to stay with Colette while I step into the next room."

Mlle. Doncoeur understood that he wanted her to keep the child busy while he questioned the foster-mother. Madame Martin must have understood, too, but she gave no indication.

"Please come in. Do you mind if I take off my things?"

Madame Martin put her packages in the kitchen. She took off her hat and fluffed out her pale blonde hair. When she had closed the bedroom door, she said: "Mlle. Doncoeur is all excited. This is quite an event, isn't it, for an old maid—particularly an old maid who cuts out every newspaper article about a certain police inspector, and who finally has the inspector in her own house. . . . Do you mind?"

She had taken a cigarette from a silver case, tapped the end, and snapped a lighter. The gesture somehow prompted Maigret's next question:

"You're not working, Madame Martin?"

"It would be difficult to hold a job and take care of the house and the little girl, too, even when the child is in school. Besides, my husband won't allow me to work."

"But you did work before you met him?"

"Naturally. I had to earn a living. Won't you sit down?"

He lowered himself into a rude raffia-bottomed chair. She rested one thigh against the edge of a table.

"You were a typist?"

"I have been a typist."

"For long?"

"Quite a while."

"You were still a typist when you met Martin? You must forgive me for asking these personal questions."

"It's your job."

"You were married five years ago. Were you working then? Just a moment. May I ask your age?"

"I'm thirty-three. I was twenty-eight then, and I was working for a Monsieur Lorilleux in the Palais-Royal arcades."

"As his secretary?"

"Monsieur Lorilleux had a jewelry shop. Or more exactly, he sold souvenirs and old coins. You know those old shops in the Palais-Royal. I was salesgirl, bookkeeper, *and* secretary. I took care of the shop when he was away."

"He was married?"

"And father of three children."

"You left him to marry Martin?"

"Not exactly. Jean didn't want me to go on working, but he wasn't making very much money then and I had quite a good job. So I kept it for the first few months."

"And then?"

"Then a strange thing happened. One morning I came to work at 9 o'clock as usual, and I found the door locked. I thought Monsieur Lorilleux had overslept, so I waited. . . ."

"Where did he live?"

"Rue Mazarine with his family. At half-past 9 I began to worry."

"Was he dead?"

"No. I phoned his wife, who said he had left the house at 8 o'clock as usual."

"Where did you telephone from?"

"From the glove shop next door. I waited all morning. His wife came down and we went to the commissariat together to report him missing, but the police didn't take it very seriously. They just asked his wife if he'd ever had heart trouble, if he had a mistress—things like that. But he was never seen again, and nobody ever heard from him. Then some Polish people bought out the store and my husband made me stop working."

"How long was this after your marriage?"

"Four months."

"Your husband was already traveling in the southwest?"

"He had the same territory he has now."

"Was he in Paris when your employer disappeared?"

"No, I don't think so."

"Didn't the police examine the premises?"

"Nothing had been touched since the night before. Nothing was missing."

"Do you know what became of Madame Lorilleux?"

"She lived for a while on the money from the sale of the store. Then she bought a little dry-goods shop not far from here, in the Rue du Pas-de-la-Mule. Her children must be grown up now, probably married."

"Do you still see her?"

"I go into her shop once in a while. That's how I know she's in business in the neighborhood. The first time I saw her there I didn't recognize her."

"How long ago was that?"

"I don't know. Six months or so."

"Does she have a telephone?"

"I don't know. Why?"

"What kind of man was Lorilleux?"

"You mean physically?"

"Let's start with the physical."

"He was a big man, taller than you, and broader. He was fat, but flabby, if you know what I mean. And rather sloppy-looking."

"How old?"

"Around fifty. I can't say exactly. He had a little salt-and-pepper moustache, and his clothes were always too big for him."

"You were familiar with his habits?"

"He walked to work every morning. He got down fifteen minutes ahead of me and cleared up the mail before I arrived. He didn't talk much. He was a rather gloomy person. He spent most of the day in the little office behind the shop."

"No romantic adventures?"

"Not that I know of."

"Didn't he try to make love to you?"

197

"No!" The monosyllable was tartly emphatic.

"But he thought highly of you?"

"I think I was a great help to him."

"Did your husband ever meet him?"

"They never spoke. Jean sometimes came to wait for me outside the shop, but he never came in." A note of impatience, tinged with anger, crept into her voice. "Is that all you want to know?"

"May I point out, Madame Martin, that you are the one who came to get me?"

"Only because a crazy old maid practically dragged me there so she could get a close-up look at you."

"You don't like Mlle. Doncoeur?"

"I don't like people who can't mind their own business."

"People like Mlle. Doncoeur?"

"You know that we've taken in my brother-in-law's child. Believe me or not, I've done everything I can for her. I treat her the way I'd treat my own child. . . ." She paused to light a fresh cigarette, and Maigret tried unsuccessfully to picture her as a doting mother. ". . . And now that old maid is always over here, offering to help me with the child. Every time I start to go out, I find her in the hallway, smiling sweetly, and saying 'You mustn't leave Colette all alone, Madame Martin. Let me go in and keep her company.' I sometimes wonder if she doesn't go through my drawers when I'm out."

"You put up with her, nevertheless."

"How can I help it? Colette asks for her, especially since she's been in bed. And my husband is fond of her because when he was a bachelor, she took care of him when he was sick with pleurisy."

"Have you already returned the doll you bought for Colette's Christmas?"

She frowned and glanced at the door to the child's bedroom. "I see you've been questioning the little girl. No, I haven't taken it back for the very good reason that all the big department stores are closed today. Would you like to see it?"

She spoke defiantly, expecting him to refuse, but he said nothing. He examined the cardboard box, noting the price tag. It was a very cheap doll.

"May I ask where you went this morning?"

"I did my marketing."

"Rue Amelot or Rue du Chemin-Vert?"

"Both."

"If I may be indiscreet, what did you buy?"

Furious, she stormed into the kitchen, snatched up her shopping bag, and dumped it on the dining room table. "Look for yourself!"

There were three tins of sardines, butter, potatoes, some ham, and a head of lettuce.

She fixed him with a hard, unwavering stare. She was not in the least nervous. Spiteful, rather.

"Any more questions?"

"Yes. The name of your insurance agent."

"My insurance. . . ." She was obviously puzzled.

"Insurance agent. The one who came to see you."

"I'm sorry. I was at a loss for a moment because you spoke of *my* agent as though he were really handling a policy for me. So Colette told you that, too? Actually, a man did come to see me twice, trying to sell me a policy. He was one of those door-to-door salesmen, and I thought at first he was selling vacuum cleaners, not life insurance. I had a terrible time getting rid of him."

"Did he stay long?"

"Long enough for me to convince him that I had no desire to take out a policy."

"What company did he represent?"

"He told me but I've forgotten. Something with 'Mutual' in it."

"And he came back later?"

"Yes."

"What time does Colette usually go to sleep?"

"I put out her light at 7:30, but sometimes she talks to herself in the dark until much later."

"So the second time the insurance man called, it was later than 7:30?"

"Possibly." She saw the trap. "I remember now I was washing the dishes."

"And you let him in?"

"He had his foot in the door."

"Did he call on other tenants in the building?"

"I haven't the slightest idea, but I'm sure you will inquire. Must you cross-examine me like a criminal, just because a little girl imagines she saw Santa Claus? If my husband were here—"

"By the way, does your husband carry life insurance?"

"I think so. In fact, I'm sure he does."

Maigret picked up his hat from a chair and started for the door. Madame Martin seemed surprised.

"Is that all?"

"That's all. It seems your brother-in-law promised to come and see his daughter today. If he should come, I would be grateful if you let me know. And now I'd like a few words with Mlle. Doncoeur."

There was a convent smell about Mlle. Doncoeur's apartment, but there was no dog or cat in sight, no antimacassars on the chairs, no bric-a-brac on the mantelpiece.

"Have you lived in this house long, Mlle. Doncoeur?"

"Twenty-five years, Monsieur l'Inspecteur. I'm one of the oldest tenants. I remember when I first moved in you were already living across the street, and you wore long moustaches."

"Who lived in the next apartment before Martin moved in?"

"A public works engineer. I don't remember his name, but I could look it up for you. He had a wife and daughter. The girl was a deaf-mute. It was very sad. They went to live somewhere in the country."

"Have you been bothered by a door-to-door insurance agent recently?"

"Not recently. There was one who came around two or three years ago."

"You don't like Madame Martin, do you?"

"Why?"

"I asked if you liked Madame Martin?"

"Well, if I had a son . . ."

"Go on."

"If I had a son I don't think I would like Madame Martin for a daughter-in-law. Especially as Monsieur Martin is such a nice man, so kind."

"You think he is unhappy with his wife?"

"I wouldn't say that. I have nothing against her, really. She can't help being the kind of woman she is."

"What kind of woman is she?"

"I couldn't say, exactly. You've seen her. You're a better judge of those things than I am. In a way, she's not like a woman at all. I'll wager she never shed a tear in her life. True, she is bringing up the child properly, decently, but she never says a kind word to her. She acts exasperated when I tell Colette a fairy tale. I'm sure she's told the girl there is no Santa Claus. Luckily Colette doesn't believe her."

"The child doesn't like her either, does she?"

"Colette is always obedient. She tries to do what's expected of her. I think she's just as happy to be left alone."

"Is she alone much?"

"Not much. I'm not reproaching Madame Martin. It's hard to explain. She wants to live her own life. She's not interested in others. She doesn't even talk much about herself."

"Have you ever met her brother-in-law—Colette's father?"

"I've seen him on the landing, but I've never spoken to him. He walks with his head down, as if he were ashamed of something. He always looks as if he slept in his clothes. No, I don't think it was he last night, Monsieur Maigret. He's not the type. Unless he was terribly drunk."

On his way out Maigret looked in at the concierge's lodge, a dark cubicle where the light burned all day.

200

It was noon when he started back across the boulevard. Curtains stirred at the windows of the house behind him. Curtains stirred at his own window, too. Mme. Maigret was watching for him so she would know when to put the chicken in the oven. He waved to her. He wanted very much to stick out his tongue and lick up a few of the tiny snow flakes that were drifting down. He could still remember their taste.

"I wonder if that little tike is happy over there," sighed Mme. Maigret as she got up from the table to bring the coffee from the kitchen.

She could see he wasn't listening. He had pushed back his chair and was stuffing his pipe while staring at the purring stove. For her own satisfaction she added: "I don't see how she could be happy with that woman."

He smiled vaguely, as he always did when he hadn't heard what she said, and continued to stare at the tiny flames licking evenly at the mica windows of the salamander. There were at least ten similar stoves in the house, all purring alike in ten similar dining rooms with wine and cakes on the table, a carafe of cordial waiting on the sideboard, and all the windows pale with the same hard, gray light of a sunless day.

It was perhaps this very familiarity which had been confusing his subconscious since morning. Nine times out of ten his investigations plunged him abruptly into new surroundings, set him at grips with people of a world he barely knew, people of a social level whose habits and manners he had to study from scratch. But in this case, which was not really a case since he had no official assignment, the whole approach was unfamiliar because the background was too familiar. For the first time in his career something professional was happening in his own world, in a building which might just as well be his building.

The Martins could easily have been living on his floor, instead of across the street, and it would probably have been Mme. Maigret who would look after Colette when her aunt was away. There was an elderly maiden lady living just under him who was a plumper, paler replica of Mlle. Doncoeur. The frames of the photographs of Martin's father and mother were exactly the same as those which framed Maigret's father and mother, and the enlargements had probably been made by the same studio.

Was that what was bothering him? He seemed to lack perspective. He was unable to look at people and things from a fresh, new viewpoint.

He had detailed his morning activities during dinner—a pleasant little Christmas dinner which had left him with an overstuffed feeling—and his wife had listened while looking at the windows across the street with an air of embarrassment.

"Is the concierge sure that nobody could have come in from outside?"

"She's not so sure any more. She was entertaining friends until after midnight. And after she had gone to bed, there were considerable comings and goings, which is natural for Christmas Eve."

"Do you think something more is going to happen?"

That was a question that had been plaguing Maigret all morning. First of all, he had to consider that Madame Martin had not come to see him spontaneously, but only on the insistence of Mlle. Doncoeur. If she had got up earlier, if she had been the first to see the doll and hear the story of Father Christmas, wouldn't she have kept the secret and ordered the little girl to say nothing?

And later she had taken the first opportunity to go out, even though there was plenty to eat in the house for the day. And she had been so absentminded that she had bought butter, although there was still a pound in the cooler.

Maigret got up from the table and resettled himself in his chair by the window. He picked up the phone and called Quai des Orfèvres.

"Lucas?"

"I got what you wanted, Chief. I have a list of all prisoners released for the last four months. There aren't as many as I thought. And none of them has lived in the Boulevard Richard-Lenoir at any time."

That didn't matter any more now. At first Maigret had thought that a tenant across the street might have hidden money or stolen goods under the floor before he was arrested. His first thought on getting out of jail would be to recover his booty. With the little girl bedridden, however, the room was occupied day and night. Impersonating Father Christmas would not have been a bad idea to get into the room. Had this been the case, however, Madame Martin would not have been so reluctant to call in Maigret. Nor would she have been in so great a hurry to get out of the house afterward on such a flimsy pretext. So Maigret had abandoned that theory.

"You want me to check each prisoner further?"

"Never mind. Any news about Paul Martin?"

"That was easy. He's known in every station house between the Bastille and the Hotel de Ville, and even on the Boulevard Saint-Michel."

"What did he do last night?"

"First he went aboard the Salvation Army barge to eat. He's a regular there one day a week and yesterday was his day. They had a special feast for Christmas Eve and he had to stand in line quite a while."

"After that?"

"About 11 o'clock he went to the Latin Quarter and opened doors for motorists in front of a nightclub. He must have collected enough money in tips to get himself a sinkful, because he was picked up dead drunk near the Place Maubert at 4 in the morning. He was taken to the station house to sleep it off, and was there until 11 this morning. They'd just turned him loose when I phoned, and they promised to bring him to me when they find him again. He still had a few francs in his pocket."

"What about Bergerac?"

"Jean Martin is taking the afternoon train for Paris. He was quite upset by a phone call he got this morning."

"He got only one call?"

"Only one this morning. He got a call last night while he was eating dinner."

"You know who called him?"

"The desk clerk says it was a man's voice, asking for Monsieur Jean Martin. He sent somebody into the dining room for Martin but when Martin got to the phone, the caller had hung up. Seems it spoiled his whole evening. He went out with a bunch of traveling salesmen to some local hot-spot where there were pretty girls and whatnot, but after drinking a few glasses of champagne, he couldn't talk about anything except his wife and daughter. The niece he calls his daughter, it seems. He had such a dismal evening that he went home early. 3 A.M. That's all you wanted to know, Chief?"

When Maigret didn't reply, Lucas had to satisfy his curiosity. "You still phoning from home, Chief? What's happening up your way? Somebody get killed?"

"I still can't say. Right now all I know is that the principals are a seven-year-old girl, a doll, and Father Christmas."

"Ah?"

"One more thing. Try to get me the home address of the manager of Zenith Watches, Avenue de l'Opéra. You ought to be able to raise somebody there, even on Christmas Day. Call me back."

"Soon as I have something."

Mme. Maigret had just served him a glass of Alsatian plum brandy which her sister had sent them. He smacked his lips. For a moment he was tempted to forget all about the business of the doll and Father Christmas. It would be much simpler just to take his wife to the movies. . . .

"What color eyes has she?"

It took him a moment to realize that the only person in the case who interested Mme. Maigret was the little girl.

"Why, I'm not quite sure. They can't be dark. She has blonde hair."

"So they're blue."

"Maybe they're blue. Very light, in any case. And they are very serious."

"Because she doesn't look at things like a child. Does she laugh?"

"She hasn't much to laugh about."

"A child can always laugh if she feels herself surrounded by people she can trust, people who let her act her age. I don't like that woman."

"You prefer Mlle. Doncoeur?"

"She may be an old maid but I'm sure she knows more about children than that Madame Martin. I've seen *her* in the shops. Madame Martin is one of those women who watch the scales, and take their money out of their pocketbooks, coin by coin. She always looks around suspiciously, as though everybody was out to cheat her."

The telephone rang as Mme. Maigret was repeating, "I don't like that woman."

It was Lucas calling, with the address of Monsieur Arthur Godefroy, general manager in France for Zenith Watches. He lived in a sumptuous villa at Saint-Cloud, and Lucas had discovered that he was at home. He added:

"Paul Martin is here, Chief. When they brought him in, he started crying. He thought something had happened to his daughter. But he's all right now—except for an awful hangover. What do I do with him?"

"Anyone around who can come up here with him?"

"Torrence just came on duty. I think he could use a little fresh air. He looks as if he had a hard night, too. Anything more from me, Chief?"

"Yes. Call Palais-Royal station. About five years ago a man named Lorilleux disappeared without a trace. He sold jewelry and old coins in the Palais-Royal arcades. Get me all the details you can on his disappearance."

Maigret smiled as he noted that his wife was sitting opposite him with her knitting. He had never before worked on a case in such domestic surroundings.

"Do I call you back?" asked Lucas.

"I don't expect to move an inch from my chair."

A moment later Maigret was talking to Monsieur Godefroy, who had a decided Swiss accent. The Zenith manager thought that something must have happened to Jean Martin, for anyone to be making inquiries about him on Christmas Day.

"Most able . . . most devoted . . . I'm bringing him into Paris to be assistant manager next year. . . . Next week, that is . . . Why do you ask? Has anything—? Be still, you!" He paused to quiet the juvenile hubbub in the background. "You must excuse me. All my family is with me today and—"

"Tell me, Monsieur Godefroy, has anyone called your office these last few days to inquire about Monsieur Martin's current address?"

"Yesterday morning, as a matter of fact. I was very busy with the holiday rush, but he asked to speak to me personally. I forget what name he gave. He said he had an extremely important message for Jean Martin, so I told him how to get in touch with Martin in Bergerac."

"He asked you nothing else?"

"No. He hung up at once. Is anything wrong?"

"I hope not. Thank you very much, Monsieur."

The screams of children began again in the background and Maigret said goodbye.

"Were you listening?"

"I heard what you said. I didn't hear his answers."

"A man called the office yesterday morning to get Martin's address. The same man undoubtedly called Bergerac that evening to make sure Martin was still there, and therefore would not be at his Boulevard Richard-Lenoir address for Christmas Eve."

"The same man who appeared last night as Father Christmas?"

"More than likely. That seems to clear Paul Martin. He would not have to make two phone calls to find out where his brother was. Madame Martin would have told him."

"You're really getting excited about this case. You're delighted that it came up, aren't you? Confess!" And while Maigret was racking his brain for excuses, she added: "It's quite natural. I'm fascinated, too. How much longer do you think the child will have to keep her leg in a cast?"

"I didn't ask."

"I wonder what sort of complications she could have had?"

Maigret looked at her curiously. Unconsciously she had switched his mind onto a new track.

"That's not such a stupid remark you just made."

"What did I say?"

"After all, since she's been in bed for two months, she should be up and around soon, barring really serious complications."

"She'll probably have to walk on crutches at first."

"That's not the point. In a few days then, or a few weeks at most, she will no longer be confined to her room. She'll go for a walk with Madame Martin. And the coast will be clear for anyone to enter the apartment without dressing up like Father Christmas."

Mme. Maigret's lips were moving. While listening to her husband and watching his face, she was counting stitches.

"First of all, the presence of the child forced our man to use trickery. She's been in bed for two months—two months for him to wait. Without the complications the flooring could have been taken up several weeks ago. Our man must have had urgent reasons for acting at once, without further delay."

"Monsieur Martin will return to Paris in a few days?"

"Exactly."

"What do you suppose the man found underneath the floor?"

"Did he really find anything? If not, his problem is still as pressing as it was last night. So he will take further action."

"What action?"

"I don't know."

"Look, Maigret, isn't the child in danger? Do you think she's safe with that woman?"

"I could answer that if I knew where Madame Martin went this morning on the pretext of doing her shopping." He picked up the phone again and called Police Judiciaire.

"I'm pestering you again, Lucas. I want you to locate a taxi that picked up a passenger this morning between 9 and 10 somewhere near Boulevard Richard-Lenoir. The fare was a woman in her early thirties, blonde, slim but solidly built. She was wearing a gray suit and a beige hat. She carried a brown shopping bag. I want to know her destination. There couldn't have been so many cabs on the street at that hour."

"Is Paul Martin with you?"

"Not yet."

"He'll be there soon. About that other thing, the Lorilleux matter, the Palais-Royal boys are checking their files. You'll have the data in a few minutes."

Jean Martin must be taking his train in Bergerac at this moment. Little Colette was probably taking her nap. Mlle. Doncoeur was doubtless sitting behind her window curtain, wondering what Maigret was up to.

People were beginning to come out now, families with their children, the children with their new toys. There were certainly queues in front of the cinemas. . . .

A taxi stopped in front of the house. Footsteps sounded in the stairway. Mme. Maigret went to the door. The deep bass voice of Torrence rumbled: "You there, Chief?"

Torrence came in with an ageless man who hugged the walls and looked humbly at the floor. Maigret went to the sideboard and filled two glasses with plum brandy.

"To your health," he said.

The man looked at Maigret with surprised, anxious eyes. He raised a trembling, hesitant hand.

"To your health, Monsieur Martin. I'm sorry to make you come all the way up here, but you won't have far to go now to see your daughter."

"Nothing has happened to her?"

"No, no. When I saw her this morning she was playing with her new doll. You can go, Torrence. Lucas must need you."

Mme. Maigret had gone into the bedroom with her knitting. She was sitting on the edge of the bed, counting her stitches.

"Sit down, Monsieur Martin."

The man had touched his lips to the glass and set it down. He looked at it uneasily.

"You have nothing to worry about. Just tell yourself that I know all about you."

"I wanted to visit her this morning," the man sighed. "I swore I would go to bed early so I could wish her a Merry Christmas."

"I know that, too."

"It's always the same. I swear I'll take just one drink, just enough to pick me up. . . ."

"You have only one brother, Monsieur Martin?"

"Yes, Jean. He's six years younger than I am. He and my wife and my daughter were all I had to love in this world."

"You don't love your sister-in-law?"

He shivered. He seemed both startled and embarrassed.

"I have nothing against Loraine."

"You entrusted your child to her, didn't you?"

"Well, yes, that is to say, when my wife died and I began to slip. . . ."

"I understand. Is your daughter happy?"

"I think so, yes. She never complains."

"Have you ever tried to get back on your feet?"

"Every night I promise myself to turn over a new leaf, but next day I start all over again. I even went to see a doctor. I followed his advice for a few days. But when I went back, he was very busy. He said I ought to be in a special sanatorium."

He reached for his glass, then hesitated. Maigret picked up his own glass and took a swallow to encourage him.

"Did you ever meet a man in your sister-in-law's apartment?"

"No. I think she's above reproach on that score."

"Do you know where your brother first met her?"

"In a little restaurant in the Rue Beaujolais where he used to eat when he was in Paris. It was near the shop where Loraine was working."

"Did they have a long engagement?"

"I can't say. Jean was on the road for two months and when he came back he told me he was getting married."

"Were you his best man?"

"Yes. Loraine has no family in Paris. She's an orphan. So her landlady acted as her witness. Is there something wrong?"

"I don't know yet. A man entered Colette's room last night dressed as Father Christmas. He gave your girl a doll, and lifted two loose boards from the floor."

"Do you think I'm in fit condition to see her?"

"You can go over in a little while. If you feel like it you can shave here. Do you think your brother would be likely to hide anything under the floor?"

"Jean? Never!"

"Even if he wanted to hide something from his wife?"

"He doesn't hide things from his wife. You don't know him. He's one of those rare humans—a scrupulously honest man. When he comes home from the road, she knows exactly how much money he has left, to the last centime."

"Is she jealous?"

Paul Martin did not reply.

"I advise you to tell me what you know. Remember that your daughter is involved in this."

"I don't think that Loraine is especially jealous. Not of women, at least. Perhaps about money. At least that's what my poor wife always said. She didn't like Loraine."

"Why not?"

"She used to say that Loraine's lips were too thin, that she was too polite, too cold, always on the defensive. My wife always thought that Loraine set her cap for Jean because he had a good job with a future and owned his own furniture."

"Loraine had no money of her own?"

"She never speaks of her family. I understand her father died when she was very young and her mother did housework somewhere in the Glacière quarter. My poor wife used to say, 'Loraine knows what she wants.'"

"Do you think she was Lorilleux's mistress?"

Paul Martin did not reply. Malgret poured him another finger of plum brandy. Martin gave him a grateful look, but he did not touch the glass. Perhaps he was thinking that his daughter might notice his breath when he crossed the street later on.

"I'll get you a cup of coffee in a moment. . . . Your wife must have had her own ideas on the subject."

"How did you know? Please note that my wife never spoke disparagingly about people. But with Loraine it was almost pathological. Whenever we were to meet my sister-in-law, I used to beg my wife not to show her antipathy. It's funny that you should bring all that up now, at this time in my life. Do you think I did wrong in letting her take Colette? I sometimes think so. But what else could I have done?"

"You didn't answer my question about Loraine's former employer."

"Oh, yes. My wife always said it was very convenient for Loraine to have married a man who was away from home so much."

"You know where she lived before her marriage?"

"In a street just off Boulevard Sébastopol, on the right as you walk from Rue de Rivoli toward the Boulevard. I remember we picked her up there the day of the wedding."

"Rue Pernelle?"

"That's it. The fourth or fifth house on the left side of the street is a quiet rooming house, quite respectable. People who work in the neighborhood live there. I remember there were several little actresses from the Châtelet."

"Would you like to shave, Monsieur Martin?"

"I'm ashamed. Still, since my daughter is just across the street. . . ."

"Come with me."

Maigret took him through the kitchen so he wouldn't have to meet Mme. Maigret in the bedroom. He set out the necessary toilet articles, not forgetting a clothes brush.

When he returned to the dining room, Mme. Maigret poked her head through the door and whispered: "What's he doing?"

"He's shaving."

Once more Maigret reached for the telephone. He was certainly giving poor Lucas a busy Christmas Day.

"Are you indispensable at the office?"

"Not if Torrence sits in for me. I've got the information you wanted."

"In just a moment. I want you to jump over to Rue Pernelle. There's a rooming house a few doors down from the Boulevard Sébastopol. If the proprietor wasn't there five years ago, try to dig up someone who lived there then. I want everything you can find out on a certain Loraine. . . ."

"Loraine who?"

"Just a minute, I didn't think of that."

Through the bathroom door he asked Martin for the maiden name of his sister-in-law. A few seconds later he was on the phone again.

"Loraine Boitel," he told Lucas. "The landlady of this rooming

209

house was witness at her marriage to Jean Martin. Loraine Boitel was working for Lorilleux at the time. Try to find out if she was more than a secretary to him, and if he ever came to see her. And work fast. This may be urgent. What have you got on Lorilleux?"

"He was quite a fellow. At home in the Rue Mazarine he was a good respectable family man. In his Palais-Royal shop he not only sold old coins and souvenirs of Paris, but he had a fine collection of pornographic books and obscene pictures."

"Not unusual for the Palais-Royal."

"I don't know what else went on there. There was a big divan covered with red silk rep in the back room, but the investigation was never pushed. Seems there were a lot of important names among his customers."

"What about Loraine Boitel?"

"The report barely mentions her, except that she waited all morning for Lorilleux the day he disappeared. I was on the phone about this when Langlois of the Financial Squad came into my office. The name Lorilleux rang a bell in the back of his mind and he went to check his files. Nothing definite on him, but he'd been making frequent trips to Switzerland and back, and there was a lot of gold smuggling going on at that time. Lorilleux was stopped and searched at the frontier several times, but they never found anything on him."

"Lucas, old man, hurry over to Rue Pernelle. I'm more than ever convinced that this is urgent."

Paul Martin appeared in the doorway, his pale cheeks close-shaven.

"I don't know how to thank you. I'm very much embarrassed."

"You'll visit your daughter now, won't you? I don't know how long you usually stay, but today I don't want you to leave until I come for you."

"I can't very well stay all night, can I?"

"Stay all night if necessary. Manage the best you can."

"Is the little girl in danger?"

"I don't know, but your place today is with your daughter."

Paul Martin drank his black coffee avidly, and started for the stairway. The door had just closed after him when Mme. Maigret rushed into the dining room.

"You can't let him go to see his daughter empty-handed on Christmas Day!"

"But—" Maigret was about to say that there just didn't happen to be a doll around the house, when his wife thrust a small shiny object into his hands. It was a gold thimble which had been in her sewing basket for years but which she never used.

"Give him that. Little girls always like thimbles. Hurry!"

He shouted from the landing: "Monsieur Martin! Just a minute, Monsieur Martin!"

He closed the man's fingers over the thimble. "Don't tell a soul where you got this."

Before reentering the dining room he stood for a moment on the threshold, grumbling. Then he sighed: "I hope you've finished making me play Father Christmas."

"I'll bet she likes the thimble as well as a doll. It's something grown-ups use, you know."

They watched the man cross the boulevard. Before going into the house he turned to look up at Maigret's windows, as if seeking encouragement.

"Do you think he'll ever be cured?"

"I doubt it."

"If anything happens to that woman, to Madame Martin. . . ."

"Well?"

"Nothing. I was thinking of the little girl. I wonder what would become of her."

Ten minutes passed. Maigret had opened his newspaper and lighted his pipe. His wife had settled down again with her knitting. She was counting stitches when he exhaled a cloud of smoke and murmured: "You haven't even seen her."

Maigret was looking for an old envelope, on the back of which he had jotted down a few notes summing up the day's events. He found it in a drawer into which Mme. Maigret always stuffed any papers she found lying around the house.

This was the only investigation, he mused, which he had ever conducted practically in its entirety from his favorite armchair. It was also unusual in that no dramatic stroke of luck had come to his aid. True, luck had been on his side, in that he had been able to muster all his facts by the simplest and most direct means. How many times had he deployed scores of detectives on an all-night search for some minor detail. This might have happened, for instance, if Monsieur Arthur Godefroy of Zenith had gone home to Zurich for Christmas, or if he had been out of reach of a telephone. Or if Monsieur Godefroy had been unaware of the telephone inquiry regarding the whereabouts of Jean Martin.

When Lucas arrived shortly after 4 o'clock, his nose red and his face pinched with the cold, he too could report the same kind of undramatic luck.

A thick yellow fog, unusual for Paris, had settled over the city. Lights shone in all the windows, floating in the murk like ships at sea or distant beacons. Familiar details had been blotted out so completely that Maigret half-expected to hear the moans of foghorns.

For some reason, perhaps because of some boyhood memory, Maigret was pleased to see the weather thicken. He was also pleased to see Lucas walk into his apartment, take off his overcoat, sit down, and stretch out his frozen hands toward the fire.

In appearance, Lucas was a reduced-scale model of Maigret—a head shorter, half as broad in the shoulders, half as stern in expression although he tried hard. Without conscious imitation but with conscious admiration, Lucas had copied his chief's slightest gestures, postures, and changes of expression—even to the ceremony of inhaling the fragrance of the plum brandy before touching his lips to the glass.

The landlady of the rooming house in the Rue Pernelle had been killed in a subway accident two years earlier, Lucas reported. Luckily, the place had been taken over by the former night watchman, who had been in trouble with the police on morals charges.

"So it was easy enough to make him talk," said Lucas, lighting a pipe much too large for him. "I was surprised that he had the money to buy the house, but he explained that he was front man for a big investor who had money in all sorts of enterprises but didn't like to have his name used."

"What kind of dump is it?"

"Looks respectable. Clean enough. Office on the mezzanine. Rooms by the month, some by the week, and a few on the second floor by the hour."

"He remembers Loraine?"

"Very well. She lived there more than three years. I got the impression he didn't like her because she was tight-fisted."

"Did Lorilleux come to see her?"

"On my way to the Rue Pernelle I picked up a photo of Lorilleux at the Palais-Royal station. The new landlord recognized him right away."

"Lorilleux went up to her room often?"

"Two or three times a month. He always had baggage with him, he always arrived around 1 o'clock in the morning, and always left before 6. I checked the timetables. There's a train from Switzerland around midnight and another at 6 in the morning. He must have told his wife he was taking the 6 o'clock train."

"Nothing else?"

"Nothing, except that Loraine was stingy with tips, and always cooked her dinner on an alcohol burner, even though the house rules said no cooking in the rooms."

"No other men?"

"No. Very respectable except for Lorilleux. The landlady was witness at her wedding."

Maigret glanced at his wife. He had insisted she remain in the room when Lucas came. She stuck to her knitting, trying to make believe she was not there.

Torrence was out in the fog, going from garage to garage, checking the trip-sheets of taxi fleets. The two men waited serenely, deep in their easy chairs, each holding a glass of plum brandy with the same pose. Maigret felt a pleasant numbness creeping over him.

His Christmas luck held out with the taxis, too. Sometimes it took days to run down a particular taxi driver, particularly when the cab in question did not belong to a fleet. Cruising drivers were the hardest to locate; they sometimes never even read the newspapers. But shortly before 5 o'clock Torrence called from the Saint-Ouen.

"I found one of the taxis," he reported.

"One? Was there more than one?"

"Looks that way. This man picked up the woman at the corner of Boulevard Richard-Lenoir and Boulevard Voltaire this morning. He drove her to Rue de Maubeuge, opposite the Gare du Nord, where she paid him off."

"Did she go into the railway station?"

"No. The chauffeur says she went into a luggage shop that keeps open on Sundays and holidays. After that he doesn't know."

"Where's the driver now?"

"Right here in the garage. He just checked in."

"Send him to me, will you? Right away. I don't care how he gets here as long as it's in a hurry. Now I want you to find me the cab that brought her home."

"Sure, Chief, as soon as I get myself a coffee with a stick in it. It's damned cold out here."

Maigret glanced through the window. There was a shadow against Mlle. Doncoeur's curtains. He turned to Lucas.

"Look in the phone book for a luggage shop across from the Gare du Nord."

Lucas took only a minute to come up with a number, which Maigret dialed.

"Hello, this is the Police Judiciaire. Shortly before 10 this morning a young woman bought something in your shop, probably a valise. She was a blonde, wearing a gray suit and a beige hat. She carried a brown shopping bag. Do you remember her?"

Perhaps trade was slack on Christmas Day. Or perhaps it was easier to remember customers who shopped on Christmas. In any case, the voice on the phone replied:

"Certainly, I waited on her myself. She said she had to leave suddenly for Cambrai because her sister was ill, and she didn't have time to go home for her bags. She wanted a cheap valise, and I sold her a fiber model we have on sale. She paid me and went into the bar next door. I was standing in the doorway and a little later I saw her walking toward the station, carrying the valise."

"Are you alone in your shop?"

"I have one clerk on duty."

"Can you leave him alone for half an hour? Fine! Then jump in a taxi and come to this address. I'll pay the fare, of course."

"And the return fare? Shall I have the cab wait?"

"Have him wait, yes."

According to Maigret's notes on the back of the envelope, the first taxi driver arrived at 5:50 P.M. He was somewhat surprised, since he had been summoned by the police, to find himself in a private apartment. He recognized Maigret, however, and made no effort to disguise his curious interest in how the famous inspector lived.

"I want you to climb to the fourth floor of the house just across the street. If the concierge stops you, tell her you're going to see Madame Martin."

"Madame Martin. I got it."

"Go to the door at the end of the hall and ring the bell. If a blond opens the door and you recognize her, make some excuse—You're on the wrong floor, anything you think of. If somebody else answers, ask to speak to Madame Martin personally.

"And then?"

"Then you come back here and tell me whether or not she is the fare you drove to Rue de Maubeuge this morning."

"I'll be right back, Inspector."

As the door closed, Maigret smiled in spite of himself.

"The first call will make her worry a little. The second, if all goes well, will make her panicky. The third, if Torrence has any luck—"

Torrence, too, was having his run of Christmas luck. The phone rang and he reported:

"I think I've found him, Chief. I dug up a driver who picked up a woman answering your description at the Gare du Nord, only he didn't take her to Boulevard Richard-Lenoir. He dropped her at the corner of Boulevard Beaumarchais and the Rue du Chemin-Vert."

"Send him to me."

"He's a little squiffed."

"No matter. Where are you?"

"The Barbès garage."

"Then it won't be much out of your way to stop by the Gare du Nord. Go to the check room. Unfortunately it won't be the same man on duty, but try to find out if a small new valise was checked between 9:30 and 10 this morning. It's made of fiber and shouldn't be too heavy. Get the number of the check. They won't let you take the valise without a warrant, so try to get the name and address of the man on duty this morning."

"What next?"

"Phone me. I'll wait for your second taxi driver. If he's been drinking, better write down my address for him, so he won't get lost."

Mme. Maigret was back in the kitchen, preparing the evening meal. She hadn't dared ask whether Lucas would eat with them.

Maigret wondered if Paul Martin was still across the street with his daughter. Had Madame Martin tried to get rid of him?

The bell rang again. Two men stood at the door.

The first driver had come back from Madame Martin's and had climbed Maigret's stairs behind the luggage dealer.

"Did you recognize her?"

"Sure. She recognized me, too. She turned pale. She ran to close a door behind her, then she asked me what I wanted."

"What did you tell her?"

"That I had the wrong floor. I think maybe she wanted to buy me off, but I didn't give her a chance. But she was watching from the window when I crossed the street. She probably knows I came here."

The luggage dealer was baffled and showed it. He was a middle-aged man, completely bald and equally obsequious. When the driver had gone, Maigret explained what he wanted, and the man objected vociferously.

"One just doesn't do this sort of thing to one's customers," he repeated stubbornly. "One simply does not inform on one's customers, you know."

After a long argument he agreed to call on Madame Martin. To make sure he didn't change his mind, Maigret sent Lucas to follow him.

They returned in less than ten minutes.

"I call your attention to the fact that I have acted under your orders, that I have been compelled—"

"Did you recognize her?"

"Will I be forced to testify under oath?"

"More than likely."

"That would be very bad for my business. People who buy luggage at the last minute are very often people who dislike public mention of their comings and goings."

"You may not have to go to court. Your deposition before the examining magistrate may be sufficient."

"Very well. It was she. She's dressed differently, but I recognized her all right."

"Did she recognize you?"

"She asked immediately who had sent me."

"What did you say?"

"I . . . I don't remember. I was quite upset. I think I said I had rung the wrong bell."

"Did she offer you anything?"

"What do you mean? She didn't even offer me a chair. Luckily. It would have been most unpleasant."

Maigret smiled, somewhat incredulously. He believed that the taxi driver had actually run away from a possible bribe. He wasn't so sure about this prosperous-looking shopkeeper who obviously begrudged his loss of time.

"Thank you for your cooperation."

The luggage dealer departed hastily.

"And now for Number Three, my dear Lucas."

Mme. Maigret was beginning to grow nervous. From the kitchen door she made discreet signs to her husband, beckoning him to join her. She whispered: "Are you sure the father is still across the street?"

"Why?"

"I don't know. I can't make out exactly what you're up to, but I've been thinking about the child, and I'm a little afraid. . . ."

Night had long since fallen. The families were all home again. Few windows across the street remained dark. The silhouette of Mlle. Doncoeur was still very much in evidence.

While waiting for the second taxi driver, Maigret decided to put on his collar and tie. He shouted to Lucas:

"Pour yourself another drop. Aren't you hungry?"

"I'm full of sandwiches, Chief. Only one thing I'd like when we go out: a tall beer, right from the spigot."

The second driver arrived at 6:20. At 6:35 he had returned from across the street, a gleam in his eye.

"She looks even better in her négligée than she does in her street clothes," he said thickly. "She made me come in and she asked who sent me. I didn't know what to say, so I told her I was a talent scout for the Folies Bergère. Was she furious! She's a fine hunk of woman, though, and I mean it. Did you get a look at her legs?"

He was in no hurry to leave. Maigret saw him ogling the bottle of plum brandy with envious eyes, and poured him a glass—to speed him on his way.

"What are you going to do next, Chief?" Lucas had rarely seen Maigret proceed with such caution, preparing each step with such care that he seemed to be mounting an attack on some desperate criminal. And yet the enemy was only a woman, a seemingly insignificant little housewife.

"You think she'll still fight back?"

"Fiercely. And what's more, in cold blood."

"What are you waiting for?"

"The phone call from Torrence."

As if on cue, the telephone rang. Torrence, of course.

"The valise is here all right. It feels practically empty. As you predicted, they won't give it to me without a warrant. The checkroom attendant who was on duty this morning lives in the suburbs, near La Varenne-Saint-Hilaire." A snag at last? Or at least a delay? Maigret frowned. But Torrence continued. "We won't have to go out there, though. When he finishes his day's work here, he plays cornet in a *bal musette* in the Rue de Lappe."

"Go get him for me."

"Shall I bring him to your place?"

Maigret hesitated, thinking of Lucas's yearning for a glass of draft beer.

"No, I'll be across the street. Madame Martin's apartment, fourth floor."

He took down his heavy overcoat. He filled his pipe.

"Coming?" he said to Lucas.

Mme. Maigret ran after him to ask what time he'd be home for dinner. After a moment of hesitation, he smiled.

"The usual time," was his not very reassuring answer.

"Look out for the little girl, will you?"

At 10 o'clock that evening the investigation was still blocked. It was unlikely that anyone in the whole building had gone to sleep, except Colette. She had finally dozed off, with her father sitting in the dark by her bedside.

Torrence had arrived at 7:30 with his part-time musician and checkroom attendant, who declared:

"She's the one. I remember she didn't put the check in her handbag. She slipped it into a big brown shopping bag." And when they took him into the kitchen he added, "That's the bag. Or one exactly like it."

The Martin apartment was very warm. Everyone spoke in low tones, as if they had agreed not to awaken the child. Nobody had eaten. Nobody, apparently, was even hungry. On their way over, Maigret and Lucas had each drunk two beers in a little cafe on the Boulevard Voltaire.

After the cornetist had spoken his piece, Maigret took Torrence aside and murmured fresh instructions.

Every corner of the apartment had been searched. Even the photos of Martin's parents had been taken from their frames, to make sure the baggage check had not been secreted between picture and backing. The dishes had been taken from their shelves and piled on the kitchen table. The larder had been emptied and examined closely. No baggage check.

Madame Martin was still wearing her pale blue négligée. She was chain-smoking cigarettes. What with the smoke from the two men's pipes, a thick blue haze swirled about the lamps.

"You are of course free to say nothing and answer no questions. Your husband will arrive at 11:17. Perhaps you will be more talkative in his presence."

"He doesn't know any more than I do."

"Does he know as much?"

"There's nothing to know. I've told you everything."

She had sat back and denied everything, all along the line. She had conceded only one point. She admitted that Lorilleux had dropped in to see her two or three times at night when she lived in the Rue Pernelle. But she insisted there had been nothing between them, nothing personal.

"In other words he came to talk business—at 1 o'clock in the morning?"

"He used to come to town by a late train, and he didn't like to walk the streets with large sums of money on him. I already told you he might have been smuggling gold, but I had nothing to do with it. You can't arrest me for his activities."

"Did he have large sums of money on him when he disappeared?"

"I don't know. He didn't always take me into his confidence."

"But he did come to see you in your room at night?"

Despite the evidence, she clung to her story of the morning's marketing. She denied ever having seen the two taxi drivers, the luggage dealer, or the check-room attendant.

"If I had really left a package at the Gare du Nord, you would have found the check, wouldn't you?"

She glanced nervously at the clock on the mantel, obviously thinking of her husband's return.

"Admit that the man who came last night found nothing under the floor because you changed the hiding place."

"I know of nothing that was hidden under the floor."

"When you learned of his visit, you decided to move the treasure to the check room for safekeeping."

"I haven't been near the Gare du Nord. There must be thousands of blonds in Paris who answer my description."

"I think I know where we'll find the check."

"You're so very clever."

"Sit over here at this table." Maigret produced a fountain pen and a sheet of paper. "Write your name and address."

She hesitated, then obeyed.

"Tonight every letter mailed in this neighborhood will be examined, and I'll wager we will find one addressed in your handwriting, probably to yourself."

He handed the paper to Lucas with an order to get in touch with the postal authorities. Much to his surprise, the woman reacted visibly.

"You see, it's a very old trick, Little One." For the first time he called her "Little One," the way he would have done if he were questioning her in his office, Quai des Orfèvres.

They were alone now. Maigret slowly paced the floor, while she remained seated.

"In case you're interested," Maigret said slowly, "the thing that shocks me most about you is not what you have done but the cold-blooded way you have done it. You've been dangling at the end of a slender thread since early this morning, and you still haven't blinked an eye. When your husband comes home, you'll try to play the martyr. And yet you know that sooner or later we'll discover the truth."

"But I've done nothing wrong."

"Then why do you lie?"

She did not reply. She was still far from the breaking point. Her nerves were calm, but her mind was obviously racing at top speed, seeking some avenue of escape.

"I'm not saying anything more," she declared. She sat down and pulled the hem of her négligée over her bare knees.

"Suit yourself." Maigret made himself comfortable in a chair opposite her.

"Are you going to stay here all night?" she asked.

"At least until your husband gets home."

"Are you going to tell him about Monsieur Lorilleux's visits to my room?"

"If necessary."

"You're a cad! Jean knows nothing about all this. He had no part in it."

"Unfortunately he is your husband."

When Lucas came back, they were staring at each other in silence.

"Janvier is taking care of the letter, Chief. I met Torrence downstairs. He says the man is in that little bar, two doors down from your house."

She sprang up. "What man?"

Maigret didn't move a muscle. "The man who came here last night. You must have expected him to come back, since he didn't find what he was looking for. And he might be in a different frame of mind this time."

She cast a dismayed glance at the clock. The train from Bergerac was due in twenty minutes. Her husband could be home in 40. She asked: "You know who this man is?"

"I can guess. I could go down and confirm my suspicion. I'd say it is Lorilleux and I'd say he is very eager to get back his property."

"It's not his property!"

"Let's say that, rightly or wrongly, he considers it his property. He must be in desperate straits, this man. He came to see you twice without getting what he wanted. He came back a third time disguised as Father Christmas. And he'll come back again. He'll be surprised to find you have company. I'm convinced that he'll be more talkative than you. Despite the general belief, men always speak more freely than women. Do you think he is armed?"

"I don't know."

"I think he is. He is tired of waiting. I don't know what story you've been telling him, but I'm sure he's fed up with it. The gentleman has a vicious face. There's nothing quite as cruel as a weakling with his back up."

"Shut up!"

"Would you like us to go so that you can be alone with him?"

The back of Maigret's envelope contained the following note: "10:38 P.M.—she decides to talk."

It was not a very connected story at first. It came out in bits and pieces, fragments of sentences interlarded with venomous asides, supplemented by Maigret's own guesses which she either confirmed or amended.

"What do you want to know?"

"Was it money that you left in the check room?"

"Bank notes. Almost a million."

"Did the money belong to Lorilleux?"

"No more to him than to me."

"To one of his customers?"

"Yes. A man named Julian Boissy."

"What became of him?"

"He died."

"How?"

"He was killed."

"By whom?"

"By Monsieur Lorilleux."

"Why?"

"Because I gave him to understand that if he could raise enough money—real money—I might run away with him."

"You were already married?"

"Yes."

"You're not in love with your husband?"

"I despise mediocrity. All my life I've been poor. All my life I've been surrounded by people who have had to scrimp and save, people who have had to sacrifice and count centimes. I've had to scrimp and sacrifice and count centimes myself." She turned savagely on Maigret, as if he had been responsible for all her troubles. "I just didn't want to be poor any more."

"Would you have gone away with Lorilleux?"

"I don't know. Perhaps for a while."

"Long enough to get your hands on his money?"

"I hate you!"

"How was Boissy murdered?"

"Monsieur Boissy was a regular customer of long standing."

"Pornographic literature?"

"He was a lascivious old goat, sure. So are all men. So is Lorilleux. So are you, probably. Boissy was a widower. He lived alone in a hotel room. He was very rich and very stingy. All rich people are stingy."

"That doesn't work both ways, does it? You, for instance, are not rich."

"I would have been rich."

"If Lorilleux had not come back. How did Boissy die?"

"The devaluation of the franc scared him out of his wits. Like everybody else at that time, he wanted gold. Monsieur Lorilleux used to shuttle gold in from Switzerland pretty regularly. And he always demanded payment in advance. One afternoon Monsieur Boissy came in the shop with a fortune in currency. I wasn't there. I had gone out on an errand."

"You planned it that way?"

"No."

"You had no idea what was going to happen?"

"No. Don't try to put words in my mouth. When I came back, Lorilleux was packing the body into a big box."

"And you blackmailed him?"

"No."

"Then why did he disappear after having given you the money?"

"I frightened him."

"You threatened to go to the police?"

"No. I merely told him that our neighbors in the Palais-Royal had been looking at me suspiciously and that I thought he ought to put the money in a safe place for a while. I told him about the loose floor board in my apartment. He thought it would only be for a few days. Two days later he asked me to cross the Belgian frontier with him."

"And you refused?"

"I told him I'd been stopped and questioned by a man who

looked like a police inspector. He was terrified. I gave him some of the money and promised to join him in Brussels as soon as it was safe."

"What did he do with the corpse?"

"He put the box in a taxi and drove to a little country house he owned on the banks of the Marne. I suppose either he buried it there or threw it into the river. Nobody ever missed Monsieur Boissy."

"So you sent Lorilleux to Belgium without you. How did you keep him away for five years?"

"I used to write him, general delivery. I told him the police were after him, and that he probably would read nothing about it in the papers because they were setting a trap for him. I told him the police were always coming back to question me. I even sent him to South America."

"He came back two months ago?"

"About. He was at the end of his rope."

"Didn't you send him any money?"

"Not much."

"Why not?"

She did not reply. She looked at the clock.

"Are you going to arrest me? What will be the charge? I didn't kill Boissy. I wasn't there when he was killed. I had nothing to do with disposing of his body."

"Stop worrying about yourself. You kept the money because all your life you wanted money—not to spend, but to keep, to feel secure, to feel rich and free from want."

"That's my business."

"When Lorilleux came back to ask for money, or to ask you to keep your promise and run away with him, you used Colette as a pretext. You tried to scare him into leaving the country again, didn't you?"

"He stayed in Paris, hiding." Her upper lip curled slightly. "What an idiot! He could have shouted his name from the housetops and nobody would have noticed."

"The business of Father Christmas wasn't idiotic."

"No? The money wasn't under the floorboard any longer. It was right under his nose, in my sewing basket."

"Your husband will be here in ten or fifteen minutes. Lorilleux across the street probably knows it. He's been in touch with Bergerac by phone, and he can read a timetable. He's surely armed. Do you want to wait here for your two men?"

"Take me away! I'll slip on a dress. . . ."

"The check-room stub?"

"General delivery, Boulevard Beaumarchais."

"She did not close the bedroom door after her. Brazenly she

222

dropped the négligée from her shoulders and sat on the edge of the bed to pull on her stockings. She selected a woolen dress from the closet, tossed toilet articles and lingerie into an overnight bag.

"Let's hurry!"

"Your husband?"

"That fool? Leave him for the birds."

"Colette?"

She shrugged.

Mlle. Doncoeur's door opened a crack as they passed.

Downstairs on the sidewalk she clung fearfully to the two men, peering into the fog.

"Take her to the Quai des Orfèvres, Lucas, I'm staying here."

She held back. There was no car in sight, and she was obviously frightened by the prospect of walking into the night with only Lucas to protect her. Lucas was not very big.

"Don't be afraid. Lorilleux is not in this vicinity."

"You lied to me! You—you—"

Maigret went back into the house.

The conference with Jean Martin lasted two hours.

When Maigret left the house at one thirty, the two brothers were in serious conversation. There was a crack of light under Mlle. Doncoeur's door, but she did not open the door as he passed.

When he got home, his wife was asleep in a chair in the dining room. His place at the table was still set. Mme. Maigret awoke with a start.

"You're alone?" When he looked at her with amused surprise, she added, "Didn't you bring the little girl home?"

"Not tonight. She's asleep. You can go for her tomorrow morning."

"Why, then we're going to . . ."

"No, not permanently. Jean Martin may console himself with some decent girl. Or perhaps his brother will get back on his feet and find a new wife. . . ."

"In other words, she won't be ours?"

"Not in fee simple, no. Only on loan. I thought that would be better than nothing. I thought it would make you happy."

"Why, yes, of course. It will make me very happy. But . . . but . . ."

She sniffled once and fumbled for her handkerchief. When she couldn't find it, she buried her face in her apron.

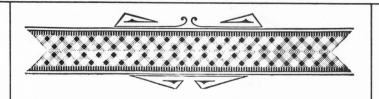

5 − 4 = MURDERER

BY BAYNARD KENDRICK

Baynard Kendrick (b. Philadelphia, April 8, 1894) was
the first president of the Mystery Writers of America. His
service experience in World War I and work with veterans in hospitals led to his creation of the blind detective,
Duncan Maclain (*The Last Express*, 1937). Long fascinated
by Florida, where he now lives, he wrote a historical novel
about the state, *The Flames of Time*, in 1948. His films
include *The Last Express, Eyes in the Night* and *Bright Victory*.
During World War II he received a plaque for his work
with blinded veterans from General Omar Bradley.

THIRTY-FIVE YEARS OF BLINDNESS, and twenty-one years as a private investigator, had driven home one unassailable truth to Captain Duncan Maclain. He lived in a world of blackness, but it was lighted with hearing, touch, taste, and smell. To disregard any notion conveyed to his mind by those four keen senses working together, no matter how foolish it seemed for the moment, was to court trouble, and sometimes to invite death . . .

It lacked five minutes of midnight when Maclain got out of the heavy truck that had picked him up hitchhiking three miles away on 17-E, plodding carefully along with his left foot on the macadam and his right on the grassy shoulder. The friendly driver hadn't guessed he was blind, but had felt Maclain's urgency to reach a telephone.

"That's Nick's Diner over there." People were always uselessly pointing out places to Duncan Maclain. "This is the junction of 303 and 17-E. I'd pull up closer but I bogged there once. You can't put these trucks where you can put a car."

"Thanks a million," said Duncan Maclain.

The truck rolled off. Twenty minutes before, a December storm in the southland had broken with a freezing wind and an icy deluge. Using a stick he had cut in the woods as an emergency cane, the captain stepped out swiftly toward the smell of the diner, strong on the breeze through the pouring rain.

He was miserable, and strung as taut as an overtuned wire. A long-distance call from Philip Barstow, the state's attorney, had brought the captain without Schnucke, his Seeing-Eye dog, from New York to Red Platte that morning by plane. They'd driven 30 miles out to Barstow's one-room hunting cabin, and hunted quail all day. Barstow was one of the captain's oldest friends, and he was never surprised at Maclain's ability to knock down three out of five singles, shooting merely at the sound.

There had been trouble and graft in the State Police, according to Phil Barstow, and the Crime Commission had started a probe on four recent unsolved shootings and on the unrestrained gambling in the vicinity. Colonel William Yerkes, in charge of the State Police, had finally asked Barstow to call in Duncan Maclain. A blind man interested in criminology, looking over the workings of the department, could accomplish more than any sighted investigator, in Yerkes's estimation.

Then, sitting over highballs after dinner in the hunting camp,

Phil Barstow had toppled out of his chair, seized with a sudden heart attack just as he started to explain. He had given the captain Yerkes's private telephone number, 3-2111, and that was about all.

It was the start of a vivid grueling nightmare for Duncan Maclain. He had made Phil Barstow as comfortable as he could, and then left the camp in a panic. Working with his braille hunting-case compass, and following the sand woods-road with a foot in one six-inch-deep rut, he had by some miracle of direction made the state road, 17-E, by 11:30.

His cigarettes, holder, and lighter were on the table when Barstow fell. His wallet, with identification card and money, was in a pocket of his hunting jacket hanging on the cabin wall. A search of his hunting pants and the pockets of the ancient woolen shirt he wore rewarded him with a badly rumpled handkerchief and a single dime. That, at least, was a break, for when he reached a phone he could make his call.

Exactly ninety-six steps from the truck his improvised cane struck an artificial hedge in front of the diner. The captain found an opening a little to his right, took two steps up, and briefly stood listening before he went in.

It might have been a cough he'd heard, or the clearing of a throat. It might have been imagination carried to his overstrung nerves and tired body on the driving rain and rising wind. Whatever it was, it conveyed a feeling of being watched. His listening brought no recurrence. He shrugged and dismissed it as he opened the door and went in.

Nobody spoke and he heard no breathing. He took two steps forward and found the counter. Muffled sounds of running water and the clatter of dishes drifted in toward him—from a pantry, probably, with a swinging-door entrance in back of the counter.

He followed thirteen stools to the right and found a cigarette machine partly blocking a window. A hinged flap there gave a passage through the counter.

He retraced his steps to where he had started and walked on down to the other end, twelve stools more. There he found a telephone booth.

He went inside and shut the door and sat for a space holding on to his dime. A call to Colonel Yerkes would solve everything—get a police car to pick him up at Nick's Diner and dispatch an ambulance to the camp for Phil. It would also do something else—tie Duncan Maclain and Yerkes inextricably together. Maclain was supposed to be looking over the department on his own as Barstow's friend. He wasn't supposed to know the colonel, and didn't. The uncanny judgment that had made the captain what he was, told him in every fiber that to call the colonel was wrong.

He put in his dime, dialed the operator, and asked for the Chief, saying he wanted to report an emergency call.

When he hung up he felt certain an ambulance would get to the camp for Phil and that the Red Platte Hotel would send a car for him. He had explained everything to the chief operator. There was always one great light burning steadily through the blackness, the friendliness of all the world to people who couldn't see.

His dime had even been returned. It would buy a cup of coffee. He put it in his pocket and sat for a space with his forehead wrinkled.

Life was full of patterns to Duncan Maclain and the pattern of the phone booth seemed somehow awry. His hand went over the dial box and paused on top. A double bell was there. That seemed natural enough, although different from the type of dial box he knew in New York. But under the shelf where the telephone sat he found two more boxes fastened to the phone-booth wall. Each of the boxes had bells on top—bells of different shape, designed to give a different sound. It was those boxes that had been cramping him since he first sat down, pressing up against his knee.

He came out, found a stool near the phone booth, and sat down; then he called out, quite loudly, "Hello, is there anybody here?"

"Who do you think I am?" a voice demanded from behind the counter farther down. "Do you think I'm deaf or can't you see?"

"The last one's right," said Duncan Maclain. "I'm blind."

"Well, whatta ya know!"

Steps came toward him in back of the counter. He was conscious of an odor of pomade and clothes long impregnated with cooking. Someone breathed on him—a short man from the location of his head, and heavy, judging from the weight of his steps as he walked along the duckboards in back of the counter. The captain was suddenly conscious of his two-day growth of beard, his damp ragged shirt, and tousled hair.

"You must be that blind guy who goes hunting with Phil Barstow."

"That's right." The captain held out his hand. "I'm Duncan Maclain."

"Well, whatta ya know! I'm Nick Gherigis. I own the joint."

A pudgy hand, freshly wiped but not too dry of dishwater, shook the captain's, confirming his estimation of Nick's height and girth by its feel.

"Phil's been stopping in here for over ten years now. Where is he?"

The captain told Nick what had happened.

"Well whatta ya know!" said Nick Gherigis. "My old lady's got a bum ticker, too. We live out back. She's having to take it easy.

Usually she helps, but right now all the work is on me. I'd drive you back to the camp now, but I don't like to leave her."

"I feel sure the ambulance will get there," Maclain told him.

"It'll get there for Barstow. He's the big wheel around here. You hungry?"

"Plenty."

"I'll fix you up some ham and eggs."

"I only have a dime with me."

"Skip it," Nick said. "Phil will pay me if you don't." He hesitated briefly. "Hell, I suppose if you can shoot a bird you can eat ham and eggs without me feeding you."

The captain said, "I usually manage to find my mouth."

The telephone rang in the booth.

"Shall I answer that for you?" Maclain got up from his stool.

Nick said, "Let it ring. The joint's closed. It's ten past 12. If you'll excuse me a minute I think the old lady's calling me."

Over the intermittent ringing the captain heard the swish of a swinging door. He could follow Nick for a few quick steps. The phone bell rang again and at its pause he felt quite certain that out in the pantry Nick had closed another door.

Maclain sat down on a stool right by the booth. A quick thought struck him that someone might be calling him at Nick's—from the hospital or hotel. Cursing his own stupidity, he reached in the booth without leaving the stool, found the receiver, and put it to his ear.

Nick's voice came over the telephone, trembling in intensity: "A hundred a week is cleaning me now. I'll blow the works before I'll double it. Kate don't know nothing, but I'm leaving her a list that'll jail everyone in the whole damn state if anything happens to me. Now go to hell!"

When the swinging door swished as Nick came back, the captain was sitting with his elbows on the counter.

There was a tinkle of keys, the snip of a lock, and the unmistakable ring of a bell and slide of a drawer as the cash register opened. A clink of change followed, and the crisp dry rustle of currency. Then came the tap of bills being straightened on edge against the top of the counter.

Nick went back through the swinging door. An instant later something clanged.

An atmosphere of menace had suddenly seeped into the diner. The captain was as sensitive to the coming of trouble as he was to the brewing of a storm. Nick was frightened. His voice and words had told all that on the extension of the pay phone. Now, after locking the cash register up for the night, he'd opened it again and removed all the money to hide it somewhere in the pantry.

"I hope he'll trust me for some cigarettes," muttered Maclain.

Nick came back, shut the cash register drawer, and said, "It's a helluva night. If that car don't show from the hotel, you'd better stay here. There's an extra little room at the back. It ain't much, but it's dry. I'll fix your eats."

Gas popped under a grill, ignited from the pilot light that Nick turned on. It was followed by the soft slap of a piece of ham tossed on the grill. The captain heard the crack of eggs against the edge of a bowl, and a second later, a comforting sizzle.

The captain nerved himself, as if for a great ordeal. "I left my cigarettes at the camp—with all my money. I hate to impose on your kindness, but I was wondering—"

"Name your brand," Nick said.

Then it happened.

Accompanied by a gust of wind, someone came through the diner door, about ten stools from where Maclain was sitting. In a voice that was high with terror, a woman screamed from behind the swinging door: "Nicky, don't shoot! Don't kill anyone!"

A gun went off, firing three times. The muffled footsteps of slippered feet stumbled off in the pantry.

Nick went down, slithering more than falling, collapsing forever with the feeble dead flap of his pudgy hand against the counter.

The captain sat like a man of bronze, his cup half-raised. Any second the gun would go off again and his own career would be finished.

Unhurried footsteps walked away—toward the other end of the diner where the cigarette machine stood. The captain listened, counting, and let a sound-etched photograph develop in his brain of a man about the size of Nick, with an overcoat rapping against his legs.

The captain remembered the hinged counter-flap. He heard it raised, and he could feel the vibrations as the man swung it over and dropped it against the counter.

He counted the footsteps along the duckboards and jumped involuntarily at the sound of the bell and the opening of the cash drawer.

For three long seconds he listened to heavy and muffled breathing, as the man stared in the drawer. The captain knew then why the man hadn't shot him.

The man was masked with something covering his nose and mouth—a handkerchief perhaps. He couldn't know Maclain was blind, but he didn't care; he couldn't be recognized.

The clank of metal sounded from the duckboards near where the captain figured Nick lay. "He's disposed of the gun beside his victim," the captain thought, and wondered why.

The heavy footsteps retraced their course, paused for a second inside the door, then went on out.

For 30 seconds the captain waited, tense and listening. There had been no sound of a car.

He set his coffee cup down and began to function again. When he knew his way, he could move much faster than most sighted people. He went to the end of the counter and through the opening almost on a run. Then he grew more curious. He felt along, with his fingers brushing shelves of condiments and canned goods, until he reached the swinging door. As he had already pictured, a large round porthole of glass was set in the door.

The woman who had screamed was undoubtedly Mrs. Gherigis. She must have seen the gunman through the window in the door. The captain figured swiftly that she couldn't have seen Nick standing in front of the grill out of range of vision.

Why had she screamed, "Nicky, don't shoot! Don't kill anyone!"?

The captain snapped his fingers in sudden understanding. The masked killer must have been wearing some of Nick's clothes. Mrs. Gherigis didn't know her husband had been shot—she had thought *he* was the killer!

"Of whom?"

Obviously the man, whoever he was, who was shaking Nick down.

The aroma of the cooking ham and eggs grew sharper, mixed with the smell of simmering coffee.

If Duncan Maclain knew any fear, it was that of fire. With even greater caution, he located the gas knob and turned off the grill.

His foot touched Nick's head. The captain knelt and let his perceptive fingers roam lightly over Nick's body. The gunman was an expert and he had shot to kill, wasting nothing. All three bullets had hit, one in Nick's stomach, one in his mouth, and one in his eye.

Water was gurgling softly in the Monel-metal sink, under the counter close to the captain's head. He cleansed the blood from his fingers.

Anxious now to check the accuracy of his hearing, he felt around Nick's body until he found the gun. With his hand resting on it, he froze.

The swinging door had opened gently behind him, but that wasn't the sound that held him rigid. It was the unmistakable click of a hammer as someone cocked a .38 revolver.

"Mrs. Gherigis?" a man's voice called out.

The captain made no move to turn.

"You there! Don't bother to look around—just leave that automatic where it is. Stand slowly and put your hands behind you.

I'm Corporal Walsh of the state police and I've got you covered."

The captain obeyed. The chill of steel on his wrists was cold as Walsh snapped handcuffs on. He felt himself frisked by an expert hand that relieved him of his pocket knife and laid it on the counter. The frisking seemed to throw Maclain off balance and he leaned against Walsh to right himself. Walsh was tall and thin, and he pushed the captain angrily away.

Then Walsh yelled, "Burzak—come in here!"

A blast of icy wind struck the captain as another man came in.

Seconds ticked by, then Burzak asked, "Isn't that the guy that got off the truck?"

"The same," said Walsh. "Get Lieutenant Corman personally on the phone and tell him exactly what happened—that we were parked down there on 303 at the crossroads, saw this man get off the truck, and were watching the place when we heard the shots. We drove up with our lights off and nailed him."

"Efficiently, too," muttered Duncan Maclain. "I was so busy checking my marvelous powers of hearing that I didn't hear you fellows come."

The captain's braille-watch said five to 1. The two police cars, with Lieutenant Corman and his three technicians from Homicide, had rolled up twenty minutes before. The captain had heard them brake to a stop.

Corman was thickset, quiet, efficient, and deadly. It hadn't been very difficult to identify himself to Corman. The lieutenant had checked by phone with the hospital and found that an ambulance was on its way to Barstow. Then he checked with the Red Platte Hotel and learned that they had not yet been able to send a car out to Nick's because of the storm. "Cancel it," Corman told them smoothly. "We'll bring him in."

"Dead or alive," thought Maclain.

Corman had then ordered the captain's handcuffs taken off and had grown quite friendly.

The captain sat on a stool, with Corman next to him, between him and the door, and listened to the pop of another flashlight bulb. The measurements, photographing, and fingerprinting were almost finished. The ambulance and intern would arrive any minute to cart Nick away.

"Mrs. Gherigis killed her husband," said Duncan Maclain. "Make a ten minute tour of the place with me and I'll show you how."

"That's a hot one," said Burzak from farther down. "The lieutenant just got through talking to her in back. She says you were the only one in the diner. She was looking through that glass in the swinging door and saw you shoot the gun."

"Which narrows it down to her word against mine," said Maclain. "But she made one mistake—a big one—in picking me for a witness while she tried to look like a man. She thought I was a bum who had wandered in here and that my story would be disbelieved. What she overlooked was that I couldn't have shot him and couldn't even see her, because I'm totally blind."

Corman stood up. "I'll make a tour with you. If you can make that story stick, Maclain, it's the very first thing I've heard that sounds like sense."

There were two things in the pantry that interested Duncan Maclain—a big deep-freeze that clanged when the lid dropped down, and a closet. The closet door stood ajar and had a Yale lock on it. What caught Maclain up was the fact that the door was lined with heavy asbestos.

"There's nothing in there but supplies and beer," said Corman. "We've already looked around. Nick had it insulated against moisture."

Duncan Maclain was already inside the closet, his fingers traveling along the wall and back of the stacked-up cases of beer. The wires he was searching for led up in back of the shelves. He came out and checked the Yale lock again, making sure it was on the thumb latch and that even if the door were shut it would open without the key.

"When I search for things," said Duncan Maclain, "I first have to find where they aren't. That's what proves to me that my thinking is right." He hooked his fingers on Corman's arm. "The washroom seems to be the logical place. Let's look there."

Two coats and a hat were hanging in the washroom, with four of Nick's soiled aprons and two suits of his overalls. Corman stood in silence as the captain's fingers brushed them all. For twelve inches up from the bottom of the legs, one of the suits of white overalls was damp and muddy.

"Those were what Mrs. Gherigis wore when she did the shooting." The captain pointed to the hat and one of the overcoats and the muddy overalls. "They're damp and Nick hasn't been out of this place since the rain started. I think if you turn them over to your technicians, lieutenant, and check the sweatband in that hat, you can prove that's what Mrs. Gherigis had on."

"Well, I'll be—" said Corman. "I'll take them now."

"No, wait." The captain stretched out his hand. "Take me out and around in front. There's a hedge out there. I felt it coming in. I'll show you how she got in and out of the diner and yet was not seen by Walsh and Burzak in their car."

They came out of the washroom, and a couple of steps to the right Corman opened another door.

"There's a storm vestibule here," Corman said. He opened a second door, letting in a gust of wind and rain. "Wait here a second," Corman went on. "We'll get drowned in this. I'll get the slickers from Walsh's car." Corman went out.

The captain raised both his sensitive hands and swept them up and down along each side of the inner vestibule door. It was the logical place to put an electric meter, fuse box, and cutout switch for the diner. He grunted in satisfaction as he found them.

An automobile door slammed and Corman came back with two slickers. They put them on and went out into the rain.

He struck the fronds of the prickly hedge in front of the diner a few feet farther on. It ran from the end of the diner to the door. It was more than head-high and planted about eighteen inches out from the diner wall.

"Have you a flashlight, lieutenant?"

"Yes."

"Shine it in back of this hedge and see if there are any footprints."

"There's nothing but water," Corman said. "It's an inch deep, at least."

"Well, that's one up for Mrs. Gherigis," said Duncan Maclain. "Let's follow briefly what she did. You'll find when you make an investigation that Nick Gherigis had been paying out dough."

"To whom?" Corman rasped.

"To a dame," said the captain. "I have very keen ears. Mrs. Gherigis called Nick in while I was in the diner, and I heard them quarreling. He's been keeping a woman some place and it's been on her mind for a long time. Tonight was the finish.

"She went in back and got Nick's gun, put on his white overalls, hat, and coat in the washroom, came around here in back of this hedge, shot him, and went back the same way, leaving the clothes in the washroom. With only Nick and me and her in the diner, she felt sure you'd hang it on me—a bum."

"I'll buy it," Corman said suddenly. "Driving up here from the road with their lights off, Walsh and Burzak couldn't have seen her from the police car."

There was a swish of tires and a splashing of water as a heavy car turned from 17-E to stop in front of the diner.

Corman said, "We might as well go inside. The morgue wagon is here."

"Do you mind if I talk with Mrs. Gherigis?" the captain asked.

"Go ahead," said Corman.

The captain stood and listened while two men carrying a stretcher went in through the diner door. Corman went in with them.

When the granite of anger set in Maclain, he ceased to be a human being and turned into a machine. He was blind, but with the inexorable blindness of justice. He hated a killer, but in his code there were worse . . .

Maclain was part of the rain and the raging wind as he took the keys from Corman's car and the ambulance. There were none in the car that had brought the technicians, so the captain swiftly raised the hood of that car and jerked the distributor wires loose, disabling the machine. A moment later he sped around the diner and was down on all fours, crawling about to pat the ground beside and underneath Walsh's and Burzak's official car. Then he got to his feet, opened the door, and removed the keys.

Beside him, Burzak's gritty voice said suddenly, "What are you doing?"

"I was about to put your slicker back in," said Duncan Maclain.

"Wait till Walsh hears this one," Burzak said. "You lying bum, I knew that you could see!"

The captain hit him, one straight right, backed with one hundred and ninety pounds of fury. It landed just an inch and a half underneath the sound of Burzak's words.

He slid out of the dripping slicker and draped it over the fallen trooper, then stepped into the vestibule and pulled the main light-switch beside the door. His feet made no noise as he sped past the washroom, across the pantry, into the insulated closet.

There wasn't even the tiniest snip as he shut himself in by pushing up the button and releasing the Yale lock on the inside of the door. He brailled the closet with frantic speed and stopped with every sense alert at three big, round cans set together on a shelf before him.

They were fastened with little tin hasps, like those on a bread box. The captain tried to lift a can and found it wouldn't move. He opened the hasp and raised the lid to stick in a probing finger. Sugar—but only on top! His finger had struck a metal bottom less than an inch and a half down.

He shut the top and twisted the can around. It was cut out at the back and set in a groove. He hadn't been wrong when he had traced the wires. He reached inside and lifted from its cradle the combination mouth-and-earpiece of a French-style telephone.

The dial signal clicked in his ear and settled to a buzzing sound. Maclain reached in through the opening and dialed 3-2111.

"Colonel Yerkes?"

"Yes. Who is it?" The colonel's voice sounded sleepy.

"It's Duncan Maclain. Phil Barstow's—"

"I know all about you." The voice was wide awake now. "I thought you were out at Barstow's camp."

"Do you know Nick's Diner?"

"Of course!"

"Fine," said Maclain. "Then get together six of your best men—ones you're positive you can trust. Arm them to the ears and get out here as fast as you can. Nick was shot an hour ago by one of your own troopers—Burzak—while Corporal Walsh was waiting outside in the car."

"Good Lord!" said Yerkes. "Why?"

"Nick was running a wire room, receiving and sending bets on the races. He has an extension to the pay booth and two dial phones concealed in a sound-proof room off the pantry. I'm locked in and telephoning from it."

"Who else is at the diner?"

"Lieutenant Corman, three technicians, two men from the morgue, Walsh and Burzak, and Mrs. Gherigis," said Maclain. "None of them are leaving—I have all the car keys. At the moment they're probably hunting for me. I put out all the lights in the place and I had to knock Trooper Burzak cold when he started to move their police car."

"Can you hold it a minute?" Yerkes demanded. "I've got another phone here. I'm going to start out the riot car. Hang on!"

The colonel was back in a few moments. "Tell me briefly what happened and I'll be right along. The riot squad is already on its way."

"Phil had a heart attack," said Duncan Maclain. "I came here to get to a phone. An ambulance is on its way to pick up Phil.

"Walsh and Burzak were parked outside by the end of the diner, where I couldn't have seen them even if I had eyes. But they saw me come in. The telephone rang and Nick left to take the call in this closet, where I am now. He told me he'd heard his wife call. I thought somebody might be phoning me back about the ambulance for Phil, so I picked up the phone in the booth.

"Nick was on the extension and I overheard part of the call. He said that a hundred a week was cleaning him and he'd blow the works before he'd double it. He said he was leaving his wife a list that would jail them all."

"You don't know who he was talking to?"

"I don't," said Maclain. "Maybe Corman."

"What makes you think that?"

"It's an idea I got when Walsh told Burzak to get Lieutenant Corman personally and to tell him exactly what had happened—that they had been parked down there on 303 at the crossroads, had seem me get off the truck, had driven up with their lights off, and had nailed me. It sounded like an awful lot of yackety-yak to send in on a murder call."

235

"Do you have any proof, Captain Maclain?" Yerkes's voice was grim.

"Plenty, but I haven't much time to tell you—somebody has just started pounding on the door. I guess they've got the lights back on.

"Walsh and Burzak saw me come in, decided it was a good time to rub out Nick and hang it on someone they thought was only a bum. Right now I look like one. Burzak put on Nick's hat, coat, and overalls—he found them in the washroom inside the side entrance. Then he came around through the front, shot Nick, and took a look in the cash register. I think he wanted that list Nick had talked about, but Nick had cleaned out the cash drawer and hidden the stuff after the warning call.

"Burzak was scarcely out of the diner when Walsh came in and put me under a gun. It was the world's fastest piece of police work, Colonel.

"Anyway, Burzak had dressed up to look like Nick and had blasted him. Mrs. Gherigis saw a man through the window of the pantry door and thought it was Nick. She still doesn't know Nick's dead."

"You sound pretty sure, Maclain."

"Of course I'm sure; get this, Colonel: five of us were here. Nick was shot. Mrs. Gherigis couldn't have done it—she was back of a door and out of range of vision. I didn't, and Walsh is tall and thin—too tall to get Nick's things on and be mistaken for him by Nick's wife. Five minus four equals one—Burzak."

"Just a second, Captain Maclain. What evidence have you got?"

"I think you'll find Nick's list of names in the deep-freeze, Colonel—I heard the lid clang. Your laboratory can prove that Burzak had Nick's clothes on . . . I'd better hang up now—they're breaking the door."

"One more second," Yerkes pleaded. "Can you *prove* that Burzak and Walsh were there all the time—from *before* the murder?"

"I have to hurry, Colonel. Burzak's and Walsh's police car hasn't moved from right beside this diner since before 11:30 when it started to rain. Everything around here is soaking, but it's bone dry under their car."

"I'll be right over," said Yerkes. "Is there anything I can bring you?"

"Cigarettes, Colonel," said Duncan Maclain, "I never did get any. And maybe just a wee drop of scotch. I'm dryer inside than the ground under Walsh's and Burzak's car."

GIDEON'S WAR

BY J. J. MARRIC

John Creasey (J. J. Marric), probably the most prolific of all mystery writers, with well over 500 books published, was born on September 17, 1908. He founded Great Britain's Crime Writers Association in 1953. Hans Santesson wrote of him, "I remember one afternoon when I was with him at Scotland Yard as he went over and over again with a senior officer there a possible incident in a Marric novel. There was obvious mutual respect as two working professionals explored possibilities that might be passed over by most readers." Mr. Creasey died in 1973.

WHEN THE EVENING NEWSPAPERS came out with their headlines:
Western Summit for London
Big Four Meet in June
and gave details already released by the Home Office about the
procession route for the State Visits, some men's eyes sparkled at
thought of the illegal profit likely to come their way as a result.

One of these was a little perky man named Alec Sonnley. He had
bright green-gray eyes in a shiny little pink-and-red face, and was
always smartly dressed. When the sun shone on him he looked
rather like an apple half hidden by leaves, for he wore a green hat
and his clothes were always gray-green or browny-green. The most
noticeable things about him, apart from his rosy, shiny complexion, were his hands and feet, which were much larger than average,
making a man of five feet six look a little ridiculous.

Everyone called him Sonny Boy, partly because of his name,
partly because of his habit of whistling popular songs—like an
errand boy. He had carefully and very skillfully organized a business in London which had all the outward appearance of being
legitimate. He ran a large wholesale warehouse in the Petticoat
Lane district of the East End, from which he supplied street traders
and hawkers, as well as small shopkeepers from the Greater London area.

In addition to this he owned thirty shops, all in popular shopping
areas, all dealing in what he called 'Fancy Goods, Jewellery, Gold and
Silver Articles'. In each shop he had a manager and two or three
assistants, and each member of the staff was strictly honest—none
of them knew that he or she was dealing in stolen goods.

To make discovery much less likely, Alec Sonnley bought up a
great deal of bankrupt stocks, salvaged goods, and low-priced
ornaments, in all of which he did good business. No single item in
any of his stores cost over five pounds, and he had a series of
"Special Advertising Offers" at five shillings and ten shillings each.
At least half his stocks were stolen goods.

He also had the third aspect of the business worked out just as
carefully as the retail and wholesale angles. He used six shoplifters
and eight handbag and pocket pickers, or snatchers and dips. This
team operated in big shopping areas, concentrating on stealing
famous-brand goods, which were taken to the retail outlets and
sold quickly.

Every now and then, especially when he believed that the police suspected one of them, Sonnley "rested" these operatives, but because of the retainer he paid them they were ready to work again the moment he felt it safe.

The great simplicity of his system helped Sonnley to his huge success. Quick-selling goods stolen from one part of London were often on sale in another part on the same day, for he had a plain truck driven by his chief operative, a man named Benny Klein, who made the rounds regularly, collecting and delivering. Anything of high value, Sonnley disposed of through ordinary receivers.

No one knew quite how much he was worth, but it probably approached half a million pounds.

Any attraction which drew the crowds to the heart of London would set Sonny Boy whistling chirpily. His pickpockets, bag snatchers, and shoplifters often quadrupled their takings on such occasions, and his wholesale warehouse supplied hundreds of street traders with souvenirs.

That Tuesday he drove from the small suite of offices in a narrow street near Baker Street Station, and out of the corner of his eye saw a newspaper placard: *Western Summit for London.*

He slowed down by the next newsboy and bought a newspaper. Very soon he began to whistle, and the whistle became positively gay while he drove to St. John's Wood, where he had an apartment near Regent's Park. He turned into the underground garage, then whistled his way across to the elevator which would take him up to the seventh floor, and his wife. She was a plump, good-natured woman with thin metallic-looking reddish yellow hair. She loved expensive clothes, loved her Sonny Boy, and, rather unexpectedly, loved cooking. So Sonnley went home to lunch whenever he could.

His tune was rounded and full as he stepped out opposite his apartment, Number 17, and let himself in. There was a faint aroma of frying onions, which suggested a steak or mixed grill. When he went into the kitchen, the steaks were sizzling and the onions clucking.

Rosie glanced round, saw him, and immediately plunged a basket of newly sliced chips into a saucepan of boiling fat, causing a great hiss and a cloud of steam.

Sonnley went across and slid his arm round his wife's comfortable bosom, squeezed, gave her neck a peck of a kiss, and said:

"I hope it's good. We've got a lot to celebrate."

"Oh, have we, Sonny dear?" said Rose. "What is it?"

"Believe it or not, sweetie-pie, we're going to have a State Procession for a great big Western Four Power Summit meeting in li'l old London Town," declared Sonnley, and held the newspaper up.

Reading, Rosie looked more and more puzzled.

"I'm sure it will be very nice, dear. Can I have a seat?"

"A what?"

"There are bound to be some wonderful stands put up for the Procession. In the Mall, I shouldn't wonder, or perhaps near the Abbey. You know, where the Houses of Parliament are." Rosie prodded a steak. "It's a pity it isn't a wedding, really. I do love to see them coming out of the Abbey with their lovely dresses. There will be stands, won't there?"

"You can bet your life there will!"

"And can I have a seat?"

"Front row, dead center, the best there is," Sonnley promised. "Rosie, that steak smells wonderful. How long will it be?"

"About ten minutes."

"Just time for me to make a phone call," said Sonnley.

He went out in the hallway, rubbing his hands, turned into a big drawing room which overlooked the park, beyond the gardens of the building. The drawing room had been furnished by a large London store, and although Sonnley was never sure why, he realized that it was as nearly perfect as it could be. The colorings were wine-red and pale blue, setting off the mid-Nineteenth Century French furniture.

He sat at the end of a long couch, dialed a Whitehall number, and was answered almost at once by a man with a slightly foreign accent.

"Benny, you seen the papers?" Sonnley asked.

"Sure, I've seen the papers," answered Benny Klein. "I thought I'd be hearing from you."

"Just have a word with all the boys and girls, and tell them to take a week or two off," said Sonnley. "I don't want anyone in trouble between now and you-know-when. All okay?"

"Holiday with pay, is it?"

"You've got it in one, Benny," Sonnley agreed. "And I've got a little vacation planned for you, too."

"*Me?* I'm going to the Riviera, Sonny Boy. You know that."

"Not now you're not," Sonnley declared. "Buy your doll a nice diamond bracelet, and tell her to stay home and be a good girl."

"I'm not going to alter my plans for anybody." Klein was suddenly harsh-voiced.

"Now take it easy, Benny, take it easy! No one said anything about altering your plans. It's just a little postponement, that's all. You can take the girl with you if she loves you so much! You're going up to Glasgow, Liverpool, Manchester, and Birmingham, and you're going to tell the boys up there to keep out of the Big Smoke when the V.I.P.s are here. We don't want any of those provincials muscling in on our London, do we?"

When Klein didn't answer, Sonnley repeated sharply, "Do we?"

Klein said gruffly; "No, we don't."

"And I don't know anyone who can tell them better than Benny Klein," went on Sonnley. "Just make them understand that they keep out. See? If they don't, they'll run into a lot of trouble."

"They'll understand," Klein asserted in a stronger voice.

"That's more like it," Sonnley approved. "Tell them I'll organize every gang of razor and chain-boys in London if provincials come down here. And when you've warned them good and proper, Benny, you can come down here and talk to the London gangs."

After a pause, Klein said, "The London gangs will want some dough."

"They'll get it, don't you worry. The same terms as for Maggie's wedding—they'll be okay. And tell your lady friend you'll buy her a mink stole as well, if she forgets all about the Contingong." Sonnley chuckled. "Okay, Benny?"

"I suppose so."

"I thought it would be," Sonnley said. "See you, boy."

He rang off, stood for a moment by the telephone, frowning. If Klein should get awkward, it would create a lot of difficulties.

"But he won't get awkward," Sonnley reassured himself, and began to whistle, if on a slightly subdued note.

After a few minutes he joined Rosie, who had now laid the table. A steak which looked juicy and tender teased Sonnley from the silver dish. The chips were a golden brown, and there were peas and broad beans as well as deep-fried onion rings.

"What's the matter, Sonny? Doesn't it look nice?" inquired Rosie.

"Blimey, it looks as if it's sitting up and begging to be eaten! I was just thinking about a business acquaintance who might need a little watching. Now, let's go!"

Sitting in a small Chelsea café and tucking into a plate of bacon, sausages, eggs, and chips was Michael Lumati, well known to Alec Sonnley, and also well known to the police, although it was now three years since he had been under suspicion of any crime, and five since he had been in prison.

On that occasion he had earned full remission after a three-year sentence for issuing forged banknotes. Nowadays, he now earned a reasonable living by selling lightning portraits at fairs and race tracks, and designing calendars, programs and catalogs—including Sonnley's.

Lumati had a small studio at the top of an old condemned building of Chelsea, and he spent a lot of time in the studio, usually cooking his own breakfast and evening meal, but going out for lunch. Today he sat in a corner of the cafe, a man nearing fifty, rather thin, with a healthy-looking tanned complexion, very clear gray eyes, and a small Vandyke beard. That, and the faded beret which he always wore at the back of his head, made him look the part of an artist.

Some of his craftsmanship, at its best in copies of currency notes, was unbelievably good.

He had a copy of the London *Standard* propped up against the wall at his side and kept reading the story of the coming State Procession. There was a calculating expression in his eyes. The police did not know that, after years of experiment and error, Lumati had succeeded in drawing a line which looked as if it were a tiny thread through the paper—making visual detection nearly impossible; nor did the police know that he had tens of thousands of these one-pound and ten-shilling notes printed and ready for distribution.

He knew a man who would want plenty of paper money at the time of the Visit, too.

Sonny Boy Sonnley.

The following Saturday morning Commander Gideon of the Criminal Investigation Department at New Scotland Yard felt irritable without quite knowing why. Preparations for the Visit were going reasonably well and no particular crime was worrying him. On Saturdays he always had a roll call of unsolved crimes, and investigations all seemed to be ticking over nicely.

Nevertheless, he had a sense that he had missed some factor of importance.

He had told Joe Bell, his chief assistant, to contact all the provincial forces, asking them to arrange to send men to London for the Visit, and they had all promised to get busy. It was too early to expect any squeals from the East End, or to guess what the wide boys were planning. His mood might be due to the weather, it was cold and blustery.

Standing by his window he could see the choppy waters of the Thames; why did the weather always seem to break at weekends?

At a quarter past ten there was a bang at the door and Superintendent Lemaitre came in. An old friend of Gideon's, Lemaitre was a senior detective with one big fault, which somehow showed in his Cockney voice, with its overtone of slick confidence.

"Hiyah, George!" He came in briskly, waved to Bell, and added, "Joe," and shook Gideon's hand. He sat on a corner of Gideon's desk, bony fists clenched, a confident and happy-looking man given to taking too much for granted and jumping too quickly to conclusions. "I'm back full of the joys and ready for anything. Just had ten days down by the briny—got in a couple of dips every day. My wife's so brown you wouldn't think she'd been decent! She wants to know if you and Kate can come round to tea or supper tomorrow."

"If Kate hasn't booked anything, we'd like to," said Gideon. "Then you can make your wife a police widow for a week or so."

"What's all this? I'm just the man you want for the Big Visit."

"So you are. For Glasgow, Liverpool, Manchester, and the rest, to check whether any of their boys are planning an offensive in London during the Visit."

"Okay, okay," said Lemaitre. "When do you want me to go?"

"Tuesday."

"Right-i-ho!" Lemaitre slapped his hands together. "Won't be sorry to get out of this den of vice for a bit. Don't forget to ask Kate about tomorrow."

On the Sunday when the Gideons had afternoon tea with the Lemaitres, Benny Klein and Jack Gorra, the leader of Glasgow's Blacks, were considering the other side of the picture. They felt very pleased with themselves, for they had hatched out a plot together—one man who had been adopted by Great Britain and given its nationality, the other the leader of the most vicious gang north of the Tweed. Their plan was simple, and depended entirely on perfect timing.

Instead of Sonny Boy Sonnley's pickpockets and bag snatchers reaping a harvest during the Visit, the Glasgow Blacks would descend on London.

Whenever they had done this in the past there had been a clash with the London crooks, often a pitched battle. Klein had suggested, and Gorra had agreed, that this was a crazy way to do it.

"All you want to do is put Sonny Boy's artists out of action for a few days," Klein had said. "Then London's wide-open."

"You're telling me what to do. Just go ahead and tell me how." Gorra was a thickset man with a small round head covered with a gingery bristle. His short, pale eyelashes and stubby eyebrows made him look almost like an albino; his pale blue eyes seemed to stare fixedly all the time.

"You ever seen a dip or a bagman work with burned fingers?" Klein inquired.

At first that did not make sense to Gorra, but the light began to dawn as Klein went on:

"We've only got to work out a way to burn the fingers of Sonnley's artists, and we're a winner."

"Acid would do the trick, a hot acid. Corrosive acid, that's what we want," Gorra put in eagerly. "The only question is how to get it onto the right fingers."

Klein grinned.

On the Thursday of the same week Gideon drove past the Mint, reflecting that hordes of people would come here during the Visit; he must soon have a word with the City Police, who would be in charge here.

He turned into Aldgate, where London seemed suddenly to become a working-class suburb. Traffic was moving at a crawl, fumes were stinking, motors growled on a sullen note. He worked his way round the mean streets to NE Divisional Police Headquarters and it was a quarter to one when he entered Christy's office.

Hugh Christy was fairly new at NE Division, which was the toughest in London. He was in his middle-forties, military in appearance and manner, brisk in movement and in speech, with rather a big head, and a manner which often seemed aggressive. Bighead was the nickname most often applied to him, but it was no longer harsh and censorious. Christy had proved in two years that he was able and shrewd.

As he shook hands and showed Gideon a chair, all in one movement, he said:

"I've got a couple of big steaks on order; they're ready to go under the grill when I press the button."

"Suits me fine," Gideon approved.

Christy's finger prodded a bell push, twice. Then he squared his shoulders and sat very erect behind his flat-topped desk.

"They'll come in and get the table ready ten minutes before we start to eat," he announced. "Any complaints, George?"

"Lot of worry," replied Gideon mildly. "I'll need all the men you can spare uniformed and C.I.D., for the big show, and there's a lot of spade work between now and then."

"Any special angles?" Christy inquired. "I heard a buzz that Benny Klein, Alec Sonnley's right-hand man, is out of town."

"He went off north with the blonde he's living with, and didn't tell anyone where he was going."

"Come to think, a lot of Sonnley's boys have gone off on holiday," Christy reported thoughtfully. "I noticed that earlier in the week, and doubt if they're just taking advantage of the weather. Think Sonny Boy Sonnley is preparing for the big show?"

"Probably. How many shops has he got in your manor?"

"Three."

"Concentrate on them," urged Gideon. "I'll have all his others closely watched, too. With luck we'll get him on this job. But don't have any of Sonnley's or Klein's boys followed unless Lemaitre asks you to. He's gone to find out what Klein's up to."

"Everyone on the ball," Christy approved.

They were in the middle of thick steaks, chips, and fried onions when a call came for Gideon from Liverpool. He soaked up a tempting pool of rich gravy into a piece of bread before taking the telephone.

"Having a nice quiet time down there, George?" It was Lemaitre. "That's good—get your strength up. I've nearly finished this job, so save Soho for me, will you?"

"It's sold," said Gideon.

"Lecherous old devil! Well, I gotta bit of news for you, pal," Lemaitre rejoiced. "Benny Klein spent the weekend in Glasgow, with a girl friend and Jack Gorra. He's been using Glasgow as a center and moving about the north. I've been to Glasgow, Edinburgh, Manchester, and Liverpool. None of the top coppers has heard of any exodus of their bad boys—all the best provincial crooks seem to be staying at home."

"Any idea why?" inquired Gideon.

"Got a coupla squeaks," Lemaitre reported with deep satisfaction. "Benny Klein's paying each leader five hundred quid to keep his boys local. He's been here in Manchester and talked to all the big boys. Now he's going back to Glasgow. The word is that the Glasgow group will be in London for the Visit, but the others will stay home."

"You mean Gorra of Glasgow is going to defy Klein?"

Gideon could see the inevitable consequences of such an invasion, and it wasn't a reassuring picture. It would almost certainly lead to warfare between powerful gangs of pickpockets and shoplifters, and might well bring out the razors and the bicycle chains, the coshes and the flick knives. If that happened, police urgently needed for normal crowd control would have to be diverted, which would create a lot of difficulties.

"That's the fishy smell," Lemaitre told him. "Klein and Jack Gorra are like old buddies."

"Think Klein's fooled Gorra?" Gideon wanted to know.

"I don't know what it means," Lemaitre confessed. "I just don't like it."

"I'll warn the Divisions," Gideon promised. "Lem, while you're on—ask Manchester, Liverpool, and Birmingham if they could spare us a hundred men, say. Just see how the wind blows. If they'll play I'll get an official request sent up from the Commissioner, but we don't want to ask and be refused."

"Right," said Lemaitre. "I'm going down to Bristol tonight, and should be back on Saturday. Okay?"

"Fine."

"Take care of Soho for me," Lemaitre quipped, and rang off.

In Glasgow at that particular moment Benny Klein was experimenting with a little water pistol, using corrosive acid in the rubber holder instead of water. Tomorrow morning he would know how the rubber stood up to the acid. If it burned through, he would have to think of something else.

Jack Gorra was watching, when one of his runners tapped at the door. He went to answer it, talked in undertones, then came back and waited until the end of the experiment before repeating:

"Lemaitre's been in Glasgow, asking questions."

"I hope it keeps fine for him," Benny Klein said.

Without a pause he moved to a small cage, where a mouse was squealing and squirming.

His sharp-featured, sallow face was twisted in an expression of beastly delight as he watched the helpless creature. It was stuck to a small chromium-plated tube which he had smeared with vitriol overnight, and left to dry. Only it hadn't dried; the squeals and antics of the mouse proved that.

"Pity that's not Sonny Boy," Klein said, and Gorra laughed.

Michael Lumati was also thinking about Sonnley. He was sitting pretty with fifteen thousand pounds of near-perfect currency notes, and still his only worry was how to get them distributed.

He had to admit that he needed someone with a lot of shops, or a lot of barrows, and someone with a big turnover during the Visit. The real truth was that he ought to use Sonnley, who had already ordered artwork for special *Souvenir Programmes* for the occasion.

"Mr. Sonnley, I've got an idea for a special Visit Souvenir Catalog, and another way of making a bit of quick dough," Lumati said on the telephone. "Could you spare me half an hour?"

"Let's have a drink together," said Sonnley, who prided himself that he never missed a chance.

Michael Lumati left his studio, took a Number 11 bus to Fulham Broadway, then sauntered toward North End Road, where the litter from the previous day's market had not been properly cleared. He turned into a public house and went upstairs to a private lounge. He could hear a man whistling *Some Enchanted Evening*. He tapped at the door, the whistling stopped, and Alec Sonnley called:

"That you, Lummy?"

"It's me, Sonny Boy."

"Come right in." Sonnley was standing by a window hung with dark green curtains. An aspidistra stood on a small table in the middle of the room, which was like one preserved as a mid-Victorian relic.

"What are you going to have?" he asked, and turned to a table on which there were dozens of bottles of beer.

"I'll have a pale." Lumati sat down in an old-fashioned saddle-back armchair as Sonnley poured.

"Got those samples?" Sonnley asked.

Lumati didn't answer.

"Now listen, Lummy, have you got them or haven't you? If you're still worrying about the busies, forget it—we've got those souvenir programs to show we're in legitimate business together. But if you're thinking of asking for more than fifty-fifty, forget that too. I'm taking just as big a risk as you are. You know that as well as I do."

"Yes, I know," said Lumati.

"Telling me you don't trust me?"

"I trust you," said Lumati, eyeing the little man closely. "But I'm not sure I trust your pal, Klein."

"Listen, Lummy," said Sonnley. "I've worked with Klein for over ten years. They don't come any smarter, but I wouldn't trust him round the corner. Klein's not in this. He's looking after the usual business for me. He's been up in the North and the Midlands, making sure we don't have trouble with those boys. I'll spread your stuff round myself with the takings from my branches, and I'll pay a lot of my bills with them. I'll spread some out with bookies, too. Don't worry. I'll get rid of most of it in a week. Now, where's the samples?"

Lumati took an envelope from his pocket, and handed it over. Sonnley slit it open and pulled out the notes inside; there were five. He rustled one in his fingers, put the five down on a table, and flipped them like a bank teller. Then he took them to a window, and, standing to one side, held one up to the light.

The thread showed through clearly, and so did the watermark; it was a remarkable job of counterfeiting. He swung round and clapped Lumati on the shoulder.

"That's the best job I've ever seen in my life, Lum! It's an absolute winner."

"It's the best job that's ever been done," said Lumati. His little beard waggled in his excitement. "And I've got fifteen thousand quids' worth of them. It's a deal, then. You won't tell Klein?"

"Cross my heart."

"And you pay me fifty percent of the face value, on delivery."

"Lum, just to show how much I trust you, I've brought three thousand quid in real English dough along with me—it's in that little case over there. Don't get it mixed up with your own specialty, will you?"

When Sonnley left soon afterward, he was whistling as merrily as could be, his green Tyrolean hat stuck jauntily on one side of his head. He whistled all the way home, all the way up to Rosie, and all the time he was washing his hands before lunch. He was halfway through a steamed steak-and-kidney pudding of mouth-watering succulence when the telephone bell rang.

"I'll get it, Sonny," Rosie said, and puffed a few straying hairs away from her nose, got up, and waddled across to the telephone in a corner; she knew how Sonny Boy disliked being interrupted while eating.

"Hello, who's that?" she inquired disinterestedly, and then she said, "Oh, Mrs. Whittaker, hello dear, how are you? . . . Well, I *am* sorry . . . Well I never . . . Well, what a funny thing to happen. Has he tried olive oil? It's ever so soothing . . . Oh, I see . . . Well, he's busy now, dear—"

She glanced across at Sonnley, who was scooping up a forkful of succulent brown meat and gravy-soaked suet crust. He waved his knife at her, and she went on, "He's just come in, dear, wait a minute."

She covered the mouthpiece with her podgy hand as she called to Sonnley, "Dick Whittaker's burned his hands something cruel. He's had to go to a doctor."

"The damn fool, he's due to start work next week," Sonnley said disgustedly, and grabbed the telephone. "Sonnley speaking. What's all this about . . .?"

He broke off, listening more intently, and when he spoke again his voice was subdued and the expression in his eyes was very different, and very thoughtful.

"All right, tell him not to worry. I'll stake him," he said curtly, and rang off.

He stared at his wife, who sat down placidly although she had just learned that one of the cleverest pickpockets in the business had burned his hands so badly that he would not be able to operate during the Visit.

Someone had smeared vitriol on the handlebars of his motorscooter.

When Klein came into his office the next morning, Sonnley sat reading some letters, without looking up. Klein took out cigarettes, lit one, and dropped the spent match into an ashtray close to Sonnley's right hand.

"Remember me?" he said. "I've got news for you."

Sonnley looked straight into his eyes, paused, and asked: "What news?"

Sonnley never admitted it to a soul, but Klein's answer took him completely by surprise, and almost broke up his poker face. The answer was one word, spoken with that gutteral accent, taking on a kind of menace which Sonnley had not known for a long time.

"Cops," said Klein.

"What the hell do you mean, cops?"

"I mean busies, dicks, bloody flatfoots," said Klein. "They're watching my van. They followed me this morning. There's a couple outside now—one of them was at the station when I got back last night, one was outside here when I arrived. Think he was waiting to pass the time of day with me? What have you been doing?"

"I don't believe—" Sonnley began.

"You take a look," invited Klein.

Sonnley stood up, slowly, and went to the window. On the other side of the street, standing by a telephone booth and reading a newspaper, was a tall heavily built man; another, taller, thinner man was strolling along.

"What have you been up to, to bring them as close as this?" demanded Klein.

"It's just routine," Sonnley said.

"Okay, then, it's just routine," said Klein. "But if I start collecting the stuff from the boys and girls and get copped, I'll be back on the Moor, and that's a routine I don't like. I've got some more news for you."

"Now, listen, Benny—"

"I want out," said Klein. "I want five thousand quid as a golden handshake, and then I'll fade. I'm not taking any chances."

Sonnley returned to his desk, sat down, and looked again into the other man's bright gray eyes. He had known that one day a break would come, but he hadn't expected blackmail, and hadn't expected trouble to come so suddenly.

He took out a checkered green and white handkerchief, and dabbed at his forehead. Klein didn't shift his gaze. He had one hand clenched on the desk, another with the palm upward, the fingers crooked and beckoning.

"Give," he said.

Sonnley still didn't speak. Klein leaned across the desk so that Sonnley could feel the warmth of his breath, and repeated:

"Give."

Sonnley said thinly, "Not a penny."

"Say that again and I'll break your neck."

"Then you'll go inside for the rest of your life."

Klein's eyes narrowed, as if he hadn't expected such tough resistance.

"Sonny Boy, don't get me wrong," he said. "I want out and I want five thousand quid, and that's how it's going to be."

"Benny," said Sonnley, in a voice which shook a little, "you aren't going to get another penny from me unless you see the next ten days through—until the Visit's over. You can please yourself."

Klein was towering over him, lips drawn back. There was silence in the room for what seemed a very long time, and with every second it looked as if Klein would explode into action. Before he did, while the breath was hissing through his mouth, Sonnley said in a soft voice:

"Who smeared vitriol on Dicky Whittaker's motorscooter?"

For a moment Klein's expression did not change; he still looked as if he would burst into violent action. Then he blinked. He closed his lips, moistened them, and said, "What's that?" and drew back a pace, as if his rage had suddenly died away. "What's that?"

"You heard."

"Come again."

"Who smeared vitriol on the handlebars of Dicky Whittaker's motorscooter?"

"Someone did *that*?" Klein sighed.

"You've been back in London since last night and no one told you?"

Klein said, still sighingly, "You're telling me, aren't you?" He moistened his lips again. "Because the cops were watching, I kept away from all the boys. I didn't hear anything. Can't Dicky work?"

"He can't work."

Klein said "Who did it, that's what I want to know?"

"That's what I want to know, too," said Sonnley. "If you want that five thousand quid you find out who did it."

"Who would hate Dicky as much as that?"

"Just find out and let me know quick," said Sonnley. "Because when I find out who did it I'll break him. Understand?" He stared levelly, coldly, into Klein's eyes. "Whoever it was, I'll break him for good. Just remember that."

"I'll find him," Klein said. "I'll find the swine."

Sonnley watched him as he turned away and went out, and saw no change in his expression. Sonnley jumped up from the desk, stepped swiftly to the door, pulled it open, and saw Klein halfway across the room beyond, still looking astounded. If he knew more than he pretended, he was covering it well.

Did he know? Or was he as shocked as he made out?

Gideon reached his office at a quarter to eight next morning, Saturday, to find Bell already there. Only the night staff was at the Yard, and Gideon had the usual Saturday morning feeling, that everyone was anxious to get through his job as soon as possible.

A messenger came in with a huge bundle of mail, and envelopes of all shapes and sizes were piled high in front of Bell. He scowled. It was too early for the secretarial staff to be here.

"Has Lemaitre been in?"

"No," answered Bell.

"I'm still puzzled about that Glasgow business," Gideon remarked. "Telephone them and ask for the latest on Jack Gorra, will you?"

There was no special news of Gorra, or of any of the provincial gangs, but Lemaitre seemed convinced that Gorra's boys would come down to work with Sonnley's.

Gideon's telephone rang, and he lifted it while glancing at another report. It was Christy of NE Division.

"Yes, Hugh?"

"Funny thing happened you ought to know about," said Christy. "Remember Dicky Whittaker?" On the instant Gideon pictured a tall, very thin, sorrowful-looking man, who had often been inside for picking pockets and snatching handbags; he was probably the cleverest man in London at either job.

"I remember him."

"He's burned the skin off his hands. Someone smeared his scooter handles with vitriol, and put him out of business." Christy gave a snort, smothering a laugh.

"Sonny Boy won't be pleased," remarked Gideon, thoughtfully. "I wish I knew what was going on with that crowd. Thanks, Hugh."

He felt uneasy, as he often did, but there was no time to sit back and think this problem out. He sent a chit round to other Divisions, asking for reports of any similar hand-burning incidents, and also told Lemaitre to keep on the lookout. That was as much as he could do, for the Visit was almost on top of them.

Security men from France, Germany and the United States were virtually in possession at the Yard, where the tempo of the preparations was reaching fever pitch. Reinforcements from all over the country were arriving in London hourly, and plans had to be made to house and feed them.

Tension was building up on high, too. The Commissioner was pushed by the Home Secretary, who was being pressured by the Cabinet to make sure that nothing went wrong.

The situation was complicated by the mood of Cox, Deputy Commander of *Uniform*, who seemed convinced that he, Gideon, had deliberately stolen his thunder. Together, they toured the routes from the airport, and checked the Procession route thoroughly, looking for any possible weakness in the security plans. In spite of it all, his first job when he returned to the office was to call Lemaitre.

"Don't you worry, Gee-Gee," Lemaitre said cockily. "I'll look after Sonny Boy."

"You'll have to," Gideon said almost sourly. "Keep your eyes wide open tomorrow, Lem."

Saturday, the first day London was likely to be flooded with visitors, was also the first day planned for a mass attack by Sonnley's men. Sonnley had not whistled very much in the past few days. He was worried, although there were some reasons for thinking that the worst of his worries might be over. The police were taking comparatively little notice of him, and he knew that they were stretched very thin. Probably the surveillance earlier in the week had been in an effort to scare him and Klein.

After the news of the "accident" to Whittaker, Klein seemed to have become obsessed with the idea of finding out who had smeared those handlebars, but he had failed. No other burned fingers had been reported, and as far as Sonnley's scouts in the big provincial cities knew, there was no movement toward London. Klein seemed to have paid them to stay out of the big smoke, as instructed, and that was just as Sonnley wanted it.

He told himself that Klein was reliable at least until he had been paid off, but would have to be watched very carefully afterward. Meanwhile, Sonnley double-checked his own arrangements.

He meant to have an alibi which no one could possibly break. He had to make sure that the money was collected and paid into the bank quickly and that no time was lost moving the stolen goods. He also wanted to distribute Lumati's money which was stored in the cellar of one of his shops—but for some subconscious reason he held that back.

At the back of Sonnley's mind there was one way in which he could use the slush, but his immediate concern was to see that his own plans worked smoothly.

On Saturday morning he gave Rosie a peck of a kiss and went outside. It was bright and sunny, and by the time he reached the garage at the back of the flats he was whistling cheerfully; good weather was just what his "artists" wanted.

He slid into the driving seat, switched on the ignition, and took the wheel. Immediately he felt something sticky and wet, and for a moment it puzzled him. Then, seconds before the acid began to burn, he realized what it was.

He snatched his hands away and sat absolutely still, eyes glaring, hands crooked, the burning getting worse with every passing second. Soon he made choking noises in his throat, as if he were fighting for breath.

That day, the day which should have been Sonny Boy Sonnley's greatest harvest, his "artists" left home for the West End of London, all of them on bicycles, scooters, and motorcycles; none of them used cars, because of the need for quick getaways.

All went among the crowds for the first of their jobs. The

weather was so lovely that it made the people happy and careless, and pockets and handbags were easy plucking. In all, fourteen of the men made good first pickings, and hurried back to their machines.

Exactly the same thing happened in each case, though in different places.

Each man gripped the handlebars and started off; after a few seconds each pulled into the curb, snatching his hands from the bars and looking down. Each saw hands and fingers which were already red and blistering and beginning to cause agony.

Man after man jumped off his machine, bystanders staring at them as they waved their hands about wildly.

The police were soon alerted.

Superintendent Lemaitre pulled up in his blue Humber outside Gideon's front door early that afternoon and Gideon saw him from the bedroom, where he was mending a spring blind. Kate was out shopping. Gideon was on call, and judging from Lemaitre's expression, this was an urgent one.

He smiled to himself as Lemaitre disappeared along the path, and carried a mind-picture of the tall, thin, rather gawkish man, with spotted red-and-white bow tie, gray overcheck suit which somehow contrived to be loud, and narrow-brimmed trilby set at a jaunty angle on the side of his head.

The bell rang twice before Gideon could get to the door.

"In a hurry, Lem?" he asked.

"In a blurry hurry," Lemaitre cracked, and there was excitement but not anxiety in his eyes. "Gotta-bitta news for you!"

He came in, almost as familiar with the house as Gideon, and went on boisterously, "Remember old Dicky Whittaker? Poor old Dicky with the blistered fingers?"

"Well?"

"We've had nine cases of blistered fingers reported this afternoon," Lemaitre announced joyfully. "Every one of them a Klein and Sonny Boy man! How about that, George?"

Without giving Gideon a chance to respond, Lemaitre careered on, taking a slip of paper from his pocket. "Every one of the baskets was caught with his pockets stuffed with loot, George. Every one's a dead cert for three years inside, after hospital treatment. Some of their hands—you should see! Raw isn't the word. But the thing is, I know what's on."

Gideon said cautiously, "Do you?"

"That's right, that's right, tell me I'm jumping to conclusions again. This time I'm bang on the ball."

Lemaitre waved the slip of paper in front of Gideon's nose. "Now listen to me, George. Here is a list of the boys who've been burned. They can't work, understand? One might have been an accident, but nine makes a campaign, and there may be more to come. So as soon as I heard there were several of them I checked round with the provincial cities. You want to know something?"

"Try me."

"Jack Gorra's boys left Glasgow last night and this morning. Some by train, some by road. And remember, Klein was up there with Gorra and they behaved like dear old pals. You can take it from me, the Glasgow Blacks are coming to take over from Sonnley, and all we've got to do is pick 'em up as they arrive, and have 'em sent back to Glasgow.

"Now wait a minute, wait a minute!" pleaded Lemaitre, as Gideon tried to get a word in. "I've telephoned Glasgow. They've put out an official request for all of Gorra's gang to be sent back for questioning. It's only a matter of putting our hand on them. They won't be likely to come by road, not all the way, it's a hell of a drive. I think those who started out by road will catch a train farther south, maybe to pick them up at Euston."

"Get the stations watched," ordered Gideon.

"Attaboy," said Lemaitre, and his grin seemed to split his face in two. "Action, that's me. We got seven of the so-and-so's off the Flying Scot, and nine more at the Bus Station. Don't they hate London!"

Gideon joined in his laugh, and felt a deep satisfaction.

His hands bandaged and free from pain, Sonnley was sitting at the window of his apartment, staring down into the street. Now and again he muttered harshly:

"I'll get the swine. I'll get him."

Soon afterward he went out by himself, to collect the tickets for the Procession stand. When he had them, he stepped into a telephone booth and, with great difficulty, inserted the coppers and dialed the number where he expected to find Klein.

It rang on and on for a long time, while Sonnley scowled straight ahead at people passing in the street.

At last the ringing stopped, and Klein answered:

"Benny Klein speaking."

"Benny," Sonnley said in a low-pitched voice; he managed to make himself sound anxious.

"Who's that?" demanded Klein, and then caught his breath. "Is that you, Sonny Boy?"

"Listen, Benny," said Sonnley with soft urgency, "I know who fixed that acid now. It was that flicker from Glasgow, Jack Gorra. I can't do anything to Gorra yet, but the day will come. Listen, Benny—" he broke off.

"I'm listening," Klein said, as if he could not really believe that Sonnley was affable.

"I'm throwing my hand in," Sonnley declared. "I can't take any more of it, Benny. I'm past it. So I'm throwing my hand in, and I want to make sure the cops don't get anything on me over the grapevine. I want you to keep your mouth shut about me, Benny."

Klein asked swiftly, "What's it worth, Sonny Boy?"

That was the moment when Sonnley felt sure that Klein had taken the bait, and after a long pause he smiled for the first time since his fingers had been burned. Then he said as if anxiously:

"We agreed on five thou', didn't we?"

"*How* much, Sonny Boy?"

"Five thou—"

"It's a deal for ten thousand," Klein said quickly. "Ten thousand will make a lot of difference to me, but a rich man like you won't notice it." There was a sneer in his voice.

Sonnley muttered, "I'm not so rich, but—well, I don't want trouble, Benny. I'll make it ten. But my hands are all burned. You'll have to collect the dough. You'll find it in the cellar at the Norvil Street shop."

"I've got some keys," Klein said. "Okay, Sonny Boy. You can sleep easy."

When he stepped out of the telephone booth Sonnley stood for a moment, wiping his forehead with the back of one bandaged hand. Then he turned toward his home.

His lips puckered as he began to whistle.

"Got a squeal on the blower, went along to Benny Klein's place, and caught him with ten thousand quids' worth of slush," Lemaitre reported to Gideon in great high spirits. "Klein swore that he'd picked it up on Sonnley's orders, but there isn't a way of proving it, and only Klein's dabs are on the money. Looks to me as if Sonnley found a way of dealing with a rat."

"All right, so we've got Klein," Gideon said. "But we haven't the engraver and printer who can turn out this kind of stuff—it's nearly perfect."

He held one of the pound notes up to the light from the window, where the "water mark" showed. "Work on Klein, work on Sonnley, work on anyone who might be able to help us put a finger on that engraver. Make it your first job when the Visit's over."

"Okay, George," Lemaitre said.

He went out, leaving Gideon at his desk, with a pile of reports about the Visit in front of him, and with a deep awareness that the war against crime kept up. There was never any rest; there never would be.

His eyes brightened at the thought that Klein was going to get a longer rest than he'd bargained for.

THE BABY IN THE ICEBOX

BY JAMES M. CAIN

James Mallahan Cain was born in Maryland on July 1, 1892. After reporting for the Baltimore *American* and the Baltimore *Sun*, he taught journalism at St. John's College, Annapolis. Later he was an editorial writer for the New York *World* and managing editor of *The New Yorker*. His first novel, *The Postman Always Rings Twice*, was published in 1934. He spent seventeen years as a screenwriter in Hollywood and his novel, *Double Indemnity*, is a film classic. His major theme has been the potentially evil dream that comes true, with terrifying consequences.

Of course there was plenty pieces in the paper about what happened out at the place last Summer, but they got it all mixed up, so I will now put down how it really was, and specially the beginning of it, so you will see it is not no lies in it.

Because when a guy and his wife begin to play leapfrog with a tiger, like you might say, and the papers put in about that part and not none of the stuff that started it off, and then one day say X marks the spot and next day say it wasn't really no murder but don't tell you what it was, why I don't blame people if they figure there was something funny about it or maybe that somebody ought to be locked up in the booby-hatch. But there wasn't no booby-hatch to this, nothing but plain onriness and a dirty rat getting it in the neck where he had it coming to him, as you will see when I get the first part explained right.

Things first begun to go sour between Duke and Lura when they put the cats in. They didn't need no cats. They had a combination autocamp, filling-station, and lunch-room out in the country a ways, and they got along all right. Duke run the filling-station, and got me in to help him, and Lura took care of the lunch-room and shacks. But Duke wasn't satisfied. Before he got this place he had raised rabbits, and one time he had bees, and another time canary birds, and nothing would suit him now but to put in some cats to draw trade. Maybe you think that's funny, but out here in California they got every kind of a farm there is, from kangaroos to alligators, and it was just about the idea that a guy like Duke would think up. So he begun building a cage, and one day he showed up with a truckload of wildcats.

I wasn't there when they unloaded them. It was two or three cars waiting and I had to gas them up. But soon as I got a chance I went back there to look things over. And believe me, they wasn't pretty. The guy that sold Duke the cats had went away about five minutes before, and Duke was standing outside the cage and he had a stick of wood in his hand with blood on it. Inside was a dead cat. The rest of them was on a shelf, that had been built for them to jump on, and every one of them was snarling at Duke.

I don't know if you ever saw a wildcat, but they are about twice as big as a house cat, brindle gray, with tufted ears and a bobbed tail. When they set and look at you they look like a owl, but they wasn't setting and looking now. They was marching around, coughing and spitting, their eyes shooting red and green fire, and it was a ugly sight, specially with that bloody dead one down on the ground. Duke was pale, and the breath was whistling through his nose, and it didn't take no doctor to see he was scared to death.

"You better bury that cat," he says to me. "I'll take care of the cars."

I looked through the wire and he grabbed me. "Look out!" he says. "They'd kill you in a minute."

"In that case," I says, "how do I get the cat out?"

"You'll have to get a stick," he says, and shoves off.

I was pretty sore, but I begun looking around for a stick. I found one, but when I got back to the cage Lura was there. "How did that happen?" she says.

"I don't know," I says, "but I can tell you this much: If there's any more of them to be buried around here, you can get somebody else to do it. My job is to fix flats, and I'm not going to be no cat undertaker."

She didn't have nothing to say to that. She just stood there while I was trying the stick, and I could hear her toe snapping up and down in the sand, and from that I knowed she was choking it back, what she really thought, and didn't think no more of this here cat idea than I did.

The stick was too short. "My," she says, pretty disagreeable, "that looks terrible. You can't bring people out here with a thing like that in there."

"All right," I snapped back. "Find me a stick."

She didn't make no move to find no stick. She put her hand on the gate. "Hold on," I says. "Them things are nothing to monkey with."

"Huh," she says. "All they look like to me is a bunch of cats."

There was a kennel back of the cage, with a drop door on it, where they was supposed to go at night. How you got them back there was bait them with food, but I didn't know that then. I yelled at them, to drive them back in there, but nothing happened. All they done was yell back. Lura listened to me a while, and then she give a kind of gasp like she couldn't stand it no longer, opened the gate, and went in.

Now believe me, that next was a bad five minutes, because she wasn't hard to look at, and I hated to think of her getting mauled up by them babies. But a guy would of had to of been blind if it didn't show him that she had a way with cats. First thing she done, when she got in, she stood still, didn't make no sudden motions or nothing, and begun to talk to them. Not no special talk. Just "Pretty pussy, what's the matter, what they been doing to you?"—like that. Then she went over to them.

They slid off, on their bellies, to another part of the shelf. But she

259

kept after them, she got her hand on one, and stroked him on the back. Then she got a-hold of another one, and pretty soon she had give them all a pat. Then she turned around, picked up the dead cat by one leg, and come out with him. I put him on the wheelbarrow and buried him.

Now, why was it that Lura kept it from Duke how easy she had got the cat out and even about being in the cage at all? I think it was just because she didn't have the heart to show him up to hisself how silly he looked. Anyway, at supper that night, she never said a word. Duke, he was nervous and excited and told all about how the cats had jumped at him and how he had to bean one to save his life, and then he give a long spiel about cats and how fear is the only thing they understand, so you would of thought he was Martin Johnson just back from the jungle or something.

But it seemed to me the dishes was making quite a noise that night, clattering around on the table, and that was funny, because one thing you could say for Lura was: she was quiet and easy to be around. So when Duke, just like it was nothing at all, asks me by the way how did I get the cat out, I heared my mouth saying, "With a stick," and not nothing more. A little bird flies around and tells you, at a time like that. Lura let it pass. Never said a word. And if you ask me, Duke never did find out how easy she could handle the cats, and that ain't only guesswork, but on account of something that happened a little while afterwards, when we got the mountain-lion.

A mountain-lion is a cougar, only out here they call them a mountain-lion. Well, one afternoon about five o'clock this one of ours squat down on her hunkers and set up the worst squalling you ever listen to. She kept it up all night, so you wanted to go out and shoot her, and next morning at breakfast Duke come running in and says come on out and look what happened. So we went out there, and there in the cage with her was the prettiest he mountain-lion you ever seen in your life. He was big, probably weighed a hundred and fifty pounds, and his coat was a pearl gray so glossy it looked like a pair of new gloves, and he had a spot of white on his throat. Sometimes they have white.

"He come down from the hills when he heard her call last night," says Duke, "and got in there somehow. Ain't it funny? When they hear that note nothing can stop them."

"Yeah," I says. "It's love."

"That's it," says Duke. "Well, we'll be having some little ones soon. Cheaper'n buying them."

After he had went on to town to buy stuff for the day, Lura sat down to the table with me. "Nice of you," I says, "to let Romeo in last night."

"Romeo?" she says.

"Yes, Romeo. That's going to be papa of twins soon, out in the lion cage."

"Oh," she says, "didn't he get in there himself?"

"He did not. If she couldn't get out, how could he get in?"

All she give me at that time was a dead pan. Didn't know nothing about it at all. Fact of the matter, she made me a little sore. But after she brung me my second cup of coffee she kind of smiled. "Well?" she says. "You wouldn't keep two loving hearts apart, would you?"

So things was, like you might say, a little gritty, but they got a whole lot worse when Duke come home with Rajah, the tiger. Because by that time, he had told so may lies that he begun to believe them hisself, and put on all the airs of a big animal-trainer. When people come out on Sundays, he would take a black snake whip and go in with the mountain-lions and wildcats, and snap it at them, and they would snarl and yowl, and Duke acted like he was doing something. Before he went in, he would let the people see him strapping on a big six-shooter, and Lura got sorer by the week.

For one thing, he looked so silly. She couldn't see nothing to going in with the cats, and specially she couldn't see no sense in going in with a whip, a six-shooter, and a ten-gallon hat like them cow people wears. And for another thing, it was bad for business. In the beginning, when Lura would take the customers' kids out and make out the cat had their finger, they loved it, and they loved it still more when the little mountain-lions come and they had spots and would push up their ears to be scratched. But when Duke started that stuff with the whip it scared them to death, and even the fathers and mothers was nervous, because there was the gun and they didn't know what would happen next. So business begun to fall off.

And then one afternoon he put down a couple of drinks and figured it was time for him to go in there with Rajah. Now it had took Lura one minute to tame Rajah. She was in there sweeping out his cage one morning when Duke was away, and when he started sliding around on his belly he got a bucket of water in the face, and that was that. From then on he was her cat. But what happened when Duke tried to tame him was awful. The first I knew what he was up to was when he made a speech to the people from the mountain-lion cage telling them not to go away yet, there was more to come. And when he come out he headed over to the tiger.

"What's the big idea?" I says. "What you up to now?"

"I'm going in with that tiger," he says. "It's got to be done, and I might as well do it now."

"Why has it got to be done?" I says.

He looked at me like as though he pitied me.

261

"I guess there's a few things about cats you don't know yet," he says. "You got a tiger on your hands, you got to let him know who's boss, that's all."

"Yeah?" I says. "And who *is* boss?"

"You see that?" he says, and cocks his finger at his face.

"See what?" I says.

"The human eye," he says. "The human eye, that's all. A cat's afraid of it. And if you know your business you'll keep him afraid of it. That's all I'll use, the human eye. But of course, just for protection, I've got these too."

"Listen, sweetheart," I says to him. "If you give me a choice between the human eye and a Bengal tiger, which one I got the most fear of, you're going to see a guy getting a shiner every time. If I was you, I'd lay off that cat."

He didn't say nothing: hitched up his holster, and went in. He didn't even get a chance to unlimber his whip. That tiger, soon as he saw him, begun to move around in a way that made your blood run cold. He didn't make for Duke first, you understand. He slid over, and in a second he was between Duke and the gate. That's one thing about a tiger you better not forget if you ever meet one. He can't work examples in arithmetic, but when it comes to the kind of brains that mean meat, he's the brightest boy in the class and then some. He's born knowing more about cutting off a retreat than you'll ever know, and his legs do it for him, just automatic, so his jaws will be free for the main business of the meeting.

Duke backed away, and his face was awful to see. He was straining every muscle to keep his mouth from sliding down in his collar. His left hand fingered the whip a little, and his right pawed around, like he had some idea of drawing the gun. But the tiger didn't give him time to make up his mind what his idea was, if any.

He would slide a few feet on his belly, then get up and trot a step or two, then slide on his belly again. He didn't make no noise, you understand. He wasn't telling Duke, Please go away: he meant to kill him, and a killer don't generally make no more fuss than he has to. So for a few seconds you could even hear Duke's feet sliding over the floor. But all of a sudden a kid begun to whimper, and I come to my senses. I run around to the back of the cage, because that was where the tiger was crowding him, and I yelled at him.

"Duke!" I says. "In his kennel! Quick!"

He didn't seen to hear me. He was still backing, and the tiger was still coming. A woman screamed. The tiger's head went down, he crouched on the ground, and tightened every muscle. I knew what that meant. Everybody knew what it meant, and specially Duke knew what it meant. He made a funny sound in his throat, turned, and ran.

That was when the tiger sprung. Duke had no idea where he was going, but when he turned he fell through the trap door and I snapped it down. The tiger hit it so hard I thought it would split. One of Duke's legs was out, and the tiger was on it in a flash, but all he got on that grab was the sole of Duke's shoe. Duke got his leg in somehow and I jammed the door down tight.

It was a sweet time at supper that night. Lura didn't see this here, because she was busy in the lunch-room when it happened, but them people had talked on their way out, and she knowed all about it. What she said was plenty. And Duke, what do you think he done? He passed it off like it wasn't nothing at all. "Just one of them things you got to expect," he says. And then he let on he knowed what he was doing all the time, and the only lucky part of it was that he didn't have to shoot a valuable animal like Rajah was. "Keep cool, that's the main thing," he says. "A thing like that can happen now and then, but never let a animal see you excited."

I heard him, and I couldn't believe my ears, but when I looked at Lura I jumped. I think I told you she wasn't hard to look at. She was a kind of medium size, with a shape that would make a guy leave his happy home, sunburned all over, and high cheekbones that give her eyes a funny slant. But her eyes was narrowed down to slits, looking at Duke, and they shot green where the light hit them, and it come over me all of sudden that she looked so much like Rajah, when he was closing in on Duke in the afternoon, that she could of been his twin sister.

Next off, Duke got it in his head he was such a big cat man now that he had to go up in the hills and do some trapping. Bring in his own stuff, he called it.

I didn't pay much attention to it at the time. Of course, he never brought in no stuff, except a couple of raccoons that he probably bought down the road for $2, but Duke was the kind of a guy that every once in a while has to sit on a rock and fish, so when he loaded up the flivver and blew, it wasn't nothing you would get excited about. Maybe I didn't really care what he was up to, because it was pretty nice, running the place with Lura with him out of the way, and I didn't ask no questions. But it was more to it than cats or 'coons or fish, and Lura knowed it, even if I didn't.

Anyhow, it was while he was away on one of them trips of his that Wild Bill Smith the Texas Tornado showed up. Bill was a snake-doctor. He had a truck, with his picture painted on it, and two or three boxes of old rattlesnakes with their teeth pulled out, and he sold snake-oil that would cure what ailed you, and a Indian herb medicine that would do the same. He was a fake, but he was big and brown and had white teeth, and I guess he really wasn't no bad guy.

The first I seen of him was when he drove up in his truck, and told me to gas him up and look at his tires. He had a bum differential that made a funny rattle, but he said never mind and went over to the lunch-room.

He was there a long time, and I thought I better let him know his car was ready. When I went over there, he was setting on a stool with a sheepish look on his face, rubbing his hand. He had a snake ring on one finger, with two red eyes, and on the back of his hand was red streaks. I knew what that meant. He had started something and Lura had fixed him. She had a pretty arm, but a grip like iron, that she said come from milking cows when she was a kid. What she done when a guy got fresh was take hold of his hand and squeeze it so the bones cracked, and he generally changed his mind.

She handed him his check without a word, and I told him what he owed on the car, and he paid up and left.

"So you settled his hash, hey?" I says to her.

"If there's one thing gets on my nerves," she says, "It's a man that starts something the minute he gets in the door."

"Why didn't you yell for me?"

"Oh, I didn't need no help."

But the next day he was back, and after I filled up his car I went over to see how he was behaving. He was setting at one of the tables this time, and Lura was standing beside him. I saw her jerk her hand away quick, and he give me the bright grin a man has when he's got something he wants to cover up. He was all teeth. "Nice day," he says. "Great weather you have in this country."

"So I hear," I says. "Your car's ready."

"What I owe you?" he says.

"Dollar twenty."

He counted it out and left.

"Listen," says Lura: "we weren't doing anything when you come in. He was just reading my hand. He's a snake doctor, and knows about the zodiac."

"Oh, wasn't we?" I says. "Well, wasn't we nice!"

"What's it to you?" she says.

"Nothing," I snapped at her. I was pretty sore.

"He says I was born under the sign of Yin," she says. You would of thought it was a piece of news fit to put in the paper.

"And who is Yin?" I says.

"It's Chinese for tiger," she says.

"Then bite yourself off a piece of raw meat," I says, and slammed out of there. We didn't have no nice time running the joint *that* day.

Next morning he was back. I kept away from the lunch-room, but I took a stroll, and seen them back there with the tiger. We had hauled a tree in there by that time, for Rajah to sharpen his claws on, and she was setting on that. The tiger had his head in her lap, and Wild Bill was looking through the wire. He couldn't even draw his breath. I didn't go near enough to hear what they was saying. I went back to the car and begin blowing the horn.

He was back quite a few times after that, in between while Duke was away. Then one night I heard a truck drive up. I knowed that truck by its rattle. And it was daylight before I heard it go away.

Couple weeks after that, Duke come running over to me at the filling-station. "Shake hands with me," he says. "I'm going to be a father."

"Gee," I says, "that's great!"

But I took good care he wasn't around when I mentioned it to Lura.

"Congratulations," I says. "Letting Romeos into the place seems to be about the best thing you do."

"What do you mean?" she says.

"Nothing," I says. "Only I heard him drive up that night. Look like to me the moon was under the sign of Cupid. Well, it's nice if you can get away with it."

"Oh," she says.

"Yeah," I says. "A fine double cross you thought up. I didn't know they tried that any more."

She set and looked at me, and then her mouth begin to twitch and her eyes filled with tears. She tried to snuffle them up but it didn't work. "It's not any double cross," she says. "That night, I never went out there. And I never let anybody in. I was supposed to go away with him that night, but—"

She broke off and begin to cry. I took her in my arms. "But then you found this out?" I says. "Is that it?" She nodded her head. It's awful to have a pretty woman in your arms that's crying over somebody else.

From then on, it was terrible. Lura would go along two or three days pretty nice, trying to like Duke again on account of the baby coming, but then would come a day when she looked like some kind of a hex, with her eyes all sunk in so you could hardly see them at all, and not a word out of her.

Them bad days, anyhow when Duke wasn't around she would spend with the tiger. She would set and watch him sleep, or maybe play with him, and he seemed to like it as much as she did. He was young when we got him, and mangy and thin, so you could see his slats. But now he was about six years old, and had been fed good, so he had got his growth and his coat was nice, and I think he was the biggest tiger I ever seen. A tiger, when he is really big, is a lot bigger than a lion, and sometimes when Rajah would be rubbing around Lura, he looked more like a mule than a cat.

His shoulders come up above her waist, and his head was so big it would cover both her legs when he put it in her lap. When his tail would go sliding past her it looked like some kind of a constrictor snake. His teeth were something to make you lie awake nights. A tiger has the biggest teeth of any cat, and Rajah's must have been four inches long, curved like a cavalry sword, and ivory white. They were the most murderous looking fangs I ever set eyes on.

When Lura went to the hospital it was a hurry call, and she didn't even have time to get her clothes together. Next day Duke had to pack her bag, and he was strutting around, because it was a boy, and Lura had named him Ron. But when he come out with the bag, he didn't have much of a strut. "Look what I found," he says to me, and fishes something out of his pocket. It was the snake ring.

"Well?" I says. "They sell them in any ten-cent store."

"H'm," he says, and kind of weighed the ring in his hand. That afternoon, when he come back, he says: "Ten-cent store, hey? I took it to a jeweler today, and he offered me two hundred dollars for it."

"You ought to sold it," I says. "Maybe save you bad luck."

Duke went away again right after Lura come back, and for a little while things was all right. She was crazy about the little boy, and I thought he was pretty cute myself, and we got along fine. But then Duke come back and at lunch one day he made a crack about the ring. Lura didn't say nothing, but he kept at it, and pretty soon she wheeled on him.

"All right," she says. "There was another man around here, and I loved him. He gave me that ring, and it meant that he and I belonged to each other. But I didn't go with him, and you know why I didn't. For Ron's sake, I've tried to love you again, and maybe I can yet, God knows. A woman can do some funny things if she tries. But that's where we're at now. That's right where we're at. And if you don't like it, you better say what you're going to do."

"When was this?" says Duke.

"It was quite a while ago. I told you I give him up, and I give him up for keeps."

"It was just before you knowed about Ron, wasn't it?" he says.

"Hey," I cut in. "That's no way to talk."

"Just what I thought," he says. not paying no attention to me. "Ron. That's a funny name for a kid. I thought it was funny, right off when I heard it. Ron. Ron. That's a laugh, ain't it?"

"That's a lie," she says. "That's a lie, every bit of it. And it's not the only lie you've been getting away with around here. Or think you have. Trapping up in the hills, hey? And what do you trap?"

But she looked at me, and choked it back. I begun to see that the cats wasn't the only things that had been gumming it up.

"All right," she wound up. "Say what you're going to do. Go on. Say it!"

But he didn't.

"Ron," he cackles, "that's a hot one," and walks out.

Next day was Saturday, and he acted funny all day. He wouldn't speak to me or Lura, and once or twice I heard him mumbling to himself. Right after supper he says to me, "How are we on oil?"

"All right," I says. "The truck was around yesterday."

"You better drive in and get some," he says. "I don't think we got enough."

"Enough?" I says. "We got enough for two weeks."

"Tomorrow is Sunday," he says, "and there'll be a big call for it. Bring out a hundred gallon and tell them to put it on the account."

By that time, I would give in to one of his nutty ideas rather than have an argument with him, and besides, I never tumbled that he was up to anything. So I wasn't there for what happened next, but I got it out of Lura later, so here is how it was:

Lura didn't pay much attention to the argument about the oil, but washed up the supper dishes, and then went in the bedroom to make sure everything was all right with the baby. When she come out she left the door open, so she could hear if he cried. The bedroom was off the sitting-room, because these here California houses don't have but one floor, and all the rooms connect. Then she lit the fire, because it was cool, and sat there watching it burn. Duke come in, walked around, and then went out back. "Close the door," she says to him. "I'll be right back," he says.

So she sat looking at the fire, she didn't know how long, maybe five minutes, maybe ten minutes. But pretty soon she felt the house shake. She thought maybe it was a earthquake, and looked at the pictures, but they was all hanging straight. Then she felt the house shake again. She listened, but it wasn't no truck outside that would cause it, and it wouldn't be no State road blasting or nothing like that at that time of night. Then she felt it shake again, and this time it shook in a regular movement, one, two, three, four, like that. And then all of a sudden she knew what it was, why Duke had acted so funny all day, why he had sent me off for the gas, why he had left the door open, and all the rest of it. There was five hundred pound of cat walking through the house, and Duke had turned him loose to kill her.

She turned around, and Rajah was looking at her, not five foot away. She didn't do nothing for a minute, just set there thinking what a boob Duke was to figure on the tiger doing his dirty work for him, when all the time she could handle him easy as a kitten, only Duke didn't know it. Then she spoke. She expected Rajah to come and put his head in her lap, but he didn't. He stood there and growled, and his ears flattened back. That scared her, and she thought of the baby. I told you a tiger had that kind of brains. It no sooner went through her head about the baby than Rajah knowed she wanted to get to that door, and he was over there before she could get out of the chair.

He was snarling in a regular roar now, but he hadn't got a whiff of the baby yet, and he was still facing Lura. She could see he meant business. She reached in the fireplace, grabbed a stick that was burning bright, and walked him down with it. A tiger is afraid of fire, and she shoved it right in his eyes. He backed past the door, and she slid in the bedroom. But he was right after her, and she had to hold the stick at him with one hand and grab the baby with the other.

But she couldn't get out. He had her cornered, and he was kicking up such a awful fuss she knowed the stick wouldn't stop him long. So she dropped it, grabbed up the baby's covers, and threw them at his head. They went wild, but they saved her just the same. A tiger, if you throw something at him with a human smell, will generally jump on it and bite at it before he does anything else, and that's what he done now. He jumped so hard the rug went out from under him, and while he was scrambling to his feet she shot past him with the baby and pulled the door shut after her.

She run in my room, got a blanket, wrapped the baby in it, and run out to the electric icebox. It was the only thing around the place that was steel. Soon as she opened the door she knowed why she couldn't do nothing with Rajah. His meat was in there, Duke hadn't fed him. She pulled the meat out, shoved the baby in, cut off the current, and closed the door. Then she picked up the meat and went around the outside of the house to the window of the bedroom. She could see Rajah in there, biting at the top of the door, where a crack of light showed through. He reached to the ceiling. She took a grip on the meat and drove at the screen with it. It give way, and the meat went through. He was on it before it hit the floor.

Next thing was to give him time to eat. She figured she could handle him once he got something in his belly. She went back to the sitting-room. And in there, kind of peering around, was Duke. He had his gun strapped on, and one look at his face was all she needed to know she hadn't made no mistake about why the tiger was loose.

"Oh," he says, kind of foolish, and then walked back and closed the door. "I meant to come back sooner, but I couldn't help looking at the night. You got no idea how beautiful it is. Stars is bright as anything."

"Yeah," she says. "Beautiful."

"Was you expecting burglars or something?" she says, looking at the gun.

"Oh, that," he says. "No. Cats been kicking up a fuss. I put it on, case I have to go back there. Always like to have it handy."

"The tiger," she says. "I thought I heard him, myself."

"Loud," says Duke. "Awful loud."

He waited. She waited. She wasn't going to give him the satisfaction of opening up first. But just then there come a growl from the bedroom, and the sound of bones cracking. A tiger acts awful sore when he eats. "What's that?" says Duke.

"I wonder," says Lura. She was hell-bent on making him spill it first.

They both looked at each other, and then there was more growls, and more sound of cracking bones. "You better go in there," says Duke, soft and easy, with the sweat standing out on his forehead and his eyes shining bright as marbles. "Something might be happening to Ron."

"Do you know what I think it is?" says Lura.

"What's that?" says Duke. His breath was whistling through his nose like it always done when he got excited.

"I think it's the tiger you sent in here to kill me," says Lura. "So you could bring in that woman you been running around with for over a year. That redhead that raises rabbit fryers on the Ventura road. That cat you been trapping!"

"And stead of getting you he got Ron," says Duke. "Little Ron! Oh my, ain't that tough? Go in there, why don't you? Ain't you got no mother love? Why don't you call up his pappy, get him in there? What's the matter? Is he afraid of a cat?"

Lura laughed at him. "All right," she says. "Now you go." With that she took hold of him. He tried to draw the gun, but she crumpled up his hand like a piece of wet paper and the gun fell on the floor. She bent him back on the table and beat his face in for him. Then she picked him up, dragged him to the front door, and threw him out. He run off a little ways. She come back and saw the gun. She picked it up, went to the door again, and threw it after him. "And take that peashooter with you," she says.

That was where she made her big mistake. When she turned to go back in the house, he shot, and that was the last she knew for a while.

Now, for what happened next, it wasn't nobody there, only Duke and the tiger, but after them State cops got done fitting it all together, combing the ruins and all, it wasn't no trouble to tell how it was, anyway most of it, and here's how they figured it out:

Soon as Duke seen Lura fall, right there in front of the house, he knowed he was up against it. So the first thing he done was run to where she was and put the gun in her hand, to make it look like she had shot herself. That was where he made *his* big mistake, because if he had kept the gun he might of had a chance. Then he went inside to telephone, and what he said was, soon as he got hold of the State police: "For God's sake come out here quick. My wife has went crazy and throwed the baby to the tiger and shot herself and I'm all alone in the house with him and—*Oh, my God, here he comes!*"

Now, that last was something he didn't figure on saying. So far as he knowed, the tiger was in the room, having a nice meal off his son, so everything was hotsy-totsy. But what he didn't know was that that piece of burning firewood that Lura had dropped had set the room on fire and on account of that the tiger had got out. How did he get out? We never did quite figure that out. But this is how I figure it, and one man's guess is good as another's:

The fire started near the window, we knew that much. That was where Lura dropped the stick, right next to the cradle, and that was where a guy coming down the road in a car first seen the flames. And what I think is that soon as the tiger got his eye off the meat and seen the fire, he begun to scramble away from it, just wild. And when a wild tiger hits a beaver-board wall, he goes through, that's all. While Duke was telephoning, Rajah come through the wall like a clown through a hoop, and the first thing he seen was Duke, at the telephone, and Duke wasn't no friend, not to Rajah he wasn't.

Anyway, that's how things was when I got there, with the oil. The State cops was a little ahead of me, and I met the ambulance with Lura in it, coming down the road seventy mile an hour, but just figured there had been a crash up the road, and didn't know nothing about it having Lura in it. And when I drove up, there was plenty to look at all right. The house was in flames, and the police was trying to get in, but couldn't get nowheres near it on account of the heat, and about a hundred cars parked all around, with people looking, and a gasoline pumper cruising up and down the road, trying to find a water connection somewheres they could screw their hose to.

But inside the house was the terrible part. You could hear Duke screaming, and in between Duke was the tiger. And both of them was screams of fear, but I think the tiger was worse. It is a awful thing to hear a animal letting out a sound like that. It kept up about five minutes after I got there, and then all of a sudden you couldn't hear nothing but the tiger. And then in a minute that stopped.

There wasn't nothing to do about the fire. In a half hour the whole place was gone, and they was combing the ruins for Duke. Well, they found him. And in his head was four holes, two on each side, deep. We measured them fangs of the tiger. They just fit.

Soon as I could I run in to the hospital. They had got the bullet

270

out by that time, and Lura was laying in bed all bandaged around the head, but there was a guard over her, on account of what Duke said over the telephone. He was a State cop. I sat down with him, and he didn't like it none. Neither did I. I knowed there was something funny about it, but what broke your heart was Lura, coming out of the ether. She would groan and mutter and try to say something so hard it would make your head ache. After a while I got up and went in the hall. But then I see the State cop shoot out of the room and line down the hall as fast as he could go. At last she had said it. The baby was in the electric icebox. They found him there, still asleep and just about ready for his milk. The fire had blacked up the outside, but inside it was as cool and nice as a new bathtub.

Well, that was about all. They cleared Lura, soon as she told her story, and the baby in the icebox proved it. Soon as she got out of the hospital she got a offer from the movies, but stead of taking it she come out to the place and her and I run it for a while, anyway the filling-station end, sleeping in the shacks and getting along nice. But one night I heard a rattle from a bum differential, and I never even bothered to show up for breakfast the next morning.

I often wish I had. Maybe she left me a note.

THE FLOWERING FACE

BY MIGNON G. EBERHART

Mignon G. Eberhart was born in Lincoln, Nebraska. She married civil engineer Alan Eberhart in 1923 and his job took them all over the world. From their travels she was able to set many of her stories and novels in varied locales. Although she does not shy away from danger in her fiction, she was horrified when she came face to face with real murder in covering a celebrated murder case for the Hearst newspapers. In 1971 she won the Grand Master Award from the Mystery Writers of America.

THERE WAS A KNOCK AND THEN another knock, and Susan Dare left a murder half completed and went to the door.

The murder—that particular murder—was, however, entirely fictional. The caller was Katherine Vandeman, who said, "Darling," breezily, entered with a rush and then saw the sheet of paper on the typewriter.

"Oh, my dear," she said contritely. "I've interrupted you. Sorry. But I had to see you."

She rushed on breathlessly: "We are going up on French Crescent today. And we want you to go along. Now please don't say you can't."

Susan hesitated, and Katherine came closer to her so that Susan caught a whiff of cigarette smoke and lemon verbena, curiously mingled. Katherine Vandeman was a tall woman, angularly built; there was about her a kind of hard, bright surface which made people feel that she was herself hard and superficial. Only her eyes, to Susan, were like bright clear holes through a stage curtain, for they were sober and clear, and somehow let you through to the Katherine Vandeman who was behind all that brightness and loudness and hardness. Her eyes and, amended Susan, the way she cared for and nursed her invalid brother-in-law. His name was Cecil Vandeman, he was perhaps ten years younger than Katherine and had been, since the death of Katherine's husband, her only close personal tie. Thinking of him Susan said:

"Who's we?"

"Cecil," said Katherine, bright eyes looking past Susan. "Norman Bridges. Sally Lee Sully. You."

"How's Cecil?" asked Susan because it was the customary inquiry. Katherine was slow about replying.

"We've had another specialist," she said finally. "I'm not altogether sure that I agree with him."

"He doesn't think Cecil is worse?" said Susan quickly.

"Oh, no, no. He thinks—or says he thinks—there's definite improvement." Katherine pulled off her gloves slowly. "You'll go with us, won't you? We'll drive up to the inn, then leave the car and take the trail to the top. It isn't much of a climb—two hours, perhaps. And Norman just telephoned the weather bureau and says it will be clear."

She looked again into Susan's eyes and caught the indecision.

And quite suddenly she said in a still voice that had lost all its bright vivacity:

"Please come, Susan Dare."

There was something urgent, something indefinably compelling about it. Susan said lamely: "But there's a friend of mine coming from Chicago."

"Who?" said Katherine.

"His name is Byrne. Jim Byrne. I had a note this moring—written sort of hurriedly." Susan fished among the papers on the table and found a sheet of yellow copy paper with a few scrawled lines on it—"Dear Susie: Have an unexpected weekend and am coming down to stay at Hunt Club. Find two good riding horses and don't plan any work. Arrive Thursday or Friday night ten o'clock train. Have greatest regard for you and your stories but kindly do not mention six-letter word meaning to destroy by violence in my hearing. JIM."

"He's just finished reporting the Blank case," said Susan explanatorily. "It must have been pretty awful."

"Reporting. Why, that's—" Katherine stopped abruptly.

"Yes, that's the Jim Byrne."

"Oh—oh, yes, I see. I remember his name now. Well—we shall be home before ten. But you might leave a message at the Hunt Club, just in case we are delayed. "Tell him—" Katherine hesitated again. "Tell him to join us—if he wants to. We'll stop for you after lunch. Goodbye, my dear."

Susan didn't really know Katherine Vandeman very well, although the Vandeman place, a huge old Southern home with stables and bluegrass meadows, lay in the valley only two miles distant from Susan's own small cabin. Susan knew in a vague way that Katherine's husband, considerably older than Katherine, had left his widow a sizable chunk of the Vandeman money. She knew, too, that Norman Bridges, a lawyer and an old friend of the Vandeman family, was, in a rather prolonged and desultory way, a suitor of Katherine's.

They called for Susan shortly after noon. Katherine at the wheel of her long convertible coupe, with Cecil beside her and Norman Bridges' tweed shoulders beside Sally Lee Sully's green sweater in the rumble.

Sally Lee Sully, a slim, dark-eyed girl with the sweet languid loveliness of a magnolia, waved prettily to Susan. Norman Bridges' white teeth flashed below his dark moustache, and Cecil got out slowly, unfolding his slender length and explaining to Susan that the seat was wide enough for the three of them if Susan didn't mind a little crowding.

Afterward Susan tried desperately to recall anything at all significant that was said or done during the trip to French Crescent. But there was nothing. Katherine drove furiously with bursts of speed and sudden brakings which threatened to send her passengers through the windshield but somehow never did.

They wound higher and higher. The road became narrow and the hairpin curves sharper. Great expanses of sky and space would appear suddenly ahead and then would vanish as the car swerved, and be replaced by a tangled wall of pines and mountain growth.

It was perhaps four o'clock when they reached the inn, from which only a footpath continued to the mountaintop. Katherine parked expertly in the space reserved for cars. And it took expert parking. They had emerged upon a small plateau backed by the steep rise of the mountain but dropping suddenly away upon sheer space and distance with only a little line of white stones to mark that irregular, precipitous edge. Katherine turned, backed, turned until Cecil, looking rather pale, said: "That's enough, K. You're only a few feet from the edge."

Katherine stopped at last, and Susan took a long breath of relief and Cecil slid out of the car. He turned and smiled, holding out his thin hand to Susan to help her. "Are your legs cramped?" he asked.

"A little," said Susan, "I've kept my foot on a brake that wasn't there practically all the way up the mountain."

"I know," said Cecil. "One does when K is driving. She—" He stopped so abruptly that Susan glanced up into his thin young face and followed the direction of his gaze. Norman Bridges had climbed down from the rumble seat and was holding up his arms for Sally Lee Sully. He was laughing, his white teeth flashing and his face red from the wind, and Sally Lee, blown and lovely, was looking down and laughing, too, so that her eyes were half-closed and darkly shadowed. As she stood above them her green sweater and knitted skirt clung to her body like wet cloth to a clay model and outlined breast and hips and slim young waist against the dull sky. Still smiling gently she brought up one knee in order to step over the side of the car and poised there for an unforgettable instant, one lovely line of grace flowing into another.

The instant that she stood there against the sky became sharp and terribly clear. The still, pearly sky. The pines. The consciousness of space and a plateau and a precipice at its edge, and a great spreading valley below.

And Norman Bridges holding his strong arms up toward Sally, with the laugh on his face becoming fixed while Sally Lee Sully poised there with her beautiful body against the sky.

Katherine banged the heavy door of the car, and the scene dissolved. Sally Lee slid into Norman's arms. Somebody cried: "What a view!" And Katherine was walking away from the car, and they had all turned to look out across space and valley.

"Don't go too near the edge," said Katherine sharply to somebody and Susan realized that she was speaking to Cecil and that, insensibly drawn, they had all drifted toward the little line of stones that marked the edge of the cliff.

Susan stepped nearer, resisting her inborn dread of high places, and looked over. A sheer drop of how many feet—a hundred—three hundred? She couldn't guess.

"Over here," said Cecil to Susan, "is the Crescent. At the right. Just behind the car." She turned at his gesture toward the car again. "It's really just a ravine but it's so sharp and sudden that it's like a gash. It's a queer sort of thing—like a cleft in the face of the plateau. Probably made in some past geological age by a mountain torrent, though it's dry now. Nothing but rocks at the bottom."

No wonder he'd been uneasy when Katherine backed and turned and maneuvered! Susan stood at the rear of the long car and observed with frozen horror that the gleaming left fenders of the car were actually not more than four feet from that sharp, jagged cut.

It was, as Cecil said, an irregular, gash-like cleft interrupting the smooth floor of the plateau. The ravine was narrow, not more than fifteen feet wide where it began at the cliff edge and narrowing to a point. Beyond it was the small plateau again, except that, there, it was not cleared except for a path that ran from the edge of the parking space, around the end of the short, sharp ravine and out again to a bench which was almost directly opposite the car. Katherine spoke quickly and loudly.

"There's a grand view from the other side of the Crescent," she said. "The view from the bench over there is better even than from the plateau on this side. Shall we walk around?"

But Sally Lee Sully, strolling toward them across the parking space, vetoed that. "We'd better get started up the mountain, if we're going."

"Right," agreed Cecil. "Weatherman to the contrary, it's going to be cloudy."

So they started, Katherine plunging ahead and becoming flushed and panting after the first half-mile. Norman trudged along easily beside Susan, smoking a pipe. Sally Lee Sully strolled behind them with an appearance of laziness and fatigue until you realized that she remained exactly twenty feet behind the whole way and might as easily have kept with them. Cecil stayed behind. It was the accustomed thing and occasioned no comment and no offers of company. As they reached a turn in the sharply climbing path that brought them out above the inn and the plateau, they could see him, clear and small below them. It was Norman who saw him first.

"There's Cecil—over on the Crescent. On the bench. See him? He's reading."

"He's always reading." That was Sally Lee.

They went on. And it was a pleasant enough climb. Except that it was cloudy. So cloudy that by the time they reached the top there was no view at all and nothing to do but sit on dampish boulders above a faintly moving, pearly gray blanket and smoke and rest before they started down again.

By the time they reached the inn it was twilight, with the car looming ghostily out of the mist, its sleek gray sides wet, and the windows of the inn lighted and showing distant-looking blobs of radiance.

"Light looks good," said Norman who was by that time merely a thick black bulk trudging beside Susan. "Hope they've got a fire. Hi, Katherine—I'd better turn on the car lights—did you lock the door?"

"Only the ignition. Do turn on the lights, Norm. I don't suppose anybody will be coming up tonight in this fog, though."

Norman vanished, a glow appeared before the car, and Katherine was the first to reach the inn. And at the sound of her step on the porch, the door flung open, letting out light and warmth, with Cecil outlined against the light welcoming them and exclaiming about the fog.

And it was Cecil who suggested that they have dinner at the inn before attempting the descent.

"You are all tired and cold. And the fog is bad. Anyway I've already ordered dinner."

Katherine hesitated and looked at Susan, and afterward Susan wondered what would have happened had she herself insisted on undertaking their trip down the mountain at once. Or rather when it would have happened.

But she did not insist. The open fire leaping in the huge fireplace, the smells of dinner, the table already laid and drawn up to the fire, and more than anything, the prospect of the fog's eventually lifting, were irresistible. And Norman, entering, looked at Katherine and looked at Cecil and closed the door behind him.

"The fog can't get worse," he said. "And it may lift a bit. Tell the girl to bring on the steaks, Cecil. I'm hungry as a bear." Then Norman added abruptly: "Golly, I forgot to bring in the champagne."

"Champagne!" Katherine's voice was strained.

Sally Lee Sully lifted languorous dark eyes to look at Katherine, and Norman said: "Of course. Champagne is the official betrothal toaster. I doubt very much if an engagement to marry is legal without champagne."

"Engagement," said Norman, facing her solidly. "Sally Lee Sully engaged to marry Cecil Vandeman. Announcement made by old friend of family, Norman Bridges." He paused. Cecil somehow was standing between Sally Lee Sully and Katherine—his hand was on Sally Lee but he looked at Katherine. Then Norman crossed to Katherine and forced her to look away from Cecil and at him. "Come now, dear—they've waited patiently till Cecil is better. Now he's well enough to marry—"

Katherine jerked away from him.

"He's not well enough!" she cried.

In the stricken, uncomfortable silence, the door from the kitchen opened brusquely and the waitress entered, laden tray in her hands.

"How do you do?" she said chattily to Norman, who was nearest the table. "Shall I serve dinner now?"

"All right," said Cecil. His hand on Sally Lee increased its pressure, as if comfortingly, before he left her. "I'll get the champagne," he said, obviously thankful for the interruption. And Norman nodded quickly: "Do. It's in the rumble seat."

Cecil picked up his hat and reached the door and paused there, looking at Katherine's rigid back, and Norman said: "Fog is bad, Cecil. Don't stumble and drop the champagne. The car lights are on, you can see all right. Look here, my girl, have you got some glasses?"

Cecil's eyes waited another instant for Katherine to turn. She did not move and he glanced then at Sally Lee, made a cheerful little gesture with his hand, and the door opened, letting in black fog, and closed.

"Goblets will do," said Norman to the waitress. "Bring 'em on. Anything will do when it's champagne."

Katherine whirled from the window.

"You had planned this all along," she said harshly. "You and Cecil. You were going to tell me like this when Sally Lee was here—and Susan—because you thought that in their presence I would say nothing."

"It was Cecil's plan—"

"And yours too, Norman. And Sally Lee's. Probably Sally Lee's plan first. She knew I would object."

"Suppose we did plan it, Katherine," Norman said with stubborn gentleness. "I have waited too."

Sally Lee looked at her ankles and drawled: "Don't be that way, Katherine. I won't eat Cecil."

"You!" said Katherine simply.

"The main thing," drawled Sally Lee, "is that Cecil loves me. And he's free, white and twenty-one, in spite of the sick baby you've tried to make him."

It was a dreadful silence—dreadful to sit there and see Sally Lee's languid sweetness, to watch that dull red slowly sweep out of Katherine's face and her long angular hands double themselves as if she could strike Sally Lee's smiling, pretty face.

Finally Norman said fumblingly: "Now, Sally Lee—" And Katherine said in a choked way: "Did you hear that, Norman? Did you hear what she said? And I've put everything away, you and everything, to nurse and care for Cecil. Yet you say let them marry. Norman, is it possible you do not realize that she's marrying him only for his money?"

Sally Lee Sully showed herself suddenly and pettishly angry.

"I meant you were making him spineless and childish. He's not half the invalid you've made him think he is. You've tried to dominate him. Well, you can't any more. He loves me. Suppose I am marrying him for his money. It's going to make him happy. If you are so devoted to him I should think that would please you."

Katherine's clenched hands relaxed hopelessly. She said to Norman:

"You see what you've done."

"I've done nothing," said Norman, standing his ground solidly. "Be reasonable, Katherine. Sally Lee isn't marrying him just for his money. He wants her. And she'll make him a good wife."

"It divides the Vandeman fortune in half if Cecil—" Sally Lee Sully checked herself as if frightened at what her vicious little tongue had been about to say and looked from Katherine quickly and supplicatingly to Norman. "You see, Norm—if Cecil doesn't marry, the whole thing would come to Katherine."

"Be reasonable," said Norman pleadingly again. "You angered her, Katherine. After all, you didn't exactly welcome her into the family." He approached Katherine and put his hand on her arm but she jerked savagely away from him and went to the door, her sport shoes making heavy, angry footfalls. She opened the door and fog poured in and it was black beyond.

"Cecil ought to be coming," she said as if detached from the painful, ugly quarrel. She peered into the fog.

"He'll be back in a minute," said Norman, relievedly pouncing upon a new topic. "Hope the fog lifts before we go down the mountain. Ah, here come the glasses. And the steaks."

The waitress entered again, glasses clinking faintly and musically and the fragrance of broiling steaks filling the room.

Sally Lee Sully looked at the steaks smoking on the table, hesitated, shrugged, let her skirt drop over her beautiful knees, and rose. Her walk across to where Katherine stood, still peering into the fog beyond the open door, was to Susan's awakened eyes a thing of potent grace. Odd, she'd never perceived the danger in the girl before.

Sally Lee put her hand on Katherine's arm. She was all wooing, all tender and sweet. "K, dear, forgive me. I didn't mean anything —You've been so good to Cecil. I'll try to be as good a wife as you've been a sister."

Norman beamed. Katherine finally tore her seeking eyes from the fog and darkness and looked slowly and searchingly into the girl's flower-like face. And it was then that she said a very strange and dreadful thing.

"Sally Lee," she said, "you will never be Cecil's wife."

Under that searching, bright regard, Sally Lee shrank back. And Norman said roughly: "Shut the door, Katherine. It's cold. Cecil will be here in a moment."

"He ought to be here now," said Katherine. "I'm going to look for him."

"Don't be silly, K, he's all right."

"He ought to have returned," she said stubbornly. "You know, Norm, he has no sense of direction. He's probably wandering about somewhere."

"Nonsense. He can see the lights from the inn."

It was just there, Susan realized later, that from somewhere, stealthily, cautiously, scarcely observed, there crept into the situation a strange sense of tension, of foreshadowing.

But it was a good ten minutes before it became definite. Observable. Tangible, even.

Ten minutes of discussion—of increasingly anxious watching, of Norman first and then Katherine vanishing into the fog and shouting from the edge of the porch into the whirling darkness beyond, soft and black and impenetrable, with not a gleam of light anywhere except from the open door and windows behind them.

But Cecil did not return. And did not reply.

And he was not at the dark and silent car, nor anywhere between the car and the inn; and the lights and the hurriedly summoned proprietor and the two servants and themselves could not discover him and could not make him hear. They were all somehow out in the fog and there were blobs of lights from electric torches and the streaming lights again from the car, and shouting voices everywhere and then that diapason of sound became suddenly still, silenced by one scream.

That was Katherine's scream when they found him.

He was at the bottom of the ravine, huddled on the rocks, dead.

It was the proprietor and Norman who crawled down there with flashlights and ropes. Mercifully the darkness and the fog veiled the thing from Katherine's eyes. And during those black moments while the men painfully, slowly, with difficulties which were too readily to be surmised, managed to remove the slender, broken body and carry it at last toward the inn, Susan sat in the blank dampness beside Katherine and held the woman's strong, angular hands.

Norman, panting, returned at last and put his arm around Katherine and drew her toward the inn. Susan and Sally Lee followed. The light gravel crunched under their feet.

All at once after that black interlude of horror they were again in the long dining room. The fire was stirred to flames. Katherine, looking like a sleepwalker, was sitting before it. The men, Norman and the proprietor and the fat, frightened cook, were talking—talking in circles, repeating themselves, exclaiming, saying how it happened. Sally Lee Sully was crouched, slim and white and silent. The waitress—white, now, and incoherent with excitement—was saying they ought to have turned on the light on the point beyond the Crescent.

And the whole thing was as the proprietor said: Cecil had gone across the open space toward the car. Had become confused in the fog and darkness. Had passed the car without knowing it. Had stepped over the edge of the ravine. It was all perfectly—terribly—clear.

"It's a cruel drop," said the proprietor. "But I never thought of anybody just walking over it like that. The lights ought to have been turned on."

"Lights?" said Norman.

"The light beyond the Crescent. Have it strung up on a wire. It is connected on the same switch with the porch light. But it was so foggy tonight—nobody here but you folks here in the dining-room."

"Don't you make a habit of turning it on every night?"

But they didn't. Why should they? So few people came up at night. It was only during the summer that people from town came up for parties and liked to walk out and sit on the ledge beyond the ravine.

Norman, shuddering, was reproaching himself bitterly.

"I sent him out, Katherine. But I never thought—how could I? He walked out into the fog—aiming toward the car—he was excited, poor Cecil. Never had a head for direction. I ought to have realized the danger. It's all my fault."

Katherine finally spoke. "It's nobody's fault," she said. Her voice was heavy and slow, each word dropping like a weight. "Well—what are we going to do?"

Telephone? But there was no telephone.

"We're so far from town," said the innkeeper. "But I'll watch the—I'll watch while you send to town."

And the waitress sobbed and said again, if she'd only turned on the lights, but how was she to know?

"Him going out into pitch-dark and the fog besides," she said, wiping her eyes.

Something stirred in Susan and quite automatically began to function. The suddenness of the thing, the confusion and, submerging everything, the blinding, swirling fog had shocked and, in a sense, submerged her. Even now she spoke without conscious purpose. And she said only, in a small, clear voice:

"Darkness! But the lights of the car were turned on. He would have been guided by that."

There was an odd, short silence. Then they looked at her.

No one spoke. Under all those eyes Susan smoothed back her hair and heard herself saying quite definitely: "The lights of the car were on. Norman turned them on when we returned from the mountaintop." She paused and added because she couldn't help it and because it was so very obvious: "But there were no lights anywhere when we went to the porch to look for Cecil. There were certainly no lights at all, then."

It was a puzzle.

Not a very great puzzle, to be sure; one doubtless with the simplest of explanations. Norman had turned on the car lights. The doors of the car were not locked. For some trivial reason someone had turned out those lights.

But it was a puzzle that all at once assumed significance.

The car lights would have guided Cecil safely to the car. He would not have passed beyond it in the darkness. Those front lights would have made a blob of yellow that would have served as a beacon.

She thought that far and realized that no one was speaking.

But presently the tensely ruminative look in the waitress's face bore fruit. She said with a burst: "Oh, yes, there were lights. I saw them from the window."

"When did you see them?" asked Susan.

"I remember exactly. I was just going from this room into the kitchen after glasses and I looked out the window and saw a light. And it was right after Mr. Vandeman had gone out for the champagne. I'm sure about it."

"Why yes," said Katherine slowly. "The lights of the car were turned on. I'm sure Cecil could have seen them from the porch. And they were on, when he left. I could see the glow myself from the window as he went out the door. The light was dim and looked far away on account of the fog but quite clear enough to guide him. Who turned them off?"

Again no one spoke for a moment. Then Norman said: "I certainly turned on the lights. And when we stepped out on the porch to call for Cecil I remember thinking how dark it was. If Katherine saw the lights as Cecil left and they were gone when we went to call him—"

The proprietor interrupted anxiously.

"None of us touched your car, Mrs. Vandeman. I was in the kitchen the whole time after you arrived. The cook was there, too, and Jennie"—he indicated the waitress—"was coming and going from the dining room. None of us was anywhere near your car."

Katherine's hand made a weary gesture and Sally Lee Sully said suddenly:

"Perhaps Cecil himself turned out the lights."

There was another thoughtful moment. Then Katherine said: "You mean he reached the car, for some reason turned out the lights and then accidentally stepped over the edge?"

Katherine rose abruptly as if she could not bear talking.

"We'll never know what happened," she said, staring into the flames. "Never. Come—we'd better go down the mountain. It's impossible, of course, to take"—she did not say "Cecil"; instead she simply stopped and then continued: "The coupe is so small. I'll get hold of Dr. Benham. He'll know what to do."

But before they started Susan did a bit of private exploring—the odd little puzzle of the lights was still a puzzle.

The switch beside the door did control both the light on the long porch, a single bare bulb set into its sloping rustic roof, and another light high up in the trees above the bench on the far side of the ravine; too, the car lights were on now, streaming dully into the fog. The fog veiled their brilliance. Still it would have been impossible, even in the fog, to miss those lights.

And Susan herself had seen that resultant glow when Norman turned them on. And Katherine had seen it from the window at the time Cecil went out toward it. And Susan herself had seen that there was no light anywhere at the moment when all four of them stepped from the dining room to the porch in order to call Cecil.

Then had he reached the car? And if he had reached the car, why had he turned off the lights before returning to the inn?

Susan walked slowly across the gravel toward the car. Back at the inn were lights and muffled voices. But the mountain was silent and dark, and felt rather than seen. Off toward the right, veiled by that soft, damp blackness was the sharp edge of the plateau. Just before her was the car and beyond the car was the narrow wedge of blackness, cruel and masked by fog, dividing the plateau from the ledge beyond. She measured her steps, noted how the strong lights of the car were blurred and veiled and only gradually became perceptible as lights, and reached the car. Across that dark space which she knew lay at her feet and away up in the trees was the light; that, too, had it been lighted, would have been a guide to Cecil. Or rather not a guide but a warning. Then the confused sound of footsteps was on the gravel and shadows were emerging from the fog.

"Let me drive, K." That was Norman's voice.

And Katherine said wearily: "No, Norman. It will give me something to do. You and Sally Lee can ride in the rumble."

But when she had got into the car and fumbled for the ignition, she said quite suddenly to Susan: "I was wrong, Susan. I can't drive."

"I'll drive," offered Susan quickly.

Susan found the road and entered it, and very cautiously made the first of those fumbling, fog-blinded curves.

It wasn't going to be any fun, getting that long car down the mountain. It hadn't been so bad coming up. Cecil had been with them, then. Cecil.

But Cecil was dead now. In an accident. Cecil who had been the focus of a queer, dreadful quarrel. They were peaceful now, Norman and Katherine and Sally Lee. Peaceful now that Cecil was dead and they had him no longer to quarrel about.

Susan peered into the fog and turned and watched for the road. It was somehow hypnotic, that constant moving through dense swirling mists, that constant heightening of tension in all the nerves, that straining for perception, that groping, groping into fog. Groping into fog. Trying to feel out imperceptible things.

Murder!

The word suddenly entered and possessed Susan's consciousness. It was unexpected. And it was like an alarm.

Now why should she think of that? No reason at all. Murder.

If it was Cecil's death she was trying to connect with murder, that was all wrong. Cecil had stepped over a cliff while all four of them were together in that lighted dining-room. Talking. Quarreling about Cecil.

But Cecil was not murdered.

Now look here, Susan, she thought, let's examine this. Don't dismiss it as if you were afraid of it; prove to yourself that there's no murder. No murder. No murder because he couldn't have been murdered when there was no one to murder him.

And there was no motive. No one who would profit by his death and no one to whom that death would be welcome.

Katherine, of course, would inherit the whole of the Vandeman fortune instead of only half of it, if Cecil died without heirs. Without a wife. But Katherine was devoted to Cecil. And she had enough money as it was. Sally Lee Sully stood to lose at Cecil's death. And Norman Bridges, unless he married Katherine, was not affected in any way. Although if he married Katherine, Cecil's death just now doubled Katherine's (and thus in a sense, Norman's own) fortune.

Katherine stirred and said abruptly: "But he's better off dead. Marriage with Sally Lee—" she did not finish.

The broken sentence fitted into a small groove in Susan's thoughts.

No motive. No murderer. Then there was no murder.

On through the fog, carrying consciousness of murder. Murder becoming part of the fog.

Against her will, against her reason, the thing persisted. Against—

If Cecil had turned out the lights of the car after leaving it, then where was the champagne? It should be in that case shattered somewhere in that deadly steep ravine. But was it?

The question was sharp and sudden like an unexpected flash of lightning.

Susan consciously and clearly began to think and build and remember. It was as if that flash of light had briefly illumined a dark room and she knew not what the objects it contained were, but merely that they were there.

And Susan knew that she had to go back. To go back now before others came. Before—a glow of yellow was rounding a curve twenty feet ahead. Susan put on brakes and clutched for the horn, and its long mellow notes echoed in unseen valleys. Susan's car stopped. The other car stopped. There were voices and men's figures before the lights.

And out of the fog came Jim Byrne. Out of the fog and up to the car.

"Susan?" he cried. "Good Lord! Why didn't you stay where you were till the fog lifted!"

Susan said something; she never knew what. Another man—Jim called him vaguely Landy—approached and Susan heard Katherine speaking to him.

"There was an accident," she was saying as if she knew him. "Cecil fell into the ravine."

Terse explanations, horrified low-voiced talk, Norman there, too, telling them. Somehow she must let Jim know that it was no accident. That it was murder. And that they must go back. That they must discover that evidence before it was destroyed.

Jim's blunted, agreeably irregular face loomed rather sternly from the blackness. His sensitive mouth looked tight, his chin, as always, faintly pugnacious.

Susan touched his hand. And as he looked directly at her, she said in a voice that was scarcely more than a whisper: "It's murder."

He heard it. His eyes became aware and his face very still. She whispered: "We must go back. Arrange it—somehow. And let me ride with you."

He arranged it. Smoothly and with his customary resource and aplomb. She believed that there was some general feeling that they were to bring the body down the mountain in Landy's sedan. No one objected. Norman took Susan's place at the wheel. With Jim and Landy at the side of the road watching lest the wheels go over the edge and shouting directions, he managed to reverse the long coupe.

And Susan, shaking a little, was beside Jim, in the front seat of the Landy sedan.

The moving rear light of the coupe ahead made a small red signal, warning them of curves. But the man Landy and Sally Lee were in the tonneau. Sally Lee was drenched with fog and chilled, and white, and very appealing. She had to ride inside, now that she could. Susan could hear Landy being comforting.

The trouble was Susan couldn't talk to Jim. The story came out but only in outline, only the surface of it, and she could not tell Jim that first they must make sure about the champagne bottles. That they must look for a string or a rope with a weight on one end. Or neither, but instead something unpredictable.

That because the motive was what she felt it was, they must prevent another murder. That was what made it so urgent. That was why they had to find evidence, conclusive evidence— somehow.

One murder and then, after a while, another. The murder of Cecil was only half that grim program. The second murder would complete it.

"He never had a head for direction," Sally Lee was saying plaintively.

Faintly, ironically, the little red gleam ahead led them over that blind, winding journey.

Once Susan said, under cover of Landy's heavier voice: "Why did you start up the mountain?"

"Nerves." He grinned at her and then sobered. "One of my fey nights. Fog and general unrest. I got your note; you hadn't returned."

There was the inn, lights in the windows and on the porch. Across, beyond the Crescent, the light in the trees made a blur. The coupe was already parked before it, and as the gravel spattered under the sedan tires the door opened. And still there was no chance to talk to Jim. Suppose she had made a mistake. Jim helped her out of the car.

"What shall I do?"

"Talk. Ask questions. Especially about the lights."

"You girls had better go inside to the fire," Landy was saying, speaking to both of them and looking at Sally Lee.

It was not difficult to approach, in the confusion and shifting lights, the rumble seat of the coupe and search for champagne bottles that *were not there*. Not difficult either to walk quietly in the shadows behind the parked cars toward the Crescent. The lights from the cars, the porch light, enabled her to pick her way along. Here was the place where the Vandeman car had been parked— here were its tire marks. That dark rift was the edge of the ravine. Across it and considerably to the right was the light in the trees.

She hesitated. She could, if she was very careful not to make a misstep, find her way along the path that skirted the ravine. The others had gone into the inn. The light among the trees over there would serve as a guide. But the fog was treacherous, inconceivably bewildering.

She took a few steps and stopped sharply. Was there a curious faint echo of crunching gravel? If so, it was silent now. Susan swallowed her heart and went on, feeling her way cautiously, step by step.

There were shrubs now as she passed the curve of the ravine and the path rose a little. Somewhere beyond the clouds there must be a rising moon, full and white, for the fog had taken on a kind of gray gleam. Her feet were yet on the path and it was easier than she'd expected. But she didn't like being alone in the fog.

Something white loomed out of it and she stopped dead still and terrified before she saw that it was only the bench. The bench where Cecil had sat reading during the afternoon.

Above her was the light and she could see it now as a light and not as just a bright glow. It was a bulb, shaded by a reflector, swathed in mist. As this side of the plateau was a little higher than the inn side, the light looked from the side of the inn much higher than it proved actually to be. For it was not more than twelve feet off the ground. It was a makeshift affair, strung as if for only temporary use on a drop-cord and hanging over a convenient branch with the slack taken up and tied in a loop.

Something rustled again in a dripping thicket nearby and Susan turned with a kind of gasp of comprehension and something very like terror. Her return over that path and around the black depth that was the ravine was, in spite of its caution, like a flight. Yet she knew that there was no one there in the fog. Everyone was at the inn. Once on the cleared space and headed toward the parked cars and the inn she lost some of her unreasoning terror. It was only murder that she was afraid of; the fact of it; the presence of it which was like a tangible thing.

The instrument of murder was there beyond that opened door, where light made a long, broad radiance.

She was panting though, when she reached the porch of the inn. What had they done? What had they decided? She controlled her breath and smoothed her hair back tightly under her brown beret and entered. And walked upon a tableau.

Katherine stood, tall and vigorous, though her long face was pale, before the fire. Sally Lee was seated languidly in a chair, looking very helpless and very beautiful. Norman was standing beside Sally Lee. Landy was leaning lazily over the back of a chair and looked perplexed. The innkeeper and the fat cook with his white apron twisted around his waist were looking worried and the waitress, Jennie, was peering in at the kitchen door.

And Jim was sitting casually on the edge of a table. He had just finished saying something, for there was about them an air of intent listening, and Jim was very definitely the focus of that strained attention. No one seemed to be aware of Susan's entrance but she knew that Jim had noted it. Norman cleared his throat and said:

"I don't understand you."

Jim flicked a glance toward Susan.

"It's a question of satisfying the coroner. It makes no difference to me of course. It's nothing to me—except a very regrettable affair. But you see, the—body *was removed*. And it was a death by violence. I'm only telling you that the coroner will be bound to ask questions. It's just as well to be perfectly clear in your minds about what happened. This business of the lights, now, seems to me confusing. Probably it isn't, really. In the excitement of the moment"—he turned suddenly and directly to Katherine.

"You turned on the car lights? When was that?"

"When we came down from the mountain. About six o'clock. But I didn't turn them on. Norman did it for me."

"Then it was you, Mr. Bridges, who turned on the lights?"

"Why, yes, of course," said Norman.

"You are sure? I mean, your sleeve didn't catch on the switch as you turned from the car and turn them off again—something like that?"

"Certainly, I'm sure. Anyway, Katherine saw the car lights from the window just as Cecil left this room and went into the fog."

"That's right," said Jim agreeably. Evidently from the talk in the

288

car and from the questions that had preceded Susan's entrance he had got a fairly complete version of the thing.

"Did anybody else see the lights after you arrived at the inn?"

Susan started to mention the waitress when the girl darted forward. "I did," she said eagerly. "Just after Mr. Vandeman went out the door."

"I see," said Jim. "Then what happened to the car lights between the time when Mrs. Vandeman and Jennie saw them, and the time when you opened the door and went out to call for Cecil? You have all said that there was no light anywhere then."

"That's just the point. There's only one thing that could have happened. Cecil must have turned them out."

"Why?" said Jim again, gently.

But Katherine's long face was beginning to look angry.

Norman said with decision: "We don't know. One never knows exactly how accidents happen. But since we were all here in this room when it must have happened (or in the kitchen), there is no other explanation. Cecil for some reason turned out those lights, started into the fog away from the car, perhaps turned back for something. We'll never know just what happened. Except that somehow—he misjudged the distances—missed his footing—"

Sally Lee looked up at Jim.

"Poor Cecil," she said. "He always got confused so easily." She dabbed her lovely eyes with her handkerchief and the Landy person looked altogether fatuous.

Jim said to her: "What did *you* do when Cecil did not return?"

Sally Lee looked blank and stopped dabbing her eyes. She said after a moment: "Well, it was like this. Katherine and Norman walked out on the porch and shouted. Pretty soon I went out too. There wasn't any light. Somebody said something about lights and Norman said he'd call the proprietor. Katherine said maybe Cecil was in the car and started across the space toward the car. Norman ran along the porch and knocked on the kitchen door, I think, and shouted something. Then—I don't know what happened. I started out toward the car and—it was very dark and I could hear people but couldn't see anything. Pretty soon I bumped into Katherine and we were all calling Cecil. It's pretty confused. I don't know what happened really. The innkeeper was out there, too."

"Were there any lights?"

Sally Lee looked thoughtful.

"After a while," she achieved presently. "Somebody turned on the lights of the car. And the innkeeper, I suppose, had some flashlights. And there was a light on the porch. And another up in the trees over there. That's all I can remember. Except that Katherine and I—and Miss Dare, I suppose—stood there together while they were climbing down into the ravine. And Katherine started to cry. Then they said he was dead and they were bringing—him up."

"I see," said Jim. "Does everybody agree to that—or has Miss Sully forgotten something?"

No one spoke for a moment. Then the proprietor said:

"I guess that's right."

Norman Bridges nodded.

"Exactly right, I think."

"Who finally turned on the porch light?"

Jennie stepped forward again.

"I did. He"—she looked at Norman—"pounded on the door from the porch and shouted that somebody was lost. My father"—(The cook, thought Susan parenthetically, or the innkeeper? The latter, for the girl added definitely, "Him," and pointed to the innkeeper)—"got some flashlights and went outdoors and the cook went too. I came in here to find out what had happened. Nobody was here. I went to the door and it was all dark outside except that just as I looked the car lights shone up all at once, as if somebody had just turned them on. They looked real near and I started out to see what had happened. Everybody was shouting and calling Cecil and pretty soon I saw the flashlights over beyond the Crescent and I thought about the light over there, so I ran back to the porch—the switch is right there beside the door—and turned it on."

"Lights," said Katherine suddenly, "are extremely confusing when there's such a dense fog."

Jim looked at her.

"Are these stories as you remember things, Mrs. Vandeman?"

Katherine hesitated. "I think so. I was very frightened. Terrified."

"Terrified?"

"I am always nervous about Cecil. I have cared for him so long. I—I was afraid he would become chilled, staying out in the fog so long."

"You didn't think of an accident?"

"No," said Katherine. "That is—yes, when he did not return. One's mind always flashes ahead to catastrophe."

Norman moved restively.

"Don't you think we'd better get under way," he suggested rather diffidently. "We'll just tell the coroner the truth. That's all we can do. And we—well, we had to move the body. We couldn't just leave him there."

Jim said: "You were certain that he was dead?"

Katherine choked back a gasping cry and Norman said quickly:

"Certainly. There was no doubt." He turned definitely to Katherine. "Warm enough to start again, dear? I think we'd better get down to town. There's nothing we can do here."

There was a general air of assent. Landy stood up and Sally Lee began to fasten her green sweater around her throat. And Jim looked at Susan.

Susan's heart leaped to her throat and pounded there. Time to act. Time to start that inexorable process going. And it had to be started. It had been a cruel and dreadful thing; terribly cruel, terribly simple, terribly brutal. It had been even stupid. Yet its very stupidity was baffling. But for one thing it would have succeeded. And that one thing was so trivial. So little. She took a long breath. Jim's eyes glowed and urged her to speak.

But she couldn't even then until he said quite clearly—so clearly that everyone in the room stopped and turned to look.

"Tell them what you know."

It was like Jim. And there was all at once a taut line about his jaw and sparks of light in his eyes like phosphorescence in a deep-lying sea. What he really said was: "Go ahead, Susie, spill it. I'm with you." But that was only with his eyes.

She said, under that compulsion: "Katherine, you said that when you were standing at the window and Cecil left, you could see the lights of the car?"

"Yes." Katherine looked tired and angry. "Let's not talk any more, Susan. It doesn't help. He's dead."

"Were the lights very clear?"

"Well"—Katherine considered—"of course, the car was at an angle with the inn so that I could see only the glow of the light. No, it wasn't exactly clear. But I knew, of course, what it was."

"You said that it seemed far away."

Katherine hesitated. "Why—yes. It did seem far away."

"Did you see two lights or one?" persisted Susan.

"I didn't see any lights," said Katherine, frowning. "There was only a kind of radiance. The way the car was facing I couldn't have seen the headlights themselves, if that is what you mean."

"But you saw a radiance, close to the ground, that seemed far away and was very dim in the fog? That's really all you could swear to seeing, isn't it?"

"I suppose so. What are you getting at, Susan?"

Susan turned to the waitress. "Tell us exactly why you are so sure you saw the lights from the car."

Jennie looked shrewd. "Because," she said quickly, "the light was close to the ground."

Something had happened in that long, firelit room. Something strange had passed over it and its chill breath had touched them all.

291

No one moved. Susan said to the innkeeper, "When Cecil Vandeman stepped over the edge of the ravine he is supposed to have had some bottles of champagne with him. I suppose they would have dropped and been broken in the fall. Did you see anything of the kind?"

"N-no," said the innkeeper. He looked perplexed and very worried. There was something going on here that he didn't understand. "But there may be something. We can look in the morning."

Susan felt inexpressibly tired. She said wearily: "You might look, too, for some thread. Thrown probably into the bushes somewhere."

The chill, queer thing that had entered that room became possessive, like a spell. Susan was aware that Jim slipped very gently from the table and was standing so that he faced the others and was between them and Susan. His hand was in his pocket. And Katherine said:

"What do you mean, Susan?"

"I mean," said Susan slowly, "that Cecil was murdered."

Jim said very quietly: "You are perfectly sure, Susan?"

Susan turned to Sally Lee Sully.

"Do you know," she said, "that an accessory to murder, either before or after the fact, is criminally liable?"

"Is—*what*—"

"Can be tried for murder. That includes—concealing evidence."

There was another silent—yet packed—moment while Sally Lee considered it. Then suddenly, pale and deadly in her beauty, she whirled to Norman Bridges.

"Tried for murder!" she screamed. "I *can't* be—I *can't* be—He did it! I don't know how, but he did it!"

Confusion. Shouts. A rush of movement. Norman's wide hands closing down across Sally Lee's beautiful, treacherous mouth. Men's figures intervening, and the firelight blotted out intermittently.

"He did it," screamed Sally Lee again frantically. "That's why he threw the champagne bottles out of the car. He hated Cecil. He was jealous. He wanted me. But I had nothing to do with the murder. Nothing—nothing—"

They were holding Norman who was struggling, and Susan said to Sally Lee: "Why do you think he wanted you?"

Above its white and selfish terror, Sally Lee's face was scornful—not of men but of Susan's ignorance. "He wanted the money too," she cried sharply. "He was going to marry Katherine."

"Why?"

"To get the money, of course."

Jim said abruptly, cutting through the confusion: "These are only accusations. You have no proof."

Sally Lee paused. An accessory—tried for murder. Concealing evidence. Her eyes glittered; nothing soft about them now, nothing languorous. She cried:

"He threw the champagne bottles, three of them, out of the car on the way down the mountain after Cecil's death. He told me not to tell. He made love to me, when Katherine didn't know. But I"—she hesitated, then plunged on: "but he could never have got me without money. I know my market, and he knew it."

In the shocked silence Katherine moved and said with a kind of groan: "That was why, Susan. That was why I needed you. There was something—I didn't know quite what. I wanted your advice."

Susan thought: Cecil first. Then Katherine. She said to Katherine: "Come, Katherine, we'll go home."

But they were not to go yet. Not before Jim had asked certain questions. Had put together logically and with conclusiveness the thing that had thrust itself with such dreadful persistence upon Susan.

"The proof," she said to Jim. "I don't know." She considered slowly. They were on the porch, cool air touching her cheek. Inside there were preparations.

"There's the electric light bulb. Fingerprints are on it."

"What bulb?"

Susan dug into that queer subterranean storehouse where all things are assembled and labeled, to emerge as conclusions.

"He turned on the car lights. We saw the glow. But Katherine and I and then Sally Lee entered the house. While the lights were on, he ran around the path and let down the light on the point. (It's on a drop-cord with the slack taken up in a loop. All he had to do was pull a string he had previously tied to the loop.) By that time we had reached the house. He turned out the car lights as he passed, leaving the light (then not burning) across the ravine. The fog was so thick that the light (when he turned it on as he entered the house) made only a bright glow and as it was about two feet off the ground, anybody would think, seeing that low light off in the fog, that it was the lights of a car. Particularly if that idea was fixed in one's mind. If you were told it was the light from a car. If you expected it to be that. But Katherine, you see, said it seemed far away."

"Wait. Was the light on the point beyond the ravine burning then—when you came down the mountain?"

"No. He had to let it down first. But he reached the house after we had entered it. The switch is just beside the door. He could have turned it on as he entered."

"The porch light would have been turned on too. They are on the same switch. Someone would have seen it."

"That's where his fingerprints must be. You see he had to unscrew the bulb before turning on the light. It would be very simple, the work of an instant. The whole thing is simple; it was only a matter of accomplishing promptly every step in the process at the right time. There was really only one point of danger in the whole thing."

"Wait," said Jim again, looking thoughtful. "Let's go chronologically. So far it's all clear. You are all in the house: the lights of the car are turned out but across the ravine a light is shining which, owing to the fog and distance and its being so close to the ground, looks very like the lights of a car. Now what?"

"Well—the waitress saw it and, naturally, merely registered that it was a low light; hence car lights. Remember that the fog actually changed and confused everything; and we would all make allowances for it. Also, Katherine saw that light and, fortunately from the murderer's viewpoint, saw it just as Cecil left the house."

"He left to get the champagne?"

"Yes. They'd quarrelled—Norman and Cecil had evidently talked of announcing the engagement; had planned to have dinner up here, and Norman must have suggested bringing the champagne. That was evident too. His only problem was to get Cecil to go to the car, and that wasn't a problem. Both men would offer to get the champagne. He would let Cecil go. Of course, if Cecil himself had already brought in the champagne Norman would have made some other pretext to take Cecil into the fog. The next step was simple; the only necessary thing was to do it. He waited until he knew Cecil would have reached the ravine. He had said as Cecil went out the door: 'The car lights are on,' thus fixing the idea in Cecil's mind—to go straight for the glow of light."

"But it might have failed."

"No. Not when he had succeeded with the preparations and had actually got Cecil started. Cecil was worried, upset on account of the quarrel. He was always easily confused about directions. And once really into the fog—no, it was pretty sure to succeed. But if it hadn't, he would have tried some other way."

"It's pretty complicated," he said and reflected. "No," he said, then. "It's just a series of trivialities, nothing about it that was difficult. And—if it worked—almost proof against detection. And I can see how it would appeal to a mind accustomed to detail and acutely aware of the need to make it look like an accident." He looked at Susan thoughtfully. "Go on."

"Then—he went to the door. Casually—as if to glance out at the fog. And by doing so, had a chance to press the switch for the

294

outside lights again. Thus when we opened the door there was no light anywhere. So what more likely than to assume what we did assume—that Cecil had reached the car, had for some reason turned out the lights and become confused starting back toward the inn. When we stood there in the darkness calling for Cecil, and Cecil didn't reply, he knew that his plan had worked. Of course, Cecil might be still alive—he couldn't know. But it was a deadly fall. It was just then Norman reached his dangerous moment. And that was to accomplish three things before the porch light and, simultaneously, the other light was turned on by somebody. He had to screw that bulb up there tight in the socket again, he had to pound on the kitchen door and shout for the innkeeper, he had to run along the path, push the bench up to the light, climb on the back of the bench and loop up the drop-cord again so that, when the switch was turned on, the light would be high in the tree again. It was his only dangerous moment. And, of course, he had as nearly as he was able, rehearsed it."

"Rehearsed?"

"When the waitress came into the room and saw him she said, "How do you do?" As if she recognized him. As if he'd been up here before—and recently. You can ask her in order to verify it. But I'm sure. I'm sure, too, that if you'll telephone the weather bureau they'll tell you that their real forecast was cloudy weather. Not fair, as Norman reported."

"The light," said Jim, "would have silhouetted the car."

"It's too far to one side. You can look tomorrow. The car tracks will still be there."

The door opened. They had an instant's view of people moving about and a lovely, graceful figure against the light.

"So that was the motive," said Jim.

"Yes," said Susan. "It was—I don't know—it was just there. Between them."

"It was a gamble on her selfishness," said Jim. "It was a risk." He paused. Fog swirled in and around them and, outside, it was quiet and cold. Presently he said: "Not such a gamble, perhaps. 'Oh, serpent heart, hid with a flowering face' "—he quoted absently, stopped and laughed unsteadily—"Shakespeare said everything. Get into the car, Sue. I'll—see to the rest."

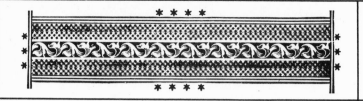

I ALWAYS GET THE CUTIES

BY JOHN D. MACDONALD

John D. MacDonald was born on July 24, 1916. Many of his more than sixty books and 500 short stories are part of the colorful Travis McGee series (*The Deep Blue Good-by, The Dreadful Lemon Sky, The Girl in the Plain Brown Wrapper, The Turquoise Lament*). He makes his home in Sarasota, Florida. Kurt Vonnegut, Jr., wrote that "To diggers a thousand years from now, the works of John D. MacDonald would be a treasure on the order of the tomb of Tutankhamen."

KEEGAN CAME INTO MY APARTMENT, frosted with winter, topcoat open, hat jammed on the back of his hard skull, bringing a noisy smell of the dark city night. He stood in front of my birch fire, his great legs planted, clapping and rubbing hard palms in the heat.

He grinned at me and winked one narrow gray eye. "I'm off duty, Doc. I wrapped up a package. A pretty package."

"Will bourbon do, Keegan?"

"If you haven't got any of that brandy left. This is a brandy night."

When I came back with the bottle and the glasses, he had stripped off his topcoat and tossed it on the couch. The crumpled hat was on the floor, near the discarded coat. Keegan had yanked a chair closer to the fire. He sprawled on the end of his spine, thick ankles crossed, the soles of his shoes steaming.

I poured his brandy and mine, and moved my chair and the long coffee table so we could share either end of it. It was bursting in him. I knew that. I've only had the vaguest hints about his home life. A house crowded with teen-age daughters, cluttered with their swains. Obviously no place to talk of his dark victories. And Keegan is not the sort of man to regale his co-workers with talk of his prowess. So I am, among other things, his sounding board. He bounces successes off the politeness of my listening, growing big in the echo of them.

"Ever try to haggle with a car dealer, Doc?" he asked.

"In a mild way."

"You are a mild guy. I tried once. Know what he told me? He said, 'Lieutenant, you try to make a car deal maybe once every two years. Me, I make ten a day. So what chance have you got?'"

This was a more oblique approach than Keegan generally used. I became attentive.

"It's the same with the cuties, Doc—the amateurs who think they can bring off one nice clean safe murder. Give me a cutie every time. I eat 'em alive. The pros are trouble. The cuties leave holes you can drive diesels through. This one was that woman back in October. At that cabin at Bear Paw Lake. What do you remember about it, Doc?"

I am always forced to summarize. It has got me into the habit of reading the crime news. I never used to.

"As I remember, Keegan, they thought she had been killed by a prowler. Her husband returned from a business trip and found the body. She had been dead approximately two weeks. Because it was the off season, the neighboring camps weren't occupied, and the people in the village thought she had gone back to the city. She had been strangled, I believe." .

"Okay. So I'll fill you in on it. Then you'll see the problem I had. The name is Grosswalk. Cynthia and Harold. He met her ten years ago when he was in med. school. He was twenty-four and she was thirty. She was loaded. He married her and he never went back to med. school. He didn't do anything for maybe five, six years. Then he gets a job selling medical supplies, surgical instruments, that kind of stuff. Whenever a wife is dead, Doc, the first thing I do is check on how they were getting along. I guess you know that."

"Your standard procedure," I said.

"Sure. So I check. They got a nice house here in the city. Not many friends. But they got neighbors with ears. There are lots of brawls. I get the idea it is about money. The money is hers—was hers, I should say. I put it up to this Grosswalk. He says okay, so they weren't getting along so good, so what? I'm supposed to be finding out who killed her, sort of coordinating with the State Police, not digging into his home life. I tell him he is a nice suspect. He already knows that. He says he didn't kill her. Then he adds one thing too many. He says he couldn't have killed her. That's all he will say. Playing it cute. You understand. I eat those cuties alive."

He waved his empty glass. I went over and refilled it.

"You see what he's doing to me, Doc. He's leaving it up to me to prove how it was he couldn't have killed her. A reverse twist. That isn't too tough. I get in touch with the sales manager of the company. Like I thought, the salesmen have to make reports. He was making a western swing. It would be no trick to fly back and sneak into the camp and kill her, take some money and junk to make it look good, and then fly back out there and pick up where he left off. She was killed on maybe the tenth of October, the medical examiner says. Then he finds her on the twenty-fourth. But the sales manager tells me something that needs a lot of checking. He says that this Grosswalk took sick out west on the eighth and went into a hospital, and he was in that hospital from the eighth to the fifteenth, a full seven days. He gave me the name of the hospital. Now you can see how the cutie made his mistake. He could have told me that easy enough. No, he has to be cute. I figure that if he's innocent he would have told me. But he's so proud of whatever gimmick he rigged for me that he's got to let me find out the hard way."

"I suppose you went out there," I said.

"It took a lot of talk. They don't like spending money for things like that. They kept telling me I should ask the L.A. cops to check because that's a good force out there. Finally I have to go by bus, or pay the difference. So I go by bus. I found the doctor. Plural—doctors. It is a clinic deal, sort of, that this Grosswalk went to. He gives them his symptoms. They say it looks to them like the edge of a nervous breakdown just beginning to show. With maybe some organic complications. So they run him through the course. Seven days of tests and checks and observations. They tell me he was there, that he didn't leave, that he *couldn't* have left. But naturally I check the hospital. They reserve part of one floor for patients from the clinic. I talked to the head nurse on that floor, and to the nurse that had the most to do with Grosswalk. She showed me the schedule and charts. Every day, every night, they were fooling around with the guy, giving him injections of this and that. He couldn't have got out. The people at the clinic told me the results. He was okay. The rest had helped him a lot. They told him to slow down. They gave him a prescription for a mild sedative. Nothing organically wrong, even though the symptoms seemed to point that way."

"So the trip was wasted?"

"Not entirely. Because on a hunch I ask if he had visitors. They keep a register. A girl came to see him as often as the rules permitted. They said she was pretty. Her name was Mary MacCarney. The address is there. So I go and see her. She lives with her folks. A real tasty kid. Nineteen. Her folks think this Grosswalk is too old for her. She is tall Irish, all black and white and blue. It was warm and we sat on the porch. I soon find out this Grosswalk has been feeding her a line, telling her that his wife is an incurable invalid not long for this world, that he can't stand hurting her by asking for a divorce, that it is better to wait, and anyway, she says, her parents might approve of a widower, but never a guy who has been divorced. She has heard from Grosswalk that his wife has been murdered by a prowler and he will be out to see her as soon as he can. He had known her for a year. But of course I have told him not to leave town. I tell her not to get her hopes too high because it begins to look to me like this Grosswalk has knocked off his wife. Things get pretty hysterical, and her old lady gets in on it, and even driving away in the cab I can hear her old lady yelling at her.

"The first thing I do on getting back is check with the doctor who took care of Mrs. Grosswalk, and he says, as I thought he would, that she was as healthy as a horse. So I go back up to that camp and unlock it again. It is a snug place, Doc. Built so you could spend the winter there if you wanted to. Insulated and sealed, with a big fuel-oil furnace, and modern kitchen equipment, and so on. It was aired out a lot better than the first time I was in it. Grosswalk stated that he hadn't touched a thing. He said it was unlocked. He saw her and backed right out and went to report it. And the only thing touched had been the body.

"I poked around. This time I took my time. She was a tidy woman. There are twin beds. One is turned down. There is a very fancy nightgown laid out. That is a thing which bothered me. I looked at her other stuff. She had pajamas which are the right thing for October at the lake. They are made from that flannel stuff. There is only one other fancy nightgown, way in the back of a drawer. I have found out here in the city that she is not the type to fool around. So how come a woman who is alone wants to sleep so pretty? Because the husband is coming back from a trip. But he couldn't have come back from the trip. I find another thing. I find deep ruts off in the brush beside the camp. The first time I went there, her car was parked in back. Now it is gone. If the car was run off where those ruts were, anybody coming to the door wouldn't see it. If the door was locked they wouldn't even knock maybe, knowing she wouldn't be home. That puzzles me. She might do it if she didn't want company. I prowl some more. I look in the deep freeze. It is well stocked. No need to buy stuff for a hell of a while. The refrigerator is the same way. And the electric is still on."

He leaned back and looked at me expectantly.

"Is that all you had to go on?" I asked.

"A murder happens here and the murderer is in Los Angeles at the time. I got him because he tried to be a cutie. Want to take a try, Doc?"

I knew I had to make an attempt. "Some sort of device?"

"To strangle a woman? Mechanical hands? You're getting too fancy, Doc."

"Then he hired somebody to do it?"

"There are guys you can hire, but they like guns. Or a piece of pipe in an alley. I don't know where you'd go to hire a strangler. He did it himself, Doc."

"Frankly, Keegan, I don't see how he could have."

"Well, I'll tell you how I went after it. I went to the medical examiner and we had a little talk. Cop logic, Doc. If the geography is wrong, then maybe you got the wrong idea on timing. But the medico checks it out. He says definitely the woman has been dead twelve days to two weeks when he makes the examination. I ask him how he knows. He says because of the extent of the decomposition of the body. I ask him if that is a constant. He says no—you use a formula. A sort of rule-of-thumb formula. I ask him the factors. He says cause of death, temperature, humidity, physical characteristics of the body, how it was clothed, whether or not insects could have got to it, and so on.

"By then I had it, Doc. It was cute. I went back to the camp and

300

looked around. It took me some time to find them. You never find a camp without them. Candles. They were in a drawer in the kitchen. Funny looking candles, Doc. Melted down, sort of. A flat side against the bottom of the drawer, and all hardened again. Then I had another idea. I checked the stove burners. I found some pieces of burned flaked metal down under the heating elements.

"Then it was easy. I had this Grosswalk brought in again. I let him sit in a cell for four hours and get nervous before I took the rookie cop in. I'd coached that rookie for an hour, so he did it right. I had him dressed in a leather jacket and work pants. I make him repeat his story in front of Grosswalk. 'I bought a chain saw last year,' he says, acting sort of confused, 'and I was going around to the camps where there are any people and I was trying to get some work cutting up fireplace wood. So I called on Mrs. Grosswalk. She didn't want any wood, but she was nice about it.' I ask the rookie when that was. He scratches his head and says, 'Sometime around the seventeenth I think it was.' That's where I had to be careful. I couldn't let him be positive about the date. I say she was supposed to be dead a week by then and was he sure it was her. 'She wasn't dead then. I know her. I'd seen her in the village. A kind of heavy-set woman with blonde hair. It was her all right, Lieutenant.' I asked him was he sure of the date and he said yes, around the seventeenth like he said, but he could check his records and find the exact day.

"I told him to take off. I just watched that cutie and saw him come apart. Then he gave it to me. He killed her on the sixteenth, the day he got out of the hospital. He flew into Omaha. By then I've got the stenographer taking it down. Grosswalk talks, staring at the floor, like he was talking to himself. It was going to be a dry run. He wasn't going to do it if she'd been here in the city or into the village in the previous seven days. But once she got in the camp she seldom went out, and the odds were all against any callers. On his previous trip to Omaha he had bought a jalopy that would run. It would make the fifty miles to the lake all right. He took the car off the lot where he'd left it and drove to the lake. She was surprised to see him back ahead of schedule. He explained the company car was being fixed. He questioned her. Finally she said she hadn't seen or talked to a living soul in ten days. Then he knew he was set to take the risk.

"He grabbed her neck and hung on until she was dead. He had his shoulders hunched right up around his ears when he said that. It was evening when he killed her, nearly bedtime. First he closed every window. Then he turned on the furnace as high as it would go. There was plenty of oil in the tank. He left the oven door open and the oven turned as high as it would go. He even built a fire in the fireplace, knowing it would be burned out by morning and there wouldn't be any smoke. He filled the biggest pans of water he could find and left them on the top of the stove. He took money and some of her jewelry, turned out the lights and locked the doors. He ran her car off in the brush where nobody would be likely to see it. He said by the time he left the house it was like an oven in there.

"He drove the jalopy back to Omaha, parked it back in the lot, and caught an 11:15 flight to Los Angeles. The next morning he was making calls. And keeping his fingers crossed. He worked his way east. He got to the camp on the twenty-fourth—about 10 in the morning. He said he went in and turned things off and opened up every window, and then went out and was sick. He waited nearly an hour before going back in. It was nearly down to normal temperature. He checked the house. He noticed she had turned down both beds before he killed her. He remade his. The water had boiled out of the pans and the bottoms had burned through. He scaled the pans out into the lake. He said he tried not to look at her, but he couldn't help it. He had enough medical background to know that it had worked, and also to fake his own illness in L. A. He went out and was sick again, and then he got her car back where it belonged. He closed most of the windows. He made another inspection trip and then drove into the village. He's a cutie, Doc, and I ate him alive."

There was a long silence. I knew what was expected of me. But I had my usual curious reluctance to please him. He held the glass cradled in his hand, gazing with a half smile into the dying fire. His face looked like stone.

"That was very intelligent, Keegan," I said.

"The pros give you real trouble, Doc. The cuties always leave holes. I couldn't bust geography, so I had to bust time." He yawned massively and stood up. "Read all about it in the morning paper, Doc."

"I'll certainly do that."

I held his coat for him. He's a big man. I had to reach up to get it properly onto his shoulders. He mashed the hat onto his head as I walked to the door with him. He put his big hand on the knob, turned, and smiled down at me without mirth.

"I always get the cuties, Doc. Always."

"You certainly seem to," I said.

"They are my favorite meat."

"So I understand."

He balled one big fist and bumped it lightly against my chin, still grinning at me. "And I'm going to get you too, Doc. You know that. You were cute. You're just taking longer than most. But you know how it's going to come out, don't you?"

I don't answer that any more. There's nothing to say. There hasn't been anything to say for a long time now.

He left, walking hard into the wild night. I sat and looked into my fire. I could hear the wind. I reached for the bottle. The wind raged over the city, as monstrous and inevitable as Keegan. It seemed as though it was looking for food—the way Keegan is always doing.

But I no longer permit myself the luxury of imagination.

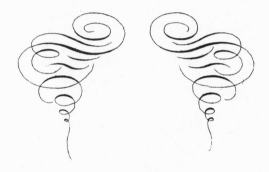

THE DAY
THE CHILDREN VANISHED

BY HUGH PENTECOST

Judson Philips was born on August 10, 1903. His pseudonym, Hugh Pentecost, originally the name of his maternal great-uncle who was a criminal lawyer in New York, emerged when a book he wrote under that name won the Dodd, Mead Red Badge Mystery Competition in 1939. He has published over 100 novels, many of those by Hugh Pentecost about Pierre Chambrun, John Jericho and Julian Quist; many by Judson Philips about Peter Styles. Ellery Queen has calied him "a pro among pros."

On a bright, clear winter's afternoon the nine children in the town of Clayton who traveled each day to the Regional School in Lakeview disappeared from the face of the earth, along with the bus in which they traveled and its driver, as completely as if they had been sucked up into outer space by some monstrous interplanetary vacuum cleaner.

Actually, in the time of hysteria which followed the disappearance, this theory was put forward by some distraught citizen of Clayton, and not a few people, completely stumped for an explanation, gave consideration to it.

There was, of course, nothing interplanetary or supernatural about the disappearance of nine children, one adult, and a special-bodied station wagon which was used as a school bus. It was the result of callous human villainy. But, because there was no possible explanation for it, it assumed all the aspects of black magic in the minds of tortured parents and a bewildered citizenry.

Clayton is seven miles from Lakeview. Clayton is a rapidly growing quarry town. Lakeview, considerably larger and with a long history of planning for growth, recently built a new school. It was agreed between the boards of education of the two towns that nine children living at the east end of Clayton should be sent to the Lakeview School where there was adequate space and teaching staff. It was to be just a temporary expedient.

Since there were only nine children, they did not send one of the big, forty-eight-passenger school buses to get them. A nine-passenger station wagon was acquired, properly painted and marked as a school bus, and Jerry Mahoney, a mechanic in the East Clayton Garage, was hired to make the two trips each day with the children.

Jerry Mahoney was well liked and respected. He had been a mechanic in the Air Force during his tour of duty in the armed services. He was a wizard with engines. He was engaged to be married to Elizabeth Deering, who worked in the Clayton Bank and was one of Clayton's choice picks. They were both nice people, responsible people.

The disappearance of the station wagon, the nine children, and Jerry Mahoney took place on a two-mile stretch of road where disappearance was impossible. It was called the "dugway," and it wound along the side of the lake. Heavy wire guardrails protected

305

the road from the lake for the full two miles. There was not a gap in it anywhere.

The ground on the other side of the road rose abruptly upward into thousands of acres of mountain woodlands, so thickly grown that not even a tractor could have made its way up any part of it except for a few yards of deserted road that led to an abandoned quarry. Even over this old road nothing could have passed without leaving a trail of torn brush and broken saplings.

At the Lakeview end of the dugway was a filling station owned by old Jake Nugent. On the afternoon of the disappearance the bus, with Jerry Mahoney at the wheel and his carload of kids laughing and shouting at each other, stopped at old man Nugent's. Jerry Mahoney had brought the old man a special delivery letter from the post office, thus saving the RFD driver from making a special trip. Jerry and old Jake exchanged greetings, the old man signed the receipt for his letter—which was from his son in Chicago asking for a loan of fifty dollars—and Jerry drove off into the dugway with his cargo of kids.

At the Clayton end of the dugway was Joe Gorman's Diner, and one of the children in Jerry's bus was Peter Gorman, Joe's son. The Diner was Jerry's first stop coming out of the dugway.

It was four thirty in the afternoon when Joe Gorman realized that the bus was nearly three-quarters of an hour late. Worried, he called the school in Lakeview and was told by Miss Bromfield, the principal, that the bus had left on schedule.

"He may have had a flat, or something," Miss Bromfield suggested.

This was one of seven calls Miss Bromfield was to get in the next half hour, all inquiring about the bus. Nine children; seven families.

Joe Gorman was the first to do anything about it seriously. He called Jake Nugent's filling station to ask about the bus, and old Jake told him it had gone through from his place on schedule. So something had happened to Jerry and his bus load of kids in the dugway. Joe got out his jeep and headed through the dugway toward Lakeview. He got all the way to Jake Nugent's without seeing the bus or passing anyone coming the other way.

Jake Nugent was a shrewd old gent, in complete possession of all his faculties. He didn't drink. When he said he had seen the bus—that it had stopped to deliver his letter—and that he had watched it drive off into the dugway, you had to believe it. Cold sweat broke out on Joe Gorman's face as he listened. The dugway had a tendency to be icy. He had noticed coming over that it hadn't been sanded. Joe hadn't been looking for a major tragedy. But if the bus had skidded, gone through the guard-rail . . .

He used Jake's phone to call the Dicklers in Clayton. The Dicklers' two children, Dorothy and Donald, were part of Jerry's load and they were the next stop after Joe's Diner. The Dicklers were already alarmed because their children hadn't come home.

Joe didn't offer any theories. He was scared, though. He called the trooper barracks in Lakeview and told them about the missing bus. They didn't take it too seriously, but said they'd send a man out.

Joe headed back for Clayton. This time his heart was a lump in his throat. He drove slowly, staring at every inch of the wire guard-rails. There was not a break anywhere, not a broken or bent post. The bus simply couldn't have skidded over the embankment into the lake without smashing through the wire guard-rail.

Joe Gorman felt better when he came out at his diner at the Clayton end. He felt better, but he felt dizzy. Five minutes later Trooper Teliski came whizzing through from Lakeview and stopped his car.

"What's the gag?" he asked Joe.

Joe tried to light a cigarette and his hands were shaking so badly he couldn't make it. Teliski snapped on his lighter and held it out. Joe dragged smoke deep into his lungs.

"Look," he said. "The bus started through the dugway at the regular time." He told about Jerry's stop at Nugent's. "It never came out this end."

A nerve twitched in Teliski's cheek. "The lake," he said.

Joe shook his head. "I—I thought of that, right off. I just came through ahead of you—looking. Not a break in the guard-rail anywhere. Not a scratch. Not a bent post. The bus didn't go into the lake. I'll stake my life on that."

"Then what else?" Teliski asked. "It couldn't go up the mountain."

"I know," Joe said, and the two men stared at each other.

"It's some kind of a joke," Teliski said.

"What kind of a joke? It's no joke to me—or the Dicklers. I talked to them."

"Maybe they had permission to go to a special movie or something," Teliski said.

"Without notifying the parents? Miss Bromfield would have told me, anyway. I talked to her. Listen, Teliski. The bus went into the dugway and it didn't come out. It's not in the dugway now, and it didn't go into the lake."

Teliski was silent for a moment, and then he spoke with a solid attempt at common sense. "It didn't come out this end," he said. "We'll check back on that guard-rail, but let's say you're right. It didn't skid into the lake. It couldn't go up the mountain. So where does that leave us?"

"Going nuts!" Joe said.

"It leaves us with only one answer. The station wagon never went into the dugway."

Joe Gorman nodded. "That's logic," he said. "But why would Jake Nugent lie? Jerry's an hour and three-quarters late now. If he didn't go in the dugway, where is he? Where *could* he go? Why hasn't he telephoned if everything is okay?"

A car drove up and stopped. A man got out and came running toward them. It was Karl Dickler, father of two of the missing children. "Thank God you're here, Teliski. What's happened?"

"Some kind of a gag," Teliski said. "We can't figure it out. The bus never came through the dugway."

"But it did!" Karl Dickler said.

"It never came out this end," Joe Gorman said. "I was watching for Pete, naturally."

"But it did come through!" Dickler said. "I passed them myself on the way to Lakeview. They were about half a mile this way from Jake Nugent's. I saw them! I waved at my own kids!"

The three men stared at each other.

"It never came out this end," Joe Gorman said, in a choked voice.

Dickler swayed and reached out to the trooper to steady himself. "The lake!" he whispered.

But they were not in the lake. Joe Gorman's survey proved accurate; no broken wire, no bent post, not even a scratch . . .

It was nearly dark when the real search began. Troopers, the families of the children, the selectmen, the sheriff and twenty-five or thirty volunteer deputies, a hundred or more school friends of the missing children.

The lake was definitely out. Not only was the guard-rail intact, but the lake was frozen over with about an inch of ice. There wasn't a break in the smooth surface of the ice anywhere along the two miles of shore bordering the dugway.

Men and women and children swarmed through the woods on the other side of the road, knowing all the time it was useless. The road was called the "dugway" because it had been dug out of the side of the mountain. There was a gravel bank about seven feet high running almost unbrokenly along that side of the road. There was the one old abandoned trail leading to the quarry. It was clear, after walking the first ten yards of it, that no car had come that way. It couldn't.

A hundred phone calls were made to surrounding towns and

villages. No one had seen the station wagon, the children, or Jerry Mahoney. The impossible had to be faced.

The bus had gone into the dugway and it hadn't come out. It hadn't skidded into the lake and it hadn't climbed the impenetrable brush of the mountain. It was just gone! Vanished into thin air!

Everyone was deeply concerned for and sympathetic with the Dicklers, and Joe Gorman, and the Williams, the Trents, the Ishams, the Nortons, and the Jennings, parents of the missing children. Nobody thought much about Jerry Mahoney's family, or his girl.

It wasn't reasonable, but as the evening wore on and not one speck of evidence was found or one acceptable theory advanced, people began to talk about Jerry Mahoney. He was the driver. The bus had to have been driven somewhere. It couldn't navigate without Jerry Mahoney at the wheel. Jerry was the only adult involved. However it had been worked—this disappearance—Jerry must have had a hand in it.

It didn't matter that, until an hour ago, Jerry had been respected, trusted, liked. Their children were gone and Jerry had taken them somewhere. Why? Ransom. They would all get ransom letters in the morning, they said. A mass kidnapping. Jerry had the kids somewhere. There weren't any rich kids in Clayton, so he was going to demand ransom from all seven families.

Thus Jerry Mahoney became a villain because there was no one else to suspect. Nobody stopped to think that Jerry's father and Jerry's girl might be as anxious about his absence as the others were about the missing children.

At nine thirty Sergeant Mason and Trooper Teliski of the State Police, George Peabody, the sheriff, and a dozen men of the community including Joe Gorman and Karl Dickler stormed into the living room of Jerry Mahoney's house where an old man with silvery white hair sat in an overstuffed armchair. Elizabeth Deering, Jerry's fiancée, was huddled on the floor beside him, her face buried on his knees, weeping.

The old man wore a rather sharply cut gray flannel suit, a bright scarlet vest with brass buttons, and a green necktie that must have been designed for a St. Patrick's Day parade. As he stroked the girl's blonde hair, the light from the lamp reflected glittering shafts from a square-cut diamond in a heavy gold setting he wore on his little finger. He looked up at Sergeant Mason and his small army of followers, and his blue eyes stopped twinkling as he saw the stern look on the Sergeant's face.

"All right, Pat," Sergeant Mason said. "What's Jerry done with those kids?" Pat Mahoney's pale-blue eyes met the Sergeant's stare steadily. Then crinkles of mirth appeared at the corners of his eyes and mouth.

"I'd like to ask you something before I try to answer that," Pat Mahoney said.

"Well?"

"Have you stopped beating your wife, Sergeant?" Pat Mahoney asked. His cackle of laughter was the only sound in the room . . .

There are those who are old enough to remember the days when Mahoney and Faye were listed about fourth on a bill of eight star acts all around the Keith-Orpheum vaudeville circuit. Pat Mahoney was an Irish comic with dancing feet, and Nora Faye—Mrs. Mahoney to you—could match him at dancing and had the soprano voice of an angel.

Like so many people in show business, Pat was a blusterer, a boaster, a name dropper, but with it all a solid professional who would practice for hours a day to perfect a new routine, never missed an entrance in forty years, and up to the day young Jerry was born in a cheap hotel in Grand Rapids, Michigan, had given away half what he earned to dead beats and hopeless failures.

The diamond ring he wore today had been in and out of a hundred hock shops. It had been the basis of his and Nora's security for more years than he liked to remember.

If you were left alone with Pat for more than five minutes, he went back to the old days—to the people he had idolized, like Sophie Tucker, and Smith and Dale, and Williams and Wolfus, and Joe Jackson. He'd known them all, played on the same bills with them. "But," he would tell you, and a strange radiance would come into the pale-blue eyes, "the greatest of them all was Nora Faye—Mrs. Mahoney to you."

Once he was started on his Nora, there was no way of stopping Pat Mahoney. He told of her talents as a singer and dancer, but in the end it was a saga of endless patience, of kindness and understanding, of love for a fat-headed, vain little Irish comic, of tenderness as a mother, and finally of clear-eyed courage in the face of stark tragedy.

Mahoney and Faye had never played the Palace, the Broadway goal of all vaudevillians. Pat had worked on a dozen acts that would crack the ice and finally he'd made it.

"We'd come out in cowboy suits, all covered with jewels, and jeweled guns, and jeweled boots, and we'd do a little soft shoe routine, and then suddenly all the lights would go out and only the jewels would show—they were made special for that—and we'd go into a fast routine, pulling the guns, and twirling and juggling them, and the roof would fall in! Oh, we tried it out of town, and our agent finally got us the booking at the Palace we'd always dreamed of."

There'd be a long silence then, and Pat would take a gaudy handkerchief from his hip pocket and blow his nose with a kind of angry violence. "I can show you the costumes still. They're packed away in a trunk in the attic. Just the way we wore them—me and Nora—the last time we ever played. Atlantic City, it was. And she came off after the act with the cheers still ringing in our ears, and down she went on the the floor of the dressing room, writhing in pain.

"Then she told me. It had been getting worse for months. She didn't want me to know. The doctor had told her straight out. She'd only a few months she could count on. She'd never said a word to me—working toward the Palace—knowing I'd dreamed of it. And only three weeks after that—she left us. Me and Jerry—she left us. We were standing by her bed when she left—and the last words she spoke were to Jerry. 'Take care of Pat,' she says to him. 'He'll be helpless without someone to take care of him.' And then she smiled at me, and all the years were in that smile."

And then, wherever we happened to be when he told the story, Pat Mahoney would wipe the back of his hand across his eyes and say, "If you'll excuse me, I think I'll be going home" . . .

Nobody laughed when Pat pulled the old courtroom wheeze on Sergeant Mason about "have you stopped beating your wife." Pat looked past the Sergeant at Trooper Teliski, and Joe Gorman, and Karl Dickler, and Mr. and Mrs. Jennings, whose two daughters were in the missing bus, and George Peabody, the fat, wheezing sheriff.

"The question I asked you, Sergeant," he said, "makes just as much sense as the one you asked me. You asked me what Nora's boy has done with those kids? There's no answer to that question. Do I hear you saying, 'I know what you must be feeling, Pat Mahoney, and you, Elizabeth Deering? And is there anything we can do for you in this hour of your terrible anxiety.' I don't hear you saying that, Sergeant."

"I'm sorry, Pat," Mason said. "Those kids are missing. Jerry had to take them somewhere."

"No!" Liz Deering cried. "You all know Jerry better than that!"

They didn't, it seemed, but they could be forgiven. You can't confront people with the inexplicable without frightening them and throwing them off balance. You can't endanger their children

311

and expect a sane reaction. They muttered angrily, and old Pat saw the tortured faces of Joe Gorman and Karl Dickler and the swollen red eyes of Mrs. Jennings.

"Has he talked in any way queerly to you, Pat?" Mason asked. "Has he acted normal of late?"

"Nora's boy is the most normal boy you ever met," Pat Mahoney said. "You know that, Sergeant. Why, you've known him since he was a child."

Mrs. Jennings screamed out, "He'd protect his son. Naturally he'd protect his son. But he's stolen our children!"

"The Pied Piper rides again," Pat Mahoney said.

"Make him talk!" Mrs. Jennings cried, and the crowd around her muttered louder.

"When did you last see Jerry, Pat?"

"Breakfast," Pat said. "He has his lunch at Joe Gorman's Diner." The corner of his mouth twitched. "He should have been home for dinner long ago."

"Did he have a need for money?" Mason asked.

"Money? He was a man respected—until now—wasn't he? He was a man with a fine girl in love with him, wasn't he? What need would he have for money?"

"Make him answer sensibly!" Mrs. Jennings pleaded in a despairing voice.

Joe Gorman stepped forward. "Pat, maybe Jerry got sick all of a sudden. It's happened to men who saw action overseas. Maybe you saw signs of something and wouldn't want to tell of it. But my Pete was on that bus, and Karl's two, and Mrs. Jennings' two. We're nowhere, Pat—so if you can tell us anything! Our kids were on that bus!"

Pat Mahoney's eyes, as he listened to Joe Gorman, filled with pain. "My kid is on that bus, too, Joe," he said.

They all stared at him, some with hatred. And then, in the distance, they heard the wail of a siren. The trooper's car was coming from Lakeview, hell-bent.

"Maybe it's news!" someone shouted.

And they all went stumbling out of the house to meet the approaching car—all but Elizabeth Deering, who stayed behind, clinging to the old man.

"I don't understand it," she said, her voice shaken. "They think he's harmed their children, Pat! Why? Why would they think he'd do such a thing? Why?"

Old Pat's eyes had a faraway look in them. "Did I ever tell you about the Great Thurston?" he asked. "Greatest magic act I ever saw."

"Pat!" Elizabeth said, her eyes widening in horror.

"First time I ever caught his act was in Sioux City," Pat said. "He came out in a flowing cape, and a silk hat, and he . . ."

Dear God, he's losing his reason, Elizabeth Deering told herself. Let the news be good! Let them be found safe!

The police car with its wailing siren carried news, but it was not the sort the people of Clayton were hoping to hear.

It was reassuring to know that within a few hours of the tragedy the entire area was alerted, that the moment daylight came a fleet of army helicopters would cover the area for hundreds of miles around, that a five-state alarm was out for the missing station wagon and its passengers, and that the Attorney General had sent the best man on his staff to direct and coordinate the search.

Top officials, viewing the case coldly and untouched by the hysteria of personal involvement, had a theory. Of course there had to be a rational explanation of the disappearance of the bus, and Clyde Haviland, tall, stoop-shouldered, scholarly-looking investigator from the Attorney General's office, was ordered to produce that explanation as soon as possible upon his arrival in Clayton. But beyond that, officials had no doubt as to the reason for the disappearance: this was a mass kidnaping—something novel in the annals of crime.

Since none of the families involved had means, Haviland and his superiors were convinced the next move in this strange charade would be a demand on the whole community to pay ransom for the children. The F.B.I. was alerted to be ready to act the moment there was any indication of involvement across state lines.

While mothers wept and the menfolk grumbled angrily that Jerry Mahoney, the driver, was at the bottom of this, officialdom worked calmly and efficiently. The Air Force turned over its complete data on Technical Sergeant Jerry Mahoney to the F.B.I. Men who had known Jerry in the service were wakened from their sleep or pulled out of restaurants or theatres to be questioned. Had he ever said anything that would indicate he might move into a world of violence? Did his medical history contain any record of mental illness?

Sitting at a desk in the town hall, Clyde Haviland reported on some of this to George Peabody, the sheriff, the town's three selectmen, Sergeant Mason, and a couple of other troopers. Haviland, carefully polishing his shell-rimmed glasses, was a quiet, reassuring sort of man. He had a fine reputation in the state. He was not an unfamiliar figure to people in Clayton because he had solved a particularly brutal murder in the neighboring town of Johnsville, and his investigation had brought him in and out of Clayton for several weeks.

"So far," he said, with a faint smile, "The report on Jerry Mahoney is quite extraordinary."

"In what way?" Sergeant Mason asked, eager for the scent of blood.

"Model citizen," Haviland said. "No one has a bad word for him. No bad temper. Never held grudges. Never chiseled. Saves his money. His savings account in the Clayton bank would surprise some of you. On the face of it, he's the last person in the world to suspect."

"There has to be a first time for everything," Karl Dickler said. He was a selectman as well as one of the bereaved parents.

"It's going down toward zero tonight," George Peabody, the sheriff, said glumly. "If those kids are out anywhere—"

"They're one hell of a long way from here by now, if you ask me," Sergeant Mason said.

Haviland looked at him, his eyes unblinking behind the lenses of his glasses. "Except that they never came out of the dugway."

"Nobody saw them," Mason said. "But they're not there so they did come out."

"They didn't come out," Joe Gorman said. "I was watching for them from the window of my diner."

"There were the three seconds you were getting something out of the icebox in your pantry," Mason said.

"And I suppose everyone else along Main Street had his head in a closet at just that time!" Joe Gorman said.

"Or someone reached down out of the heavens and snatched that station wagon up into space," Haviland said. He was looking at Peabody's pudgy face as he spoke, and something he saw there made him add quickly, "I'm kidding, of course."

Peabody laughed nervously. "It's the only explanation we've had so far."

Karl Dickler put his hand up to his cheek. There was a nerve there that had started to twitch, regularly as the tick of a clock. "I like Jerry. I'd give the same kind of report on him you've been getting, Mr. Haviland. But you can't pass up the facts. I'd have said he'd defend those kids with his life. But did he? And the old man—his father. He won't answer questions directly. There's something queer about him. Damn it, Mr. Haviland, my kids are—out there, somewhere!" He waved toward the frost-coated window panes.

"Every highway within two hundred miles of here is being patrolled, Mr. Dickler," Haviland said. "If they'd driven straight away from here in daylight—granting Mason is right and everybody was in a closet when the station wagon went through town—they'd have been seen a hundred times after they left Clayton. There isn't one report of anyone having seen the station wagon with the school-bus markings." Haviland paused to light a cigarette. His tapering fingers were nicotine-stained.

"If you'd ever investigated a crime, Mr. Dickler, you'd know we usually are swamped with calls from people who think they've seen the wanted man. A bus—a bus load of kids. Somebody *had* to see it! But there isn't even a crackpot report. If there was some place he could have stayed under cover—and don't tell me, I know there isn't—and started moving after dark, he might get some distance. But alarms are out everywhere. He couldn't travel five miles now without being trapped."

"We've told ourselves all these things for hours!" Dickler said, pinching savagely at his twitching cheek. "What are you going to *do*, Haviland?"

"Unless we're all wrong," Haviland said, "we're going to hear from the kidnapers soon. Tonight—or maybe in the morning—by mail, or phone, or in some unexpected way. But we'll hear. They'll demand money What other purpose can there be? Once we hear, we'll have to start to play it by ear. That's the way these cases are."

"Meanwhile you just sit here and wait!" Dickler said, a kind of despair rising in his voice. "What am I going to say to my wife?"

"I think all the parents of the children should go home. You may be the one the kidnapers contact. It may be your child they put on the phone to convince you the kids are safe," Haviland said. "As soon as it's daylight—"

"You think the kids *are* safe?" Dickler cried out.

Haviland stared at the distraught father for a minute. Then he spoke, gently. "What kind of assurance could I give you, Mr. Dickler? Even if I tried, you wouldn't believe me. People who play this kind of game are without feelings, not rational. When you fight them, you have to walk quietly. If you scare them, God knows what to expect. That's why I urge you all to go home and wait." He dropped his cigarette on the floor and heeled it out. "And pray," he said. . . .

Elizabeth Deering, Jerry Mahoney's girl, was sick with anxiety. Jerry was foremost in her mind; Jerry, missing with the children; Jerry, worse than that, suspected by his friends. But on top of that was old Pat Mahoney.

He hadn't made the slightest sense since the angry crowd had left his house. He had talked on endlessly about the old days in vaudeville. He seemed obsessed with the memory of the first time he had seen The Great Thurston in Sioux City. He remembered card tricks, and sawing the lady in half, and his wife Nora's childish delight in being completely bewildered. He seemed to remember everything he had seen the man do.

315

Elizabeth tried, but she could not bring Pat back to the present. The tragedy seemed to have tipped him right out of the world of reason. She was partly relieved when she heard firm steps on the front porch. The other part of her, when she saw Sergeant Mason and the tall stranger, was the fear that they had news—bad news about Jerry.

Mason was less aggressive than he had been on his first visit. He introduced Haviland and said they wanted to talk to Pat. Elizabeth took them back into the living room where old Pat still sat in the overstuffed armchair.

Mason introduced Haviland. "Mr. Haviland is a special investigator from the Attorney General's office, Pat."

Pat's eyes brightened. "Say, you're the fellow that solved that murder over in Johnsville, aren't you?" he said. "Smart piece of work."

"Thanks," Haviland said. He looked at Pat, astonished at his gaudy vest and tie and the glittering diamond on his finger. He had been prepared for Pat, but not adequately.

"Sit down," Pat said. "Maybe Liz would make us some coffee if we asked her pretty."

Mason nodded to Liz, who went out into the kitchen. He followed her to tell her there was no news. Haviland sat down on the couch next to Pat, stretched out his long legs, and offered Pat a cigarette.

"Don't smoke," Pat said. "Never really liked anything but cigars. Nora hated the smell of 'em. So what was I to do? You go to vaudeville in the old days, Mr. Haviland?"

"When I was a kid," Haviland said, lighting a cigarette. "I never had the pleasure of seeing you though, Mr. Mahoney."

"Call me Pat," Pat said. "Everyone does. I was nothing, Mr. Haviland. Just a third-rate song-and-dance man. But Nora—well, if you ever saw my Nora . . ."

Haviland waited for him to go on, but Pat seemed lost in his precious memories.

"You must be very worried about your son, Pat," he said.

For a fractional moment the mask of pleasant incompetence seemed to be stripped from Pat's face. "Wouldn't you be?" he asked, harshly. Then, almost instantly, the mask was fitted back into place, and old Pat gave his cackling laugh. "You got theories, Mr. Haviland? How're you going to handle this case?"

"I think," Haviland said conversationally, "that the children and your son have been kidnaped. I think we'll hear from the kidnapers soon. I think, in all probability, the whole town will be asked to get up a large ransom."

Pat nodded. "I'll chip in this diamond ring," he said. "It's got Jerry out of trouble more than once."

Haviland's eyes narrowed. "He's been in trouble before?"

"His main trouble was his Pop," Pat said. "Sometimes there wasn't enough to eat. But we could always raise eating money on this ring." He turned his bright, laughing eyes directly on Haviland. "You figured out how the bus disappeared?"

"No," Haviland said.

"Of course it doesn't really matter, does it?" Pat said.

"Well, if we knew—" Haviland said.

"It wouldn't really matter," Pat said. "It's what's going to happen now that matters."

"You mean the demand for money?"

"If that's what's going to happen," Pat said. The cackling laugh suddenly grated on Haviland's nerves. The old joker did know something!

"You have a different theory, Pat?" Haviland asked, keeping his exasperation out of his voice.

"You ever see The Great Thurston on the Keith-Orpheum circuit?" Pat asked.

"I'm afraid not," Haviland said.

"Greatest magic act I ever saw," Pat said. "Better than Houdini. Better than anyone. I first saw him in Sioux City—"

"About the case here, Pat," Haviland interrupted. "You have a theory?"

"I got no theory," Pat said. "But I know what's going to happen."

Haviland leaned forward. "What's going to happen?"

"One of two things," Pat said. "Everybody in this town is going to be looking. They're going to be looking for that station wagon in the lake, where they know it isn't, and they're going to be looking for it in the woods, where they know it isn't. That's one thing that may happen. The other thing is, they buy this theory of yours, Mr. Haviland—and it's a good theory, mind you—and they all stay home and wait to hear something. There's one same result from both things, isn't there?"

"Same result?"

"Sure. Nobody in Clayton goes to work. The quarries don't operate. The small businesses will shut down. People will be looking and people will be waiting . . ."

"So?"

"So what good will that do anyone?" Pat asked.

Haviland ground out his cigarette in an ashtray. "It won't do anyone any good. The quarry owners will lose some money. The small businesses will lose some."

"Not much point in it, is there?" Pat said, grinning.

Haviland rose. He'd had about enough. Mason and Elizabeth were coming back from the kitchen with coffee. "There isn't much point to anything you're saying, Mr. Mahoney."

Pat's eyes twinkled. "You said you never saw The Great Thurston, didn't you?"

"I never saw him," Haviland said.

"Well, we'll see. If they're supposed to stay home and wait, they'll stay home and wait. If they're supposed to be out searching, they'll be out searching. Ah, coffee! Smells real good. Pull up a chair, Sergeant. By the way, Mr. Haviland, I'll make you a bet," Pat said.

"I'm not a betting man," Haviland said.

"Oh, just a manner-of-speaking bet," Pat said. "I'll make you a bet that tomorrow morning they'll be out searching. I'll make you a bet that *even if you order them to stay home and wait*, they'll be out searching!"

"Look here, Pat, if you know something . . ."

A dreamy look came into Pat's eyes. "Nora was so taken with The Great Thurston that time in Sioux City I went around to see him afterwards. I thought maybe he'd show me how to do a few simple tricks. I pretended it was for Nora, but really I thought we might use 'em in our act. He wouldn't tell me anything—that is, not about any of his tricks. But he told me the whole principle of his business."

"Sugar?" Elizabeth asked Haviland. Poor old man, she thought.

"The principle is," Pat said, "to make your audience think only what you want them to think, and see only what you want them to see." Pat's eyes brightened. "Which reminds me, there's something I'd like to have you see, Mr. Haviland."

Haviland gulped his coffee. Somehow he felt mesmerized by the old man. Pat was at the foot of the stairs, beckoning. Haviland followed.

Elizabeth looked at Mason and there were tears in her eyes. "It's thrown him completely off base," she said. "You know what he's going to show Mr. Haviland?" Sergeant Mason shook his head.

"A cowboy suit!" Elizabeth said, and dropped down on the couch, crying softly. "He's going to show him a cowboy suit."

And she was right. Haviland found himself in the attic, his head bowed to keep from bumping into the sloping beams. Old Pat had opened a wardrobe trunk and with the gesture of a waiter taking the silver lid off a tomato surprise, revealed two cowboy suits, one hanging neatly on each side of the trunk—Nora's and his. Chaps, shirt, vest, boots, Stetsons, and gun belt—all studded with stage jewelry.

". . . and when the lights went out," Pat was saying, "all you could see was these gewgaws, sparkling. And we'd take out the guns . . ."

And suddenly Pat had the two jeweled six-shooters in his hands, twirling and spinning them. "In the old days I could draw these guns and twirl 'em into position faster than Jesse James!"

The spell was broken for Haviland. The old guy was cuckoo. "I enjoyed seeing them, Mr. Mahoney," he said. "But now, I'm afraid I've got to get back . . ."

As soon as dawn broke, Haviland had Sergeant Mason and Sheriff George Peabody take him out to the scene of the disappearance. Everyone else was at home, waiting to hear from the kidnapers. It had been a terrible night for the whole town, a night filled with forebodings and dark imaginings. Haviland covered every inch of the two mile stretch of the dugway. And he couldn't get away from the facts. There was no way for it to have happened— but it happened.

About eight thirty he was back in Clayton in Joe's Diner, stamping his feet to warm them and waiting eagerly for eggs and toast to go with his steaming cup of black coffee. All the parents had been checked. There'd been no phone calls, no notes slipped under doors, nothing in the early-morning mail.

Haviland never got his breakfast. Trooper Teliski came charging into the diner just as Joe Gorman was taking the eggs off the grill. Teliski, a healthy young man, was white as parchment, and the words came out of him in a kind of choking sob. "We've found 'em," he said. "Or at least we know where they are. Helicopters spotted 'em. I just finished passing the word in town."

Joe Gorman dropped the plate of eggs on the floor behind the counter. Haviland spun around on his counter stool. Just looking at Teliski made the hair rise on the back of his neck.

"The old quarry off the dugway," Teliski said, and gulped for air. "No sign of the bus. It didn't drive up there. But the kids." Teliski steadied himself on the counter. "Schoolbooks," he said. "A couple of coats—lying on the edge of the quarry. And in the quarry —more of the same. A red beret belonging to one of the kids—"

"Peter!" Joe Gorman cried out.

Haviland headed for the door. The main street of Clayton was frightening to see. People were running out of houses, screaming at each other, heading crazily toward the dugway. Those who went for their cars scattered the people in front of them. There was no order—only blind panic.

Haviland stood on the curb outside the diner, ice in his veins. He looked down the street to where old Pat Mahoney lived, just in time to see a wildly weeping woman pick up a stone and throw it through the front window of Pat's house.

"Come on—what's the matter with you?" Teliski shouted from behind the wheel of the State Police car.

Haviland stood where he was, frozen, staring at the broken window of Pat Mahoney's house. The abandoned quarry, he knew, was sixty feet deep, full to within six feet of the top with icy water fed in by constantly bubbling springs.

A fire engine roared past. They were going to try to pump out the quarry. It would be like bailing out the Atlantic Ocean with a tea cup.

"Haviland!" Teliski called desperately.

Haviland still stared at Pat Mahoney's house. A cackling old voice rang in his ears. "I'll make you a bet, Mr. Haviland. I'll make you a bet that even if you order them to stay at home and wait, they'll be out searching."

Rage such as he had never known flooded the ice out of Haviland's veins. So Pat had known! The old codger had known *last night!*

Special Investigator Haviland had never witnessed anything like the scene at the quarry.

The old road, long since overgrown, which ran about 200 yards in from the dugway to the quarry, had been trampled down as if by a herd of buffalo.

Within three-quarters of an hour of the news reaching town, it seemed as if everyone from Clayton and half the population of Lakeview had arrived at the quarry's edge.

One of the very first army helicopters, which had taken to the air at dawn, had spotted the clothes and books at the edge of the abandoned stone pit.

The pilot had dropped down close enough to identify the strange objects and radioed immediately to State Police. The stampede had followed.

Haviland was trained to be objective in the face of tragedy, but he found himself torn to pieces by what he saw. Women crowded forward, screaming, trying to examine the articles of clothing and the books. Maybe not all the children were in this icy grave. It was only the hope of desperation. No one really believed it. It seemed, as Trooper Teliski had said, to be the work of a maniac.

Haviland collected as many facts about the quarry as he could from a shaken Sheriff Peabody.

"Marble's always been Clayton's business," Peabody said. "Half the big buildings in New York have got their marble out of Clayton quarries. This was one of the first quarries opened up by the Clayton Marble Company nearly sixty years ago. When they started up new ones, this one was abandoned."

In spite of the cold, Peabody was sweating. He wiped the sleeve of his plaid hunting shirt across his face. "Sixty feet down, and sheer walls," he said. "They took the blocks out at ten-foot levels, so there is a little ledge about every ten feet going down. A kid couldn't climb out of it if it was empty."

Haviland glanced over at the fire engine which had started to pump water from the quarry. "Not much use in that," he said.

"The springs are feeding it faster than they can pump it out," Peabody said. "There's no use telling them. They got to feel they're doing something." The fat sheriff's mouth set in a grim slit. "Why would Jerry Mahoney do a thing like this? *Why?* I guess you can only say the old man is a little crazy, and the son has gone off his rocker too."

"There are some things that don't fit," Haviland said. He noticed his own hands weren't steady as he lit a cigarette. The hysterical shrieking of one of the women near the edge of the quarry grated on his nerves. "Where is the station wagon?"

"He must have driven up here and—and done what he did to the kids," Peabody said. "Then waited till after dark to make a get-away."

"But you searched this part of the woods before dark last night," Haviland said.

"We missed it somehow, that's all," Peabody said stubbornly.

"A nine-passenger station wagon is pretty hard to miss," Haviland said.

"So we missed it," Peabody said. "God knows how, but we missed it." He shook his head. "I suppose the only thing that'll work here is grappling hooks. They're sending a crane over from one of the active quarries. Take an hour or more to get it here. Nobody'll leave here till the hooks have scraped the bottom of that place and they've brought up the kids."

Unless, Haviland thought to himself, the lynching spirit gets into them. He was thinking of an old man in a red vest and a green necktie and a diamond twinkling on his little finger. He was thinking of a broken window pane—and of the way he'd seen mobs act before in his time.

Someone gripped the sleeve of Haviland's coat and he looked down into the horror-struck face of Elizabeth Deering, Jerry Mahoney's girl.

"It's true, then," she whispered. She swayed on her feet, holding tight to Haviland for support.

"It's true they found some things belonging to the kids," he said. "That's all that's true at the moment, Miss Deering." He was a little astonished by his own words. He realized that, instinctively, he was not believing everything that he saw in front of him. "This whole area was searched last night before dark," he said. "No one found any schoolbooks or coats or berets then. No one saw the station wagon."

321

"What's the use of talking that way?" Peabody said. His eyes were narrowed, staring at Liz Deering. "I don't want to believe what I see either, Mr. Haviland. But I got to." The next words came out of the fat man with a bitterness that stung like a whiplash. "Maybe you're the only one in Clayton that's lucky, Liz. You found out he was a homicidal maniac in time—before you got married to him."

"Please, George!" the girl cried. "How can you believe—"

"What can anyone believe but that?" Peabody said, and turned away.

Liz Deering clung to Haviland, sobbing. The tall man stared over her head at the hundreds of people grouped around the quarry's edge. He was reminded of a mine disaster he had seen once in Pennsylvania: a whole town waiting at the head of the mine shaft for the dead to be brought to the surface.

"Let's get out of here," he said to Liz Deering, with sudden energy.

Clayton was a dead town. Stores were closed. Joe's Diner was closed. The railroad station agent was on the job, handling dozens of telegrams that were coming in from friends and relatives of the parents of the missing children. The two girls in the telephone office, across the street from the bank, were at their posts.

Old Mr. Granger, a teller in the bank, and one of the stenographers were all of the bank staff that had stayed on the job. Old Mr. Granger was preparing the payroll for the Clayton Marble Company. He didn't know whether the truck from the company offices with the two guards would show up for the money or not.

Nothing else was working on schedule today. Even the hotel down the street had closed. One or two salesmen had driven into town, heard the news, and gone off down the dugway toward the scene of the tragedy. A few very old people tottered in and out the front doors of houses, looking anxiously down Main Street toward the dugway. Even the clinic was closed. The town's doctors and nurses had all gone to the scene of the disaster.

Down the street a piece of newspaper had been taped over the hole in Pat Mahoney's front window. Pat Mahoney sat in the big overstuffed armchair in his living room. He rocked slowly back and forth, staring at an open scrapbook spread across his knees. A big black headline from a show-business paper was pasted across the top.

MAHONEY AND FAYE
BOFFO BUFFALO

Under it were pictures of Pat and Nora in their jeweled cowboy suits, their six-shooters drawn, pointing straight at the camera. There was a description of the act, the dance in the dark with only the jewels showing and the six-shooters spouting flame. "Most original number of its kind seen in years," a Buffalo critic had written. "The ever popular Mahoney and Faye have added something to their familiar routines that should please theater audiences from coast to coast. We are not surprised to hear that they have been booked into the Palace."

Pat closed the scrapbook and put it down on the floor beside him. From the inside pocket of his jacket he took a wallet. It bulged with papers and cards. He was an honorary Elk, honorary police chief of Wichita in 1927, a Friar, a Lamb.

Carefully protected by isinglass were some snapshots. They were faded now, but anyone could see they were pictures of Nora with little Jerry at various stages of his growth. There was Jerry at six months, Jerry at a year, Jerry at four years. And Nora, smiling gently at her son. The love seemed to shine right out of the pictures, Pat thought.

Pat replaced the pictures and put the wallet back in his pocket. He got up from his chair and moved toward the stairway. People who knew him would have been surprised. No one had ever seen Pat when his movements weren't brisk and youthful. He could still go into a tap routine at the drop of a hat, and he always gave the impression that he was on the verge of doing so. Now he moved slowly, almost painfully—a tired old man, with no need to hide it from anyone. There was no one to hide it from; Jerry was missing, Liz was gone.

He climbed to the second floor and turned to the attic door. He opened it, switched on the lights, and climbed up to the area under the eaves. There he opened the wardrobe trunk he'd shown to Haviland. From the left side he took out the cowboy outfit—the chaps, the boots, the vest and shirt and Stetson hat, and the gun belt with the two jeweled six-shooters. Slowly he carried them down to his bedroom on the second floor. There Pat Mahoney proceeded to get into costume.

He stood, at last, in front of the full-length mirror on the back of the bathroom door. The high-heeled boots made him a couple of inches taller than usual. The Stetson was set on his head at a rakish angle. The jeweled chaps and vest glittered in the sunlight from the window. Suddenly old Pat jumped into a flat-footed stance, and the guns were out of the holsters, spinning dizzily and then pointed straight at the mirror.

"Get 'em up, you lily-livered rats!" old Pat shouted. A bejeweled gunman stared back at him fiercely from the mirror.

Then, slowly, he turned away to a silver picture frame on his bureau. Nora, as a very young girl, looked out at him with her gentle smile.

"It'll be all right, honey," Pat said. "You'll see. It'll be another boffo, honey. Don't you worry about your boy. Don't you ever worry about him while I'm around."

It was a terrible day for Clayton, but Gertrude Naylor, the chief operator in the telephone office, said afterward that perhaps the worst moment for her was when she spotted old Pat Mahoney walking down the main street—right in the middle of the street—dressed in that crazy cowboy outfit. He walked slowly, looking from right to left, staying right on the white line that divided the street.

"I'd seen it a hundred times before in the movies," Gertrude Naylor said afterward. "A cowboy, walking down the street of a deserted town, waiting for his enemy to appear—waiting for the moment to draw his guns. Old Pat's hands floated just above those crazy guns in his holster, and he kept rubbing the tips of his fingers against his thumb. I showed him to Millie, and we started to laugh, and then, somehow, it seemed about the most awful thing of all. Jerry Mahoney had murdered those kids and here was his old man, gone nutty as a fruitcake."

Old Mr. Granger, in the bank, had much the same reaction when the aged, bejeweled gun toter walked up to the teller's window.

"Good morning, Mr. Granger," Pat said, cheerfully.

"Good morning, Pat."

"You're not too busy this morning, I see," Pat said.

"N-no," Mr. Granger said. The killer's father—dressed up like a kid for the circus. He's ready for a padded cell, Mr. Granger thought.

"Since you're not so busy," Pat said, "I'd like to have a look at the detailed statement of my account for the last three months." As he spoke, he turned and leaned against the counter, staring out through the plate-glass bank window at the street. His hands stayed near the guns, and he kept rubbing his fingertips against the ball of his thumb.

"You get a statement each month, Pat," Mr. Granger said.

"Just the same, I'd like to see the detailed statement for the last three months," Pat said.

"I had to humor him, I thought," Mr. Granger said later. "So I went back in the vault to get his records out of the files. Well, I was just inside the vault door when he spoke again, in the most natural way, 'If I were you, Mr. Granger,' he said, 'I'd close that vault door, and I'd stay inside, and I'd set off all the alarms I could lay my hands on. You're about to be stuck up, Mr. Granger.'

"Well, I thought it was part of his craziness," Mr. Granger said, later. "I thought he meant *he* was going to stick up the bank. I thought that was why he'd got all dressed up in that cowboy outfit.

324

Gone back to his childhood, I thought. I was scared, because I figured he was crazy. So I *did* close the vault door. And I *did* set off the alarm, only it didn't work. I didn't know then all the electric wires into the bank had been cut."

Gertrude and Millie, the telephone operators, had a box seat for the rest of it. They saw the black sedan draw up in front of the bank and they saw the four men in dark suits and hats get out of it and start up the steps of the bank. Two of them were carrying small suitcases and two of them were carrying guns.

Then suddenly the bank doors burst open and an ancient cowboy appeared, hands poised over his guns. He did a curious little jig step that brought him out in a solid square stance. The four men were so astonished at the sight of him they seemed to freeze.

"Stick 'em up, you lily-livered rats!" old Pat shouted. The guns were out of the holsters, twirling. Suddenly they belched flame, straight at the bandits.

The four men dived for safety, like men plunging off the deck of a sinking ship. One of them made the corner of the bank building. Two of them got to the safe side of the car. The fourth, trying to scramble back into the car, was caught in the line of fire.

"I shot over your heads that first time!" Pat shouted. "Move another inch and I'll blow you all to hell!" The guns twirled again and then suddenly aimed steadily at the exposed bandit. "All right, come forward and throw your guns down," Pat ordered.

The man in the direct line of fire obeyed at once. His gun bounced on the pavement a few feet from Pat and he raised his arms slowly. Pat inched his way toward the discarded gun.

The other men didn't move. And then Gertrude and Millie saw the one who had gotten around the corner of the bank slowly raise his gun and take deliberate aim at Pat. She and Millie both screamed, and it made old Pat jerk his head around. In that instant there was a roar of gunfire.

Old Pat went down, clutching at his shoulder. But so did the bandit who'd shot him and so did one of the men behind the car. Then Gertrude and Millie saw the tall figure of Mr. Haviland come around the corner of the hotel next door, a smoking gun in his hand. He must have spoken very quietly because Gertrude and Millie couldn't hear him, but whatever he said made the other bandits give up. Then they saw Liz Deering running across the street to where old Pat lay, blood dripping through the fingers that clutched at his shoulder.

Trooper Teliski's car went racing through the dugway at breakneck speed, siren shrieking. As he came to the turn-in to the old quarry, his tires skidded in and up the rugged path, car bounding

325

over stones, ripping through brush. Suddenly just ahead of him on the path loomed the crane from the new quarry, inching up the road on a caterpillar tractor. Trooper Teliski sprang out of his car and ran past the crane, shouting at the tractor driver.

"To hell with that!" Teliski shouted.

Stumbling and gasping for breath, he raced out into the clearing where hundreds of people waited in a grief-stricken silence for the grappling for bodies to begin.

"Everybody!" Teliski shouted. "Everybody! Listen!" He was half laughing, half strangling for breath. "Your kids aren't there! They're safe! They're all safe—the kids, Jerry Mahoney, everyone! They aren't here. They'll be home before you will! Your kids—" And then he fell forward on his face, sucking in the damp, loam-scented air.

Twenty minutes later Clayton was a madhouse. People running, people driving, people hanging onto the running boards of cars and clinging to bumpers. And in the middle of the town, right opposite the bank, was a station wagon with a yellow school-bus sign on its roof, and the children were spilling out of it, waving and shouting at their parents, who laughed and wept. And a handsome young Irishman with bright blue eyes was locked in a tight embrace with Elizabeth Deering.

Haviland's fingers shook slightly as he lit a cigarette. Not yet noon and he was on his second pack.

"You can't see him yet," he said to Jerry Mahoney. "The doctor's with him. In a few minutes."

"I still don't get it," Jerry said. "People thought *I* had harmed those kids?"

"You don't know what it's been like here," Liz Deering said, clinging tightly to his arm.

Jerry Mahoney turned and saw the newspaper taped over the broken front window, and his face hardened. "Try and tell me, plain and simple, about Pop," he said.

Haviland shook his head, smiling like a man still dazed. "Your Pop is an amazing man, Mr. Mahoney," he said. "His mind works in its own peculiar ways . . . The disappearance of the bus affected him differently from some others. He saw it as a magic trick, and he thought of it as a magic trick—or, rather, as *part* of a magic trick. He said it to me and I wouldn't listen. He said it is a magician's job to get you to think what he wants you to think and see what he wants you to see. The disappearance of the children, the ghastly faking of their death in the quarry—it meant one thing to your Pop, Mr. Mahoney. Someone wanted all the people in Clayton to be out of town. Why?

"There was only one good reason that remarkable Pop of yours could think of. The quarry payroll. Nearly a hundred thousand dollars in cash, and not a soul in town to protect it. Everyone would be looking for the children, and all the bandits had to do was walk in the bank and take the money. No cops, no nothing to interfere with them."

"But why didn't Pop tell you his idea?" Jerry asked.

"You still don't know what is was like here, Mr. Mahoney," Haviland said. "People thought you had done something to those kids; they imagined your Pop knew something about it. If he'd told his story, even to me, I think I'd have thought he was either touched in the head or covering up. So he kept still—although he did throw me a couple of hints. And suddenly, he was, to all intents and purposes alone in the town. So he went upstairs, got dressed in those cowboy clothes, and went, calm as you please, to the bank to meet the bandits he knew must be coming. And they came."

"But why the cowboy suit?" Liz Deering asked.

"A strange and wonderful mind," Haviland said. "He thought the sight of him would be screwy enough to throw the bandits off balance. He thought if he started blasting away with his guns they might panic. They almost did."

"What I don't understand," Liz said, "is how, when he fired straight at them, he never hit anybody!"

"Those were stage guns—prop guns," Jerry said. "They only fire blanks."

Haviland nodded. "He thought he could get them to drop their own guns and then he'd have a real weapon and have the drop on them. It almost worked. But the one man who'd ducked around the corner of the building got a clean shot at him. Fortunately, I arrived at exactly the same minute, and I had them from behind."

"But how did you happen to turn up?" Jerry asked.

"I couldn't get your father out of my mind," Haviland said. "He seemed to know what was going to happen. He said they'd be searching for the kids, whether I told them to wait at home or not. Suddenly I had to know why he'd said that."

"Thank God," Jerry said. "I gather you got them to tell you where we were?"

Haviland nodded. "I'm still not clear how it worked, Jerry."

"It was as simple as pie a la mode," Jerry said. "I was about a half mile into the dugway on the home trip with the kids. We'd just passed Karl Dickler headed the other way when a big trailer truck loomed up ahead of me on the road. It was stopped, and a couple of guys were standing around the tail end of it.

"Broken down, I thought. I pulled up. All of a sudden guns were pointed at me and the kids. They didn't talk much. They just said to do as I was told. They opened the back of the big truck and rolled out a ramp. Then I was ordered to drive the station wagon right up into the body of the truck. I might have tried to make a break for it except for the kids. I drove up into the truck, they closed up the rear end, and that was that. They drove off with us—right through the main street of town here!

"Not ten minutes later," Jerry went on, "they pulled into that big deserted barn on the Haskell place. We've been shut up there ever since. They were real decent to the kids—hot dogs, ice cream, soda.

"So we just waited there, not knowing why, but nobody hurt, and the kids not as scared as you might think," Jerry laughed. "Oh, we came out of the dugway all right—and right by everybody in town. But nobody saw us."

The doctor appeared in the doorway. "You can see him for a minute now, Jerry," he said. "I had to give him a pretty strong sedative. Dug the bullet out of his shoulder and it hurt a bit. He's sleepy—but he'll do better if he sees you, I think. Don't stay too long, though."

Jerry bounded up the stairs and into the bedroom where Pat Mahoney lay, his face very pale, his eyes half closed. Jerry knelt by the bed.

"Pop," he whispered. "You crazy old galoot!"

Pat opened his eyes. "You okay, Jerry?"

"Okay, Pop."

"And the kids?"

"Fine. Not a hair of their heads touched." Jerry reached out and covered Pat's hand with his. "Now look here, Two-Gun Mahoney . . ."

Pat grinned at him. "It was a boffo, Jerry. A real boffo."

"It sure was," Jerry said. He started to speak, but he saw that Pat was looking past him at the silver picture frame on the dresser.

"I told you it'd be all right, honey," Pat whispered. "I told you not to worry about your boy while I was around to take care of him." Then he grinned at Jerry, and his eyes closed and he was asleep.

Jerry tiptoed out of the room to find his own girl.

GUILT-EDGED BLONDE

BY ROSS MACDONALD

Ross Macdonald (Ken Millar) was born on December 13, 1915, in California, where he now lives with his wife, mystery writer Margaret Millar. He was raised in Canada and received his doctorate from the University of Michigan. The modern mystery, he says, "deals with the worst things that can happen to people and the worst things people can do to each other." His style is hard-boiled and metaphorical and his detective Lew Archer has been called the natural successor to Dashiell Hammett's Sam Spade and Raymond Chandler's Philip Marlowe.

A man was waiting for me at the gate at the edge of the runway. He didn't look like the man I expected to meet. He wore a stained tan windbreaker, baggy slacks, a hat as squashed and dubious as his face. He must have been 40 years old, to judge by the gray in his hair and the lines around his eyes. His eyes were dark and evasive, moving here and there as if to avoid getting hurt. He had been hurt often and badly, I guessed.

"You Archer?"

I said I was. I offered him my hand. He didn't know what to do with it. He regarded it suspiciously, as if I was planning to try a Judo hold on him. He kept his hands in the pockets of his windbreaker.

"I'm Harry Nemo." His voice was a grudging whine. It cost him an effort to give his name away. "My brother told me to come and pick you up. You ready to go?"

"As soon as I get my luggage."

I collected my overnight bag at the counter in the empty waiting room. The bag was very heavy for its size. It contained, besides a toothbrush and spare linen, two guns and the ammunition for them. A .38 special for sudden work, and a .32 automatic as a spare.

Harry Nemo took me outside to his car. It was a new seven-passenger custom job, as long and black as death. The windshield and side windows were very thick, and they had the yellowish tinge of bullet-proof glass.

"Are you expecting to be shot at?"

"Not me." His smile was dismal. "This is Nick's car."

"Why didn't Nick come himself?"

He looked around the deserted field. The plane I had arrived on was a flashing speck in the sky above the red sun. The only human being in sight was the operator in the control tower. But Nemo leaned toward me in the seat, and spoke in a whisper:

"Nick's a scared pigeon. He's scared to leave the house. Ever since this morning."

"What happened this morning?"

"Didn't he tell you? You talked to him on the phone."

"He didn't say very much. He told me he wanted to hire a bodyguard for six days, until his boat sails. He didn't tell me why."

"They're gunning for him, that's why. He went to the beach this morning. He has a private beach along the back of his ranch, and he went down there by himself for his morning dip. Somebody took a shot at him from the top of the bluff. Five or six shots. He was in the water, see, with no gun handy. He told me the slugs were splashing around him like hailstones. He ducked and swam under water out to sea. Lucky for him he's a good swimmer, or he wouldn't of got away. It's no wonder he's scared. It means they caught up with him, see?"

"Who are 'they,' or is that a family secret?"

Nemo turned from the wheel to peer into my face. His breath was sour, his look incredulous. "Hell, don't you know who Nick is? Didn't he tell you?"

"He's a lemon-grower, isn't he?"

"He is now."

"What did he used to be?"

The bitter beaten face closed on itself. "I oughtn't to be flapping at the mouth. He can tell you himself if he wants to."

Two hundred horses yanked us away from the curb. I rode with my heavy leather bag on my knees. Nemo drove as if driving was the one thing in life he enjoyed, rapt in silent communion with the engine. It whisked us along the highway, then down a gradual incline between geometrically planted lemon groves. The sunset sea glimmered red at the foot of the slope.

Before we reached it, we turned off the blacktop into a private lane which ran like a straight hair-parting between the dark green trees. Straight for half a mile or more to a low house in a clearing.

The house was flat-roofed, made of concrete and fieldstone, with an attached garage. All its windows were blinded with heavy draperies. It was surrounded with well-kept shrubbery and lawn, the lawn with a ten-foot wire fence surmounted by barbed wire.

Nemo stopped in front of the closed and padlocked gate, and honked the horn. There was no response. He honked the horn again.

About halfway between the house and the gate a crawling thing came out of the shrubbery. It was a man, moving very slowly on hands and knees. His head hung down almost to the ground. One side of his head was bright red, as if he had fallen in paint. He left a jagged red trail in the gravel of the driveway.

Harry Nemo said, "Nick!" He scrambled out of the car. "What happened, Nick?"

The crawling man lifted his heavy head and looked at us. Cumbrously, he rose to his feet. He came forward with his legs spraddled and loose, like a huge infant learning to walk. He breathed loudly and horribly, looking at us with a dreadful hopefulness. Then he died on his feet, still walking. I saw the change in his face before it struck the gravel.

331

Harry Nemo went over the fence like a weary monkey, snagging his slacks on the barbed wire. He knelt beside his brother and turned him over and palmed his chest. He stood up shaking his head.

I had my bag unzipped and my hand on the revolver. I went to the gate, "Open up, Harry."

Harry was saying, "They got him," over and over. He crossed himself several times. "The dirty bastards."

"Open up," I said.

He found a key ring in the dead man's pocket and opened the padlocked gate. Our dragging footsteps crunched the gravel. I looked down at the specks of gravel in Nicky Nemo's eyes, the bullet hole in his temple.

"Who got him, Harry?"

"I dunno. Fats Jordan, or Artie Castola, or Faronese. It must have been one of them."

"The Purple Gang."

"You called it. Nicky was their treasurer back in the thirties. He was the one that didn't get into the papers. He handled the payoff, see. When the heat went on and the gang got busted up, he had some money in a safe-deposit box. He was the only one that got away."

"How much money?"

"Nicky never told me. All I know, he come out here before the war and bought a thousand acres of lemon land. It took them fifteen years to catch up with him. He always knew they were gonna, though. He knew it."

"Artie Castola got off the Rock last spring."

"You're telling me. That's when Nicky bought himself the bullet-proof car and put up the fence."

"Are they gunning for you?"

He looked around at the darkening groves and the sky. The sky was streaked with running red, as if the sun had died a violent death.

"I dunno," he answered nervously. "They got no reason to. I'm as clean as soap. I never been in the rackets. Not since I was young, anyway. The wife made me go straight, see?"

I said, "We better get into the house and call the police."

The front door was standing a few inches ajar. I could see at the edge that it was sheathed with quarter-inch steel plate. Harry put my thoughts into words.

"Why in hell would he go outside? He was safe as houses as long as he stayed inside."

"Did he live alone?"

"More or less alone."

"What does that mean?"

He pretended not to hear me, but I got some kind of answer. Looking through the doorless arch into the living room, I saw a leopardskin coat folded across the back of the chesterfield. There were red-tipped cigarette butts mingled with cigar butts in the ashtrays.

"Nicky was married?"

"Not exactly."

"You know the woman?"

"Naw." But he was lying.

Somewhere behind the thick walls of the house there was a creak of springs, a crashing bump, the broken roar of a cold engine, grinding of tires in gravel. I got to the door in time to see a cerise convertible hurtling down the driveway. The top was down, and a yellow-haired girl was small and intent at the wheel. She swerved around Nick's body and got through the gate somehow, with her tires screaming.

I aimed at the right rear tire, and missed. Harry came up behind me. He pushed my gun arm down before I could fire again. The convertible disappeared in the direction of the highway.

"Let her go," he said.

"Who is she?"

He thought about it, his slow brain clicking almost audibly. "I dunno. Some pig that Nicky picked up someplace. Her name is Flossie or Florrie or something. She didn't shoot him, if that's what you're worried about."

"You know her pretty well, do you?"

"The hell I do. I don't mess with Nicky's dames." He tried to work up a rage to go with the strong words, but he didn't have the makings. The best he could produce was petulance. "Listen, mister, why should you hang around? The guy that hired you is dead."

"I haven't been paid, for one thing."

"I'll fix that."

He trotted across the lawn to the body and came back with an alligator billfold. It was thick with money.

"How much?"

"A hundred will do it."

He handed me a hundred-dollar bill. "Now how about you amscray, bud, before the law gets here?"

"I need transportation."

"Take Nicky's car. He won't be using it. You can park it at the airport and leave the key with the agent."

"I can, eh?"

"Sure. I'm telling you you can."

"Aren't you getting a little free with your brother's property?"

333

"It's my property now, bud." A bright thought struck him, disorganizing his face. "Incidentally, how would you like to get off of my land?"

"I'm staying, Harry. I like this place. I always say it's people that make a place."

The gun was still in my hand. He looked down at it.

"Get on the telephone, Harry. Call the police."

"Who do you think you are, ordering me around? I took my last order from anybody, see?" He glanced over his shoulder at the dark and shapeless object on the gravel, and spat venomously.

"I'm a citizen, working for Nicky. Not for you."

He changed his tune very suddenly. "How much to go to work for me?"

"Depends on the line of work."

He manipulated the alligator wallet. "Here's another hundred. If you got to hang around, keep the lip buttoned down about the dame, eh? Is it a deal?"

I didn't answer, but I took the money. I put it in a separate pocket by itself. Harry telephoned the county sheriff.

He emptied the ashtrays before the sheriff's men arrived, and stuffed the leopardskin coat into the woodbox. I sat and watched him.

We spent the next two hours with loud-mouthed deputies. They were angry with the dead man for having the kind of past that attracted bullets. They were angry with Harry for being his brother. They were secretly angry with themselves for being inexperienced and incompetent. They didn't even uncover the leopardskin coat.

Harry Nemo left the courthouse first. I waited for him to leave, and tailed him home, on foot.

Where a leaning palm tree reared its ragged head above the pavements there was a court lined with jerry-built frame cottages. Harry turned up the walk between them and entered the first cottage. Light flashed on his face from inside. I heard a woman's voice say something to him. Then light and sound were cut off by the closing door.

An old gabled house with boarded-up windows stood opposite the court. I crossed the street and settled down in the shadows of its veranda to watch Harry Nemo's cottage. Three cigarettes later a tall woman in a dark hat and a light coat came out of the cottage and walked briskly to the corner and out of sight. Two cigarettes after that she reappeared at the corner on my side of the street, still walking briskly. I noticed that she had a large straw handbag under her arm. Her face was long and stony under the streetlight.

Leaving the street, she marched up the broken sidewalk to the veranda where I was leaning against the shadowed wall. The stairs groaned under her decisive footsteps. I put my hand on the gun in my pocket, and waited. With the rigid assurance of a WAC corporal marching at the head of her platoon, she crossed the veranda to me, a thin high-shouldered silhouette against the light from the corner. Her hand was in her straw bag, and the end of the bag was pointed at my stomach. Her shadowed face was a gleam of eyes, a glint of teeth.

"I wouldn't try it if I were you," she said. "I have a gun here, and the safety is off, and I know how to shoot it, mister."

"Congratulations."

"I'm not joking." Her deep contralto rose a notch. "Rapid fire used to be my specialty. So you better take your hands out of your pockets."

I showed her my hands, empty. Moving very quickly, she relieved my pocket of the weight of my gun, and frisked me for other weapons.

"Who are you, mister?" she said as she stepped back. "You can't be Arturo Castola, you're not old enough."

"Are you a policewoman?"

"I'll ask the questions. What are you doing here?"

"Waiting for a friend."

"You're a liar. You've been watching my house for an hour and a half. I tabbed you through the window."

"So you went and bought yourself a gun?"

"I did. You followed Harry home. I'm Mrs. Nemo, and I want to know why."

"Harry's the friend I'm waiting for."

"You're a double liar. Harry's afraid of you. You're no friend of his."

"That depends on Harry. I'm a detective."

She snorted. "Very likely. Where's your buzzer?"

"I'm a private detective," I said. "I have identification in my wallet."

"Show me. And don't try any tricks."

I produced my photostat. She held it up to the light from the street, and handed it back to me. "So you're a detective. You better do something about your tailing technique. It's obvious."

"I didn't know I was dealing with a cop."

"I was a cop," she said. "Not any more."

"Then give me back my .38. It cost me seventy dollars."

"First tell me, what's your interest in my husband? Who hired you?"

"Nick, your brother-in-law. He called me in Los Angeles today, said he needed a bodyguard for a week. Didn't Harry tell you?"

She didn't answer.

"By the time I got to Nick, he didn't need a bodyguard, or anything. But I thought I'd stick around and see what I could find out about his death. He was a client, after all."

"You should pick your clients more carefully."

"What about picking brothers-in-law?"

She shook her head stiffly. The hair that escaped from under her hat was almost white. "I'm not responsible for Nick or anything about him. Harry is my responsibility. I met him in line of duty and I straightened him out, understand? I tore him loose from Detroit and the rackets, and I brought him out here. I couldn't cut him off from his brother entirely. But he hasn't been in trouble since I married him. Not once."

"Until now."

"Harry isn't in trouble now."

"Not yet. Not officially."

"What do you mean?"

"Give me my gun, and put yours down. I can't talk into iron."

She hesitated, a grim and anxious woman under pressure. I wondered what quirk of fate or psychology had married her to a hood, and decided it must have been love. Only love would send a woman across a dark street to face down an unknown gunman. Mrs. Nemo was horsefaced and aging and not pretty, but she had courage.

She handed me my gun. Its butt was soothing to the palm of my hand. I dropped it into my pocket. A gang of boys at loose ends went by in the street, hooting and whistling purposelessly.

She leaned toward me, almost as tall as I was. Her voice was a low sibilance forced between her teeth:

"Harry had nothing to do with his brother's death. You're crazy if you think so."

"What makes you so sure, Mrs. Nemo?"

"Harry couldn't, that's all. I know Harry, I can read him like a book. Even if he had the guts, which he hasn't, he wouldn't dare to think of killing Nick. Nick was his older brother, understand, the successful one in the family." Her voice rasped contemptuously. "In spite of everything I could do or say, Harry worshiped Nick right up to the end."

"Those brotherly feelings sometimes cut two ways. And Harry had a lot to gain."

"Not a cent. Nothing."

"He's Nick's heir, isn't he?"

"Not as long as he stays married to me. I wouldn't let him touch a cent of Nick Nemo's filthy money. Is that clear?"

336

"It's clear to me. But is it clear to Harry?"

"I made it clear to him, many times. Anyway, this is ridiculous. Harry wouldn't lay a finger on that precious brother of his."

"Maybe he didn't do it himself. He could have had it done for him. I know he's covering for somebody."

"Who?"

"A blonde girl left the house after we arrived. She got away in a cherry-colored convertible. Harry recognized her."

"A cherry-colored convertible?"

"Yes. Does that mean something to you?"

"No. Nothing in particular. She must have been one of Nick's girls. He always had girls."

"Why would Harry cover for her?"

"What do you mean, cover for her?"

"She left a leopardskin coat behind. Harry hid it, and paid me not to tell the police."

"Harry did that?"

"Unless I'm having delusions."

"Maybe you are at that. If you think Harry paid that girl to shoot Nick, or had anything—"

"I know. Don't say it. I'm crazy."

Mrs. Nemo laid a thin hand on my arm. "Anyway, lay off Harry. Please. I have a hard enough time handling him as it is. He's worse than my first husband. The first one was a drunk, believe it or not." She glanced at the lighted cottage across the street, and I saw one-half of her bitter smile. "I wonder what makes a woman go for the lame ducks the way I did."

"I wouldn't know, Mrs. Nemo. Okay, I'll lay off Harry."

But I had no intention of laying off Harry. When she went back to her cottage, I walked around three-quarters of the block and took up a new position in the doorway of a dry-cleaning establishment. This time I didn't smoke. I didn't even move, except to look at my watch from time to time.

Around eleven o'clock the lights went out behind the blinds in the Nemo cottage. Shortly before midnight the front door opened and Harry slipped out. He looked up and down the street and began to walk. He passed within six feet of my dark doorway, hustling along in a kind of furtive shuffle.

Working very cautiously, at a distance, I tailed him downtown. He disappeared into the lighted cavern of an all-night garage. He came out of the garage a few minutes later, driving an old Chevrolet.

My money also talked to the attendant. I drew an old Buick which would still do 75. I proved that it would as soon as I hit the highway. I reached the entrance to Nick Nemo's private lane in time to see Harry's lights approaching the dark ranchhouse.

I cut my lights and parked at the roadside a hundred yards below the entrance to the lane, and facing it. The Chevrolet reappeared in a few minutes. Harry was still alone in the front seat. I followed it blind as far as the highway before I risked my lights. Then down the highway to the edge of town.

In the middle of the motel and drive-in district he turned off onto a side road and in under a neon sign which spelled out *TRAILER COURT* across the darkness. The trailers stood along the bank of a dry creek. The Chevrolet stopped in front of one of them, which had a light in the window. Harry got out with a spotted bundle under his arm. He knocked on the door of the trailer.

I U-turned at the next corner and put in more waiting time. The Chevrolet rolled out under the neon sign and turned toward the highway. I let it go.

Leaving my car, I walked along the creek bank to the lighted trailer. The windows were curtained. The cerise convertible was parked on its far side. I tapped on the aluminum door.

"Harry?" a girl's voice said. "Is that you, Harry?"

I muttered something indistinguishable. The door opened, and the yellow-haired girl looked out. She was very young, but her round blue eyes were heavy and sick with hangover, or remorse. She had on a nylon slip, nothing else.

"What is this?"

She tried to shut the door. I held it open.

"Get away from here. Leave me alone. I'll scream."

"All right. Scream."

She opened her mouth. No sound came out. She closed her mouth again. It was small and fleshy and defiant. "Who are you? Law?"

"Close enough. I'm coming in."

"Come in then, damn you. I got nothing to hide."

"I can see that."

I brushed in past her. There were dead Martinis on her breath. The little room was a jumble of feminine clothes, silk and cashmere and tweed and gossamer nylon, some of them flung on the floor, others hung up to dry. The leopardskin coat lay on the bunk bed, staring with innumerable bold eyes. She picked it up and covered her shoulders with it. Unconsciously, her nervous hands began to pick the wood chips out of the fur.

"Harry did you a favor, didn't he?" I said.

"Maybe he did."

"Have you been doing any favors for Harry?"

"Such as?"

"Such as knocking off his brother?"

"You're way off the beam, mister. I was very fond of Uncle Nick."

"Why run out on the killing then?"

"I panicked," she said. "It would happen to any girl. I was asleep when he got it, see, passed out if you want the truth. I heard the gun go off. It woke me up, but it took me quite a while to bring myself to and sober up enough to put my clothes on. By the time I made it to the bedroom window, Harry was back, with some guy." She peered into my face. "Were you the guy?"

I nodded.

"I thought so. I thought you were law at the time. I saw Nick lying there in the driveway, all bloody, and I put two and two together and got trouble. Bad trouble for me, unless I got out. So I got out. It wasn't nice to do, after what Nick meant to me, but it was the only sensible thing. I got my career to think of."

"What career is that?"

"Modeling. Acting. Uncle Nick was gonna send me to school."

"Unless you talk, you'll finish your education at Corona. Who shot Nick?"

A thin edge of terror entered her voice. "I don't know, I tell you. I was passed out in the bedroom. I didn't see nothing."

"Why did Harry bring you your coat?"

"He didn't want me to get involved. He's my father, after all."

"Harry Nemo is your father?"

"Yes."

"You'll have to do better than that. What's your name?"

"Jeannine. Jeannine Larue."

"Why isn't your name Nemo if Harry is your father? Why do you call him Harry?"

"He's my stepfather, I mean."

"Sure," I said. "And Nick was really your uncle, and you were having a family reunion with him."

"He wasn't any blood relation to me. I always called him uncle, though."

"If Harry's your father, why don't you live with him?"

"I used to. Honest. This is the truth I'm telling you. I had to get out on account of the old lady. The old lady hates my guts. She's a real creep, a square. She can't stand for a girl to have any fun. Just because my old man was a rummy—"

"What's your idea of fun, Jeannine?"

She shook her feathercut hair at me. It exhaled a heavy perfume which was worth its weight in blood. She bared one pearly shoulder and smiled an artificial hustler's smile. "What's yours? Maybe we can get together."

"You mean the way you got together with Nick?"

"You're prettier than him."

"I'm also smarter, I hope. Is Harry really your stepfather?"

"Ask him if you don't believe me. Ask him. He lives in a place on Tule Street—I don't remember the number."

"I know where he lives."

But Harry wasn't at home. I knocked on the door of the frame cottage and got no answer. I turned the knob, and found that the door was unlocked. There was a light behind it. The other cottages in the court were dark. It was long past midnight, and the street was deserted. I went into the cottage, preceded by my gun.

A ceiling bulb glared down on sparse and threadbare furniture, a time-eaten rug. Besides the living room, the house contained a cubbyhole of a bedroom and a closet kitchenette. Everything in the poverty-striken place was pathetically clean. There were moral mottoes on the walls, and one picture. It was a photograph of a towheaded girl in a teen-age party dress. Jeannine, before she learned that a pretty face and a sleek body could buy her the things she wanted. The things she thought she wanted.

For some reason I felt sick. I went outside. Somewhere out of sight an old car engine muttered. Its muttering grew on the night. Harry Nemo's rented Chevrolet turned the corner under the streetlight. Its front wheels were weaving. One of the wheels climbed the curb in front of the cottage. The Chevrolet came to a halt at a drunken angle.

I crossed the sidewalk and opened the car door. Harry was at the wheel, clinging to it desperately as if he needed it to hold him up. His chest was bloody. His mouth was bright with blood. He spoke through it thickly:

"She got me."

"Who got you, Harry? Jeannine?"

"No. Not her. She was the reason for it, though. We had it coming."

Those were his final words. I caught his body as it fell sideways out of the seat. Laid it out on the sidewalk and left it for the cop on the beat to find.

I drove across town to the trailer court. Jeannine's trailer still had light in it, filtered through the curtains over the windows. I pushed the door open.

The girl was packing a suitcase on the bunk bed. She looked at me over her shoulder, and froze. Her blonde head was cocked like a frightened bird's, hypnotized by my gun.

"Where are you off to, kid?"

"Out of this town. I'm getting out."

"You have some talking to do first."

She straightened up. "I told you all I know. You didn't believe me. What's the matter, didn't you get to see Harry?"

"I saw him. Harry's dead. Your whole family is dying like flies."

She half turned and sat down limply on the disordered bed. "Dead? You think I did it?"

"I think you know who did. Harry said before he died that you were the reason for it all."

"Me the reason for it?" Her eyes widened in false naïveté, but there was thought behind them, quick and desperate thought. "You mean Harry got killed on account of me?"

"Harry and Nick both. It was a woman who shot them."

"God," she said. The desperate thought behind her eyes crystallized into knowledge. Which I shared.

The aching silence was broken by a big diesel rolling by on the highway. She said above its roar:

"That crazy old bat. So *she* killed Nick."

"You're talking about your mother, Mrs. Nemo."

"Yeah."

"Did you see her shoot him?"

"No. I was blotto like I told you. But I saw her out there this week, keeping an eye on the house. She's always watched me like a hawk."

"Is that why you were getting out of town? Because you knew she killed Nick?"

"Maybe it was. I don't know. I wouldn't let myself think about it."

Her blue gaze shifted from my face to something behind me. I turned. Mrs. Nemo was in the doorway. She was hugging the straw bag to her thin chest.

Her right hand dove into the bag. I shot her in the right arm. She leaned against the door frame and held her dangling arm with her left hand. Her face was granite in whose crevices her eyes were like live things caught.

The gun she dropped was a cheap .32 revolver, its nickel plating worn and corroded. I spun the cylinder. One shot had been fired from it.

"This accounts for Harry," I said. "You didn't shoot Nick with this gun, not at that distance."

"No." She was looking down at her dripping hand. "I used my old police gun on Nick Nemo. After I killed him, I threw the gun into the sea. I didn't know I'd have further use for a gun. I bought that little suicide gun tonight."

"To use on Harry?"

"To use on you. I thought you were on to me. I didn't know until you told me that Harry knew about Nick and Jeannine."

"Jeannine is your daughter by your first husband?"

"My only daughter." She said to the girl, "I did it for you,

341

Jeannine. I've seen too much—the awful things that can happen."

The girl didn't answer.

"I can understand why you shot Nick," I said, "but why did Harry have to die?"

"Nick paid him," she said. "Nick paid him for Jeannine. I found Harry in a bar an hour ago, and he admitted it. I hope I killed him."

"You killed him, Mrs. Nemo. What brought you here? Was Jeannine the third on your list?"

"No. No. She's my own girl. I came to tell her what I did for her. I wanted her to know."

She looked at the girl on the bed. Her eyes were terrible with pain and love.

The girl said in a stunned voice, "Mother. You're hurt. I'm sorry."

"Let's go, Mrs. Nemo," I said.

THE CASE
OF THE EMERALD SKY

B Y ERIC AMBLER

Eric Ambler was born on June 28, 1909. His first novel,
The Dark Frontier, started out as a parody but it changed
halfway through, he says, into the kind of story it was
parodying. Subsequent novels revealed his special gift
for political insight. By the age of 31 he had written six
successful novels, including *A Coffin for Dimitrios*, regarded by many as his masterpiece. For a ten-year period
he was drawn to filmwriting and wrote no fiction. *Doctor
Frigo* (1975) is his most recent novel.

ASSISTANT COMMISSIONER MERCER of Scotland Yard stared, without speaking, at the card which Sergeant Flecker had placed before him.

There was no address, simply:

DR. JAN CZISSAR
Late Prague Police

It was an inoffensive-looking card. An onlooker, who knew only that Dr. Czissar was a refugee Czech with a brilliant record of service in the criminal investigation department of the Prague police, would have been surprised at the expression of dislike that spread slowly over the assistant commissioner's healthy face.

Yet, had the same onlooker known the circumstances of Mercer's first encounter with Dr. Czissar, he would not have been surprised. Just one week had elapsed since Dr. Czissar had appeared out of the blue with a letter of introduction from the mighty Sir Herbert at the home office, and Mercer was still smarting as a result of the meeting.

Sergeant Flecker had seen and interpreted the expression. Now he spoke.

"Out, sir?"

Mercer looked up sharply. "No, sergeant. In, but too busy," he snapped.

Half an hour later Mercer's telephone rang.

"Sir Herbert to speak to you from the Home Office, sir," said the operator.

Sir Herbert said, "Hello, Mercer, is that you?" And then, without waiting for a reply: "What's this I hear about your refusing to see Dr. Czissar?"

Mercer jumped but managed to pull himself together. "I did not refuse to see him, Sir Herbert," he said with iron calm. "I sent down a message that I was too busy to see him."

Sir Herbert snorted. "Now look here, Mercer; I happen to know that it was Dr. Czissar who spotted those Seabourne murderers for you. Not blaming you, personally, of course, and I don't propose to mention the matter to the commissioner. You can't be right every time. We all know that as an organization there's nothing to touch Scotland Yard. My point is, Mercer, that you fellows ought not to be above learning a thing or two from a foreign expert. Clever fellows, these Czechs, you know. No question of poaching on your preserves. Dr. Czissar wants no publicity. He's grateful to this country and eager to help. Least we can do is to let him. We don't want any professional jealousy standing in the way."

If it were possible to speak coherently through clenched teeth, Mercer would have done so. "There's no question either of poaching on preserves or of professional jealousy, Sir Herbert. I was, as Dr. Czissar was informed, busy when he called. If he will write for an appointment, I shall be pleased to see him."

"Good man," said Sir Herbert cheerfully. "But we don't want any of this red tape business about writing in. He's in my office now. I'll send him over. He's particularly anxious to have a word with you about this Brock Park case. He won't keep you more than a few minutes. Good-by."

Mercer replaced the telephone carefully. He knew that if he had replaced it as he felt like replacing it, the entire instrument would have been smashed. For a moment or two he sat quite still. Then, suddenly, he snatched the telephone up again.

"Inspector Cleat, please." He waited. "Is that you, Cleat? Is the commissioner in? . . . I see. Well, you might ask him as soon as he comes in if he could spare me a minute or two. It's urgent. Right."

He hung up again, feeling a little better. If Sir Herbert could have words with the commissioner, so could he. The old man wouldn't stand for his subordinates being humiliated and insulted by pettifogging politicians. Professional jealousy!

Meanwhile, however, this precious Dr. Czissar wanted to talk about the Brock Park case. Right! Let him! He wouldn't be able to pull that to pieces. It was absolutely watertight. He picked up the file on the case which lay on his desk.

Yes, absolutely watertight.

Three years previously, Thomas Medley, a widower of 60 with two adult children, had married Helena Merlin, a woman of 42. The four had since lived together in a large house in the London suburb of Brock Park. Medley, who had amassed a comfortable fortune, had retired from business shortly before his second marriage, and had devoted most of his time since to his hobby, gardening. Helena Merlin was an artist, a landscape painter, and in Brock Park it was whispered that her pictures sold for large sums. She dressed fashionably and smartly, and was disliked by her neighbors. Harold Medley, the son aged 25, was a medical student at a London hospital. His sister, Janet, was three years younger, and as dowdy as her stepmother was smart.

In the early October of that year, and as a result of an extra heavy meal, Thomas Medley had retired to bed with a bilious attack. Such attacks had not been unusual. He had had an enlarged liver, and had been normally dyspeptic. His doctor had prescribed in the usual way. On his third day in bed the patient had been considerably better. On the fourth day, however, at about four in the afternoon, he had been seized with violent abdominal pains, persistent vomiting, and severe cramps in the muscles of his legs.

These symptoms had persisted for three days, on the last of which there had been convulsions. He had died that night. The doctor had certified the death as being due to gastroenteritis. The dead man's estate had amounted to, roughly £110,000. Half of it went to his wife. The remainder was divided equally between his two children.

A week after the funeral, the police had received an anonymous letter suggesting that Medley had been poisoned. Subsequently, they had received two further letters. Information had then reached them that several residents in Brock Park had received similar letters, and that the matter was the subject of gossip.

Medley's doctor was approached later. He had reasserted that the death had been due to gastroenteritis, but admitted that the possibility of the condition having been brought by the willful administration of poison had not occurred to him. The body had been exhumed by license of the home secretary, and an autopsy performed. No traces of poison had been found in the stomach; but in the liver, kidneys and spleen a total of 1.751 grains of asrsenic had been found.

Inquiries had established that on the day on which the poisoning symptoms had appeared, the deceased had had a small luncheon consisting of breast of chicken, spinach (canned), and one potato. The cook had partaken of spinach from the same tin without suffering any ill effects. After his luncheon, Medley had taken a dose of the medicine prescribed for him by the doctor. It had been mixed with water for him by his son, Harold.

Evidence had been obtained from a servant that, a fortnight before the death, Harold had asked his father for £100 to settle a racing debt. He had been refused. Inquiries had revealed that Harold had lied. He had been secretly married for some time, and the money had been needed not to pay racing debts but for his wife, who was about to have a child.

The case against Harold had been conclusive. He had needed money desperately. He had quarrelled with his father. He had known that he was the heir to a quarter of his father's estate. As a medical student in a hospital, he had been in a position to obtain arsenic. The poisoning that appeared had shown that the arsenic must have been administered at about the time the medicine had been taken. It had been the first occasion on which Harold had prepared his father's medicine.

346

The coroner's jury had boggled at indicting him in their verdict, but he had later been arrested and was now on remand. Further evidence from the hospital as to his access to supplies of arsenical drugs had been forthcoming. He would certainly be committed for trial.

Mercer sat back in his chair. A watertight case. Sentences began to form in his mind. "This Dr. Czissar, Sir Charles, is merely a time-wasting crank. He's a refugee and his sufferings have probably unhinged him a little. If you could put the matter to Sir Herbert, in that light . . ."

And then, for the second time that afternoon, Dr. Czissar was announced.

Mercer was angry, yet, as Dr. Czissar came into the room, he became conscious of a curious feeling of friendliness toward him. It was not entirely the friendliness that one feels toward an enemy one is about to destroy. In his mind's eye he had been picturing Dr. Czissar as an ogre. Now, Mercer saw that, with his mild eyes behind their thick spectacles, his round, pale face, his drab raincoat and his unfurled umbrella, Dr. Czissar was, after all, merely pathetic. When, just inside the door, Dr. Czissar stopped, clapped his umbrella to his side as if it were a rifle, and said loudly: "Dr. Jan Czissar. Late Prague Police, At your service." Mercer very nearly smiled.

Instead he said: "Sit down, doctor. I am sorry I was too busy to see you earlier."

"It is so good of you . . ." began Dr. Czissar earnestly.

"Not at all, doctor. You want, I hear, to compliment us on our handling of the Brock Park case."

Dr. Czissar blinked. "Oh, no, Assistant Commissioner Mercer," he said anxiously. "I would like to compliment, but it is too early, I think. I do not wish to seem impolite, but . . ."

Mercer smiled complacently. "Oh, we shall convict our man, all right, doctor. I don't think you need to worry."

Dr. Czissar's anxiety became painful to behold. "Oh, but I do worry. You see—" He hesitated diffidently. "—he is not guilty."

Mercer hoped that the smile with which he greeted the statement did not reveal his secret exultation. He said blandly, "Are you aware, doctor, of all the evidence against him?"

"I attended the inquest," said Dr. Czissar mournfully. "But there will be more evidence from the hospital, no doubt. This young Mr. Harold could no doubt have stolen enough arsenic to poison a regiment without the loss being discovered."

The fact that the words had been taken out of his mouth disconcerted Mercer only slightly. He nodded. "Exactly."

A faint, thin smile stretched the doctor's full lips. He settled his glasses on his nose. Then he cleared his throat, swallowed hard and leaned forward. "Attention, please," he said sharply.

For some reason that he could not fathom, Mercer felt his self-confidence ooze suddenly away. He had seen that same series of actions, ending with the peremptory demand for attention, performed once before, and it had been the prelude to humiliation, to . . . He pulled himself up sharply. The Brock Park case was watertight. He was being absurd.

"I'm listening," he said.

"Good." Dr. Czissar wagged one solemn finger. "According to the medical evidence given at the inquest, arsenic was found in the liver, kidneys and spleen. No?"

Mercer nodded firmly. "One point seven five one grains. That shows that much more than a fatal dose had been administered. Much more."

Dr. Czissar's eyes gleamed. "Ah, yes. Much more. It is odd, is it not, that so much was found in the kidneys?"

"Nothing odd at all about it."

"Let us leave the point for the moment. Is it not true, Assistant Commissioner Mercer, that all postmortem tests for arsenic are for arsenic itself and not for any particular arsenic salt?"

Mercer frowned. "Yes, but it's unimportant. All arsenic salts are deadly poisons. Besides, when arsenic is absorbed by the human body, it turns to the sulphide. I don't see what you are driving at, doctor."

"My point is this, Assistant Commissioner, that usually it is impossible to tell from a delayed autopsy which form of arsenic was used to poison the body. You agree? It might be arsenious oxide, or one of the arsenates or arsenites, copper arsenite, for instance; or it might be a chloride, or it might be an organic compound of arsenic."

"Precisely."

"But," continued Dr. Czissar, "what sort of arsenic should we expect to find in a hospital, eh?"

Mercer pursed his lips. "I see no harm in telling you, doctor, that Harold Medley could easily have secured supplies of either salvarsan or neosalvarsan. They are both important drugs."

"Yes, indeed," said Dr. Czissar. "Very useful in one-tenth of a gram doses, but very dangerous in larger quantities." He stared at the ceiling. "Have you seen any of Helena Merlin's paintings, Assistant Commissioner?"

The sudden change of subject took Mercer unawares. He hesitated. Then: "Oh, you mean Mrs. Medley. No, I haven't seen any of her paintings."

"Such a chic, attractive woman," said Dr. Czissar. "After I had seen her at the inquest I could not help wishing to see some of her work. I found some in a gallery near Bond St." He sighed. "I had expected something clever, but I was disappointed. She paints what she thinks instead of what is."

"Really? I'm afraid, doctor, that I must . . ."

"I felt," persisted Dr. Czissar, bringing his cowlike eyes once more to Mercer's, "that the thoughts of a woman who thinks of a field as blue and of a sky as emerald green must be a little strange."

"Modern stuff, eh?" said Mercer shortly. "I don't much care for it, either. And now, doctor, if you've finished, I'll ask you to excuse me. I . . ."

"Oh, but I have not finished yet," said Dr. Czissar kindly. "I think, Assistant Commissioner, that a woman who paints a landscape with a green sky is not only strange, but also interesting, don't you? I asked the gentlemen at the gallery about her. She produces only a few pictures—about six a year. He offered to sell me one of them for 15 guineas. She earns £100 a year from her work. It is wonderful how expensively she dresses on that sum."

"She had a rich husband."

"Oh, yes. A curious household, don't you think? The daughter Janet is especially curious. I was so sorry that she was so much upset by the evidence at the inquest."

"A young woman probably would be upset at the idea of her brother being a murderer," said Mercer drily.

"But to accuse herself so violently of the murder. That was odd."

"Hysteria. You get a lot of it in murder cases." Mercer stood up and held out his hand. "Well, doctor, I'm sorry you haven't been able to upset our case this time. If you'll leave your address with the sergeant as you go. I'll see that you get a pass for the trial," he added with relish.

But Dr. Czissar did not move. "You are going to try this young man for murder, then?" he said slowly. "You have not understood what I have been hinting at?"

Mercer grinned. "We've got something better than hints, doctor—a first-class circumstantial case against young Medley. Motive, time and method of administration, source of the poison. Concrete evidence, doctor! Juries like it. If you can produce one scrap of evidence to show that we've got the wrong man, I'll be glad to hear it."

Dr. Czissar's back straightened, and his cowlike eyes flashed. He said, sharply, "I, too, am busy. I am engaged on a work on medical jurisprudence. I desire only to see justice done. I do not believe that on the evidence you have you can convict this young man under English law; but the fact of his being brought to trial could damage his career as a doctor. Furthermore, there is the real murderer to

349

be considered. Therefore, in a spirit of friendliness, I have come to you instead of going to Harold Medley's legal advisers. I will now give you your evidence."

Mercer sat down again. He was very angry. "I am listening," he said grimly; "but if you . . ."

"Attention, please," said Dr. Czissar. He raised a finger. "Arsenic was found in the dead man's kidneys. It is determined that Harold Medley could have poisoned his father with either salvarsan or neosalvarsan. There is a contradiction there. Most inorganic salts of arsenic, white arsenic, for instance, are practically insoluble in water, and if a quantity of such a salt had been administered, we might expect to find traces of it in the kidneys. Salvarsan and neosalvarsan, however, are compounds of arsenic and are very soluble in water. If either of them had been administered through the mouth, we should *not* expect to find arsenic in the kidneys."

He paused; but Mercer was silent.

"In what form, therefore, was the arsenic administered?" he went on. "The tests do not tell us, for they detect only the presence of the element, arsenic. Let us then look among the inorganic salts. There is white arsenic, that is arsenious oxide. It is used for dipping sheep. We would not expect to find it in Brock Park. But Mr. Medley was a gardener. What about sodium arsenite, the weed-killer? But we heard at the inquest that the weed-killer in the garden was of the kind harmful only to weeds. We come to copper arsenite. Mr. Medley was, in my opinion, poisoned by a large dose of copper arsenite."

"And on what evidence," demanded Mercer, "do you base that opinion?"

"There is, or there has been, copper arsenite in the Medleys' house." Dr. Czissar looked at the ceiling. "On the day of the in- quest, Mrs. Medley wore a fur coat. I have since found another fur coat like it. The price of the coat was 400 guineas. Inquiries in Brock Park have told me that this lady's husband, besides being a rich man, was also a very mean and unpleasant man. At the inquest, his son told us that he had kept his marriage a secret because he was afraid that his father would stop his allowance or prevent his continuing studies in medicine. Helena Medley had expensive tastes. She had married this man so that she could indulge them. He had failed her. That coat she wore, Assistant Commissioner, was unpaid for. You will find, I think, that she had other debts, and that a threat had been made by one of the creditors to ap- proach her husband. She was tired of this man so much older than she was—this man who did not even justify his existence by spend- ing his fortune on her. She poisoned her husband. There is no doubt of it."

"The commissioner to speak to you, sir," said the operator.

"All right. Hello . . . Hello, Sir Charles. Yes, I did want to speak to you urgently. It was—" He hesitated. "—it was about the Brock Park case. I think that we will have to release young Medley. I've got hold of some new medical evidence that . . . Yes, yes, I realize that, Sir Charles, and I'm very sorry that . . . All right, Sir Charles, I'll come immediately."

He replaced the telephone and went.

"Nonsense!" said Mercer. "Of course we know that she was in debt. We are not fools. But lots of women are in debt. It doesn't make them murderers. Ridiculous!"

"All murderers are ridiculous," agreed Dr. Czissar solemnly; "especially the clever ones."

"But how on earth . . .?" began Mercer.

Dr. Czissar smiled gently. "It was the spinach that the dead man had for luncheon before the symptoms of poisoning began that interested me," he said. "Why give spinach when it is out of season? Canned vegetables are not usually given to an invalid with gastric trouble. And then, when I saw Mrs. Medley's paintings, I understood. The emerald sky, Assistant Commissioner. It was a fine, rich emerald green, that sky—*the sort of emerald green that the artist gets when there is aceto-arsenite of copper in the paint!* The firm which supplies Mrs. Medley with her working materials will be able to tell you when she bought it. I suggest, too, that you take the picture—it is in the Summons Gallery—and remove a little of the sky for analysis. You will find that the spinach was prepared at her suggestion and taken to her husband's bedroom by her. Spinach is *green* and *slightly bitter* in taste. *So is copper arsenite.*" He sighed. "If there had not been anonymous letters . . ."

"Ah!" interrupted Mercer. "The anonymous letters! Perhaps you know . . ."

"Oh, yes," said Dr. Czissar simply. "The daughter Janet wrote them. Poor child! She disliked her smart stepmother and wrote them out of spite. Imagine her feelings when she found that she had—how do you say?—put a noose about her brother's throat. It would be natural for her to try to take the blame herself." He looked at his watch. "But it is late and I must get to the museum reading-room before it closes." He stood up, clapped his umbrella to his side, clicked his heels and said loudly: "Dr. Jan Czissar. Late Prague Police. At your service!"